Samuel Beckett and the Problem of Irishness

Samuel Beckett and the Problem of Irishness

Emilie Morin

palgrave
macmillan

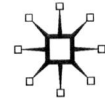

© Emilie Morin 2009

All rights reserved. No reproduction, copy or transmission of this publication may be made without written permission.

No portion of this publication may be reproduced, copied or transmitted save with written permission or in accordance with the provisions of the Copyright, Designs and Patents Act 1988, or under the terms of any licence permitting limited copying issued by the Copyright Licensing Agency, Saffron House, 6-10 Kirby Street, London EC1N 8TS.

Any person who does any unauthorized act in relation to this publication may be liable to criminal prosecution and civil claims for damages.

The author has asserted her right to be identified as the author of this work in accordance with the Copyright, Designs and Patents Act 1988.

First published 2009 by
PALGRAVE MACMILLAN

Palgrave Macmillan in the UK is an imprint of Macmillan Publishers Limited, registered in England, company number 785998, of Houndmills, Basingstoke, Hampshire RG21 6XS.

Palgrave Macmillan in the US is a division of St Martin's Press LLC,
175 Fifth Avenue, New York, NY 10010.

Palgrave Macmillan is the global academic imprint of the above companies and has companies and representatives throughout the world.

Palgrave® and Macmillan® are registered trademarks in the United States, the United Kingdom, Europe and other countries.

ISBN-13: 978–0–230–21986–1 hardback

This book is printed on paper suitable for recycling and made from fully managed and sustained forest sources. Logging, pulping and manufacturing processes are expected to conform to the environmental regulations of the country of origin.

A catalogue record for this book is available from the British Library.

A catalog record for this book is available from the Library of Congress.

10 9 8 7 6 5 4 3 2 1
18 17 16 15 14 13 12 11 10 09

Printed and bound in Great Britain by
CPI Antony Rowe, Chippenham and Eastbourne

For Jean Frontini

Contents

Preface ix
Acknowledgements xi

Introduction 1
1. Beckett and the Irish Literary Revival 21
2. Translation as Principle of Composition 55
3. Representing Scarcity 96
4. Writing Disappearance 127
Conclusion 161

List of Abbreviations and Notations 164
Notes 166
Bibliography 203
Index 219

Preface

Many thanks are due: as is often the case, the processes which fashioned this monograph were not linear. Michael McAteer guided the project from its earliest form, and his intellectual generosity and unfailing support made my years at Queen's University Belfast immensely rewarding. Particular thanks are due to Garin Dowd, whose comments set the process of rewriting in motion; to Julian Garforth, Liz Barry, Ronan McDonald and James Patten for their support over the years; to Seán Kennedy for drawing my attention to "L'Expulsé"; to Mark Nixon for his assistance with minute aspects of the MacGreevy correspondence; to Richard Rowland for his help during my move to York; to Robin Arma for his generosity; to Christabel Scaife for her assistance.

Thanks are also due to the School of English at Queen's University Belfast and the Department of English and Related Literature at the University of York for supporting my research. I am grateful to the F.R. Leavis Fund of the Department of English and Related Literature at the University of York for meeting the costs associated with the use of copyright materials, and to Queen's University Belfast for the University Studentship which funded my doctoral research between 2003 and 2006. Additional financial assistance from the Helena Wallace Fund, the Queen's Alumni Fund and the School of English at Queen's enabled me to work on all major Beckett archives during that time. For their assistance, I am grateful to Verity Andrews at the Beckett International Foundation and to the staff of Special Collections and the Main Library, Queen's University Belfast; the Manuscripts Department, Bibliothèque Nationale de Paris; the Harry Ransom Humanities Research Centre, University of Texas at Austin; the Manuscripts Department and Early Printed Books, Trinity College Dublin Library; the library of the Société des Auteurs et Compositeurs Dramatiques; the National Library of Ireland.

This book would not have come to fruition without the support of my friends and family. Particular thanks are due to Serge and Jacqueline Charron, Willow Coyle, Jason Dixon, Caroline Farnan, Lisa Foran and Nilantha McPartland, Georgina Hambleton, Anita Maertens, Hayley Mansfield, Helen McClements, Ioana Moraru, Aisling Mullan, Emma Murphy, Jennifer and Thomas Regan-Lefèbvre and Rhona Trench. The unconditional support of Jean, Anne, Jean-Baptiste and Loïse Morin pushed me forward, and I cannot thank them enough for their help during difficult times. There are also acknowledgements which are difficult to phrase. For months, I have tried to think of a way in which I might express my immense gratitude to Nicholas Melia, but have found that there is too much to say. I can only acknowledge the long hours he spent discussing and editing manuscripts with patience and care, and thank him for letting this end in laughter.

Acknowledgements

The author and publishers wish to thank the following for permission to reproduce copyright material:

© The Estate of Samuel Beckett
Extracts from Samuel Beckett's letters, notebooks and manuscripts reproduced by kind permission of the Estate of Samuel Beckett c/o Rosica Colin Limited, London

Faber and Faber, for permission to quote from Samuel Beckett's published works in English

Watt by Samuel Beckett
Copyright © 1953 by Samuel Beckett

More Pricks Than Kicks by Samuel Beckett
Copyright © 1972 by Grove Press, Inc.

Three Novels: Molloy, Malone Dies, The Unnamable by Samuel Beckett
Copyright © 1955, 1956, 1958 by Grove Press, Inc.

Murphy by Samuel Beckett
Copyright © 1957 by Grove Press, Inc.

Disjecta by Samuel Beckett
Copyright © 1984 by Grove Press, Inc.

Complete Short Prose by Samuel Beckett
Copyright © 1995 by the Estate of Samuel Beckett

Happy Days by Samuel Beckett
Copyright © 1961 by Grove Press, Inc.

Endgame and *Act Without Words* by Samuel Beckett
Copyright © 1958 by Grove Press, Inc.

Waiting for Godot by Samuel Beckett
Copyright © 1954 by Grove Press, Inc.; copyright renewed ©1982 by Samuel Beckett

Collected Shorter Plays by Samuel Beckett
Copyright © 1984 by Grove Press, Inc.

Krapp's Last Tape Copyright © 1958 by Samuel Beckett

All That Fall Copyright © 1957 by Samuel Beckett

Not I Copyright © 1973 by Samuel Beckett
Eh Joe Copyright © 1967 by Samuel Beckett
...but the clouds... Copyright © 1977 by Samuel Beckett
That Time Copyright © 1976 by Samuel Beckett
Used by permission of Grove/Atlantic, Inc.

© by Les Editions de Minuit pour toutes les citations en français des oeuvres de Samuel Beckett (by the Editions de Minuit for all French citations from the works of Samuel Beckett)

Cover painting: *Monotype* by Robin Arma
Copyright © Robin Arma
Reproduced by kind permission of Robin Arma

The Hair of the Dogma: A Further Selection from 'Cruiskeen Lawn'
The Best of Myles
The Poor Mouth
by Flann O'Brien (Copyright © Flann O'Brien)
Reprinted by kind permission of A.M. Heath & Co Ltd

Nick Hern Books Ltd, for excerpts from Mel Gussow, *Conversations with (and about) Beckett*
Copyright © 1996 Mel Gussow

The Lilliput Press of Dublin, for the excerpt from p. 56 of David Lloyd, *Anomalous States: Irish Writing and the Postcolonial Moment* (1993). By kind permission of The Lilliput Press of Dublin.

Taylor & Francis Ltd, http://www.informaworld.com, for the excerpt from p. 161 of Peter Boxall, "Samuel Beckett: Towards a Political Reading", *Irish Studies Review* (2002) volume 10 issue 2

A P Watt Ltd on behalf of Gráinne Yeats, for excerpts from Jack B. Yeats, *The Collected Plays of Jack B. Yeats* and W.B. Yeats, *Explorations*, *Collected Plays*, *The Poems*, *Uncollected Prose by W.B. Yeats I and II*

Albert Camus, *The Myth of Sisyphus*, trans. Justin O'Brien (1955) p. 13. Translation copyright © Justin O'Brien, 1955. Reproduced by permission of Penguin Books Ltd

Every effort has been made to trace rights holders, but if any have been inadvertently overlooked the publishers would be pleased to make the necessary arrangements at the first opportunity.

Introduction

It is difficult to envisage Samuel Beckett's artistic development without considering his changing relationship with Ireland. Even though he appeared to sever ties with his country of birth by settling in France and writing in French, he never ceased to wrestle with certain aspects of Ireland's political and cultural predicament, despite his work being rarely weighed down by such concerns. His French and English writings, even in later life, remained haunted by Dublin trivia, Irish place names and particular episodes of Irish history; the presence of these elements, although they are little more than traces, nonetheless reveals the extent of Beckett's intimate conflict with their distinctiveness.

These residues have facilitated Beckett's gradual assimilation into an Irish pantheon of writers, despite his avowed contempt for the insularity and narrow-mindedness of post-independence Ireland and a carefully maintained absence from the world of Irish letters. His dealings with Aosdána, the honour-granting body and patron of the arts, to which he was first nominated at its creation in 1981, were marked by his silence and absence from general assemblies and ceremonies.[1] In recent years, Beckett has been transformed into a marketable cultural icon, a development manifest in the widely publicised 2001 *Beckett on Film* project conceived by Michael Colgan of Dublin's Gate Theatre. Irish recognition of Beckett's literary genius has found many other articulations: some tributes, such as Beckett's Gold, a beer created in 1997 by the Dublin Brewing Company, have met with little success, while others have shown acceptance of Beckett's refusal to be weighed down by constraints of place: the euro coins minted in 2006 by the Irish Central Bank to commemorate his centenary, for instance, present him as an artist whose work extends beyond national borders.

Beckett's absorption into Irish cultural life is concurrent with marked changes in critical approaches to his work. As the use of archival materials becomes widespread, new facets of his writing are opening up to scholarly investigation and the focus of critical debate is shifting from an emphasis on the universality of Beckett's concerns to an acknowledgement of their historical and cultural grounding – a development illustrated in the 2005 issue of the journal *Samuel Beckett Today/Aujourd'hui* entitled *Historicising Beckett* and edited by Seán Kennedy.[2] The paucity of well-defined geographical and historical anchors in Beckett's work is no longer seen as an expression of its striving towards uncharted territories of the mind. Few scholars now dispute that, even as Beckett's writing continues to dislocate linguistic and cultural boundaries, it remains informed by the social and political events of its time.

Nevertheless, the many lives that Beckett's texts have led in French and English are rarely accounted for; this is unsurprising, given the conceptual difficulties that arise when one attempts to reconcile the plurality of Beckett's historical attachments with the debates surrounding the opacity of his position within modernism and postmodernism and his relationship to European philosophical currents. Acknowledging Beckett as a bilingual writer also means depriving oneself of the ability to rely upon national characteristics: he is neither fully Irish nor French, but an Irish author *in translation*, whose work has changing boundaries, depending on the context in which it is examined. In the case of Beckett, the label 'Irish writer' no longer corresponds to stable meanings, since his closeness to the European avant-garde and his use of French as a primary means of expression greatly complicate his relationship with the literary territories under investigation during the period known as the Irish Literary Revival.[3]

The ways in which Beckett evades strict categorisation have generated an either/or dynamic in critical approaches to his work: by virtue of his writing in French, he is not strictly an Irish writer, and is therefore frequently taken as the quintessential example of the 'European writer'. However, these two classifications are equally problematic, given the specificity of Beckett's experiences of Ireland, France, Germany and Great Britain, and the circumstances that led him to write in two languages. That Beckett was Irish and wrote in French does not necessarily make 'European' an adequate label but, rather, brings to light a diffuse association between Irishness and a form of anti-cosmopolitanism, if not a reductive worldview. In addition, this alternative configuration of Beckett rests upon theoretical and historical notions that require clarification; it does not account for the distinctiveness of Ireland's colonial history or, indeed, for the complex development of European modernist currents outside old colonial powers such as France and Great Britain, whose collapse Beckett witnessed at a remove.[4] Last but certainly not least, the adjective 'European' becomes laden with Anglocentric and Francocentric assumptions when applied to Beckett – precisely the assumptions that his bilingual work questions.

Bearing in mind the complexities that surround categorisations of Beckett as 'Irish' and/or 'European', this book attempts to define historical and theoretical frameworks within which Beckett's relationship with and to Ireland can be problematised. While Beckett's affinities with a range of Irish writers affiliated with the Revival and the post-Revival periods are evident, there is an urgent need to elucidate the means by which the residual cultural and historical specificity of the work may be understood in relation to its anti-essentialist approach to notions of identity. It is the contention of this book that the Irish echoes lingering in Beckett's bilingual *oeuvre* have a conceptual significance, determining the ways in which meaning is produced, challenged, reproduced and transformed, and instructing the processes that *enable* Beckett's questioning of identity as corresponding to stable social and historical values. Furthermore, reviewing the forms of displacement, erasure and negation surrounding Beckett's representations of Ireland brings to light a paradox central to his writing, namely that its apparent autonomy from an Irish context finds articulation only in relation to its residual attachment to Irish culture and history.

While Beckett's texts often enable indisputable connections to be made with an Irish setting, finding coherence within this aspect of his work is far more challenging, not least when an Irish idiom is used. This problem finds a particularly humorous illustration in the radio play *All That Fall*. Written in Hiberno-English, *All That Fall* is set in a caricatured Irish village called Boghill, clearly inspired by Beckett's childhood memories of Foxrock, a southern suburb of Dublin. Nevertheless, for Beckett's characters, the concept of home cannot be associated with stable memories, let alone be comprehended, as Mrs Rooney suggests. "It is suicide to be abroad. But what is it to be at home, Mr Tyler, what is it to be at home? A lingering dissolution", she says to Mr Tyler, who briefly accompanies her during her journey to the train station.[5] Mrs Rooney's declaration illustrates the capacity of Beckett's writing to generate a form of autonomy from cultural particulars by means of its attachment to an Irish location: here, Ireland operates as a site absent for memorialisation, as a residual presence that generates its own dissolution and, ultimately, negation. Yet, if the alignment between the characters and a rural Irish setting cannot be entirely sustained, this is precisely what enables an innovative approach to form: form shapes content, and it is emphasised, at all times, that one is listening to a play of voices taking place in a void. The re-attachment of these voices to an Irish location is problematic, because it necessarily takes place through Hiberno-English, a language rooted in particulars of time and place that does not sit comfortably with the play's movement towards abstraction. This tension between the concrete and the abstract affects Mrs Rooney's perception of herself; she remarks upon the strangeness of her mode of expression: "I use none but the simplest words, I hope, and yet I sometimes find my way of speaking very ... bizarre", she laments.[6] The issue of memory is here secondary; what becomes salient is the process through which Beckett preserves a residual degree of engagement with an Irish historical predicament by way of a *disengagement* from it.

Addressing this feature of Beckett's *oeuvre*, the present study examines the ways in which the avant-garde practices informing Beckett's handling of an Irish context relate to his anti-essentialist approach to identity. Theoretical debates surrounding the historicity of modernism enable a pertinent contextualisation of primitivist, exoticist and absurdist leanings within Beckett's work in relation to his response to the literature of the Revival. These debates, essentially led by Georg Lukács and Theodor Adorno, were instrumental in fashioning historical and social theories of the avant-garde in twentieth-century philosophy.[7]

It is clear from Beckett's published writings that he was eager to maintain a distance from his country of birth, and it remains difficult to understand his relationship with Ireland in terms other than estrangement and withdrawal. Certain passages in his published and unpublished correspondence confirm that his contempt for the provincialism of the Ireland he left before the Second World War did not diminish over time. In some instances, the very suggestion that his work was inspired by memories of his country of birth angered him: when the bookseller Jacob Schwartz (to whom he sold many of his manuscripts) complimented him on *Krapp's Last Tape*, remarking upon how much the play reminded him of Ireland, Beckett icily replied that it had nothing to do with Ireland and had simply been written for the actor Patrick Magee.[8] In other instances, he seems to have enjoyed the freedom that came with posing as a Dublin exile. This was evidenced with the publication of Eoin O'Brien's book *The Beckett Country* in 1986, which documents how Beckett's imagination remained haunted by the landscapes of his youth. An unlikely exchange of letters between Beckett and Bertie Ahern (who was then Lord Mayor of Dublin) ensued, in which Ahern, who had attended the launch of the book, wrote admiringly to Beckett and commented upon the impact of his work on a new generation of Irish artists and students of literature. The tongue-in-cheek character of Beckett's reply cannot have escaped its addressee: "It is indeed with pleasure that I note the growth of interest in my work among the younger generation of my countrymen and with gratitude for the contacts it affords me of which I have so long felt the want".[9]

Such responses are strongly indicative of Beckett's ambivalent attitude towards the cultural and historical weight carried by his work. However, if Beckett often described the Irish flavour of his writings as merely incidental, his distance from his country of birth remains couched in highly specific terminology, and some of his allusions to Ireland have posed problems for readers unfamiliar with their historical and political nuances. Nevertheless, this aspect of Beckett's work has never loomed large in Beckett Studies, and critics such as Gerry Dukes have rightly questioned this oversight. Taking as an example Faber's 1993 revised edition of *Waiting for Godot*, Dukes remarks that its editors, James Knowlson and Dougald McMillan, have mistaken "camogie" for "hurling"; he identifies this minor error as the manifestation of a wide-ranging critical failure to acknowledge the context formative of Beckett as a writer.[10]

Dukes's attack upon critical reluctance to acknowledge the Irish dimension of Beckett's work points to a larger problem in scholarly approaches – namely, the conceptual split between understandings of Beckett as an Irish writer burdened by his Protestant heritage and as a placeless modernist/postmodernist whose work transcends national boundaries.[11] Peter Boxall has remarked upon this issue, noting that "[w]hen a biographical or train-spotterish interest is betrayed in the odd cultural details that pepper Beckett's writing, it is shrouded in anxious caveats that assure the reader that such details are of signal unimportance in the wide and empty expanses of the Beckett poetic terrain".[12] This compartmentalisation has prevented a nuanced understanding of the postcolonial environment informing Beckett's development, the troubled nature of his relationship with Ireland being largely perceived as a matter of secondary importance until the publication in 1991 of John Harrington's *The Irish Beckett*, the only book-length scholarly analysis of this topic.[13] Taking the emergence of the Irish Free State as a backdrop for a consideration of Beckett's artistic evolution, Harrington argues that Beckett's early fiction sits uneasily between Protestant and Catholic cultures: it conveys his familiarity with a fractured Protestant heritage and his unwillingness to substitute it for an equally fractured Catholic culture. Harrington's analysis emphasises that Beckett's specificity has been fundamentally misunderstood; as he points out, Beckett has simply fallen into the gaps between revisionist and postcolonial reappraisals of Irish modernism: "For Irish revisionism, the man to beat is Yeats; for Irish revivalism, the man to beat is Joyce. At the present moment in Irish cultural studies, because those hot and cold rhetorics are in place, and because he put the argument into definite form, the man to beat is Beckett".[14]

The ingrained mechanisms denounced by Harrington and Dukes also result from early attempts to present Beckett as a passive, peripheral figure in Irish literature. Vivian Mercier's *The Irish Comic Tradition* is one such attempt: Mercier relates Beckett to a tradition running from ancient Gaelic poets to Anglo-Irish writers such as Jonathan Swift and Maria Edgeworth but presents any association with this tradition as merely accidental.[15] After being attacked for his peremptory tone, Mercier amended his claims to state, "Samuel Beckett is an Irishman but not an Irish writer".[16] Mercier's argument proved to be consensual among his contemporaries: Beckett was described, for instance, as a "Nayman from Noland" and as a less distinctively Irish writer than either Yeats or Joyce – comments which suggest that Beckett did not refer to Ireland explicitly enough or often enough to qualify as their counterpart.[17]

Other critics have, however, denounced inconsistencies in approaches to Beckett's work: in 1969, the discrepancy in Irish attitudes to Joyce, Yeats and Beckett was already bewildering to James Mays, who argued that indifference to Beckett was a measure of retaliation against his apparent independence from Irish letters.[18] Other than Mays, few scholars have questioned the mechanisms underlying Beckett's categorisation as an international writer. The assumption that his writing had very little to do with Irish history and politics was, for a time, deeply embedded in Beckett Studies: this is apparent in the stance taken by James Knowlson in his introduction to the catalogue of the 1971 Beckett exhibition in Reading, in which he dismissed critical attempts to link Beckett's work to an Irish setting. However, Knowlson did later recognise that Beckett's Irish background was worthy of critical investigation, amending his initial position in his 1986 foreword to Eoin O'Brien's *The Beckett Country* and in his biography of Beckett, in which, as in Deirdre Bair's *Samuel Beckett*, the privileged character of Beckett's upbringing is emphasised.[19]

In contrast to these critical currents, Seamus Deane, Declan Kiberd and David Lloyd have integrated Beckett into a postcolonial paradigm, providing fresh perspectives upon his peculiar position in twentieth-century Irish literature. Beckett's focus on powerlessness, master–slave relationships, linguistic instability and material deprivation may identify him as a perfect candidate for the application of theories of hybridity and the subaltern. However, several factors place him at a remove from the models offered for apprehending Irish literature as postcolonial: the multiple political contexts of his work, for instance, raise particularly problematic issues.[20] Indeed, acknowledging Beckett's importance as a French writer when placing his work in an Irish literary tradition requires the transfer of one's focus from a context of anti-colonial struggle to one of imperial collapse, since Beckett's ascent as a French writer largely took place against a backdrop of anti-colonial wars and uprisings in Tunisia, Morocco and Algeria. A configuration of Beckett's work in an Irish postcolonial context alone thus has problematic implications, which are complicated further when one considers his ambiguous relationship with French counter-colonial cultures during the disintegration of the colonial empire.

In the analyses developed by Deane, Kiberd and Lloyd, Beckett remains a liminal figure due to his bilingualism, his reluctance to engage openly and consistently with an Irish historical predicament and his proximity to European avant-garde currents.[21] In their readings, Beckett fails to establish any solidity as an anti-colonial writer and remains a signifier of otherness, on the verge of evaporation into the void. For Deane, Beckett's trajectory is perpendicular to Joyce's; Deane argues that, while the sway of history is obvious in Joyce's writing, Beckett's remains "weightless".[22] Quoting from *All That Fall*, Deane notes that "Ireland, with its dead language, its deadening politics, its illiberal legislation, is the historical correlative of the personal state of nirvana-nullity for which Beckett's people crave. Silent, ruined, given to the imaginary, dominated by the actual, it is a perfect site for a metaphysics of absence".[23] In contrast to Deane's emphasis on Beckett's transformation of Ireland into a non-place, Kiberd establishes Beckett as "the pre-eminent resistance writer", whose anti-colonial battle takes place through language.[24] He reads Beckett's famous declaration to art critic Georges Duthuit that "there is nothing to express, nothing with which to express, nothing from which to express, no power to express, no desire to express, together with the obligation to express" as a suitable description of the postcolonial artist, "reared in a cultural vacuum, fatigued by the representational naïveté of realist artists of the colonial power, and twitching with the urge to leave some trace behind him".[25] Also, in this instance, Beckett's alliance with an Irish anti-colonial tradition operates in the negative mode; his use of French merely obfuscates the terms by which he might be read as a postcolonial writer. Similarly, in Lloyd's analysis of *First Love*, Beckett's Irishness is brought to light by means of an obliteration of the French context shaping his writing. Lloyd's reading establishes *First Love* as a direct reaction to both colonial forces and the nationalist orthodoxy of the Irish Free State; however, it does not remark upon the novella's complex history and the discrepancies between its two existing versions – while the 1973 English text is clearly set in Dublin, the narrator's nationality remains unspecified in the 1946 French text, which nevertheless states clearly that he is not of French origin. Lloyd's demonstration of the ways in which Beckett's English novella blurs the relationship between individual memory, collective memory and language remains largely dissociated from its practical articulations within these two distinct textual entities; his focus remains upon Beckett's subversion of a Free State ideology of national identity and he concludes that *First Love* "approaches the threshold of another language within which a post-colonial subjectivity might begin to find articulation".[26] As in Kiberd's analysis, Beckett's response to Irish colonial history remains associated with a lack of substance, and the idea of a postcolonial Beckett remains half-articulated, at the boundaries of self-negation.

* * *

In light of these critical debates, it becomes clear that Beckett's work has accommodated understandings of modernism that vary widely in terms of their acknowledgement of colonial contexts, and that Irish readings of Beckett, in their articulation as well as their dismissal and absence, bring to light broader issues concerning the ways in which Irish literature itself is understood conceptually and historically. The crucial point is that the traits that enable the assimilation of Beckett's work into the Irish literary canon also signal its ambivalent position in relation to traditional understandings of European modernism. Features particular to his work, such as self-translation, may also be read as signs of a relationship to modernist outlooks on language that is more nuanced and complex than is commonly acknowledged: if Beckett's turn to self-translation disqualifies him from the very possibility of being understood solely in an Irish context, such a decision is also informed by his perspective on the legacy of the Irish Revival.

In an attempt to contextualise such tensions, this study emphasises the necessity of configuring Beckett's approach to the notion of Irishness in relation to debates surrounding European modernism; certain points of agreement and disagreement among Jean-Paul Sartre, Georg Lukács and

Theodor Adorno concerning issues of artistic representation and human existence in a post-Auschwitz world provide the basis for elucidating the theoretical concerns concurrent with Beckett's anti-essentialist approach to notions of identity.[27] In particular, Adorno's understanding of the avant-garde and Sartre's concept of scarcity are taken as platforms for considering the ways in which Beckett's handling of Irishness conflates problems of artistic engagement, disengagement, autonomy and responsibility. It is through the lens of Adorno's engagements with the historical role of the avant-garde that the theoretical notions capable of reflecting Beckett's complex relationship to an Irish context emerge. In keeping with Adorno's perspective in *Aesthetic Theory*, the term 'avant-garde' here designates both an art form concerned with aesthetic experimentation and a historical category within modernism. By 'experimentation' I refer to processes and methods whose objective results cannot be foreseen. Adorno relates this particular definition of experimentation to "the primacy of constructive methods over subjective imagination", an understanding of experimental art forms that is germane to the genesis of Beckett's texts.[28]

Consequently, the study highlights the complexities of form and method which characterise the anti-essentialist aspirations of Beckett's texts in relation to the use of an Irish context. Particular attention is paid to *Molloy* (in French and English), *Malone meurt* and *Malone Dies*, novels through which Beckett refined his approach to translation, and to *Waiting for Godot* and *Endgame*, plays widely recognised as central to the development of absurdist drama in the 1950s. The study opens with a discussion of the manner in which Beckett's hostility towards Irish parochialism shaped his understanding of his artistic purpose. His rejection of the nationalist ideals of the Revival, as evidenced in his critical writings of the 1930s and *Murphy*, provided him with a necessary distance from essentialist understandings of national identity. However, his response to the Revival remained ambivalent, and later experimental pieces for the theatre reveal his kinship with certain aspects of Revivalist drama. Drawing on this analysis of Beckett's formative years, the second chapter looks at translation as a transformative act in Beckett's work; it outlines a context for understanding Beckett's use of the mechanisms of translation *outside* the act of translation itself, at the level of narration and style. Using case studies from the *Three Novels* or trilogy (*Molloy, Malone Dies, The Unnamable*), this section highlights connections between Beckett's translation choices and projects of the Revival period, showing that Beckett's ambivalent response to the Revival instructs the procedures of translation through which inconsistency of meaning is generated in his work. As the chapter surveys the processes of translation shaping Beckett's approach to meaning, it calls for a re-evaluation of his relationship to existentialist definitions of the absurd. The third chapter discusses Beckett's concern with the subject of material scarcity and illustrates how this defining feature may be contextualised, paying particular attention to Beckett's early drama. Here, Beckett's approach to the issue of scarcity is read in the light of primitive leanings within Revivalist literature, showing that the influence of the Revival informed the position occupied by his work in a series of debates within Marxism and existentialism concerning the representation of historical consciousness and the role of modernism. Finally, the fourth chapter addresses the functioning of Beckett's imagination as considerably more locally rooted than is often assumed, focusing on the geneses of dramatic texts from the 1960s and 1970s and commenting upon the recurrent and careful elision of Irish traits and allusions, a mechanism which governs Beckett's interest in, and attraction to, certain avant-garde practices. This aspect of Beckett's evolution as a playwright is related to modernist experiments theorised by Wassily Kandinsky and Arnold Schoenberg, whose explorations of the concept of abstraction provide precedents for Beckett's own. The more Beckett attempted to purge his writing of its Irish echoes and reliance upon an Irish context, the more these elements insinuated themselves as structural problems: the processes of erosion, accretion and displacement that shape his representations of Ireland leave an indelible imprint on his brand of minimalism. Manuscript evidence shows that the modes of representation and non-representation favoured by Beckett in his later drama crystallise entirely around the structural problems posed by the use of an Irish context.

* * *

Before we go any further, it is necessary to point towards important biographical questions underlying Beckett's relationship to modernist concerns. Indeed, his development as a writer was, to a large extent, fashioned by an awareness of the changes taking place in Irish letters and politics. Although he lived in an environment sheltered from the experience of the Catholic majority, the Ireland he knew was a country in turmoil, and he saw the fractures and transitions that marked its progression towards a new political order. Born on 13 April 1906 in the Dublin suburb of Foxrock, he was raised in a wealthy Protestant family, in which announcing one's intention to vote for Eamon de Valera in the

1933 General Election was considered an act of rebellion.[29] What little he witnessed of political violence as a child was at a remove; nevertheless, some of the events taking place during the drive towards independence left him with tenacious memories. The vision of Dublin in flames during the Easter Rising, for instance, left a deep impression upon the young Beckett.[30] Part of his early education took place in a Dublin multi-denominational school called Earlsfort House, after which he attended institutions hostile to Irish sovereignty such as Portora Royal School in Enniskillen and Trinity College Dublin. He experienced the reality of partition directly at Portora, when the partitioning enactments were taking effect, and again during the two terms he spent teaching at Campbell College in Belfast in 1928. Between November 1928 and September 1930, he worked as *lecteur* at the Ecole Normale Supérieure in Paris, where he met Thomas MacGreevy, who would become his confidant; during this time, he also became closely acquainted with James Joyce and his circle.[31] After returning to Ireland, he lectured at Trinity College Dublin but soon resigned, stating that he could not bear teaching to others what he did not know himself.[32]

Dublin did not provide the intellectual stimulation that Beckett craved. In correspondence with MacGreevy, he deplored the apathy and narrow-mindedness of Irish intellectuals and described the Irish capital as little more than a cultural backwater. As a budding writer, he remained on the margins of the Dublin literary world, in which his fiction was, for a time, renowned for its obscenity.[33] Contact with the Dublin *literati* (among whom Austin Clarke, Percy Ussher and Liam O'Flaherty figured as a particularly loathsome battalion)[34] was merely occasional, and Beckett remained extremely sceptical about the domains of aesthetic and thematic investigation in the post-Revival period, preferring to look towards the formal experiments celebrated in modernist periodicals such as Eugene Jolas's *transition*. The lack of success of *More Pricks Than Kicks*, his first collection of short stories, published in London in 1934 and set in Dublin, was a cruel disappointment; Beckett complained to MacGreevy shortly after its publication that his book was unavailable in Dublin.[35] In articles and reviews written for a range of Irish, English and French periodicals throughout the 1930s, he manifested his concern about the orthodox logic of thought and imagination that ruled over the representation of national identity; his fear that the intellectual life of the country might have come to a standstill due to harsh censorship laws is evident, as he voices his frustration at the insularity of the Irish Free State (or the "I.F.S.", as he liked to designate it).[36] His letters to MacGreevy expressed in less covert terms his unease with

Irish economic and political isolationism, and he commented with disbelief upon Eamon de Valera's ideal of a self-supporting Ireland:

> An Italian barber told me De Valera was a great man, would never let his country down, would stick to his point. Bravo! But the night porter at the Shaftesbury, from Dublin, is very annoyed indeed about the whole business. He'll be the ruin of the country, he said. And between the two positions the rustle of Cockneys rubbing their hands.[37]

Clearly, for Beckett, the terms of the equation had not changed since the end of British rule, and de Valera was scarcely better than "cockatoo Cosgrave arrayed as a Fascist".[38] A 1934 article written in protest against censorship and entitled "Censorship in the Saorstat" provides evidence of his ongoing concern with the impact of governmental policies upon Irish literature: his plea is addressed to a society more concerned about its agricultural output than the arts.

The 1930s were also a difficult decade in terms of familial relationships: Beckett's everyday life at Cooldrinagh, the family home in Foxrock, was marked by continuous conflicts with his mother, May. He soon resolved to break free from this stifling environment; a long-term escape after the death of his father in 1933 took him to London in order to undergo psychoanalysis. He stayed in London for two years; then, in September 1936, he went to Germany, where he remained until April 1937, before making France his permanent residence in October 1937. His choice not to return to a neutral Ireland at the beginning of the war is generally seen as a radical step, an impression cultivated by Beckett himself. In an interview with Israel Shenker, he notoriously justified his choice by saying that he "preferred France in war to Ireland in peace", stating that theocracy and censorship had pushed him out of Ireland.[39] During the decade following the Second World War, he visited his family occasionally, but after the death of his mother in 1950 and that of his brother in 1954, he rarely went to Dublin.

As Beckett gradually drifted away from the concerns which had permeated his youth, the tone of his exchanges with Thomas MacGreevy also shifted; the warmth and enthusiasm of their early correspondence diminished as MacGreevy's nationalist leanings became more affirmed.[40] Their views on the role of the artist differed considerably, and an ongoing dialogue regarding the painting of Jack Yeats reveals a Beckett often angered by MacGreevy's heavy-handed use of nationalist rhetoric. Their disagreements did, however, have a salutary effect on Beckett, forcing him to refine his understanding of the purpose of the modern artist.

Their correspondence was affected by the impact of the Second World War upon Beckett's daily life: indeed, the war forced a long pause in exchanges that had otherwise been strikingly regular between 1930 and 1937. Interrupted due to Beckett's difficult circumstances, the correspondence was resumed at a slower pace in 1945. After the war, Beckett became more openly critical of MacGreevy's nationalist beliefs and questioned his motives publicly, publishing a scathing review of MacGreevy's monograph on Jack Yeats in 1945 in the *Irish Times*. At this point, it became evident that he resented MacGreevy's orthodox nationalism and wished to dissociate himself from it. It also appears that Beckett ceased to confide in his friend concerning his writing. Their divergence became clear in 1951, when MacGreevy expressed disappointment at Beckett's failure to provide him with a copy of *Molloy*. The situation was remedied immediately: Beckett sent copies of *Molloy* and the freshly published *Malone meurt*, explaining his fear that such works might upset his friend.[41]

The tensions evident in Beckett's correspondence with MacGreevy confirm that exile was a necessary step in Beckett's progress and that, while the post-Revival period may have had little to offer a writer of his stature, he also had too little in common with his Irish contemporaries to be able to develop in such an environment. Beckett keenly suggested as much in his critical reviews of 1930s Irish poetry and drama, in which he denounced the parochialism of Yeats's followers. His ferocious attacks upon Revivalist literature were not without precedent among writers of the post-Revival generation: similar reactions can be traced in the writings of Flann O'Brien and Sean O'Casey, who also searched for a counter-discourse to the idealism sutured to national character in post-independence Ireland.

For Flann O'Brien, de Valera's ideal of a Catholic, Irish-speaking, self-sufficient republic was nonsensical at best and nefarious at worst. In his famous St Patrick's Day address of 1943, de Valera equated national identity with social uniformity, dreaming of idyllic rural communities in which frugal living conditions and the pursuit of spiritual and intellectual fulfilment went hand in hand.[42] O'Brien's column in the *Irish Times*, published under the pseudonym of Myles na gCopaleen (in reference to Dion Boucicault's *The Colleen Bawn*), is replete with sarcastic comments about governmental attempts to project an idealised vision of a rural and classless Ireland:

> I read in the papers that some fine Irishmen have declared that we must all live like the good folk in the Gaeltacht, leading that simple life, speaking that far-from-simple language, presumably occupying

ourselves with the uncomplicated agricultural chores which distinguish all ethnic groups the world over which have been denied the enervating influence of H.M. English language. Uniquely, a large section of our people wish to be peasants, thus giving hope of a return to the primal balance to which I have referred. To the plain people of Ireland I will make a fair offer. If, gathering together in solemn conclave ye pledge yerselves to be humble unsophisticates unacquainted with English, innocent of all sciences save that of the smiling Irish fields, I, for my part, am prepared to be King.[43]

Beckett was familiar with the English versions of O'Brien's column; the many guises and voices adopted by O'Brien's persona Myles may have appealed to him.[44] O'Brien's keen use of national clichés did not fall on deaf ears, and his satirical writings provide a suitable precedent for viewing Beckett's caricatures of Irish political life in later works such as *Texts for Nothing*.[45] For Beckett, as with O'Brien's column, republicanism is synonymous with passivity, conservatism and an assiduous reading of the sports section:

> The sport of kings is our passion, the dogs too, we have no political opinions, simply limply republican. But we also have a soft spot for the Windsors, the Hanoverians, I forget, the Hohenzollerns is it. Nothing human is foreign to us, once we have digested the racing news.[46]

However, despite their shared hostility to the idea of a monolithic Irish national character, there is little evidence of a personal exchange between Beckett and O'Brien. Their sole meeting in Dublin, according to Beckett, was disappointing. Probably due to O'Brien's lasting animosity towards Joyce, Beckett felt that their discussion did not deserve to be commented upon.[47]

In contrast, Beckett felt a strong artistic affinity with Sean O'Casey, celebrating in a 1934 review the latter's capacity to provoke and innovate. He regretted O'Casey's estrangement from the world of Irish letters and, as he stated in later years, thought of O'Casey's exile as a crucial step in the history of Irish drama, condemning Yeats's rejection of O'Casey's expressionist play *The Silver Tassie* for production at the Abbey as a monumental error.[48] As a young critic, Beckett may also have identified with O'Casey's bitterness towards the figureheads of the Revival; indeed, "Recent Irish Poetry" is not far removed from O'Casey's *Autobiographies*, in which O'Casey casts himself as a mere spectator, watching the antics of his contemporaries and mocking the self-importance of "the long-haired poet, Yeats himself", and Lady Gregory's fascination for Celtic iconography.[49] However, O'Casey's correspondence reveals a disapproval of the pessimism and political aloofness that he perceived as features of Beckett's early drama. Initially, he rejected comparisons between his work and Beckett's, and he later objected to Beckett's "never-ending tenebre despair", which he perceived as defeatism.[50]

Nevertheless, a form of political solidarity, largely nurtured by external circumstances, gradually developed between the two writers.[51] Both contributed to Nancy Cunard's 1937 pamphlet against the Spanish Civil War; Beckett's famous one-word contribution ("¡UPTHEREPUBLIC!") contrasted with O'Casey's exuberant statement, which manifested his support for "the determined faces firing at the steel-clad slug of Fascism from the smoke and flame of the barricades".[52] Both men also asserted their unconditional resistance to Irish censorship in 1958, when a Dublin festival that planned to stage O'Casey's *The Drums of Father Ned*, a dramatic adaptation of Joyce's *Ulysses* and Beckett's mime plays was unofficially banned from showing by Archbishop McQuaid, who refused to say an opening mass at the festival.[53] O'Casey immediately imposed his own official ban on professional performances of all his plays in Ireland and maintained it for six years.[54] Beckett followed O'Casey's ban on the grounds of solidarity, stating that withdrawal was the only form of protest at his disposal.[55] Alan Simpson, director of Dublin's Pike Theatre, hoped that Beckett would soon let his work be performed in Ireland again. However, the latter maintained his stance for several years; his correspondence with Simpson reveals his scorn for "Eire or whatever the name of the place is now".[56] The ban would remain in place until May 1960, when Beckett authorised Cyril Cusack to organise two performances of *Krapp's Last Tape* in Dublin, a decision that resulted eventually in Beckett giving permission for his plays to be performed on Irish stages.[57] However, he remained, for a long time, reluctant to encourage productions of his work in Ireland, writing to the actor Jack McGowran in 1965: "As you know I'm not keen on my work being done in Ireland. But there's no point in bringing that up now".[58]

The threads linking Beckett to writers of the post-Revival generation allow for more than simple comparison, shedding light upon shared political concerns among literary figures of the period. However, Beckett's attacks upon censorship and conservatism carried little political weight, in contrast to O'Brien and O'Casey. His article against censorship was never published, and his early writings placed him in an extremely vulnerable position in 1930s Dublin, as evidenced during the trial that opposed his uncle Henry Morris Sinclair to Oliver St John Gogarty in 1937. Gogarty was an influential public figure in Dublin and the trial attracted much attention from the press. As chief witness, Beckett, newly settled in France, had to return to Dublin temporarily. It can be argued that the proceedings brought to a head many of the problems that he had faced as a budding writer in 1930s Dublin. The hearings were humiliating; as the author of a book banned six months after its publication, *More Pricks Than Kicks*, Beckett played the role of scapegoat.[59] He was discredited for his essay on "Prowst" and called a "blasphemer" and a "wretched creature" by the defending counsel. He subsequently did his best to erase this episode from his memory: when Ruby Cohn asked him how long he had stayed in Dublin for the trial, he replied in the margin of her letter: "Forget".[60] Beckett's expression of grand forgetfulness contrasts with his otherwise bitter statements on 1930s Dublin and suggests an unwillingness to dwell upon his vulnerability as an artist in the Irish Free State. Subsequently, he refused to make direct statements to the public, writing, for instance, to Jacoba van Velde, who acted as his literary agent after the war and later translated his work into Dutch: "Je ne suis pas critique et n'ai à exprimer publiquement aucun jugement d'ordre littéraire (ou autre)" [I am not a critic and refuse to make any public statement of whatever nature, literary judgement or other].[61]

In France, Beckett's friendships with artists such as Marcel Duchamp and Alberto Giacometti reveal his closeness to an artistic elite aware of the politics of its time but unwilling to present itself as having a direct political impact. Often irritated by people's attempts to impose a meaning upon his writings, Beckett treated political readings of his work as nothing more than embarrassing deflections, emphasising that he was not a social commentator.[62] Nevertheless, his concern for the defence of human rights is well known, and he took action when he thought it necessary: in South Africa, for instance, he banned the performance of his plays in theatres that insisted on maintaining racial segregation. His manifestations of support for artists persecuted by their governments often took the shape of public gestures: in 1967, he wrote to the Franco government, asking for the liberation of the playwright Fernando Arrabal, who had been imprisoned for treason and blasphemy, and, in 1982, he dedicated the play *Catastrophe* to Václav Havel, detained for his involvement in the Czech human rights movement. These displays of solidarity have been ascribed to Beckett's staunch humanist beliefs: W.J. McCormack, for instance, has emphasised Beckett's concern regarding anti-colonialist movements and the Spanish Civil War.[63] Nevertheless, notions of Beckett as liberal, left-wing and anti-racist are less convincing when one considers his formative years; his introduction to "Dante...Bruno. Vico..Joyce" and his comments on Henry Crowder (Nancy Cunard's black lover) in correspondence smack of racism.[64]

* * *

Reading Beckett's responses to the literary and artistic developments of the post-Revival period in their historical contexts brings to light rarely acknowledged political concerns, and enables, in turn, a nuanced understanding of the political tenor of his *oeuvre*.[65] Nevertheless, it remains difficult to qualify Beckett's relationship to the idea of the political, given the work's bilinguality and its antithetical relationship to the Sartrean notion of commitment. The impact of external dynamics upon published texts and resources has further obscured the possibility of an understanding of the issue based on concrete evidence: indeed, the nature of Beckett's political concerns has been obfuscated by a variety of factors, including the editing choices made in published letters and interviews. His correspondence with the theatre director Alan Schneider, for example, was edited in a manner which occasionally presents his comments on current affairs as unworthy of attention, and similar editing strategies were used in Charles Juliet's account of his conversations with Beckett.[66] Clearly, Beckett remained an outsider in the world of French letters during the post-war period, reluctant to take a stand in the debates surrounding the dissolution of the French colonial empire in North Africa and the social revolution that followed May 1968. Although his involvement in the French Resistance gave him a prominent political status after the war, his foreign resident status necessitated a cautiousness in his statements. This was particularly evident during the Algerian War of Independence, as James Knowlson illustrates in his biography.[67] Viewed in relation to his precarious position in France, Beckett's decision to preserve an Irish setting in many of his French texts thus raises difficult questions regarding his relationship with anti-colonial movements beyond Ireland. Indeed, the cultural, historical and geographical references to Ireland that linger in his French writings signal his outsider status and apparent freedom from contemporaneous political debate. Yet, in the context of the Algerian war, these Irish echoes retained provocative undertones, inflecting Beckett's work with a political content, yet deflecting the possibility of addressing the effects of colonialism, due to the various forms of erosion and elision that characterise such references to Irish culture and politics.

If Beckett's refusal to present himself as an Irish writer is best understood as a ramification of his response to a Revivalist literature dominated by Yeats's nationalism, the theoretical notions that provide elucidation of Beckett's simultaneous engagement with and disengagement from Irish culture and history remain exterior to any Irish context the work may inhabit. In particular, the question of commitment arises primarily in relation to Beckett's wider political and philosophical contexts; indeed, Beckett's persistence in associating Ireland with an ensemble of cultural and historical residues finds adequate contextualisation in the tension between Jean-Paul Sartre's notion of *littérature engagée* and Adorno's response to it.

In the 1947 *Qu'est-ce que la littérature?*, Sartre examined the link between individual responsibility and literary representation, calling for a literature of contestation able to awaken social action and turn its readers into active agents, rather than mere spectators. His definition of the nature of *engagement* or commitment was hugely influential in its establishment of an equation between literature and political protest. However, Sartre's philosophy of writing is limited in scope, as its examination of the act of writing developed from a hierarchisation of forms. Indeed, Sartre claimed that only prose could be committed, his definition effectively excluding what he considered to be non-representational art forms and mediums such as music and poetry. Despite Beckett displaying the potential to produce a fully committed form of writing, his work did not sit well with Sartre's own principles: when Sartre was asked whether he could identify writers working in accordance with his ideas (by which the interviewer meant working "towards greater freedom, within a full commitment"), he named Beckett among practitioners of the *nouveau roman* such as Alain Robbe-Grillet, Nathalie Sarraute and Michel Butor.[68] However, for Sartre, only Butor was actively looking for answers to the problem of freedom and commitment; Robbe-Grillet, Sarraute and Beckett had goals of a different nature. Sartre's exclusion of poetry and music from the possibility of engagement was not without impact on his philosophical position within Marxism; Fredric Jameson argues that his refusal to consider non-representational art forms prevented him from addressing the debates surrounding the historical and political impetus of avant-garde literary movements.[69] For Jameson, Sartre's decision to prioritise prose over other art forms was precisely the reason for his failure to tackle the nuances that preoccupied Brecht, Lukács and Adorno in their considerations of the respective merits of realism and modernism.

At the same time, Sartre's definition of engagement provided a framework within which the role of the avant-garde could be rearticulated. Adorno's polemical essay "Commitment", for instance, draws on Sartre's understanding of a committed literature to examine the avant-garde's precarious position in post-war Europe. Responding to Sartre's analysis of the relation of art to society, Adorno calls the subjectivism of Sartre's argument into question, pointing out that Sartre postulates "an identity between living individuals and the essence of society" and argues for an "absolute sovereignty of the subject".[70] He denounces another flaw in Sartre's theory, namely that a committed literature runs the risk of degenerating into ideology, if not pure propaganda. Taking Brecht's drama as an example, Adorno argues that the decision to give art a didactic purpose is self-defeating and politically naïve: he claims that Brecht trivialises political reality and fails to portray the horrors of fascism. Sartre's theatre, a "theatre of unfreedom", is equally flawed and radically at odds with Sartre's own philosophy of writing.[71] Here, Beckett's exploration of meaninglessness provides Adorno with a platform for criticising the lack of sophistication of Sartre's understanding of modernism. For Adorno, Beckett's writing questions the conceptual dimension of existentialism and represents the abdication of the subject in a post-Auschwitz world: his drama, like Kafka's, makes officially committed works look like "pantomime" by comparison, but compels a change of attitudes by arousing the kind of anguish which existentialism merely invokes.[72] This comparison between Brecht, Beckett and Kafka eventually leads Adorno to reverse Sartre's proposition entirely, emphasising that "[t]his is not a time for political art": "politics has migrated into autonomous art, and nowhere more so than where it seems to be politically dead".[73]

Aesthetic Theory questions Sartre's notion of commitment further, presenting protest as impossible in a modern world that has lost meaning. Adorno describes the autonomy of art as twofold, as an illusion and as a necessary fact, and establishes that which binds the work of art *to* society as a corollary to that which enables its autonomy *from* society. For Adorno, it is necessary to understand the twofold nature of art in order to comprehend the social importance of the avant-garde. This leads him to define resistance as the sole social function of art, which he perceives as an immanent, elusive movement *against* society:

> The relation of art and society has its locus in art itself and its development, not in immediate partisanship, in what today is called *commitment*. It is equally fruitless to seek to grasp this relationship

theoretically by constructing as an invariant the non-conformist attitudes of art through history and opposing it to affirmative attitude. There is no dearth of artworks that could only with difficulty be forced into a nonconformist tradition – which is in any case thoroughly fissured – whose objectivity nevertheless maintains a profoundly critical stance toward society.[74]

Adorno's exploration of the autonomy of art in *Aesthetic Theory* is, in fact, an attempt to negotiate the political status of the literature of the absurd in post-war Europe, where, as he points out, understanding itself has become a problematic category.[75] Beckett's work is central to his discussion, as the embodiment of a crisis of meaning that is "rooted in a problematic common to all art, the failure in the face of rationality".[76] In both form and content, Beckett's texts are expressions of this failure, an artistic choice which differentiates him from his contemporaries: according to Adorno, it is precisely Beckett's ability to *reject* meaning that differentiates him from a Sartre who attempts to *inject* meaning into his plays.[77] While Adorno identifies the disappearance of meaning as central to avant-garde literature, he also suggests that the problems of meaning raised in Beckett's work should be historicised adequately, because his work "is ruled as much by an obsession with positive nothingness as by the obsession with a meaninglessness that has developed historically and is thus in a sense merited, though this meritedness in no way allows any positive meaning to be reclaimed".[78]

Although Adorno's focus remains centred upon the role of the European avant-garde after the Second World War, his understanding of modernism provides useful access to the ways in which Beckett's use of Irishness governs his interest in, and adoption of, avant-garde techniques. More precisely, Adorno's analysis of patterns of autonomy and resistance within avant-garde movements provides a precious insight into Beckett's simultaneous engagement with and disengagement from an Irish context, making space for the ways in which Beckett's artistic development remained bound to his rejection of the imaginative realms available to the Irish writer during and after the Revival period. Drawing on Adorno's understanding of modernism, what follows is an attempt to examine the ways in which some of the pressures that Beckett negotiated as a developing artist in Ireland and France filtered into his writings, informing his turn to self-translation and search for new expressive forms.

1
Beckett and the Irish Literary Revival

The drama produced in Dublin in the 1920s and 1930s is the backdrop against which Beckett developed a genuine love for theatre. During his years of study at Trinity College Dublin, between 1923 and 1927, he was a regular theatregoer, known among his peers for his enthusiasm for the Abbey Theatre and his interest in "abstruse" plays.[1] He was particularly interested in W.B. Yeats's drama and later spoke highly of *At the Hawk's Well*, *Purgatory*, *The Words upon the Window-pane* and Yeats's two adaptations of Sophocles, *Oedipus the King* and *Oedipus at Colonus*.[2] His later declarations about the Abbey, however, were ambivalent. In 1970, the list he gave to biographer James Knowlson of the plays he remembered seeing in his youth does not indicate a noteworthy interest in the Abbey, inclusions being limited to Synge, Yeats, O'Casey, Lennox Robinson, T.C. Murray and Brinsley Macnamara.[3] In contrast, a 1989 interview with Knowlson suggests that Beckett's interest in the Abbey was far more significant than he had previously implied: he claimed to have made weekly visits to the Abbey and stated that he would always occupy the same seats; he also remembered the various ticket prices and the layout of the theatre.[4] Although the Abbey Theatre remained dominated by "peasant quality" drama throughout the 1920s and 1930s, its programmes were not exclusively devoted to Revival or post-Revival plays and left room for translations of Ibsen, Chekhov, Romains, Schnitzler and Pirandello.[5] The young Beckett may have been attracted to these incursions into European drama; there is evidence that he saw a 1932 production of Ibsen's *The Wild Duck*, for instance.[6]

During the 1930s, he frequented a variety of other theatres: some, such as the Gate, produced avant-garde European drama, while others, such as the Queen's, the Gaiety, the Olympia and the Theatre Royal, displayed more populist leanings.[7] He also occasionally attended productions of the Dublin Drama League, which was devoted to keeping the Dublin public in touch with European drama and was run by George Yeats and Lennox Robinson.[8] His interest in the theatre found other outlets: in the mid-1930s, some of his leisure time was spent sharing ideas with an amateur drama group that supported German Expressionism.[9] During this decade, he was also briefly involved in plays written by friends, such as Georges Pelorson's pastiche of Corneille's *Le Cid*, staged at the Peacock Theatre in 19 31, and Mary Manning's *Youth's the Season*, staged at the Gate Theatre in 1936.[10]

Beckett's correspondence evidences an interest in Irish drama which did not diminish after he left Ireland.[11] Shortly after moving to France, he expressed a hope to see the premiere of Yeats's *Purgatory* in Dublin in August 1938.[12] In Paris, he would keep an eye on the Abbey plays put on at the Théâtre des Nations, and,[13] in a 1947 letter to Arland Ussher, he commented upon the success of a Paris production of O'Casey's *L'Ombre d'un franc-tireur* (*The Shadow of a Gunman*).[14] He also kept himself informed regarding new plays appearing in Dublin; in a 1955 letter to Mary Manning, he evoked his dislike of Cyril Cusack's production of Synge's *The Playboy of the Western World*, which he witnessed at Dublin's Gaiety Theatre during the summer of 1954.[15] He also asked Manning for the script of Jack Yeats's Abbey play *In Sand* following Thomas MacGreevy's enthusiastic praise. Later, he made a coded allusion to this play in *Happy Days*, in which Winnie's leitmotiv "no pain – hardly any" echoes Jack Yeats's line "no pain, no fuss".[16]

Beckett's mixed feelings regarding the Abbey were not muted over time; having become established as a playwright, he maintained a clearly expressed distance from the Abbey's naturalism, despite indicating the extent of his interest in Revivalist drama. In 1956, for instance, he refused to endorse a tribute for the centenary of Shaw's birth at the Gaiety Theatre, acknowledging instead his deep admiration for Yeats's *At the Hawk's Well*, Synge's *The Well of the Saints* and O'Casey's *Juno and the Paycock*. In response to Cyril Cusack, who had asked him to write a tribute to Shaw in French for the Gaiety's commemorative booklet, Beckett stated that he "wouldn't write in French for King Street".[17] He also made clear his profound dislike of Shaw, joking that he would gladly trade "the whole unupsettable apple-cart for a sup of the Hawk's Well, or the Saints', or a whiff of Juno, to go no further". Beckett's 'tribute' reads as a token of his admiration for the innovative dramatic forms developed during the Revival period. It also registers a humorous disdain for Irish attempts to define a unified literary canon, alluding to Shaw's chosen position of outsider in relation to the Abbey (which

Shaw expressed, for instance, in his preface to *John Bull's Other Island*). Last but not least, Beckett's note contrasts with the greetings he sent to the *Irish Times* for O'Casey's eightieth birthday four years later. In this instance, he celebrated a playwright estranged from his homeland and a work able to transcend national boundaries: "To my great compatriot, Sean O'Casey, from France where he is honoured, I send my enduring gratitude and homage".[18]

Beckett's statement of dissent regarding orthodox definitions of the 'Irish writer' should not be taken at face value: indeed, his correspondence with Thomas MacGreevy during the 1930s reveals that his technical understanding of the theatre developed very much in relation to the plays he saw in Dublin at the time. His comments upon questions of dramatisation, setting and lighting are never exempt from self-mockery and he occasionally mimics the tone of a critic. Describing Balderston and Squire's *Berkeley Square* as "a ragged adaptation of the ragged Sense of the Past", he wrote in 1936: "Of course it is not a play at all, but a very interesting psychological situation with all kinds of unuttered obiters that are scarcely developed in the book either as far as I remember".[19] His judgements are often uncompromising. He loathed Synge's *Deirdre of the Sorrows*, for instance, and thought that Synge's rendering of Deirdre was inadequate in its accentuation of her childishness; nevertheless, when the play was revived at the Abbey in 1935, he thought of taking his mother to see it, explaining to MacGreevy that he would not go and see such a poor Synge play on his own account.[20] Clearly, he was immensely disappointed by Synge's recasting of this ancient legend in stylised peasant speech and found his treatment of Deirdre neglectful.[21]

His letters to MacGreevy also lament a perceived lack of professionalism on Dublin stages and reveal his dislike of the directors of the Gate Theatre, Hilton Edwards and Micheál MacLiammóir, whom he briefly met while working on Mary Manning's *Youth's the Season*.[22] The Gate, founded in 1928 as an antidote to the parochialism of the Abbey, was keen on presenting its productions as cosmopolitan and eclectic and was the first Irish theatre to treat lighting, settings and costumes as elements which had to be methodically and systematically designed.[23] However, the young Beckett judged its productions tasteless and aesthetically unadventurous. While he kept an eye on the Gate's programmes, he showed little enthusiasm for the attempts of its directors to 'Europeanise' the Irish stage. His comments regarding a 1932 production of Ibsen's *Peer Gynt* (which he did not go to) suggest that he saw Gate productions of European drama as elitist and pretentious: "Such wonderful lighting, my dear, all coming from behind instead of in front. Imagine that! And Grieg without mercy".[24] The Gate's production of Shakespeare's *Romeo and Juliet*, which succeeded *Peer Gynt*, also failed to meet with his approval:

> All wrong, fundamentally wrong. MacLiammoir said his lines nicely enough, but missed a lot of chances, slurring over things like "rejoice in splendour of mine own". The others were unspeakable, the lighting & setting flashy and crepuscular, when the whole thing should be full of sun & heat.[25]

Beckett found the level of technical mastery displayed at the Abbey Theatre equally unsatisfying, writing that, although the production of Ibsen's *The Wild Duck* was badly directed and badly acted, it remained a fine work.[26] Lady Gregory's theatrical techniques were, in his view, particularly mediocre; after witnessing a revival of *Dervorgilla* in 1934, he described the play as unconditionally vulgar in its conception and execution.[27] His negative comments recall Joyce's own stance in the early 1900s, particularly his attacks upon Lady Gregory's stylised dramatic language and his denunciation of Revivalist drama as populist, backward and vulgar.[28] Clearly, for Beckett, Lady Gregory's use of ancient myth had disturbing resonances in post-independence Ireland. This is confirmed in his account of Eileen Crowe's performance as Dervorgilla; calling her an "ineffable bitch", he compared her to "Frau Lot petrified into a symbolic condemnation of free trade", an embodiment of Irish economic isolationism.[29] He also greeted some of Yeats's late plays with little enthusiasm, criticising their slowness and pomposity. After seeing productions of *The Resurrection* and *The King of the Great Clock Tower* at the Abbey (the presence of his friend Con Leventhal among the cast of *The Resurrection* possibly being an incentive for his attendance),[30] he lamented in August 1934: "The ancient thermolater at play. Balbus building his wall would be more dramatic".[31] Ironically, similar criticisms were directed against his own plays much later: Jorge Luis Borges called him "a bore", and Vivian Mercier famously referred to *Waiting for Godot* as a play in which "nothing happens, *twice*".[32]

* * *

If Beckett was quick to chastise Abbey productions for their lack of polish, his dismissive comments nevertheless reveal an interest in their search for a new expressive force in dramatic language and stage design.

Through the agencies of Yeats and Synge, Revivalist drama remained engaged in ongoing dialogue with European artistic movements, fusing modes of representation influenced by Richard Wagner, Maurice Maeterlinck, Henrik Ibsen and Stéphane Mallarmé with themes and motifs drawn from ancient Celtic lore.[33] It is precisely this leaning towards avant-garde experiment that is pertinent in considering Revivalist drama as a formative influence upon Beckett: viewed in the light of Beckett's comments, the late Revival period is revealed as profoundly attuned to the principles and processes of modernism.

Even if its formal radicalism denotes a familiarity with contemporaneous literary currents in mainland Europe, identifying the Revival as an avant-garde movement raises difficult questions. Indeed, the term 'avant-garde' finds its source in a form of political radicalism and resistance to the established order, whereas the Revival is generally envisaged as a culturally orthodox, anti-modern phenomenon, shaped by the nationalism of Yeats's early writings – a perspective influenced by Yeats's authoritative statements on the purpose of literary representation.[34] When issuing guidelines to Irish writers in the 1890s, Yeats associated the idea of a national literature with stylistic and thematic homogeneity, gradually imposing an understanding of Irish writing that was largely defined by its proximity to folk myth and legend.[35] The elements that Yeats deemed to be indicative of national distinctiveness remained a source of disagreement among Irish writers of the period; nevertheless, differences in perspective were overcome by a shared desire to find modes of representation through which the nation might be awakened to a sense of its own cultural specificity.[36] The actual development of Revivalist literature remained informed by this reflection, as writers experimented with the dramatic stylisation of peasant speech and perfected strategies of representation that diverged from the colonial stereotypes that previously dominated artistic production.[37]

According to Terry Eagleton, the discrepancy between the nationalist aspirations of the early Revival period and its leaning towards experimentation is precisely what generates its uniqueness. In an influential essay entitled "The Archaic Avant-Garde", Eagleton utilises the example of the Revival to show that avant-garde figures such as Beckett emerged from cultures at the threshold of modernity, neither modern nor traditional. Nevertheless, he points out that the orthodox nationalism promoted in Revivalist literature remained antithetical to literary experimentation and that the Revival was not part of an avant-garde in the strict sense of the term; rather, it combined tradition and modernity in a unique way, largely remaining under the sway of tradition.[38] Such an analysis prompts a reconsideration of the Revival's relationship to the idea of the modern, yet Eagleton fails to remark upon the conceptual proximity of the Revival to nationalist projects in eighteenth- and nineteenth-century Europe (some of which involved, for instance, Herder, Kleist and Wagner in Germany). It is important to note that Irish interest in folklore was also consistent with other contemporaneous artistic currents; for instance, the *Blaue Reiter Almanac*, published in 1912 at the initiative of Wassily Kandinsky and Franz Marc, included examples of European, African and Asiatic folk art alongside recent Expressionist and Cubist paintings and atonal music scores.[39] Two exhibitions were organised prior to its printing in 1911 and 1912, one of which included a large number of Russian folk prints or *lubki*, much admired by Kandinsky. The rationale for the almanac emerged from Kandinsky's rejection of the boundaries between folk art, children's art and ethnography, which he considered to be closely related phenomena, distinguished by their shared disdain for academic and formal precepts.[40]

While it remains essential to consider the Revival an integral part of European artistic currents, the context within which Revivalist writers operated was heavily laden with anti-colonial concerns, forbidding linear comparisons with ventures such as those of the *Blaue Reiter* group. The drama of the early Revival period, in particular, was driven by an aspiration towards an ideal of faithful representation that set the movement apart from anti-naturalistic currents. At the foundation of the Abbey in 1904, Lady Gregory and Yeats asserted their wish to counter colonial representations of Irishness enshrined in nineteenth-century literature, stating that Irish dramatists should depict Ireland not as "the home of buffoonery and of easy sentiment, as it has been represented", but as "the home of an ancient idealism".[41] Abbey plays should, as Yeats suggested, present the "sincere observation and experience" of rural life in Ireland.[42]

Soon, however, the selection criteria relinquished such lofty purpose. Once the directors of the Abbey accepted Free State subsidies in 1924, performances became subjected to government control and the guidelines for writers were tightened.[43] Writers who submitted a play that fell short of the Abbey's standards but showed potential for revision received an advice form, drafted by Yeats, which specified: "A play to be suitable for performance at the Abbey should contain some criticism of life, founded on the experience or personal observation of the writer, or some vision of life, of Irish life by preference".[44] The form stated explicitly that propagandist plays and works written "mainly to serve some obvious moral purpose" would be turned down. George O'Brien, appointed in 1925 by the Irish government to the Abbey board of directors, made constant efforts to minimise the provocative character of the plays produced, particularly those of Sean O'Casey; the appearance of a prostitute in *The Plough and the Stars*, for instance, posed problems.[45] The amount of control imposed upon Abbey productions peaked during the 1930s, when the parochial character of Abbey plays was exacerbated. The adoption of a so-called peasant tone became a criterion for assessment in the selection of plays – 'peasant quality' was even abbreviated *pq*.[46]

As a playwright, Yeats gradually became estranged from the goals he had set for Irish writers in his early career: from the mid-1910s, influenced by Ezra Pound and the stage designer Edward Gordon Craig, he diverged from the Abbey's naturalism, evolving towards a highly stylised form of theatre that drew heavily on the conventions of Japanese Noh drama. His desire to find a new trajectory is evident in his comments upon the Abbey's achievements: in "A People's Theatre", a 1919 essay addressed to Lady Gregory, Yeats expressed a desire to explore "the theatre's anti-self" and to create for himself alone an "unpopular" theatre, far removed from the Abbey's attempts to reach the masses.[47] Eastern theatrical techniques provided him with a platform for such a theatre, enabling the recasting of ancient Irish myths in new dramatic forms. However, finding suitable actors and venues in Ireland was difficult, and his most innovative plays were not produced at the Abbey but shown in private performances, notably with the Dublin Drama League, which was dedicated to the promotion of modern European drama.[48] The plays Beckett admired, such as *At the Hawk's Well* and *Purgatory*, were born out of Yeats's acknowledgement that the early aspirations of the Revival were no longer attainable or relevant: they can be more accurately situated as an element of a post-Revival re-evaluation of early Revival idealism than as part of the Revival itself.

The contexts of Yeats's aesthetic choices in the theatre have been thoroughly researched, as has Beckett's long-term, assiduous interest in Yeats's drama. It is not my purpose to elaborate on these issues here, but to highlight the diffuse influence of Yeats's search for alternative theatrical techniques upon Beckett's approach to playwriting.[49] *Play*, in particular, suggests that, although Beckett did not explicitly identify Yeats as a precursor, the latter's non-naturalistic drama provided him with an example of the manner in which an Irish content could be assimilated into experimental forms. *Play* presents us with three heads speaking from beyond the grave: a man, his wife and his mistress, designated M, W1 and W2 respectively. In early drafts, the characters, named Syke,

Nickie and Conk, were differentiated by hair colour and were given more specificity. Nickie, the sole female character, was conceived as emblematically representative of Ireland, with "red hair, milky complexion, full red lips, green earrings".[50] All suggestions of an Irish background were, however, subsequently removed, and the characters were reduced to initials, recalling Yeats's use of archetypal characters. Thus, the genesis of *Play* was marked by a movement from cultural cliché towards the non-specific; at the same time, as the play developed, it drew upon certain aspects of Yeats's own experiments, exhibiting a striking similarity to *The King of the Great Clock Tower*. Yeats's play also focuses upon a love triangle, in this case between three masked characters, King, Queen and Stroller. The presentation of a severed head marks a key moment: the King, angered by the arrogance of the Stroller, orders that his head be cut off; he then places the severed head of the Stroller on a cubical throne and forces the Queen to dance while the severed head sings. The preliminary drafts of Beckett's *Play* recall this particular moment (although Beckett disliked Yeats's play when he first saw it): in early drafts, he initially intended to use three white, yard-high boxes, recalling the throne used by Yeats. He later considered using three large white urns, before finally choosing three identical grey urns.[51] However, unlike Yeats, Beckett specified that no masks should be employed. The actors' heavy make-up, which was originally a mixture of porridge, egg white and glue,[52] nevertheless results in an effect similar to Yeats's use of masks, particularly the "beautiful impassive mask" of the Queen in *The King of the Great Clock Tower*.[53] Consequently, no firm differentiation is established between actors and props in *Play*. This, for Beckett, was an essential feature of the piece, and he emphasised the importance of the stage directions repeatedly.[54]

The vision of a suspended head also dominates Yeats's last play, *The Death of Cuchulain* (1939), which ends with the presentation of seven severed heads figured by black parallelograms, six of which remain on the stage floor while the head of Cuchulain "may, if need be, be raised above the others on a pedestal".[55] It is certain that the Yeatsian echoes of Beckett's experimental piece contribute to a wider network of influences: critics have suggested, for instance, the influence of Oscar Wilde's *Salomé*, a play first written in French and clearly influenced by Maeterlinck and the French Symbolists, which features a severed head presented on a silver shield.[56] Nevertheless, Beckett's idea of trapping the actors in stage accessories in *Play* has distinctively Yeatsian undertones. While searching for means to "give poetical writing its full effect upon the stage", Yeats once asked the actors to rehearse in barrels so that they "might forget gesture and have their minds free to think of speech for a while".[57] Yeats's experiment, in this instance, imitated sound strategies used on the formal Noh stage, where resonators in the form of large earthenware jars built into the substructure enable actors to control pitch and sound at significant moments by positioning themselves strategically.[58] Yeats also thought of adding castors under the barrels so that he could move the actors about with a pole when the action required it – a strategy that Beckett later adopted in *Act without Words II*, in which a goad is used to trigger action.

* * *

Yeats is now widely recognised as a formative influence upon Beckett's approach to stage design and the dramatic use of dance and song; nevertheless, Beckett's opinion of Yeats varied widely, fluctuating between rejection and admiration. As a budding writer, he remained reluctant to view Yeats as a playwright versed in experimental forms of theatre, preferring instead to portray him as an overbearing traditionalist. Such a perspective also bears the stamp of wider concerns relating to artistic expression – concerns which are brought to light in polemical reviews that Beckett published throughout the 1930s, in which the Revival is largely presented as antagonistic to literary experiment.

In particular, in a 1934 review of O'Casey's *Windfalls*, a collection of short stories, poems and plays, Beckett relates artistic experimentation to the rejection of the stylistic and thematic constraints associated with the use of Irish subject matter in Revivalist literature. The review, entitled "The Essential and the Incidental", appeared in the *Christmas* issue of *The Bookman*; somewhat ironically, *Windfalls* was banned on 4 December 1934, around the time of the review's publication. Beckett may have become aware of the coincidence in retrospect via the background research he carried out for his article against censorship, in which he refers to the ban on O'Casey's work.[59] Reviewing *Windfalls* was, for Beckett, an opportunity to express his boundless admiration for O'Casey's capacity to innovate. However, his appreciation of O'Casey has less to do with the texts themselves than with the manner in which the latter countered policies of representation enshrined at the Abbey. The review centres upon O'Casey's innovative approach to dramatisation: apart from Yeats's rejection of the *Silver Tassie*, the Irish context of O'Casey's work is not mentioned. O'Casey's naturalism is portrayed as the expression of a modernist sensibility, with Beckett presenting O'Casey as a "master of knockabout" able to discern "the principle of disintegration in even the most complacent solidities".[60] Despite the play not being included in *Windfalls*, Beckett takes *Juno and the Paycock* as a barometer for discussing the aesthetic value of O'Casey's drama. The play ends with the return of Captain Boyle and his friend Joxer Daly to the Boyles' tenement flat and a drunken, half-articulated lament upon Ireland's "terr...ible state o'...chassis".[61] This conclusion is presented as a quintessential example of O'Casey's ability to portray sensory dislocation: for Beckett, O'Casey's humorous take on the meaninglessness of political violence signifies nothing but the instability of existence, and he equates the chaos or "chassis" described in *Juno and the Paycock* with a "dramatic dehiscence" in which "mind and world come asunder in irreparable dissociation".[62]

Beckett was aware of the strong impact of O'Casey's depictions of the Easter Rising and the Irish Civil War upon the Irish public: he had been witness to the riots that took place at the Abbey during the first production of *The Plough and the Stars* and recognised the political weight of O'Casey's representations of the Dublin slums. As in *The Plough and the Stars*, which deeply shocked Dublin patriots, O'Casey takes a provocative stance towards the newborn Free State government in *Juno and the Paycock*. The changing fortunes of the Boyle family come to symbolise the changing fortunes of the state itself against a social microcosm that is not ready for political independence. Through Joxer Daly, O'Casey voices his doubts regarding the ability of the new political order to last: Joxer laments Boyle's arrogant behaviour, describing his friend as a "mastherpiece" of Free State ideology when being informed of the Boyles' impending demise.[63] O'Casey's social and political critique is, nevertheless, far removed from Beckett's concerns, and his review discusses neither O'Casey's adoption of linguistic and phonetic conventions to portray the Dublin working class nor his attitude towards the sanctification of violence and sacrifice. Instead, Beckett presents O'Casey's work as a theatre of knockabout which focuses on the senses and the possibilities of dramatisation: "This is the energy of his theatre, the triumph of the principle of knockabout in situation, in all its elements and on all its planes, from the furniture to the higher centres".[64] His use of the word "furniture" evokes a central aspect of *Juno and the Paycock*, namely the steady addition and removal of trinkets: the Boyles' flat, relatively empty in Act One, becomes full of clutter bought with borrowed money in Act Two. The physical stripping of the set is central to Act Three, in which the removal of the furniture symbolises the extraordinary waste of energy involved in the nation's progression towards a new order. For Beckett, the movement of the props testifies to O'Casey's ability to conceive explosive theatrical situations which consume characters and props alike, his conceptualisation of the workings of the theatrical space taking precedence over the political events addressed.

* * *

Due to its emphasis on the importance of innovation, Beckett's review of *Windfalls* represents more than a declaration of influence: it illustrates a refining of his understanding of the purpose of the artist, as he sought for means to question the essentialised models of identity on offer in post-independence Ireland. This was a recurrent concern, and, in a review of 1930s Irish poetry entitled "Recent Irish Poetry", he commented in greater depth upon the nefarious effects of Irish cultural nationalism on artistic experiment. He wrote the review while in London during May and June 1934, shortly before his article against censorship; it was published in August 1934 in a special "Irish Number" of *The Bookman* under the pseudonym of Andrew Belis.[65]

Beckett's choice of pseudonym suggests that he may have conceived the review as a coded, posthumous homage to Boris Nikolaevich Bugayev, known as Andrey Bely.[66] Bely, one of the founding fathers of Russian modernism, died in Moscow on 8 January 1934, as Beckett moved to London and began psychoanalysis with Wilfred Bion; an obituary appeared in the London *Times* of 26 January, which celebrated Bely's contribution to Russian Symbolism and presented him as a precursor of James Joyce.[67] For Bely, the function of literature was to be found in a use of language that appealed both to the mind and to the emotions, and, in a series of articles on the use of symbol and the unity of form and content within the work of art, he developed an understanding of outer reality as entirely subordinate to subjective experience. His reflections culminated in a theory of symbolism that presented the fusion between content and form as central to the creative process; for Bely, what the art work unveiled was the actual transformation of objective reality through the experience of the artist.[68] Bely's thought had a strong impact upon European artistic circles from the 1910s, the search for a symbiosis between form and content proving central to later theories of abstraction.[69] In "Recent Irish Poetry", Beckett's understandings of subject and object, as well as form and content, display a striking similarity to Bely's own concerns. Such emphasis on the effect of modernist methods of composition is also a feature of preceding essays such as "Dante...Bruno. Vico..Joyce", which celebrates Joyce for his ability to fuse content and form and to ultimately prevent their differentiation, turning the act of reading into an entirely new experience. This analysis of Joyce's use of language is consonant with Bely's own perspective upon the relationship of inner experience to reality, suggesting that Bely's sensitivity to the abyss of artistic experience provided Beckett with an alternative opening from which he could reflect upon the nature of modernist experimentation, if not with an antidote to Yeats's own symbolism.

It is difficult to ascertain when Beckett discovered Bely. German translations of Bely's novels were widely available throughout the 1920s, and it is likely that Beckett was exposed to some of them.[70] It is certain that, as a young man, he had a strong fascination with contemporary Russian artistic circles. He even considered moving to Russia in the mid-1930s to study cinema: in 1936, he wrote to Sergei Eisenstein, asking to be accepted into the Moscow Film School and, having failed to receive a reply, considered studying under Vsevolod Pudovkin.[71] Beckett may also have become acquainted with Bely's work through his Russian-born friend George Reavey, who published his first collection of poems, *Echo's Bones and Other Precipitates*, and acted briefly as his agent during the 1930s. Bely was among the writers chosen by Reavey for his 1933 anthology of Soviet literature, and, from the early 1930s, Reavey began to publish a range of critical articles on Bely, in which he compared him to Irish modernist writers and commented on an intimate complicity between Bely's and Joyce's approaches to language.[72] Beckett shared his fascination; in a 1937 letter to Reavey, he recalled a lecture on "Belji" that he had heard in Dresden and advised his friend to translate *The Silver Dove* into English (Reavey took up Beckett's suggestion many years later, his translation appearing in 1974).[73]

Like Eisenstein and Pudovkin, Bely was in a delicate position in 1930s Russia. In the pre-Soviet years, he had supported a form of free experimentalism which fell out of favour in the early 1930s.[74] In 1932, all independent literary organisations were disbanded and replaced by a single Union of Soviet Writers closely controlled by the Communist Party; in 1934, the first Congress of Soviet Writers proclaimed socialist realism the only permissible method of literary representation. Bely made no attempt to integrate into the new system, which prioritised 'mass intelligibility' over experimental forms, but remained free from the threat of the Gulag.[75] However, from this point, his writing career was fraught with difficulties and he found publication practically impossible. It is difficult to identify the extent of Beckett's awareness of the considerable pressures faced by Russian artists under Stalin and it is doubtful that, in "Recent Irish Poetry", he wanted to make an association between Stalin's methods of repression and a censorship-ridden Ireland. Nevertheless, his choice of pseudonym confirms that "Recent Irish Poetry" was written in an attempt to reconfigure Irish modernism away from the shadow of Joyce and in relation to wider theoretical concerns shaping the emergence of avant-garde movements on the fringes of Europe.

Ironically, the use of a pseudonym was not sufficient to guarantee anonymity in Dublin literary circles. Beckett was, for a time, concerned that the poets under attack might have guessed the identity of Andrew Belis, especially since one of his short stories was printed in the same issue under his own name. He was relieved to hear from MacGreevy that F.R. Higgins did not get "his prop of song in a pickle" when reading "Recent Irish Poetry", but feared that Austin Clarke might have identified him as the author, concluding with relief that "the Olympic mistletoe one" didn't mind.[76] Nevertheless, he remained apprehensive about Clarke's reaction for some time, writing to MacGreevy in June 1936: "Clarke was full of hate but he didn't seem to bear me any ill for the Bookman article, if he ever saw it".[77] However, Clarke's article "Irish Poetry To-Day", which appeared in the *Dublin Magazine* of January–March 1935, suggests that he had read "Recent Irish Poetry" closely. Indeed, Clarke's argument suggests an eagerness to counter Beckett's charge of parochialism: he compares the Celtic Twilight to French Symbolism, praises Yeats's integrity as a poet and highlights the experimentalism of post-Revival poetry.

Writing "Recent Irish Poetry" was, in all likelihood, an arduous task, and Beckett rehearsed some of his phrasings in correspondence with MacGreevy. He referred to Yeats's late drama in a letter of August 1934 as "the ancient thermolater at play" – a term that reappears in the introduction to "Recent Irish Poetry" as a comment upon anti-modernist sentiment within Revivalist poetry.[78] Although Beckett stated that the article was originally based on a review of Yeats's late work, Yeats's modernism is entirely obfuscated by Beckett's rejection of his nationalist persona.[79] The canon of writing defined by Yeats during the early years of the Revival movement is, in fact, Beckett's main target, and he covertly mocks Yeats's call for Irish writers in the 1890s to use "Irish subjects" or folk legends.[80] Instead, Beckett celebrates a modernist literature immune to the propagation of national myths, concerned with adopting the "rupture of the lines of communication" and the breakdown of perception as the grounding of its aesthetic practice.[81] He denounces the self-congratulatory insularity of Revivalists and neo-Revivalists, describing the Revival as the source of an aesthetic empty of meaning – a "flight from self-awareness". This central void is surrounded by an "iridescence of themes", whose primitive iconography can be contained in no more than seven names ("Oisin, Cuchulain, Maeve, Tir-nanog, the Táin Bo Cuailgne, Yoga, the Crone of Beare").[82] The national literature, then, for Beckett, is characterised by the random reshuffling of such "accredited" themes. Nothing is spared, including Yeats's and Russell's fascination with Eastern mysticism, which is ridiculed as an interest in "Yoga".

Joyce's name does not appear, but his shadow looms large over Beckett's attack upon Revivalist aesthetics. The "Scylla and Charybdis" episode of *Ulysses*, for instance, alludes to Yeats's interest in mysticism in equally dismissive fashion: "Seven is dear to the mystic mind. The shining seven W.B. calls them".[83] Russell (AE) seen through the eyes of Stephen Dedalus remains a ghostly presence, hankering for locations more exotic than Dublin: "Dunlop, Judge, the noblest Roman of them all, A.E., Arval, the Name Ineffable, in heaven hight: K.H., their master, whose identity is no secret to adepts. [...] The life esoteric is not for ordinary person".[84] Joyce's 1901 article "The Day of the Rabblement" also provides a precedent for Beckett's concerns; praising Yeats's *The Wind among the Reeds* as superior poetry, Joyce denounces the populist leanings of the Revival movement and describes the use of popular folklore as a danger to artistic autonomy.[85] "Recent Irish Poetry" shows similar cynicism in its handling of Yeats and his followers; however, Beckett's critique of the parochialism of the Revival is considerably harsher, due mainly to the frame of reference being modernist modes of representation rather than the Revival itself.

The historical scope addressed in Beckett's convoluted attack on the Revivalist canon is nonetheless significant, as Sinéad Mooney has pointed out; indeed, "Recent Irish Poetry" ends with sarcastic comments about the sanctity of national character, dismissing nineteenth-century forefathers of the Revival such as Samuel Ferguson and Standish O'Grady.[86] As he rejects advocates of an alignment between nation and culture, Beckett celebrates the ability of modernist literature to question the boundaries of being and essentialist definitions of collective identity. Modernism is defined as a movement that undermines all stable truths and disintegrates values central to the Revival such as historical continuity and the sovereignty of the subject.

However, Beckett's opposition of tradition to experiment is far from straightforward. The progress of his argument is complicated by his familiarity with Irish modernist poets, all of whom are friends or acquaintances. MacGreevy's poetry proves particularly difficult to negotiate.[87] Indeed, MacGreevy's leanings towards religious writing and his nationalist opinions do not sit easily with Beckett's perspective on the purpose of Irish modernism, and MacGreevy is relegated to a no-man's-land between Revivalists and modernists, "in the sense that he neither excludes self-perception from his work nor postulates the object as inaccessible".[88] Brian Coffey and Denis Devlin do not rank much higher in Beckett's classification. Beckett's depiction of them as "without question the most interesting of the youngest generation of Irish poets" is faint praise, given the torrent of invective that he hurls at both older and younger generations of "antiquarians".[89] Their potential to influence the course of Irish literary life collectively is valued, but the importance of their respective artistic projects is left undefined. Beckett's correspondence and his acidic review of Devlin's *Intercessions* confirm that he did not think highly of them; in a 1933 letter to MacGreevy, he calls Devlin "a giggler" and admits: "I did not take very kindly to either of them, but I preferred Devlin to Coffey, which preference has the value of a whim available for development in accordance with what by laws I have no idea".[90] He also shows scepticism regarding Coffey's abilities as a poet: "I find him very fort on his subject, but the poetry is another pair of sleeves. Still there is far more there all round than in Devlin, I think. His fever of mind is alarming. But there is the laughter to cool it".[91]

A similar degree of ambivalence surrounds Beckett's references to Yeats's poetry.[92] Rephrasing Yeats's poem "Three Movements", he comments upon the writer's indifference towards his non-followers, or "the fish that lie gasping on the shore".[93] Beneath the sarcasm, Beckett's careful reading and appreciation of *The Winding Stair and Other Poems* is evident: the "cut-and-dried sanctity and loveliness" he mocks is also a quotation from Yeats's poem "Coole and Ballylee, 1931"[94] and the line "What, be a singer born and lack a theme!" is a misquotation from "Vacillation".[95] Another allusion to this line appears in *Murphy*, filtered through the mouth of Austin Ticklepenny: "Fear not, I have ceased to sing", the former poet tells Murphy on the occasion of their first meeting.[96] Here, the contrast between Beckett's simplistic analysis of the Revival period and his informed handling of Yeats's poetry leads the review beyond a simple opposition of tradition to experiment. It enables Beckett to parody that for which he displays resentment: not simply the parochialism of Irish letters, but the manner in which stylistic and thematic conventions hinder literary experiment.

Beckett's criticisms should not be taken at face value and can easily be read as youthful exuberance: later, on several occasions, he asserted his unshakeable admiration for the poet and spoke of how Yeats, like Goethe, had produced his best work at the end of his life.[97] His admiration for Yeats's late poetry is evident in the television play ...*but the clouds*..., written in English in 1976, which quotes from "The Tower".[98] Beckett's tribute to Yeats, however, is confined to the realm of the ghostly and the half-articulated, providing yet another illustration of his ambivalent standpoint: Yeats's poem is incorporated into a series of sequential images and reduced to fragments, which move from partial to complete intelligibility. The play centres on a male figure designated M, who tries to remember the features of his beloved and begs her to appear to him; his days and nights are consumed by his desire to see her image. Her face appears sporadically on screen; she mouths words but her murmur remains inaudible. Three shots dissolve into one another: a near shot of the man from behind, presenting him hunched over a desk in his "sanctum", a close-up of the woman's face and a long shot of the man standing, as he prepares for another day of wandering or another sleepless night. Eventually, the last four lines of Yeats's "The Tower" are heard, this time recited by a disembodied voice, that of the male character: "...but the clouds of the sky...when the horizon fades...or a bird's sleepy cry...among the deepening shades...".[99] Beckett's evocation of unrequited love clearly draws on the dilemma expressed in Yeats's poem: "Does the imagination dwell the most/Upon a woman won or woman lost?"[100] Amusingly, the manuscript drafts of ...*but the clouds*... reveal an ongoing hesitation regarding the poem's final lines. Beckett initially wrote "among the darkening shades", before committing to "among the deepening shades".[101]

Richard Ellmann interprets Beckett's use of "The Tower" in ...*but the clouds*... as a reference to Beckett's only meeting with Yeats, which was arranged by Thomas MacGreevy in September 1932.[102] During this meeting, Yeats praised Beckett's "Whoroscope" and recited a few lines of the poem. According to Ellmann, Yeats was fascinated by the conflict that these lines expressed between "helpless male love" and "female cruelty".[103] Beckett was somewhat bewildered by Yeats's praise and later suggested that he remembered a Yeats trapped between various personas. Writing to H.O. White in 1957, he mocked Yeats's grandiloquence and remarked upon the difference between the Yeats brothers: "The light of Jack Yeats will always burn with me. I met W.B. only once, in Killiney, rambling Swift and making great play with his Wellingtons. I have been re-reading his poems, and Ellmann's book [...]".[104] That Beckett should remember Yeats as "rambling Swift" is worthy of note: both writers reflected upon Swift's legacy in the early 1930s, Yeats writing a play on Swift entitled *The Words upon the Window-pane* (1934) and Beckett pursuing various projects in more haphazard fashion. A few months after meeting Yeats, Beckett considered writing a poem about Swift, but he abandoned the project. The idea came to him as he was wandering near Portrane in north Dublin in December 1932; he came across a tower often frequented by Swift, allegedly in order to visit his rumoured lover, Esther Johnson, nicknamed Stella. The episode, as reported to MacGreevy, was highly comical, and was eventually woven into *More Pricks Than Kicks*.[105]

In *The Words upon the Window-pane*, Yeats evokes the voice and personality of Swift through three women: the two women Swift loved, Stella and Esther Vanhomrigh (nicknamed Vanessa), and a medium called Mrs Henderson. Beckett admired the play and may have been familiar with Yeats's introduction to it, the first half of which appeared in the October–December 1931 issue of the *Dublin Magazine*, directly facing his own poem "Alba".[106] Yeats's play is set during a meeting of the Dublin Spiritualists' Association, in a room haunted by Stella's presence,[107] where a poem she wrote to Swift features on the window, carved by diamond into glass. The dramatic power of silent speech is emphasised; the singers witness Mrs Henderson's lips moving while a hymn is being sung, but they cannot hear the words. Echoing this image, a woman's face appears sporadically in *…but the clouds…*, speaking silently.[108] Beckett's ghostly female figure, for Katharine Worth, may be read as a response to Yeats's own portrayal of Swift through the mediation of Mrs Henderson, Stella and Vanessa; she identifies in the rituals of the play, particularly in M's change of robes, a reference to Yeats's love of ceremony, masks and mystification.[109] *…but the clouds…* may also be read as a reflection upon the nature of artistic inspiration in line with Yeats's portrayal of the figure of the muse, the blankness of Beckett's female figure echoing Vanessa's question: "Was that all, Jonathan? Was I nothing but a painter's canvas?"[110] Vanessa's half-articulated revolt, which takes place through the mediation of Mrs Henderson, finds a resonance in Beckett's character, who also resists visual and verbal articulation.

Yeats and Swift are not the only ghosts in *…but the clouds…*: years later, Beckett would allude to the presence of Synge.[111] The use of the colour grey to represent the double-edged nature of vision as both salvation and condemnation conjures images of Synge's *The Well of the Saints*, a text conceived "like a monochrome painting, all in shades of one colour", which anticipates narrative elements central to *…but the clouds…*.[112] In *The Well of the Saints*, blindness enables imaginative freedom; for Martin and Mary Doul, a couple of blind beggars, "the seeing is a queer lot".[113] They have been convinced of their beautiful and youthful appearance, yet, upon recovering sight through the intervention of a saint, they find themselves old, weather-beaten and ugly. The temporary recovery of their sight is marked by further disappointments; Martin, for instance, attempts to seduce the younger Molly Byrne, promising her a life of free wandering, but is rebuked. Trying to convince her to change her mind, he claims that he has the ability to see her like no other man has seen her before, evoking a life in which her image would stay with him wherever he walked, forever taking his mind away from "the muck that seeing men do meet all roads spread on the world".[114]

In contrast to his apparent coldness towards Yeats, Beckett was always unequivocal in presenting Synge as his dramatic precursor, despite his marked divergence from Synge's naturalism.[115] Synge's influence is prominent in the radio play *All That Fall*, in which Beckett develops a musical, stylised form of Hiberno-English that recalls Synge's dramatic language. Hiberno-English is used to emphasise the undefined existence of the characters as verbal constructs. Both Mrs Rooney and her husband remark upon the strangeness of her speech patterns: he fears that his wife might be struggling with a "dead language" and confesses that, occasionally, he is similarly afflicted.[116] Mrs Rooney confirms that it is an "unspeakably excruciating" feeling.[117] Characters move in and out of focus, one "big pale blur" after another,[118] and Mrs Rooney is particularly sensitive to her own lack of physical substance, lamenting: "I am not half-alive nor anything approaching it".[119] The debates surrounding the revival of the Irish language are evoked with tongue firmly in cheek, providing Mrs Rooney with a point of reference for her own ordeal: "Well, you know, it will be dead in time, just like our own poor dear Gaelic, there is that to be said".[120]

The play is set in Boghill, a caricatured rural town far removed from the hamlets inhabited by Synge's half-pagan peasants.[121] Beckett's characters have an acute sense of their position within class hierarchies, and religious bigotry is ridiculed through the devout Miss Fitt, who lets Mrs Rooney take her arm, remarking with resignation that "it is the Protestant thing to do".[122] An allusion to the political partition further disturbs the play's relationship to Synge's timeless and idealised Ireland; Mrs Rooney asks: "Now we are the laughing-stock of the twenty-six counties. Or is it thirty-six?"[123] The governmental policies aimed at the preservation of the Irish language are sneered at, the renaming of public toilets being presented as their main achievement: Mr Rooney goes to "the men's, or Fir as they call it now, from Vir Viris I suppose, the V becoming F, in accordance with Grimm's Law".[124] Despite such playful attempts to register the shifts taking place in Ireland after independence, the strong experimental slant of the play situates it at a remove from Irish social realities. The emphasis remains upon the spatiality of sound, the use of stylised sounds giving a comical edge to Beckett's exploration of the boundaries of articulation and perception. The possibility of using a realistic form to represent a rural landscape dissolves before the universe of the play is fully sketched out. The play begins with "rural" sounds: "Sheep, bird, cow, cock, severally, then together. Silence".[125] The use of Hiberno-English is central to the musicality of Beckett's dramatic language; it remains clear, however, that Hiberno-English is merely an instrument in Beckett's exploration of form: *one hears a radio play*, circumscribed by sounds resonating in an abstract space, form taking precedence over any specificity of content that might be introduced.

The play marks a significant moment in Beckett's exploration of the potentiality of sound and shows that, long after he found himself at the forefront of formal innovation in European drama, he continued to grapple with the legacies and the exigencies that shaped his formative years. His handling of the legacy of Yeats and Synge, in turn, encourages a reconsideration of the stance that he adopted as a budding writer. In particular, the divide outlined between traditionalists and modernists in "Recent Irish Poetry" consequently takes on new currency, becoming less absolute in its advocacy of dissent from the conventions of style and imagery surrounding the development of a national literary canon.

* * *

Furthermore, Beckett's questioning of Revivalist literature is an attempt to address the evolving political and social role of Irish literature, more than questions of structure and method. His surface claim is that the legacies of Yeats and Synge restricted the literary domains available for investigation, throwing the Irish writer eager to embrace modernist modes of composition into a void reminiscent of the breakdown the latter sought to represent. Yet, in Beckett's 1934 portrayal of the essential divide between modernists and anti-modernists, it is also possible to distinguish a concern with more pressing political issues: indeed, by the mid-1930s, the censorship laws had significantly affected Irish letters, and Beckett's attacks upon the Revivalist canon had motivations other than literary.

In 1934, coinciding with his analysis of Irish modernism, he wrote a forceful protest against censorship entitled "Censorship in the Saorstat", which shows that, while he continued to deny any affiliation with an Irish literary tradition, he remained involved in the debates surrounding its changing social and political status. However, his plea for the preservation of artistic freedom in the Irish Free State went entirely unnoticed, and the article, which had been commissioned by *The Bookman*, remained unpublished, the periodical having gone out of business before the intended publication date. Without success, Beckett then submitted the article to *transition*, having added a final section in which he identified himself as a non-existent Irish artist, number 465 in the register of prohibited writers. He was referring to very recent events: his first collection of short stories, *More Pricks Than Kicks*, was placed on Ireland's Register of Prohibited Books a few months after its publication.[126]

"Censorship in the Saorstat" is a direct attack upon the Censorship of Books and Periodicals Publication Act, passed in 1929 to enable the creation of a censorship board that had a licence to operate in virtual secrecy, answerable only to the Minister of Justice.[127] The original bill did not confine censorship simply to pornographic publications; foreign periodicals, books and films became important targets, and the censors showed remarkable industriousness, banning an estimated 1,200 books and 140 periodicals between 1930 and 1939.[128] Although W.B. Yeats, George Bernard Shaw, George Russell and Oliver St John Gogarty publicly opposed the act, comment and controversy on the subject of censorship remained scant throughout the 1930s.[129] Beckett strongly resented the passivity of the literary circles dominated by Yeats and Russell; in 1932, he sent MacGreevy an irate description of Dublin intellectuals as self-absorbed, procrastinating amateurs:

> I met R.N.D. Wilson last Sunday chez Percy Ussher. [...] I thought there was not much to him and felt vaguely uneasy with him. He read or declaimed acres of his own verse, and to be sure there were odds and ends of agreeableness here and there. He has nice thick shining black hair and his little prose-poem diapason seems to be keyed to A.E.'s. A.E. & WB play a lot of croquet together at Riversdale, Rathfarnham, and the former always wins by a mile. I suppose James Starkey holds the stakes. Austin Clarke and Monk Gibbon seek on the bank a definition of obscenity.[130]

The threat of censorship affected Beckett from the early 1930s onwards: the rumours of obscenity surrounding his work in Dublin literary circles led to delays in the publication of his first poems, the editors of the *Dublin Magazine* sifting them for obscene puns.[131] After *More Pricks Than Kicks* (which was not republished until 1970), *Watt* was banned in 1954 and *Molloy* in 1956.[132] Thus, Beckett's writings were not brought to the attention of the Irish public until the success of *Waiting for Godot*. Some writers were puzzled by his invisibility on the Irish literary scene: John Montague, for instance, referred to Beckett as "the Greta Garbo of modern literature", observing that none of his work was in print for two decades.[133] In later years, Beckett suggested that these difficult times were long forgotten, writing to John Calder in 1960: "Perhaps *Molloy* was banned at some stage, or *Malone*, I don't remember".[134]

Such grand forgetfulness runs counter to the anger and bitterness that characterises "Censorship in the Saorstat". Beckett identifies the formation of the Censorship Board and the ban on contraceptives in the Irish Free State as part of the same process of mass propaganda, equating a "sterilization of the mind" with an "apotheosis of the litter".[135] A genuine despair and anger can be detected beneath his sarcasm: "France may commit race suicide, Erin will never. And should she be found at any time deficient in Cuchulains, at least it shall never be said that they were contraceived".[136] This comment alludes to the demographic slump that characterised the inter-war period in France, which the government sought to remedy by stiffening penalties for abortion and prohibiting birth control.[137] However, if Beckett denounces inconsistencies in Irish regulations, he does not dismiss French anti-abortion laws as a "curiosity of panic legislation" of the Irish kind.[138] The difference, it seems, lies in the attempts of the Free State government to promote racial and spiritual purity by controlling modes of literary representation. For Beckett, the mechanisms of Irish censorship and anti-contraception measures have common origins, being indebted to the worldview fashioning the racialist stock symbols associated with national character. Invoking Cuchulain and "the pure Gael, drawing his breath from his heels", he contrasts an ideal Ireland "peopled with virgins" with a real Ireland swarming with "decorticated multiparas".[139]

Central to Beckett's attack on censorship is the heavy coverage from which governmental attempts to sever economic ties with Great Britain benefited in the Irish press: he points out that the sustained focus upon industrial developments and the tariff war with Great Britain defuses public debate on censorship. Among the "latest snuffles from the infant industries" which monopolise the headlines, he singles out sugar factories created in 1933 and 1934 in Tuam, Mallow and Thurles by the newly established Comhlucht Siúicre Éireann, the national sugar production company set up as part of large-scale attempts to curb dependence upon British imports.[140] These factories followed from the Beet Sugar Act of 1925, which promoted the establishment of an agrarian, self-sufficient nation by introducing direct government subsidy into Irish sugar production.[141] For Beckett, such economic policies correspond to a form of totalitarian thinking; the Irish people are no longer able to read books, but the governmental measures which regulate both agricultural and literary production lead to the same result, the fattening of Irish pigs (which, once paper is no longer needed, become the sole beneficiaries of the censorship laws), and he concludes: "We now feed our pigs on sugarbeet pulp. It is all the same to them".[142]

Beckett's sardonic conclusion reads as a denunciation of the failure of Irish intellectuals to address censorship and, more precisely, as a coded reference to George Russell's interest in the pig industry and his activity as founder of the *Irish Homestead*, the newspaper ridiculed by Joyce as "the pigs' paper".[143] There are further Joycean echoes in Beckett's grim predictions concerning the future of Irish letters, which recall Stephen Dedalus's description of Ireland as "the old sow that eats her farrow".[144] Undoubtedly, Joyce's own struggle to maintain the integrity of his work strengthened Beckett's convictions, Joyces's struggle to publish an unexpurgated version of *Ulysses* in the early 1930s greatly influencing Beckett's decision to defend freedom of expression for himself and others.[145]

At the beginning of August 1934, however, while Beckett was carrying out background research for "Censorship in the Saorstat", it was Yeats, rather than Joyce, who provided preoccupation. Beckett noted the provocative content of Yeats's play *The Resurrection* with amusement and, in a letter to MacGreevy, mocked "what Yeats, greatly daring, can compose in the way of blasphemy", alluding to Yeats's ineffectual role in the censorship debates.[146] In September 1928, prior to the passing of the Censorship Act, Yeats published two articles opposing censorship, one in the English press and one in the Irish press. The article written for the London *Spectator* remained strongly connected to Irish social realities, such as illiteracy and birth control. In contrast, the article published in the *Irish Statesman* displayed less concern for the impact of censorship upon Irish society, ridiculing the Censorship Act as an entertaining blunder instead.[147] When writing for the Irish press, Yeats appeared more eager to swipe at the Catholic Church's ignorance of St Thomas Aquinas's philosophy than to contest the necessity of censorship: he pointed out that the Act's definition of indecency entirely contradicted the official ideology of the Catholic Church, based on the thought of Aquinas. The article, however, did not question the necessity of censorship, admitting that there were such things as "immoral painting" and "immoral literature".[148] Instead, Yeats called for an amendment to the government's definition of indecency and highlighted the importance of choosing men "learned in art and letters" as censors.[149]

The Censorship Act was passed a year after Yeats left the Senate; at the time of writing the articles, Yeats retained a vested interest in the affairs of the State and was anxious to resist what he perceived as philistine nationalism. Foreseeing a dark future for the intellectual life of the nation in the wake of the censorship laws, he resolved to establish an Irish Academy of Letters in 1932, in order to create a sense of solidarity among Irish writers.[150] There were two membership categories: Academicians, who had adopted Ireland as the main focus of their work, and Associates, who could give adequate grounds for their election.[151] The attitude of this Academy towards the Censorship Board, however, was not clearly defined. Joyce refused to join and O'Casey angrily declined Yeats's invitation on the grounds that the "censorship of dull authority embattled in this Irish Academy of Letters" was more dangerous than the joint authority of Church and State.[152] Beckett held a similar opinion, describing "our lately founded Academy" as an extension of the Censorship Board in "Recent Irish Poetry". Denouncing the sterility of Yeats's academy, he evoked a literary scene dominated by "that fabulous bird, the mesozoic pelican, addicted, though childless, to self-eviscerations".[153]

Beckett's responses to censorship address different concerns from those of the writer he designated "Nobel Yeats" in *More Pricks Than Kicks*:[154] at the time of Beckett's protest, any radicalism of opinion was crushed, and de Valera was adopting a tough line on left-wing opposition, trying, in particular, to dismantle the IRA, in which a small minority displayed strong sympathies with Marxist ideals.[155] While Yeats's response to the censorship laws remains influenced by his perspective on Irish politics and former senatorial responsibilities, Beckett's stance reflects an estrangement from a general climate of conservatism, rather than from Catholic orthodoxy in particular. Subsequently, Beckett remained faithful to the position he adopted in "Censorship in the Saorstat", actively opposing any attempt to interfere with his work when matters of integrity were at stake.[156] Such an attitude implicated him in ferocious disputes, the most famous of which involved England's Lord Chamberlain, to whom he would refer as "the Lord Chamberpot".[157]

If "Censorship in the Saorstat" was written relatively quickly,[158] research for the article proved to be something of a chore, since the act was not available for public scrutiny and could not be purchased in Dublin bookshops.[159] The search for official reports of parliamentary debates, presumably at the National Library of Ireland, led to delays in writing other reviews (of Gide and Rimbaud) and Beckett approached the task with mixed feelings.[160] The article evidences careful research, documenting the debates in the Dáil and the Seanad surrounding the censorship laws and referencing the main political figures involved between February and April 1929. Beckett's main targets are the Minister for Justice James Fitzgerald-Kenney, Senator Thomas Johnson, and Deputies Ernest Henry Alton, Michael Tierney and John Joseph Byrne (who was chairman of the Censorship Board in 1934).[161] Nevertheless, his transcriptions of government publications become more slapdash as the article progresses: his account of the Seanad debate on the provocative nature of Boccaccio's poetry, for instance, is an ample paraphrase.[162]

While "Censorship in the Saorstat" reveals a deep familiarity with the nuances of the Censorship Act, it is also an extremely fanciful piece of writing. Certain sections which ridicule the workings of the Free State government read as a parody of official descriptions of Ireland such as those featured in the *Saorstát Éireann Official Handbook* of 1932. This government publication, edited by Michael Tierney, evokes in great detail the new economic attractions of the country since independence: Ireland is presented as a tourist haven, as "the motorist's paradise".[163] However, the handbook's attempts to legitimate the newborn Free State as a European country often border on the absurd; the country's geography is described as "over 2 1/3 times that of Belgium, over twice that of Holland, and 1.7 times that of Switzerland or of Denmark".[164] The country's population also gives rise to a fanciful inventory, being categorised as "slightly greater than that of Norway", "double that of New Zealand", "four-fifths that of Denmark, three-fourths that of Switzerland, and just half that of Sweden".[165] Similarly, Beckett's facts and figures are accompanied by eccentric descriptions and associations. If, in the *Saorstát Éireann Official Handbook*, the repetition of "in the Saorstát" operates as a rhetorical device to assert Ireland's cultural and political legitimacy, the value of "Saorstát" as signifier is reversed in Beckett's article, which emphasises the estrangement of the Free State government from the rest of Europe and its rejection of a European literary canon. Ireland tilts towards the absurd and becomes loaded with Swiftian undertones, in keeping with Beckett's comparison of the Irish government to the "Grand Academy of Balnibarbi", an assembly dedicated to the pursuit of futile projects at the expense of the nation's well-being.[166] Whether the second part of "Censorship in the Saorstat" was deliberately conceived as a mock-addendum to this handbook remains hypothetical; however, the parallels in style and construction seem far from coincidental, and suggest a shrewd denunciation of the government's idealisations of the nation's economy.

* * *

Beckett's disapproval of Irish cultural legislation had an immediate bearing on the composition of *Murphy*, which anticipates the reaction of potential censors: "This phrase is chosen with care, lest the filthy censors should lack an occasion to commit their filthy synecdoche".[167] A kissing scene, during which Miss Counihan sits on Wylie's knees, is set "*not* in Wynn's Hotel lest an action for libel should lie".[168] The following paragraph specifies: "The above passage is carefully calculated to deprave the cultivated reader". Beckett's resentment towards the Dublin *literati* weighs heavily upon the novel; in particular, his caricature of Austin Clarke is so ferocious that it might have constituted a case for legal proceedings, as James Mays notes.[169] Ticklepenny, a "Pot Poet from the County of Dublin", is lazy, bad-tempered, socially inept and overall undeserving of "any particular description";[170] his passivity is taken for granted and portrayed as a virtue: "It was not usual for Ticklepenny to feel slighted at all, it was unprecedented for him to do so without cause, as was the present case".[171] The prediction proved accurate, as Clarke did not file for libel. Nevertheless, Beckett was informed by Con Leventhal that Clarke had, while reviewing *Murphy* for the *Dublin Magazine*, sifted the text for libellous allusions to himself.[172] The review, which appeared anonymously, depicted *Murphy* as a nasty fantasy, unredeemed by its obvious erudition; Clarke remarked that the only character in the novel who appeared to have any human qualities was the prostitute Celia.[173]

Beckett had previously mocked Clarke's position as a follower of Yeats in "Recent Irish Poetry", commenting upon his command of the "fully licensed stock-in-trade from Aisling to the Red Branch Bundling".[174] In *Murphy*, his parody of Clarke's literary nationalism is taken a stage further, and he mocks

> [...] the class of pentameter that Ticklepenny felt it his duty to Erin to compose, as free as a canary in the fifth foot (a cruel sacrifice, for Ticklepenny hiccupped in end rhymes) and at the caesura as hard and fast as his own divine flatus and otherwise bulging with as many

minor beauties from the gaelic prosodoturfy as could be sucked out of a mug of Beamish's porter.[175]

This passage, as Mays notes, is a reference to Clarke's own comment upon the possibility of creating new rhyming patterns in *Pilgrimage*, a 1929 collection reviewed in "Recent Irish Poetry".[176] Further evidence of Beckett's familiarity with Clarke's work may be found in his correspondence: in 1930, he saw Clarke's play *The Hunger Demon* at Dublin's Gate Theatre and described it as "truly pernicious" in a letter to MacGreevy.[177] His attitude towards Clarke seems to have oscillated between frank hostility and lukewarm appreciation; recalling a meeting with Clarke after the publication of "Recent Irish Poetry", he wrote to MacGreevy: "He is really pathetic and sympathetic. Or is it that one clutches at any kind of literary contact?"[178]

For Mays, Beckett's caricature is simply a lapse of taste, particularly as regards *Murphy*'s allusions to the psychiatric treatment received by Clarke following the breakdown of his marriage.[179] Nevertheless, Beckett's parody of Clarke's literary nationalism may be more complex than has been previously assumed, as it is inscribed within a pastiche of the artistic progression described by Joyce through Stephen Dedalus. Ticklepenny is described contemptuously as a "distinguished indigent drunken Irish bard",[180] bringing to mind the Stephen addressed by Buck Mulligan as "you dreadful bard" and "the unclean bard" in *Ulysses*.[181] Ticklepenny also expresses his fondness for the word "tundish", echoing a key passage in *A Portrait of the Artist as a Young Man*.[182] In a conversation with his Dean of Studies at university, Stephen explains that the funnel of a lamp is called a "tundish" in Lower Drumcondra, where the "best English" is spoken.[183] He is convinced that "tundish" is an Irish word, but finds out that it is English prior to his departure for Paris. Beckett was particularly struck by this passage; in "Dante…Bruno. Vico..Joyce", he reads Stephen's exchange with the dean as the proof of Joyce's divergence from Vico's viewpoint on the human and the divine, and notes that the signifier takes precedence over the exchange itself: "The lamp is more important than the lamp-lighter".[184] Elsewhere, a tongue-in-cheek allusion to Yeats's "Who Goes with Fergus?" further illustrates Joyce's influence upon the compositional minutiae of *Murphy*: "[The sheep] turned their broody heads aside from the emetic, bringing them back into alignment as soon as it passed from them".[185] Yeats's original lines read: "And no more turn aside and brood/Upon love's bitter mystery".[186] In *Ulysses*, Stephen Dedalus also remains haunted by Yeats's poem, which is recited by Buck Mulligan before breakfast.[187]

Such echoes illustrate the complex manner in which, as with Stephen, the Revival occupies the margins of Murphy's consciousness.

Beckett clearly stated that he did not wish to encourage Joycean readings of *Murphy*, writing to Sighle Kennedy in 1967 that he did not see any Joycean, or indeed Proustian echoes in his writing.[188] Nevertheless, preliminary notes in the workbook known as the "Whoroscope" Notebook confirm that he had Joyce's *Bildungsroman* in mind when he drafted the novel; Murphy was then called "X":

> The picaresque inverted. Gil Blas is realised by his encounters & receives his mission from them. X is realised by his failure to encounter & his progress depends on this failure being sustained. If he made terms with people the story would come to an end.[189]

The term "encounter" is loaded with Joycean undertones, recalling the short story "An Encounter" in *Dubliners* and the concluding section of *A Portrait of the Artist as a Young Man*, which Beckett admired greatly,[190] and in which Stephen expresses his desire to "encounter for the millionth time the reality of experience and to forge in the smithy of [his] soul the uncreated conscience of [his] race".[191] Stephen's maturation is largely encouraged by his reaction to a stratified colonial society and culminates in the promise of exile. In *Murphy*, the conventions of the *Bildungsroman* utilised by Joyce as a scaffold resurface and are transposed to the metropolitan centre. However, in London, the possibility of progression is similarly precluded for Beckett's hero, even if he has achieved what is, for Joyce's Stephen, a prerequisite for his existence as an artist: exile. Indeed, the idea of social progress is, at best, meaningless in London, where opportunities for advancement amount to working in shifts at a psychiatric hospital among other "puppets".[192]

Although *Murphy* is set primarily in London, it is replete with satirical allusions to figureheads of the Revival, most of which are considerably more sophisticated than Beckett's treatment of Austin Clarke: one such example is provided in the form of Murphy's will. Murphy asks that his ashes be flushed down the toilets of the Abbey "if possible during the performance of a piece".[193] His instructions are informed by the history of the building, which had previously housed a morgue; its toilets were so famously noisy that there were strict injunctions not to use them during a performance.[194] But events take a different turn, and the bag containing Murphy's ashes explodes on the floor of a London pub, a moment which suggests an analogy with George Moore's last wishes, also frustrated, as Sighle Kennedy points out.[195] In an attempt to embarrass his conventional Catholic relatives, Moore had asked for his remains to be cremated and for his ashes to be spread over Hampstead Heath.[196] Instead, the Moore family decided to bury his ashes on an island in Lough Carra, County Mayo, opposite the ruins of Moore Hall, where the ceremony would be more likely to go unnoticed.[197]

The enduring fascination with Eastern mysticism displayed by Yeats and George Russell is an object of particular mockery in *Murphy*, as in "Recent Irish Poetry".[198] Beckett derides Yeats's attraction to the Orient and his involvement with figures such as Shri Purohit Swami through the figure of Ramaswami Krishnaswami Nayaranswami Suk, whose horoscopes are "[f]amous throughout Civilised World and Irish Free State".[199] "The Suk" may be understood as a parody of the writer whom Yeats liked to call "the Swami",[200] but also as a jibe at Yeats himself, whose recognised involvement with groups such as the Order of the Golden Dawn and Madame Blavatsky's Theosophical Society seemed incompatible with his interest in politics and his later senatorial position. George Russell's interest in the esoteric is also depicted as a practice at odds with the original aspirations of the Revival to create a national literature for Ireland. His readership is not Irish but English: Miss Carridge, Murphy's landlady in London, reads his *Candle of Vision* with delight.[201] In the French translation, the reference to Russell is removed and *The Candle of Vision* becomes a cheap paperback entitled *Roses de décembre*, by Madame Rosa Caroline Mackworth Praed, a choice of translation confirming Beckett's contempt for Russell's gnostic analysis of human speech.[202] The "Circe" episode of *Ulysses*, which parodies the study of the mystical significance of language published by the founder of the *Irish Homestead*, provides a precedent for these jibes, presenting the cries of a transformed AE: "(*with a voice of waves*) Aum! Hek! Wal! Ak! Lub! Mor! Ma! [...] Aum! Baum! Pyjaum! I am the light of the homestead! I am the dreamery creamery butter".[203] Beckett's animosity towards Russell was tenacious: in *Watt*, Russell's *Homeward Songs by the Way* finds again an enthusiastic readership of one in Mr. Case, a signal man with "a very superior taste in books".[204] Beckett's persistent hostility towards Russell can be explained by the curt rejection of his poetry for publication in the *Irish Statesman*: Russell claimed to have a copy-box full of submissions to address.[205] By the time *Murphy* was published, however, Russell was long deceased.

There is evidence in Beckett's notebooks that his satire of Revivalist iconography in *Murphy* was prepared with extreme care; an entry in the "Whoroscope" Notebook reads: "Indicate that Celia spent her childhood in Ireland".[206] In the published text, Celia is more Irish than the

Irish flag: "eyes: green", "complexion: white", "hair: yellow".[207] Another entry in Beckett's notebook emphasises women's capacity for initiative in ancient Irish tales of elopement, in which men submit to women's will: "Deirdre & Naisi, son of Usnadh (Woman always takes initiative in Celtic Mime e.g. Grainne with Diarmuid)".[208] Celia's strong character places her in line with such mythical heroines, whose ordeals were adapted for the stage by Yeats, Synge, Lady Gregory and George Russell. Yet Celia's profession identifies her as a parody of Revivalist representations of the motherland. A prostitute, she calls into question national allegories such as the young girl with the "walk of a queen" and the old woman who leads men to battle in Yeats's seminal play *Cathleen Ni Houlihan*.[209]

Beckett's distaste for Revivalist celebrations of heroism and self-sacrifice is another prominent feature of *Murphy*, in which the figure of Cuchulain is treated particularly scornfully. In the literature of the Revival, Cuchulain stood for more than a mythological figure: he embodied the "true Irish spirit" and corresponded to an "objective, communal reality", as Terence Brown emphasises.[210] In *Murphy*, the sanitised, sexless Cuchulain, hailed by W.B. Yeats and Patrick Pearse as a symbol of the nation's greatness, is endowed with prominent thighs and buttocks:

> In Dublin a week later, that would be September 19th, Neary minus his whiskers was recognized by a former pupil called Wylie, in the General Post Office, contemplating from behind the statue of Cuchulain. Neary had bared his head, as though the holy ground meant something to him. Suddenly he flung aside his hat, sprang forward, seized the dying hero by the thighs and began to dash his head against his buttocks, such as they are.[211]

Such an attack is physically impossible in reality, as Anthony Roche notes, since the buttocks of Oliver Sheppard's statue of Cuchulain are masked in the folds of its robe.[212] In its historical context, Neary's feat reads as a condemnation of the cult of commemoration that developed following de Valera's accession to power, since Sheppard's statue, which is still exhibited in Dublin's General Post Office on O'Connell Street, was selected by de Valera in the 1930s as the most appropriate memorial to the Easter Rising and thus became an official embodiment of Free State ideology.[213] Ironically, Yeats reflected upon the significance of the Cuchulain statue at the same time as Beckett, both in his poem "The Statues" and in his play *The Death of Cuchulain*.[214] In "The Statues", the "plummet-measured face" of Cuchulain represents the resilience of the national psyche against the chaos of the modern world; it is invoked as a remedy to the "filthy modern tide".[215]

Beckett faced substantial difficulties in getting *Murphy* published, possibly due to the novel's heavy reliance upon coded satire; Dublin, as a geographical entity and as a literary microcosm, becomes a signifier for the exotic and the bizarre, in relation to which London remains a largely nondescript location. The novel's Irish content led Routledge to advertise it as an expression of "Irish genius" upon publication in 1938 and to describe it as "leavened with a Celtic waywardness which is as attractive as it is elusive".[216] This quality of elusiveness is indicative of Beckett's attempts to find modes of representation that are partially autonomous from the stylistic and thematic legacy of the Revival, their residual reliance upon this legacy being deployed for parodic means. Illustrating Beckett's stance in "Recent Irish Poetry", *Murphy* rejects the idea that literature should be bound by a stylistic consensus concerning the representation of human existence. This consensus, which Beckett elsewhere calls the "approved aesthetic", is entirely alien to his own understanding of artistic freedom.[217]

* * *

For Beckett, the idea of a specifically Irish art form was anathema. In a 1954 tribute to Jack Yeats, for instance, he reiterated his belief that imagination cannot be enslaved to a particular purpose: "The artist who stakes his being is from nowhere, has no kith" [trans. James White].[218] The value of Jack Yeats's painting is here presented as entirely independent of nation, epoch and personality. Beckett had specific motivations for making this claim, which developed from an ongoing debate with Thomas MacGreevy regarding the nature of artistic engagement and autonomy; in particular, his vision of the artist as homeless acts as a belated response to MacGreevy's monograph on Jack Yeats – a celebration of "a great artist and a great Irishman".[219]

MacGreevy completed his essay while living in London, and Beckett was, at the time, somewhat concerned for his friend, fearing that he had become too concerned with Irish politics, too "Ireland-haunted".[220] Their dialogue regarding Yeats's painting spread over a number of years; MacGreevy sent the proofs of his monograph to Beckett in 1938 and Beckett reviewed it for the *Irish Times* in 1945. Beckett's review, published on 4 August, unequivocally blames MacGreevy for sacrificing the aesthetic qualities of Yeats's work to his own nationalist opinions: "The national aspects of Mr Yeats's genius have, I think, been over-stated, and for motives not always remarkable for their aesthetic purity".[221] These motives are antithetical to what Beckett describes elsewhere as Yeats's "analytical imagination".[222] In response to MacGreevy's celebration of Yeats as the perfect example of the Irish artist, Beckett argues that Yeats's painting is the result of "processes less simple, and less delicious, than those to which the plastic *vis* is commonly reduced".[223] This is a direct attack upon MacGreevy's view that Jack Yeats "paints the Ireland that matters",[224] a phrasing that suggests a leaning towards the orthodox nationalism developed in Daniel Corkery's thought, recalling Corkery's idea of "the Ireland that counts", as John Harrington notes.[225] As in his review of O'Casey's *Windfalls*, Beckett's appreciation of Jack Yeats's art rests on the partial disregard of the latter's chronicling of developments within Irish society. This was a view that he had long held: in a 1936 review of Yeats's novel *The Amaranthers* for the *Dublin Magazine*, he argued that Yeats's art refuses to adhere to the local and aspires to the universal in its celebration of "the mobility and autonomy of the imagined",[226] a comment that recalls Eugene Jolas's manifesto "Poetry Is Vertical", which Beckett signed in 1932 and which proclaimed "the autonomy of the poetic vision, the hegemony of the inner life over the outer life".[227]

A preliminary draft of "MacGreevy on Yeats" confirms that Beckett was angered by the insularity of MacGreevy's analysis and its emphasis on the unveiling of truth, beauty and goodness as art's primary purpose. A passage omitted from the published review indirectly accuses MacGreevy of desiring to assimilate Yeats's painting "to something in the nature of turf-development, or a large-scale Red Cross benevolence".[228] MacGreevy's essay begins with a rhetorical question: "Ireland, it will be said, is small. Does it matter? Does anything in Ireland matter? The answer is that every place where there are human beings matters".[229] Beckett is dismissive of such rhetoric:

> From these wild and unintelligible remarks the reader will turn with pleasure to Mr MacGreevy's naturalness and lucidity, from a Sisyphus labouring for his life in objectless chaos to a grave and gentle and good-humoured man painting the truth and goodness and beauty of Ireland. Perhaps after all it comes to much the same thing. But terms are what matter.[230]

He ridicules MacGreevy's reliance upon stereotypes traditionally conditioning Anglo-Irish colonial relations, such as the distinction between a non-secularist Irish mind and a secularist English mind, and questions with virulence the presumption of Irish uniqueness:

> Does it matter that Elsheimer, even in Italy, painted Germans, or that [ ] in Norway or wherever it was, painted Norway or wherever it was? What can it possibly matter what is painted, or whether it is painted with sympathy, or loathing, or indifference? He is among the greatest, with Kandinsky and Klee, Balliner [sic] and Soutine, because he brings light, as only the great dare bring light, to the issueless predicament of existence, reduces the dark where there might have been a door. That his manner of doing so is peculiarly Irish, whatever that means, is no doubt of interest, but of scant interest beside the matter done. There are no stones like the Cloyne stones, and few boots.[231]

Clearly, Beckett's point of reference while drafting the review was not Ireland, but post-war France, where the notion of political engagement had acquired an entirely different meaning due to the disappearance of a stable social order. The review was drafted in Foxrock in July 1945, Beckett having briefly returned to Ireland after moving back to Paris. He retained a painful awareness of the contrast between the relative affluence of Dublin and the economic distress of France and England: later, upon describing the consequences of Allied bombing raids in "The Capital of the Ruins", he expressed his exasperation at a lack of awareness among the Irish of the scarcity of material resources available on the Continent, contrasting the distress witnessed in the northern French city of St-Lô with an Ireland left untroubled by the war.[232] To Beckett, MacGreevy seemed particularly unsuited to the hardships of post-war France; when his friend mentioned that he would consider joining him to work at the Irish hospital in St-Lô, Beckett replied that he would dislike the atmosphere of "Irish bosthoonery" and the promiscuity involved.[233]

MacGreevy was well aware that Beckett disapproved of his portrayal of Yeats as the epitome of the Irish artist. Upon receiving a proof of the essay in January 1938, Beckett displayed little enthusiasm for its lengthy social and political analyses and, despite praising the discussion of the aesthetic value of Yeats's painting, he denounced MacGreevy's nationalist stance as the simplistic juxtaposition of cause and effect: "I think you have provided a clue that will be of great help to a lot of people, to the kind of people who in the phrase of Bergson can't be happy till they have 'solidified the flowing', i.e. to most people".[234] Beckett's response to the second part of the essay, which focuses on the social and political aspects of Yeats's work, betrays an anger that seems disproportionate. He refuses to share MacGreevy's enthusiasm for what he calls "our national scene" and denounces his adherence to a dangerous orthodoxy of thought entirely independent of an anti-colonial struggle:

> But perhaps that also is the fault of my mood and my chronic inability to understand as member of any proposition a phrase like "the Irish people", or to imagine that it ever gave a fart in its corduroys for any form of art whatsoever, whether before the Union or after, or that it was ever capable of any thought or act other than the rudimentary thoughts and acts belted into it by the priests and by the demagogues in service of the priests, or that it will ever care, if it ever knows, any more than the Bog of Allen will ever care or know that there was once a painter in Ireland called Jack Butler Yeats.[235]

It is possible to discern a faint echo of O'Casey's *Juno and the Paycock*, Captain Boyle's dismissive reference to "boyos that's only afther comin' up from the bog o'Allen" reading as a Dublin pejorative against rural Ireland.[236] Similar to his depictions of the effects of censorship, Beckett uses a convoluted sentence structure here to turn the parochialism of Irish cultural and political life into a vehicle for the absurd. His reference to the "demagogues in service of the priests" suggests a condemnation of the close relationships existing between Fianna Fáil and the bishops;[237] he presents Ireland as a diseased nation with little care for intellectual matters and divided along parameters dependent on religion and land ownership. This view contrasts vividly with MacGreevy's idealised portrayal of Jack Yeats's Ireland, which remains unstratified by class, as Tim Armstrong rightly notes.[238] However, the letter ends with an attempt to soften the blow: "God love thee, Tom, and don't be minding me. I can't think of Ireland the way you do".[239] This conclusion fits a pattern in their exchanges: Beckett also ended his dismissive comments on Richard Aldington (MacGreevy's previous focus of study) in an apologetic way, evoking his "literary caries".[240]

Despite his opposition to the appropriation of art for nationalist purposes, Beckett remained extremely sensitive to the cultural specificity of avant-garde writers. This is evident in his 1967 plea to the Spanish government in defence of the playwright Fernando Arrabal, imprisoned by the Franco regime. Arrabal, then a French resident, was arrested during a trip to Spain and was convicted of treason and blasphemy for writing in one of his own books an autograph reading: "Me cago en Dios, en la patria y en todos lo demás" [I shit on God, my country and everything else].[241] In his letter of support, Beckett celebrates Arrabal's ability to integrate a national quality into his work and to export his vision:

> [La Cour] va juger un écrivain espagnol qui, dans le bref espace de dix ans, s'est hissé au premier rang des dramaturges d'aujourd'hui et cela par la force d'un talent profondément espagnol. Partout où l'on joue ses pièces, et on les joue partout, l'Espagne est là.
>
> [This Court] is about to judge a Spanish writer who, in the brief space of ten years, has pulled himself up to the first rank of the playwrights of today, by the strength of a profoundly Spanish talent. Wherever his theatre is played, and it is played everywhere, Spain is there.[242]

In this instance, Beckett's praise of Arrabal's work can be seen as purely a strategic attempt to influence the court favourably by appealing to the particular brand of 'Spanishness' promoted by Franco. That Beckett should emphasise the presence of a local element in the art of someone as innovative and provocative as Arrabal constitutes a radical revision of his previous attacks on nationalist understandings of art in an Irish context, and shows that Irish debates around art's relationship to national character had an enduring impact on his view of artistic purpose. There are similarities between the trajectories of Beckett and Arrabal: Arrabal's work was banned in Spain; he wrote in Spanish and translated his work into French with the help of his wife.[243] However, Arrabal's textual bilinguality is not a defining factor in Beckett's plea; Beckett understood his own choice to write in French not as an expression of distance from his Irish origins, but as a liberation from an understanding of artistic purpose of which he disapproved. His defence of Arrabal clearly illustrates an ongoing concern for aspects of Revivalist literature that he had formerly dismissed and a persistency in his attempts to reconfigure them in a global context. The document thus retains import not only as a letter in defence of the role of the avant-garde: it reads as a fitting signifier of the manner in which Beckett displaces aspects of the legacy of the Revival in his work, even as he draws on them.

2
Translation as Principle of Composition

Beckett began dabbling with French as a medium of composition shortly before the Second World War. His correspondence reveals an artist as yet unsure of the value of his writing and unaware of the determining effect of this shift upon his development.[1] In the immediate aftermath of the war, he found himself comforted in his decision to explore new linguistic territories: "A la libération, je pus conserver mon appartement, j'y revins, et me remis à écrire – en français – avec le désir de m'appauvrir encore davantage. C'était ça le vrai mobile" [At the end of the war, I was able to keep my flat. I returned to it, and started writing again, in French, hoping to impoverish myself even more. That was my true motive].[2] A few years later, during the writing of *Molloy*, he scribbled notes in which he also identified the end of the war as the moment at which he began writing in French, claiming that he was unaware of any major influences and had no project.[3] A prolific period ensued, however, during which Beckett, moving seamlessly between French and English, became an established member of the avant-garde elect. There was little that was sudden or radical about his choice to use both languages and to translate his own work; on the contrary, this new orientation was the outcome of a lengthy reflection upon the nature of representation. Indeed, writing in French enabled Beckett to achieve some of the goals he had established for himself as a young writer: to detach himself from the ideological and thematic formulae prevalent during the post-Revival period and to explore new linguistic territories.

Although writing in French was a natural development for a bilingual writer living in France, Beckett's turn towards French has been depicted as a "contradiction", an "abandonment", a "betrayal" and a form of "linguistic self-denial".[4] Such criticism suggests that, for many, choosing another language endowed Beckett's work with a peculiar neutrality and positioned him antagonistically in relation to his Irish origins. In embracing self-translation, however, Beckett traced his own path, adopting a new approach to the modernist methods of expression prevalent in a post-Auschwitz world where, to borrow Adorno's terms, literature was reduced to an aporia, only possible as emergent and developing, and yet, notwithstanding, claiming to be complete.[5]

Beckett was an accomplished translator in his own right when he turned to French as a primary medium of expression. His first non-critical publications included translations of Arthur Rimbaud, Paul Eluard, André Breton and Guillaume Apollinaire, a collaboration with Alfred Péron and Philippe Soupault on the Anna Livia Plurabelle section of Joyce's *Work in Progress* and, later, contributions to Nancy Cunard's *Negro: An Anthology* (1934) and an anthology of Mexican poetry (1951–52). He also translated a book by Georges Duthuit on Fauvism and a preface to a catalogue of Wassily Kandinsky's paintings.[6] He retained fluctuating memories of these published translations[7] and rarely recalled them with high regard, dismissing the Mexican anthology, for instance, as the fruit of economic need, a "pot boiler".[8] However, his experience of translating poetry and prose played a crucial role in his search for a language drained of its vitality, or "exuberance", as he put it.[9] In principle, the processes involved in the act of translation brought him closer to the neutral idiom that he expressed a yearning for in his 1937 letter to Axel Kaun. In this letter, he explained his desire to reject common usage and to reach beyond language itself:

> It is indeed becoming more and more difficult, even senseless, for me to write an official English. And more and more my own language appears to me like a veil that must be torn apart in order to get at the things (or the Nothingness) behind it. Grammar and Style. To me they seem to have become as irrelevant as a Victorian bathing suit or the imperturbability of a true gentleman. A mask. Let us hope the time will come, thank God that in certain circles it has already come, when language is most efficiently used where it is being most efficiently misused.[10] [Trans. Ruby Cohn]

Clearly, an immersion in avant-garde poetry provided Beckett with a new direction: his remark on the necessity of acknowledging linguistic misuse recalls Breton's exploration of pure inspiration in his *Manifestes du surréalisme* (1924).

Ironically, Yeats may be taken as an immediate precursor to Beckett's search for a new language: prefiguring Beckett's position, Yeats asserted in 1902 that the Irish writer could reject standard English only by questioning its grammatical conventions. Quoting Zola, he observed that the greatest literature comes to life when the writer refuses to respect the rules of grammar.[11] Contrary to Yeats, whose approach to the English language developed as part of a reflection upon Gaelic poetry, Beckett's aim was not to access an Irish cultural heritage, but to reach beyond it: by writing in French, he could escape many of the stylistic pitfalls that he had denounced in relation to Irish modernism in "Recent Irish Poetry".

Beckett began to write poetry in French soon after explaining his difficulties to Kaun; his progression suggests that French was, at the time, better suited than English to his artistic vision and that it provided him with a basis for forms of misuse that had previously remained excluded from his realm of investigation. His post-war novellas *Premier amour* and "L'Expulsé" illustrate a search for specific stylistic effects germane to minimalist fiction. Both texts rely on narrators who are foreign to the French language: the anonymous narrator of *Premier amour*, for instance, states explicitly that neither he nor his first love, Lulu, whom he has just encountered, is French. Neither of them is able to pronounce her nickname, and the French-speaking reader is informed of their non-native status by their shared inability to pronounce the letter 'u' in a manner that respects the rules of French phonetics:

> Mais pour passer maintenant à un sujet plus gai, le nom de la femme avec qui je m'unis, à peu de temps de là, le petit nom, était Lulu. Du moins elle me l'affirmait, et je ne vois pas quel intérêt elle pouvait avoir à me mentir, à ce propos. Evidemment, on ne sait jamais. N'étant pas française elle disait, Loulou. *Moi aussi, n'étant pas français non plus, je disais Loulou comme elle.* Tous les deux, nous disions Loulou.[12] [Emphasis mine]

Such idiosyncratic pronunciation finds a counterpart in the redundant sentence structure used by the narrator to emphasise his alternative nationality. This facet of *Premier amour* suggests that Beckett's search for a "literature of the unword" involved an exploration of the relationship between language, culture and meaning; disturbing their alignment enabled him to create a narrative mode that thrived on its antagonism towards the exigencies of classical realism. In *Premier amour*, the simplest of acts, such as pronouncing one's own name or the name of one's 'beloved', become impossible: all events, thoughts and emotions become acts of translation.

Issues of translation are also central to both form and content in the version of "L'Expulsé" published in the December 1946–January 1947 issue of the journal *Fontaine*. This version differs from the text republished as part of *Nouvelles et textes pour rien* by Les Editions de Minuit in 1955, the later text having been revised by Beckett to suppress all evidence of the narrator's foreignness. In the *Fontaine* version, the narrator's hesitation regarding French grammar and usage operates as a central narrative element, suggesting a correspondence between his estrangement from his surroundings and his foreignness in relation to French culture. Remarking that his cherished hat has become too big for him, the narrator becomes confused between two verbal groups, "devenir" (to become) and "finir par être" (a literal translation into French of "to end up being").[13] This passage was edited out of the republished version, along with all other passages in which the narrator playfully signalled his non-Frenchness. Elsewhere, he considers infringing the rule that imposes a masculine possessive article before feminine nouns beginning with a vowel or the letter *h* for phonetic reasons. Commenting upon the smell of his own breath leads him to remark upon the gender of the word *haleine* (breath): he acknowledges in passing that he is tempted to transpose it to the feminine but does not dare to do so.[14] Literal translations of English phrases recur, such as "chute d'eau" (downpour) instead of *averse*; "les étrangers" (strangers) instead of *les inconnus*; "sans doute à faux" (wrongly, without a doubt) instead of the set expression *sans doute à tort*.[15] As the narrative voice flirts with literal translation, the effect produced is one of disorientation: one is faced with a text that appears to have a shadowy and fragmentary existence elsewhere, in another language and culture.

Such strategies correspond to stylistic choices that have been carefully calculated, and, at times, to genuine uncertainties about language use.[16] There is evidence that Mania Péron, the widow of Beckett's friend Alfred Péron,[17] was his main source of information in this regard; he would send her letters as well as *pneumatiques* or telegrams to solicit advice.[18] Their correspondence reveals Beckett's concern regarding questions of grammar and usage; for instance, he writes in 1953:

> Chauvet m'a rejoint. Très gentil. Il m'a dit que ma phrase est correcte telle quelle, c'est-à-dire avec à qui. Il m'a cité d'autres cas où il faudrait de. Il n'a pas su très bien m'expliquer ça. Je crois que l'éloignement du complément du groupe verbal y est pour beaucoup. Selon lui c'est une question d'usage X impossible à présenter sous forme de règle.
>
> [Chauvet came to meet me. Very pleasant. He told me that my sentence is correct as it is, namely with *à qui*. He evoked other cases

which require the use of *de*. He couldn't explain this very well. I think this is mostly due to the distance between the complement and the verbal group. According to him, it is a question of usage, something that cannot be presented as a rule.][19]

The passage is followed by a quotation from Rimbaud's poem "Comédie en trois baisers", intimating a sense of pressure to also justify his semantic choices:

> J'ai adopté beaucoup de vos suggestions mais pas toutes. Pour <u>malinement</u>, j'ai l'autorité de Rimbaud [...]. Il est évident que <u>malignement</u> veut dire tout autre chose.
>
> [I adopted many of your suggestions but not all. As regards *malinement*, I have the authority of Rimbaud. [...] Obviously, *malignement* means something entirely different.][20]

Beckett had little sympathy for arguments concerning 'le génie de la langue française', an expression which has permeated public discourses on French culture since Rivarol's 1793 speech on the universality of the French language. Beckett makes explicit his dislike of universalist presumptions in *Malone meurt*:

> La femme, s'arrêtant un instant entre deux courses, ou au milieu d'une, levait les bras au ciel pour les laisser retomber lourdement aussitôt, vaincue par l'exigence de leur grand poids. Puis elle leur imprimait, à chacun de son côté, des mouvements difficiles à décrire mais dont la signification n'était pas très claire. Elle les écartait de ses flancs, je dirais brandissait *si j'ignorais encore mieux le génie de votre langue*. Ça tenait du geste étrange, à la fois coléreux et désarticulé, du bras secouant un torchon, ou un chiffon, par la fenêtre, pour en faire tomber la poussière.[21] [Emphasis mine]
>
> The woman, pausing an instant between two tasks, or in the midst of one, flung up her arms and, in the same breath, unable to sustain their great weight, let them fall again. Then she began to toss them about in a way difficult to describe, and not easy to understand. The movements resembled those, at once frantic and slack, of an arm shaking a duster, or a rag, to rid it of its dust.[22]

In referring to the 'genius of your language' and subsequently omitting to refer to it, Beckett mocks the idea, implemented on a large scale by the Académie Française, that language is an essential site of national character or, to borrow Pierre Nora's term, a *lieu de mémoire*.[23] This omission also points to the absence of English equivalents for the syntactical tension at work in the French text. In French, the intricate syntax of the passage deprives the actions portrayed of a logic and forbids comprehension, however partial; in contrast, all loose meanings disappear from the English text. The French text evokes movements that remain inaccessible due to the narrator's deliberate ignorance of the 'genius of the French language', while the English text merely highlights the difficulty of describing such movements, but does not attribute this to semantics.[24] Elsewhere, Molloy reasserts his indifference to French language and literature; when speaking of the merits of newspaper for keeping warm, he explains his predilection to the *Times Literary Supplement* or "Le Supplément Littéraire du Times", which remains impermeable to flatulence.[25] This item was a symbol of luxury in post-war France, explaining Molloy's pride in his prized possession; in this instance also, the implication of cultural displacement defines the French and English texts as separate entities.

Beckett's interrogation of the hierarchical relationship traditionally associated with the act of translation, namely of the sovereignty of the 'original' text over its translation, is sustained throughout his bilingual *oeuvre*, finding particular prominence in the trilogy *Molloy, Malone meurt, L'Innommable* and its English counterpart *Molloy, Malone Dies, The Unnamable*, novels that further develop the translation effects explored in his post-war fiction.[26] Beckett was, for a time, opposed to the use of the term 'trilogy'; however, it remains fitting to speak here of what are otherwise known as the *Three Novels* as a single entity, given the remarkable continuity between these novels' explorations of linguistic processes involved in the acts of narration and translation.[27] Summarisation is irrelevant to their achievements; they exist mainly as verbal constructs, centring upon characters trapped in rooms and, in the case of *L'Innommable* and *The Unnamable*, in a jar. Any journey or search portrayed has little by way of conclusion or external justification. What becomes salient, when considering these novels as bilingual entities, is Beckett's integration of a reflection upon the processes of translation into both form and content.

* * *

Certain minutiae in the French texts suggest an adherence to anglophone norms of measurement: distances, for example, are not expressed in the metric system, but in *pouces*, or inches, and in *milles*, or miles.[28] Weight is expressed in *livres*, or pounds;[29] monetary references are to *livres* and *shillings*.[30] These traces, suggestive of the bearing of translation upon the French texts, enable the creation of a narrative mode which fails to elucidate the processes of memory and perception involved in the telling of a story. In French as in English, the narrators are frequently unable to understand the workings of the language in which they operate and which is used around them, becoming mere vehicles for the anxieties surrounding the act of translation: the sheets of paper on which Molloy writes return to him marked with ungraspable signs, for instance.[31] Likewise, Malone must alter his accent and vocabulary in order to be understood by his housekeeper; he speaks a language of a different vintage, or one that is not his mother tongue:

> In the beginning it was different. The woman came right into the room, bustled about, enquired about my needs, my wants. I succeeded in the end in getting them into her head, my needs and my wants. It was not easy. She did not understand. Until the day I found the terms, the accents, that fitted her.[32]

Irish names such as Molloy, Moran, Malone, Murphy and Quin recur in the French and English narratives, suggesting a dependence upon Ireland as a central source of meaning. Yet comparing English and French versions forbids a straightforward alignment with an Irish setting and Irish origins. Moran's first name remains Jacques in both versions of *Molloy*, for instance, but his surname could be either French or Irish. In contrast, the teddy bear of his son, Jacques Moran Junior, remains sympathetic to the language of the text: it is called Baby Jack in English and Jeannot (Johnny) in French.[33] As for the name Molloy, its pronunciation remains uncertain in French, since the ending does not necessitate the use of a diphthong.

Certain aspects of *Molloy* and *Malone Dies* suggest continuity with Beckett's earlier writings. *Molloy*, for instance, exhibits a hostile response to rural Irish landscapes that recalls the contempt for "dung poetry" registered in "Recent Irish Poetry".[34] Both Molloy and Moran are colour-blind, unable to distinguish the colour green, and share an aversion to the pastoral.[35] "Good God, what a land of breeders, you see quadrupeds everywhere", says Molloy.[36] This remark is echoed by Moran upon his arrival in Ballyba: "What a pastoral land, my God".[37] In French, their perspectives on their surroundings duplicate one another, reinforcing a psychological proximity: "Quel pays rural, mon Dieu, on voit des quadrupèdes partout", says Molloy, while Moran laments: "Quel pays pastoral, mon Dieu".[38] Molloy's town, Bally – a seaside swamp characterised by industrial underdevelopment – is clearly conceived as a caricature of Dublin and suggests a phonetic pun on Baile Átha Cliath.[39] In English, a reference to Blackpool, the translation of the name given to Dublin by its Danish founders (Dubh-Linn), confirms further the existence of a correspondence between Molloy's "part of the world" and Beckett's city of birth.[40] In *Malone Dies*, although Malone remains confined to his bedroom, the narrative displays snapshots of Dublin Bay, evoking "the sea, the islands, the headlands, the isthmuses, the coast stretching away to north and south and the crooked moles of the harbour".[41] *L'Innommable* similarly combines the fleeting with the strikingly specific in its referencing of Irish place names and cultural stereotypes. The narrator remains haunted by memories of a strict religious education and pilgrimages to Killarney; he was born in "Bally je ne sais plus quoi, endroit qui, à les en croire, m'aurait infligé le jour".[42] The English text attains a higher degree of vulgarity and physical violence: "Bally I forget what, this being the place, according to them, where the inestimable gift of life had been rammed down my gullet".[43] While describing the trials and tribulations imposed upon him by an unidentified collective designated as "they", the narrator asserts his refusal to succumb to "their" demands and to remember his behaviour "là-haut, dans l'île, au milieu de mes compatriotes, coreligionnaires, contemporains et copains", and describes a life mired in "tourbières" (boglands).[44] In *The Unnamable*, his declarations regarding his activities "above in the island, among my compatriots, contemporaries, coreligionists and companions in distress" are culturally and historically weighted and suggest Irish origins.[45] However, the narrative voice cannot be attached to a fixed location or contained within established linguistic constructions: "[...] someone says you, it's the fault of the pronouns, there is no name for me, no pronoun for me".[46]

At the time of writing *Molloy* and *Malone Dies*, Beckett had forged little distance from the self-congratulatory nationalism denounced in his critical writings. Both novels were written swiftly; *Molloy* was begun during one of Beckett's last long-term stays in Ireland, in May 1947,[47] and he started work on *Malone meurt* shortly after finishing its predecessor in November 1947 (the novel was then provisionally entitled *L'Absent*).[48] With his unruly mane of hair, the character of Malone may have been inspired by a quotation from Spenser's *A View of the Present State of Ireland* that Beckett had copied into a notebook in the 1930s, which described the Irish as wearing long "glibs" or, as stated by Spenser, "a thick curled bush of hair hanging down over their eyes, and monstrously disguising them".[49] Initially, Beckett did not intend to give *Molloy* and *Malone meurt* a successor but, rather, considered them, with *Murphy*, as a series. He wrote to MacGreevy in January 1948: "The French *Murphy* fell stillborn in the press, as I think Dr. J. [Samuel Johnson] said. *Molloy* is a long book, the second last of the series begun with *Murphy*, if it can be said to be a series. The last is begun and then I hope I'll hear no more of him".[50] Beckett's vision of these three novels as an ensemble is important, given the strong bearing of biographical factors upon the writing of *Murphy*. His dismay at the racism of 1930s London clearly influenced the composition of the novel, and he later complained: "I hated London. Everyone knew you were Irish – the taxi drivers called you 'Pat' or 'Mick'".[51] He would sometimes refuse to speak; mundane events would turn into ordeals due to his Irish accent, as he confessed to MacGreevy in August 1932: "I haven't opened my mouth except in bars & groceries since you left this day week: haughty bar-persons, and black-souled grocers".[52] His sense of remaining an outsider by dint of his Irishness nourished the composition of *Murphy*; when Murphy applies for a job in a chandlery in London, his Irishness is signalled by a play on Cockney accents: "' 'E ain't smart', said the chandler, 'not by a long chork 'e ain't' ".[53]

* * *

In French, the use of an Irish setting enables a process of cultural dislocation: for the francophone reader, Ireland is associated with the faraway, the nonsensical and the bizarre, Irish names and locations signalling a movement towards a narrative logic on the verge of intelligibility, solely identifiable by means of its otherness in relation to French language and culture. In this sense, the Irish dimension of the French trilogy can be comprehended only through its *distance* from French cultural norms; the suturing of the narrative to a French context remains minimal. Familiar clichés recur: the Fourteenth of July, designated as "fête de la liberté" in *Malone meurt*, is caricatured as a "festival of freedom" in *Malone Dies*,[54] and the evocation of Pigalle in *L'Innommable* becomes Montmartre in *The Unnamable*.[55] Within these cultural reversals, one may discern mechanisms that recall Adorno's analysis of Beckett's anti-essentialist stance (as illustrated in *Endgame*). The Beckettian subject no longer corresponds to closed and coherent forms of meaning, but, rather, to that which Adorno defines as non-identity or, in this instance, the splintering of consciousness into disparate elements.[56]

References to Irish place names lose their original meaning in the transposition into French but retain their specificity, becoming defined solely in terms of their exoticism and/or their degree of translatability.

These features are, on some occasions, signalled to the reader simultaneously, drawing attention to the cross-cultural positioning of the narrative without serving a significant purpose in terms of its meaning, progression or direction. Beckett's allusion to Dublin's Glasnevin cemetery in *Malone meurt* is one such example; Glasnevin features in a mock-version of a popular ballad, which ends with the line "La main dans la main vers Glasnevin" [hand in hand towards Glasnevin].[57] Glasnevin is, in this instance, subordinated to the rules of French phonetics in order to rhyme with "chemin". However, a note at the bottom of the page recreates a sense of dislocation: "Nom d'un cimetière local très estimé" [name of a highly regarded local cemetery]. In this particular example, the relationship between the French and English texts is entirely reversed. The note signifies a song in translation, its odd and fanciful imagery obeying a cultural logic other than French and, hence, its meaning remaining inaccessible to the French reader. There are, however, no hidden truths to be yearned for; the reference to Glasnevin is absent from the song in the English text, as is the note.

In other instances, the shadow of the French text hovers over the English version; this is evidenced in Beckett's emphasis upon the phonetic proximity of 'Ireland' and 'island' in *The Unnamable*. In this instance, the double linguistic dimension of the trilogy becomes apparent in both the form and content of the text: "The island, I'm on the island, I've never left the island, God help me. [...] The island, that's all the earth I know".[58] The narrator's complaint is double-edged: since there are no triphthongs in French, a French speaker learning English may have a tendency to turn the triphthong into a diphthong and to pronounce 'Ireland' as 'island'. This lament is endowed with a retroactive meaning that becomes apparent only when one approaches the novel as a text whose existence is multiple rather than single: the exoticism of the French text is elucidated only with reference to the English version, while Beckett's emphasis on the enigmatic character of cultural and linguistic workings is fully operative, in English, only with the support of the French text. These examples also illustrate the manner in which the use of an Irish setting generates inconsistencies of meaning: Ireland operates simultaneously as a point of origin for a reflection upon cultural mores and as a matrix of the foreign and the unknowable.

* * *

Beckett's use of features of translation in order to alter meaning has important implications, particularly with regard to the traditional contextualisation of his work in relation to philosophical principles developed in French existentialism. Indeed, considering the trilogy as a bilingual entity reveals that Beckett's relationship with existentialist notions of the absurd is considerably more complex than has previously been assumed. Two dimensions of the absurd coexist and occasionally collapse into one another via Beckett's use of Irish traits and allusions in the novel trilogy: one is indebted to the lack of a well-defined cultural frame of reference (the absurd as incongruous, illogical or opposed to reason and common sense); the other is particular to the philosophical context of Beckett's French writings and echoes aspects of Albert Camus's definition of the absurd. In *The Myth of Sisyphus* (published in French in 1942), Camus argues that the realisation of the world's meaninglessness leads to a fragmentation of perception:

> A world that can be explained even with bad reasons is a familiar world. But, on the other hand, in a universe suddenly divested of illusions and lights, man feels an alien, a stranger. His exile is without remedy since he is deprived of the memory of a lost home or the hope of a promised land. This divorce between man and his life, the actor and his setting, is properly the feeling of absurdity.[59]

For Camus, absurdity derives from a clash between the drive of the human consciousness towards meaning and the meaningless nature of the world. This drive towards meaning is also central to Sartre's existentialism in *Being and Nothingness* (published in French in 1943), in which the absurd is defined as "that which is meaningless": man's existence is absurd, Sartre argues, "because his contingency finds no external justification. His projects are absurd because they are directed towards an unattainable goal (the 'desire to become God' or to be simultaneously the free For-itself and the absolute In-itself)".[60] Sartre defines "being-for-itself" (*être-pour-soi*) as an ontological lack: "The nihilation of Being-in-itself; consciousness conceived as a lack of Being, a desire for Being, a relation to Being. By bringing Nothingness into the world the For-itself can stand out from Being and judge other beings by knowing what it is not".[61] This conscious drive towards meaning is opposed to being-in-itself (*être-en-soi*), the non-conscious Being.

These definitions of the absurd have significantly informed critical approaches to Beckett's interest in meaninglessness: drawing on Camus's philosophy, Martin Esslin established Beckett's early drama as central to the development of an absurdist tradition in post-war Europe.[62] Likewise, A. Alvarez evoked similarities between Beckett's work and

Camus's existentialism in order to argue that, in a post-atomic world, absurd behaviour is natural, circumstances forbidding any other kind of behaviour.[63] However, if the narrative alignment of the French trilogy with an Irish cultural and historical landscape provides a grounding for the estrangement evoked by Camus, applying existentialist definitions of the absurd to Beckett becomes deeply problematic once one acknowledges the unfolding of an Irish background in his bilingual *oeuvre*. A consideration of the bearing of translation upon the texts illuminates the Beckettian absurd as an experience deriving from the elusiveness of language; as linguistic process, it carries considerable historical weight and does not sit comfortably with the conceptual and ahistorical nature of existentialist outlooks upon meaning. Adorno's essay on *Endgame*, which draws on Beckett's drama to question the relevance of absurdity as general doctrine to post-war literature, emphasises Beckett's estranged position in relation to existentialism: for Adorno, Beckett exhausts the definition of the absurd as developed by Camus and Sartre precisely because their approaches to meaning remain entirely non-specific and dissociated from an appreciation of the historicity of aesthetics. Using the example of *Endgame*, Adorno argues that the evident bearing of history is what marks Beckett's distance from existentialism. For Adorno, the disappearance of meaning in Beckett's work corresponds to a form of historical inevitability: his writing is doomed to seek the "meaning that it has itself extinguished".[64]

Amusingly, Beckett did not consider himself existentialist and regarded the drama of Camus and Ionesco as "depressing" (an adjective frequently applied to his own work).[65] The difference may, in fact, be located in his humorous use of an Irish context; comparing the function of an Irish historical and cultural landscape in French and English reveals Beckett's relationship with existentialist definitions of the absurd to be considerably more complex than has been previously assumed.

The manner in which Beckett exceeds these notions of the absurd is evident in *Malone Dies*, in which Malone compares himself to the Lord Mayor of Cork, Terence MacSwiney, who died in 1920, in one of the longest hunger strikes in Irish political history. In this instance, MacSwiney stands not as a political icon capable of stirring the national imagination, but as an index against which Malone can evaluate his own situation:

> That reminds me, how long can one fast with impunity? The Lord Mayor of Cork lasted for ages, but he was young, and then he had political convictions, human ones too probably, just plain human

convictions. And he allowed himself a sip of water from time to time, sweetened probably. Water, for pity's sake! How is it I am not thirsty.[66]

The tone of the French text is slightly harsher:

En fait, combien de temps peut-on jeûner impunément? Le maire de Cork a duré un temps infini, mais il était jeune, et puis il avait des convictions politiques et même tout simplement humaines probablement. Et il se permettait une larme d'eau de temps en temps, sucrée probablement. A boire par pitié. Comment ça se fait-il que je n'aie pas soif?[67]

In 1920s Ireland, the sacrificial heritage of the nation was hailed as one of the foundational values of political nationalism, and MacSwiney was a hero.[68] His maxim was a celebration of endurance and self-sacrifice: "It is not those who can inflict the most, but those who will suffer the most who will conquer".[69] By dint of this reference to MacSwiney, the narrative diverges from Camus's ahistorical definition of the absurd, regardless of the resemblance between the respective ordeals of Camus's Sisyphus and Beckett's Malone. However, the possibility of a hunger strike no longer exists; the meaning of heroism is hollowed out by and within language. In associating a particular episode of Irish nationalism with a retreat of meaning, Beckett also departs from MacSwiney's militancy, while rejecting the narrow definition of identity offered by nationalism. Such an engagement with historical and political particulars resists Camus's all-encompassing definition of the absurd, and, here, one can see how Beckett's simultaneous engagement with and departure from an existentialist view of the absurd coincides with the critique of existentialism through which Adorno reads *Endgame*: "French existentialism had tackled history. In Beckett, history devours existentialism".[70]

The complex processes that tie Beckett's use of technical features of translation to his examination of the nature of meaning are exposed in Molloy's reflection upon the phonetic similarity of "maman" and "ma", and his interrogation of the cultural logic underlying familial kinship:

Moi je l'appelais Mag, quand je devais lui donner un nom. Et si je l'appelais Mag c'était qu'à mon idée, sans que j'eusse su dire pourquoi, la lettre g abolissait la syllabe ma, et pour ainsi dire crachait dessus, mieux que toute autre lettre ne l'aurait fait. Et en même temps je satisfaisais un besoin profond et sans doute inavoué, celui d'avoir une ma, c'est-à-dire une maman, et de l'annoncer, à haute voix. Car avant de dire mag on dit ma, c'est forcé. Et da, dans ma région, veut dire papa.[71]

While the French text emphasises the proximity of the Irish "ma" to the French "maman", the English text stresses the difference between "ma" and "mother", between Irish English and standard English:

> I called her Mag, when I had to call her something. And I called her Mag because for me, without my knowing why, the letter g abolished the syllable Ma, and as it were spat on it, better than any other letter would have done. And at the same time I satisfied a deep and doubtless unacknowledged need, the need to have a Ma, that is a mother, and to proclaim it, audibly. For before you say mag, you say ma, inevitably. And da, in my part of the world, means father.[72]

The word "ma" provides an example of Beckett's subtle use of the technical features of translation outside the process of translation itself in order to interrogate normativity and social propriety.[73] Two forms of absurdity coincide: one is linked to the failure of the English language to accommodate features specific to Irish English, the other to Molloy's relentless search for meaning within different systems of cultural values. At this point, Molloy's reflection upon the inadequacies of language illustrates further the manner in which the cultural specificity of the narrative complicates its relation to the existential anguish described by Camus.

Speculations on the nature, meaning and functioning of language are at the centre of elaborate discussions in the French texts, illustrating a hypersensitivity to syntax and phonetics. The relish of the French Malone for words derived from Latin is immediately apparent: "Je me dis nonagénaire mais je ne peux pas le prouver. Je ne suis peut-être que quinquagénaire, ou que quadragénaire. Il y a une éternité que je n'en tiens plus compte, de mes ans je veux dire".[74] In *Molloy*, the faculty of the French language to compartmentalise time into different units of value is stressed: "Je parle au présent, il est si facile de parler au présent, quand il s'agit du passé. C'est le présent mythologique, n'y faites pas attention".[75] The term "présent mythologique" designates a present tense that does not have the value of a present *per se* but reflects a form of constancy. In the English text, these considerations become non-specific, a "mythological present" evoked as equivalent.[76]

Elsewhere, while discussing the necessity of making an inventory of his possessions, Molloy comments upon his own fanciful use of syntax: "Et si je n'ai pas toujours l'air de me conformer à ce principe, c'est qu'il m'échappe, de temps en temps, et disparaît, au même titre que si je ne l'avais jamais dégagé. Phrase démente, peu importe".[77] The correspondence between tenses is straightforward in English; the subjunctive is not required. As a consequence, Molloy's final judgement is less blunt: "And if I do not always appear to observe this principle it is because it escapes me, from time to time, and vanishes, as utterly as if I had never educed it. Mad words, no matter".[78]

The infiltration of the French texts by English constructions enables an interrogation of the relationship between meaning, usage and syntax. Certain structures resist the rules of French syntax:

> Et si je me suis toujours conduit comme un cochon, *la faute n'en est pas à moi*, mais à mes supérieurs, qui me corrigeaient seulement sur des points de détail au lieu de me montrer l'essence du système, comme cela se fait dans les grands collèges anglo-saxons, et les principes dont découlent les bonnes manières et la façon de passer, sans se gourer, *de ceux-là à celles-ci*, et de remonter aux sources à partir d'une posture donnée.[79]

> And if I have always behaved like a pig, *the fault lies not with me* but with my superiors, who corrected me only on points of detail instead of showing me the essence of the system, after the manner of the great English schools, and the guiding principles of good manners, and how to proceed, without going wrong, *from the former to the latter*, and how to trace back to its ultimate source a given comportment.[80] [Emphasis mine]

Ce n'est pas ma faute and *de l'un à l'autre* are constructions that arrive naturally for the French speaker, whereas "la faute n'en est pas à moi" and "de ceux-là à celles-ci" are clearly indebted to English. The French sentence thus anticipates an English counterpart, in a manner that affects both form and content, the bearing of English syntax upon the French narrative being confirmed in Molloy's evocation of his anglophone education. However, in other instances, it remains uncertain whether syntactical interpenetration is entirely deliberate. When evoking the countryside around Bally, for instance, Molloy uses the phrase "dégradement des tons", instead of the set phrase *dégradé des tons* (*se dégrader* meaning to fall into disrepair, *dégrader* to damage or deface).[81] Similarly, *Malone meurt* features the phrase "elle souriait pour des riens", rather than the set expression *sourire pour un rien*, and "Travaillez-vous pour votre compte?", instead of the set phrase *travailler à son compte*.[82]

Patterns reminiscent of the syntax of Hiberno-English occasionally surface in the French texts, in the use of emphatic structures commencing with *et, c'est...que* and *ce qui*, in which Beckett's fondness for Hiberno-English is reflected, French being an analytical language less likely to require or accommodate such structures.[83] The order of grammatical clauses is occasionally reversed; in some instances, the complement clause or group precedes the main clause defined by subject and verb instead of following it, as illustrated in these fragments from *Molloy* and *Malone meurt*:

> L'agent venait vers moi, c'était ma lenteur qui lui déplaisait. Lui aussi on le regardait, des fenêtres. Quelque part on riait. En moi aussi il y avait quelqu'un qui riait.
>
> Et cette importante demi-vérité, il l'entrevoyait peut-être déjà.
>
> 13) Ma soupe pourquoi l'a-t-on supprimée? 14) Mes vases pour quels motifs ne les vide-t-on plus?
>
> Cet enchevêtrement de corps grisâtres, c'est eux.[84]

Such reversals do not conform to standard French usage, reading instead as adaptations of 'it is...that', a grammatical construction which is commonplace in certain strands of Hiberno-English and particularly prominent in the stylised peasant speech of the Abbey plays of Synge and Lady Gregory.[85]

Elsewhere, proximity to Irish culture and politics is asserted explicitly by means of English phrases, enabling a playful examination of the ways in which language may be used to eradicate itself.[86] An untranslated reference to Irish nationalist orthodoxy enables Malone to present a form of speech muted in and by itself, which nonetheless results in something other than silence:

> Oui, c'est ce que j'aime en moi, enfin une des choses que j'aime, le don de pouvoir dire *Up the Republic!* par exemple, ou Chérie! sans avoir à me demander si je n'aurais pas mieux fait de me taire ou de dire autre chose, oui, je n'ai pas à réfléchir, ni avant ni après, je n'ai qu'à ouvrir la bouche pour qu'elle témoigne de ma vieille histoire et du long silence qui m'a rendu muet, de sorte que tout se passe dans un grand silence.[87]

The French text has a gentleness that contrasts strongly with the harshness of the English translation:

> Yes, that's what I like about me, at least one of the things, that I can say, Up the Republic!, for example, or, Sweetheart!, for example, without having to wonder if I should not rather have cut my tongue out, or said something else. Yes, no reflection is needed, before or after, I have only to open my mouth for it to testify to the old story, my old story, and to the long silence that has silenced me, so that all is silent.[88]

'Up the Republic', 'Up the Rebels' and, later, 'Up Dev' were popular political slogans, particularly before the 1933 General Election.[89] Viewed through the lens of Beckett's estranged speaker, the slogan is purely tokenistic and the idea of a collective political experience is rendered meaningless, since speaking is tantamount to being silenced. If the two texts unite in their depiction of silence as a form of speech, reading the two passages together unveils a complex transfer of meaning. The English text is considerably harsher when considered alongside the mellifluous French text, and signals a playful passage from the feminine to the masculine. The feminine "la bouche" is neutered, and the passive verb "me taire" is translated into a brutal image – "cut my tongue out" – which actualises double meaning as a form of linguistic emasculation and the eradication of the mother tongue. In contrast, the emphasis upon the subject in French ("c'est ce que j'aime en moi", it is what I like about myself) may be read as a virtually direct translation from Hiberno-English.

Whether gendered representations of Ireland have a bearing on Beckett's translation practices is outside the scope of the present argument; nevertheless, it is worth noting that *Molloy* alludes indirectly to the gender politics surrounding colonial representations of Irishness. Lousse's reaction to the loss of her dog is, to Molloy, as bewildering as the workings of Irish Gaelic:

> I thought she was going to cry, it was the thing to do, but on the contrary she laughed. It was perhaps her way of crying. Or perhaps I was mistaken and she was really crying, with the noise of laughter. Tears and laughter, they are so much Gaelic to me.[90]

In this instance, Molloy's speculations on the nature of Lousse's emotions also read as a subversion of the racialist discourses that surrounded representations of the Irish during the Victorian period. For instance, the Celt as described by Matthew Arnold was incapable of controlling his emotions, the victim of a condition akin to emotional hysteria.[91] This allusion is absent from the French text, in which Molloy's evocation of an incoherent self is entirely disconnected from a specificity of context.[92]

* * *

The resistance of Irish references and English phrases to transposition into French raises important questions that extend beyond modernist contexts, calling for a reappraisal of Beckett's relationship to translation projects developing during the Revival period. French was, for Beckett, a virgin idiom that enabled him to "cut away the excess" and "strip away the colour".[93] Without doubt, "excess" and "colour" were stylistic flaws that Beckett associated with the stylised language characteristic of many Revivalist writers, a result of what he called "Anglo-Irish exuberance and automatisms".[94] Nevertheless, his incorporation of the process of translation into his writing allows for an echoing of the cultural anxieties regarding questions of language in Ireland during the Revival and its immediate aftermath. In particular, the lack of a teleological structure of translation in the trilogy may be read as an adaptation of certain devices of translation used by Revivalist writers in their search for means of representing an Irish voice. In the case of Beckett's trilogy, one is thus presented with two distinct, yet interrelated entities, rather than an original text and its translation: the relationship between the French and English versions is troubled by minute linguistic details such as names, currencies and systems of measurement foreign to the language used.[95] Such an investigation of the processes of translation is not without precedent; indeed, notwithstanding Beckett's radical departure from the naturalism of Revivalist writers, problems of translation tackled at the turn of the century by Douglas Hyde, W.B. Yeats, Lady Gregory and George Moore find resonance in his own questioning of the conventions of mimetic translation.[96]

Beckett manifested his sensitivity to problems of style and, in particular, the excessive stylisation potentially accompanying the use of technical features of translation exterior to the translation process, declaring, with regard to Synge's peasant speech, that no one in Ireland spoke in such a fashion.[97] Nevertheless, the dramatic language crafted by Beckett in *All That Fall* and *The Old Tune* (an adaptation of Robert Pinget's *La Manivelle* into Hiberno-English) illustrates an ongoing appreciation of the musicality of Hiberno-English, a quality celebrated in conversation with Pinget as "l'anglais du roi".[98] Beckett's approach to Irish English, in this instance, finds consonance in *A Portrait of the Artist as a Young Man*, in which Stephen argues that forms and structures that have disappeared from standard English are preserved in the English spoken in Ireland.[99] However, like Beckett, Joyce was occasionally ruthless towards the artificial character of Anglo-Irish peasant speech; this is illustrated in Buck Mulligan's parody of Synge's dramatic language in *Ulysses*:

> It's what I'm telling you, mister honey, it's queer and sick we were, Haines and myself, the time himself brought it in. 'Twas murmur we did for a gallus potion would rouse a friar, I'm thinking, and he limp with leching. And we one hour and two hours and three hours in Connery's sitting civil waiting for pints apiece.[100]

While debates surrounding issues of translation during the Revival period were primarily centred on the creation of a national literature, translation is used in Beckett's trilogy to crystallise problems related to the possibilities of form and representation. These concerns appear, in their earliest manifestation, in his essays on Proust and Joyce, in which Proust is celebrated for his ability to fuse form and content, and in which Beckett claims that Joyce's writing "is not *about* something; *it is that something itself*".[101] By using certain features of translation as a guiding principle of composition, Beckett could attune content to form and form to content utilising the same principle of resistance to classical realism. This is taken to an extreme in *L'Innommable* and *The Unnamable*, in which language itself resists assimilation to the act of telling:

> Témoigner pour eux, jusqu'à ce que j'en crève, comme si on pouvait crever à ce jeu-là, voilà ce qu'ils veulent que je fasse. Ne pouvoir ouvrir la bouche sans les proclamer, à titre de congénère, voilà ce à quoi ils croient m'avoir réduit. M'avoir collé un langage dont ils s'imaginent que je ne pourrai jamais me servir sans m'avouer de leur tribu, la belle astuce. Je vais le leur arranger, leur charabia. Auquel je n'ai jamais rien compris du reste, pas plus qu'aux histoires qu'il charrie, comme des chiens crevés. Mon incapacité d'absorption, ma faculté d'oubli, ils les ont sous-estimées.[102]

> To testify to them, until I die, as if there was any dying with that tomfoolery, that's what they've sworn they'll bring me to. Not to be

able to open my mouth without proclaiming them, and our fellowship, that's what they imagine they'll have me reduced to. It's a poor trick that consists in ramming a set of words down your gullet on the principle that you can't bring them up without being branded as belonging to their breed. But I'll fix their gibberish for them. I never understood a word of it in any case, not a word of the stories it spews, like gobbets in a vomit. My inability to absorb, my genius for forgetting, are more than they reckoned with.[103]

The French and the English versions differ in their depiction of linguistic rejection; the image of vomiting used in English is absent from the French text. However, in both cases, language disappears within and against itself, and is allied to the disappearance of the self, leading to the emergence of a vision of physical violence and self-abuse. The narrator *is* language, "made of words, others' words, what others, the place too, the air, the walls, the floor, the ceiling, all words".[104]

* * *

Evocations of weather and food give further evidence of the complementary operation of English and French texts as regards their undermining of cultural values. Weather is discussed extensively in *Molloy*; for instance, in a parody of clichéd discussion of the Irish climate, Molloy emphasises the fact that he has become immune to the continuous rain and brief sunny spells. His expertise on climatic fluctuations can be attributed to his vagabond status:

> D'ailleurs cette question de climat n'avait pas d'intérêt pour moi, je m'accommodais de toutes les sauces. J'ajouterais donc seulement qu'il faisait souvent du soleil le matin, dans cette région, jusqu'à dix heures, dix heures et demie, et qu'à ce moment-là le ciel se couvrait et la pluie tombait, tombait jusqu'au soir. Alors le soleil sortait et se couchait, la terre trempée étincelait un instant, puis s'éteignait, privée de lumière.[105]
>
> In any case this whole question of climate left me cold, I could stomach any mess. So I will only add that the mornings were often sunny, in that part of the world, until ten o'clock or coming up to eleven, and that then the sky darkened and the rain fell, fell till evening. Then the sun came out and went down, the drenched earth sparkled an instant, then went out, bereft of light.[106]

Yet Molloy is afflicted by too many physical ailments for dampness to have any significant effect upon his well-being. The impact of the rigorous weather, in addition, is lessened by his use of the *Times Literary Supplement* as insulation. In this aspect of the narrative, one may discern a deflation of Revivalist idealisations of the pastoral, particularly of Synge's celebrations of the 'authentic' mode of existence of those on the periphery of society. In his prose writings on the Wicklow Mountains, as in his depictions of the isolated communities living on the Aran Islands, Synge associated deprivation with a form of purity and authenticity.[107] Celebrating the luminosity and subtle colours of Wicklow, he emphasised the "many privileges" of the homeless, remarking in *In Wicklow, West Kerry and Connemara*: "The tramp in Ireland is little troubled by the laws, and lives in out-of-door conditions that keep him in good humour and fine bodily health".[108] Beckett, who was familiar with Synge's accounts of his wanderings in the Wicklow Mountains, may have drawn on his book in order to describe the region traversed by Molloy.

Molloy's emphasis upon his own lack of sensitivity to the weather also reinforces his ties with Moran, serving a structural purpose other than signifying a rejection of Revivalist representations of the Irish countryside. Indeed, in the French text, Molloy's disregard for the weather and the quality of food are conveyed in a single clause: "je m'accommodais de toutes les sauces". The declaration of his ability to adapt to "all sauces" is a pun on the colloquial expression *se faire saucer*, to find oneself trapped in abundant rain.[109] The translation of "je m'accommodais de toutes les sauces" into "I could stomach any mess" confirms Molloy's disinterest in food and contributes to the representation of Molloy and Moran as mirror doubles. Moran's extreme sensitivity to culinary matters is manifest in his exchanges with his maid (Marthe in French, Martha in English), who remains unperturbed by his demands and persistently cooks Irish stew:

> Je regardai un peu dans les casseroles. De l'Irish Stew. Plat nourrissant et économe, un peu indigeste. Honneur au pays dont il a popularisé le nom.[110]

In the English text, the dish loses its exotic aura and its capitals:

> I peered into the pots. Irish stew. A nourishing and economical dish, if a little indigestible. All honour to the land it has brought before the world.[111]

The stew is a disappointment, the onions having dissolved: "Where are the onions? I cried. Gone to nothing, replied Martha".[112] In French, Marthe's culinary vocabulary is more developed and precise: "Le stew me déçut. Où sont les oignons? m'écriai-je. Réduits, répondit Marthe".[113] Moran displays similar indifference towards her triumphant transformation of the week's leftovers into a "plat du berger" or shepherd's pie.[114] Here, Moran's gastronomic pretensions and dismissal of Marthe's culinary repertoire provide strong illustrations of the manner in which Beckett toys with clichés associated with French gastronomy.[115] Similarly, in *L'Innommable*, food is the locus where francophone and anglophone cultures bear upon each other. In humorous fashion, the narrator of *L'Innommable* also manifests an interest in culinary matters; he expresses general concern about the quality of corned beef, the differences between various kinds of carrots and the appropriate time of year for serving tripe. The cross-cultural positioning of the narrative concerning dietary choice is revealed in his comment upon the insubstantiality of a French breakfast in English: "I wonder if I couldn't sneak out by the fundament, one morning, with the French breakfast".[116] In contrast, the phrase used in the French text ("le petit déjeuner") is nondescript.[117]

* * *

Given the cultural and linguistic playfulness of the French novels, their translation into English raised considerable problems. These were addressed by adding an Irish flavour to the English texts, which is evident in the translation of colloquialisms: in *Molloy*, "comme un vieux con" becomes "like an old ballocks"; in *Malone Dies*, "merde alors" becomes "well I'll be buggered".[118] Beckett also deliberately hibernicised *The Unnamable* by using local Dublin expressions such as "billy in the bowl" and "faith":

> Mahood is no worse than his predecessors. But before executing his portrait, full length on his surviving leg, let me note that my next vice-exister will be a billy in the bowl, that's final, with his bowl on his head and his arse in the dust, plump down on thousand-breasted Tellus, it'll be softer for him. Faith that's an idea, yet another, mutilate, mutilate, and perhaps some day, fifteen generations hence, you'll succeed in beginning to look like yourself, among the passers-by.[119]

The Billy evoked in this passage recalls a figure from Dublin folklore, who was crippled and propelled himself around the city in a wooden bowl.[120] The French text is standard and remains confined to an examination of the literal meaning of the expression *cul-de-jatte*:

> Mahood n'est pas pire que ses devanciers. Mais avant d'en brosser le portrait, sur pied, il n'en a plus qu'un, mon prochain représentant en existence sera un cul de jatte, c'est décidé, la jatte sur la tête et le cul dans la poussière, à même Tellus aux milles mamelles, pour plus de douceur. Tiens, c'est une idée, encore une, j'arriverai presque peut-être, à coups de mutilations, d'ici une quinzaine de générations d'homme, à faire figure de moi, parmi les passants.[121]

In French, *cul-de-jatte* has a well-defined meaning, designating a legless cripple – as does the expression *portrait en pied*, meaning standing or seated portrait, to which Beckett refers in order to joke about Mahood's appearance. In French, the narrator's sensitivity to the literal meaning of set phrases recalls the perspective of a non-native speaker; foreignness is thus translated into Irishness.

A sizeable proportion of the jokes and puns that feature in the French version of the trilogy emerge from Beckett's inquisitive approach to features peculiar to the French language. Locating equivalents created intractable problems; in *Molloy* particularly, there is clearly something lost in the passage into English. Some jokes simply could not be translated, thus affecting the presentation of Molloy and Moran as mirror doubles:

> Je n'étais pas dans mon assiette. Elle est profonde, mon assiette, une assiette à soupe, et il est rare que je n'y sois pas. C'est pourquoi je le signale.[122]

And later:

> Je posai ma cuiller. Dites-moi, Marthe, dis-je, quelle est cette préparation? Elle me la nomma. J'en ai déjà mangé? dis-je. Elle m'assura qu'oui. C'est donc moi qui ne suis pas dans mon assiette, dis-je. Ce trait d'esprit me plut énormément, j'en ris tellement que je me mis à hoqueter. Il fut perdu pour Marthe qui me regardait avec hébètement.[123]

This joke disappears in the English version, because the phrase "ne pas être dans son assiette" has no equivalent:

> I was out of sorts. They are deep, my sorts, a deep ditch, and I am not often out of them. That's why I mention it.[124]
>
> I laid down my spoon. Tell me, Martha, I said, what is this preparation? She named it. Have I had it before? I said. She assured me I had.

I then made a joke which pleased me enormously. I laughed so much I began to hiccup. It was lost on Martha who stared at me dazedly.[125]

In English, Moran's joke remains unidentified and he deplores Martha's inability to understand him. In contrast, in French, his contempt for Marthe's lack of intelligence is evident in his allusion to her bad elocution, which, incidentally, mirrors her culinary neglect.

Patrick Bowles, who assisted Beckett in the translation of *Molloy*, found the work daunting, as Beckett remained adamant that the novel should not be translated, but, rather, turned into "a new book in the new language".[126] The speech patterns drawn from Hiberno-English and added to the English texts confirm that Beckett retained close control over this transformative process. For instance, Moran replies to his son, who is feeling unwell: "A stomach-ache! Have you a temperature?"[127] The French text is standard: "Mal au ventre! As-tu de la fièvre?"[128] In other cases, where the French text contained emphatic structures and repetitions that recalled Hiberno-English, translated sections are given Irish inflections. For instance, Molloy emphasises the mysteriousness of his employer, who visits him only on Sundays, by means of a series of reversals: "C'est un drôle de type, celui qui vient me voir. C'est tous les dimanches qu'il vient, paraît-il".[129] In English, this becomes: "He's a queer one the one who comes to see me. He comes every Sunday apparently".[130] Phrasings such as these require authorial endorsement and it is highly unlikely that Bowles alone chose them.

Beckett considered the translation of *Molloy* to be awful and, when he revised it in August 1954, he decided to begin translating *Malone meurt* alone: "J'essaie de réviser l'affreuse traduction qu'on a faite de *Molloy*. Un cauchemar, encore un. Je commence moi-même la traduction de *Malone*" [I am trying to revise the awful translation we did of *Molloy*. Yet another nightmare. I have started translating *Malone* myself].[131] This represented a substantial departure for Beckett; previously, he had translated his work in collaboration with other writers, including Bowles, Ludovic Janvier for *Watt*, Alfred Péron for *Murphy* and Richard Seaver for "L'Expulsé" and "La Fin" (later, Robert Pinget contributed to *Cendres* and *Tous ceux qui tombent*). However, Beckett found collaboration difficult, and this sentiment was often reciprocated by his translators.[132] Self-translation appeared to be the only solution, as Beckett explained to John Fletcher. He had hoped to save time by letting others translate his work, but soon realised that he had been mistaken.[133] Unfortunately, for Beckett, this new step did not prove to be a liberation and he clearly felt imprisoned: his letters to Thomas MacGreevy, Aidan Higgins, Kay

Boyle, Alan Schneider and Jacoba van Velde are replete with comments regarding the difficulties of self-translation, which he found extremely wearisome.[134] "Great mistake giving such work to another and a great bore having to do it oneself", he lamented to MacGreevy.[135]

* * *

When work began on the translation of the trilogy, Beckett was already accustomed to dealing with issues of cultural translation: the use of Hiberno-English had raised intractable problems during the 1930s, when he had attempted to write a play on Samuel Johnson. Since he wanted the play to be performed in Ireland, he initially decided to grant Irish inflections to the speech of his characters, while Johnson would speak only the words found in Boswell's biography. The venture was preceded by considerable research, as evidenced in three hefty notebooks, which reveal Beckett's keen interest in Johnson's perspective on Ireland and stress Johnson's condemnation of the colonial administration as a barbaric system sustained by unlawful and immoral practices.[136] Little of this nourished the play, however. Entitled *Human Wishes*, the text remained a mere fragment and was published along with other marginalia in *Disjecta* (1983). Although the play remains centred on Johnson, the writer does not appear in it; Beckett later admitted that, at the time, he was unable to solve the problems of consistency raised by the combination of different strains of English.[137]

Interestingly, the most immediate precedent for this project may be found in Lady Augusta Gregory's Irish adaptations of Molière's comedies. Indeed, in imbuing a play set in eighteenth-century England with Irish inflections, Beckett echoed the stylistic strategies adopted by Lady Gregory in her translations into Hiberno-English.[138] The intention of these translations, written between 1906 and 1926, was to adapt the "spirit" of Molière into the Galway dialect that Lady Gregory had been using in plays written for the Abbey.[139] Her texts are best described as textual reworkings, due to their erasure of all class-based plotlines upon which the dénouement depended in Molière's plays; indeed, due to Gregory's uniform use of Irish peasant speech, no speech distinction can be drawn between master and servant. In Beckett's trilogy, the simultaneous use of several cultural frameworks similarly produces an effect of equalisation; his narrators appear to be exempted from class based concerns, their mannerisms nonetheless suggesting a form of decayed gentility that is confirmed by their knowledge of classical painting and philosophy.

If the stylistic effects deployed by Beckett bear some resemblance to translation projects such as those of Lady Gregory, their respective purposes differ considerably: indeed, Gregory's decision to translate Molière into Kiltartanese originated in a belief that Hiberno-English carried a form of creative energy absent from standard English. Her idea of transposing Molière into Irish surroundings did not meet with universal approval; Joseph Holloway, a devoted theatregoer, remarked in his diaries that her choice to transform the comedies into peasant plays and to retain the French surroundings, dress and scenes constituted an affront to common sense.[140] In contrast, both Yeats and Synge discerned a considerable dramatic vitality in Lady Gregory's reworkings of Molière: Synge admired the linguistic energy of her version of *Le Docteur malgré lui*,[141] and Yeats thought that her translation of *Les Rogueries de Scapin* was better than the original play, which he found far removed from life and overly farcical.[142] In an Abbey programme of February 1909, Yeats described Lady Gregory's translations of Molière as a form of artistic rebirth, emphasising their exoticism:

> The word translation [...] which should be applied to scenery, acting, and words alike, implies, or should imply, freedom. In vital translation, and I believe that our translations are vital, a work of art does not go upon its travels: it is re-born in a strange land.[143]

In praising Gregory's adaptations, Yeats promoted the notion of translation as a creative act, rather than a technical process. In contrast, he showed little esteem for the translated poetry of the Young Ireland movement, which combined a residue of "Gaelic manner" with "borrowed rhetoric",[144] and he argued that the use of "mature English methods of utterance" in order to "sing of Irish wrongs or preach of Irish purposes" was inappropriate.[145] Nevertheless, Yeats appreciated the poetry of the period that sought to reproduce the cadences of Gaelic; the "clumsiness and crudity" of Callanan's poems, for instance, appealed to him, due to their ability to bring "into the elaborate literature of the modern world the cold vehemence, the arid definiteness, the tumultuous movement, the immeasurable dreaming of the Gaelic literature".[146] Douglas Hyde's 1893 *Love Songs of Connacht* provided Yeats with a further example of the type of "poetical thought" Irish authors should strive for; he was struck by the "haunting charm" of Hyde's divergence from standard English and praised the imaginative potential of Hyde's adaptations of Gaelic folk poetry into prose.[147] Yeats's admiration for the "dialect" thus created by Hyde emerged from a belief that English was a decaying language; for Yeats, as for many of his contemporaries, using a form of English whose imagery and cadence were inspired from Gaelic could breathe new life into literature.

Despite the considerable differences in intention and method separating Hyde's translations from Beckett's texts, Hyde's innovative use of the processes of translation provides precious insight into the ways in which Beckett's own questioning of the conventions of translation may be contextualised. Indeed, *Love Songs of Connacht* departs radically from the idea of complete transposition that had been adopted in previous translations of Gaelic poetry, such as those published by the Young Irelanders, and, instead, renders the translation process transparent. Verse translations and literal prose translations feature alongside originals texts, with the literal prose translation concealed in footnotes; the verse translations into English recreate the meter and rhyme of the folk songs from which they are derived, the prose translations their imagery. Hyde hoped that revealing the mechanisms of translation in the syntax and vocabulary of the prose translations would restore the poetic energy of the originals. However, in this instance, literalism leads to the precedence of form over content: indeed, in their rejection of English syntax, Hyde's prose translations brought to life a stylised peasant speech that subverted the rules of English prosody. For Michael Cronin, the subversive potential of these textual offshoots lies in their handling of the target language, English prosody being undermined by another syntax, sound system and lexicon during the literal translation from Gaelic into English.[148] The translations in prose and in verse are calculated to be complementary, yet the blatant disjunctions of syntax, form and imagery identify them as separate entities. Whether one should prioritise the prose translations over the verse translations or vice versa remains uncertain; the distinctions traditionally drawn between the original text and its translation are eroded, as a satellite text in prose comes into being in the footnotes.

Due to its creation of a textual entity which expands beyond the traditional limits of translation, Hyde's volume of poems constitutes an interesting forerunner to the associations and disjunctions developing within Beckett's bilingual body of work. Hyde's translations, however, were sutured to specific debates; in particular, his prose translations responded to issues of creativity and style that preoccupied the leading protagonists of the Literary Revival in the early years of the movement. His creation of stylised peasant speech addressed some of the problems of expression and consistency surrounding the creation of a national literature in English and, as such, was highly influential. As

Yeats pointed out, Hyde's poetic language proved more adequate than standard English for the exploration of Irish themes; indeed, if these themes could be *thought* in English, they could not possibly be *written* in standard English.[149] For Yeats, Hyde's prose translations brought to life a new way of thinking and opened up a "new region for the mind to wander in"; as such, they represented "the coming of a new power into literature".[150] George Moore, who had no knowledge of Gaelic, was equally fascinated by the vitality and simplicity of Hyde's peasant speech, remarking that "to write beautiful English one has only to translate literally from the Irish".[151]

Thomas MacDonagh's *Literature in Ireland*, published posthumously in 1916, reveals that Hyde's translations shaped the ways in which an 'Irish mode' came to be defined in later years. For MacDonagh, a language overburdened with conventions was not conducive to the national concerns. To bestow a new dynamism upon English, he pointed out, the Irish writer needed to suppress "the phraseology, the inversions, the poetic words, the cumbrous epithets, the mannerisms, of its pastoral and of its genteel days".[152] He was particularly sensitive to the disruptive power of Hyde's imagery and noted that Hyde's literal translations of stock phrases created not only a "strange language" but also, most importantly, a "different logic": phrases that seemed tired and ordinary in Irish gained a new life when transposed into English.[153] Echoing Yeats, MacDonagh argued that Hyde's translations represented the future of Irish literature in English and concluded that the new literature would advance of its own accord, free from translation.[154]

The prospect of a stylised peasant dialect becoming the basis of the new national literature did, however, confound Hyde's original expectations. Initially, Hyde had hoped to reveal the beauty of the Irish language to the "increasing class of Irishmen who take a just pride in their native language, and to those foreigners who, great philologists and etymologists as they are, find themselves hampered in their pursuits through their unavoidable ignorance of the modern Irish idiom".[155] His translations became self-defeating in practice: instead of promoting Irish as the language of the nation, they implied that translation could give birth to a new literary tradition in English, as Declan Kiberd notes.[156]

In this respect, *Love Songs of Connacht* is at variance with Hyde's stance in "The Necessity for De-Anglicizing Ireland", an 1892 speech that led to the formation of the Gaelic League. Hyde denounced a paradox in Irish attitudes to the use of English: while the Irish display a deep animosity towards England, they are only too willing to adopt the English language and English customs and manners. This "most anomalous position", for Hyde, could only thwart the natural progression of literature and the arts.[157] His great fear was that by adopting customs and manners that were inspired by England, the Irish might lose sense of themselves, "ceasing to be Irish without becoming English".[158] This turn towards English values reflected the growing materialism of the Irish people and was detrimental to the distinctiveness of national character, anti-materialism being precisely what distinguished the "Irish race" from the "English race" and gave the Irish people their dignity.[159] To curb the cultural and scholarly decline associated with the disappearance of Gaelic-speaking Ireland, Hyde proposed to replace all things English with their Gaelic equivalents, particularly names, sports and choices of dress. De-anglicisation, in this instance, was a necessity that involved the Irish people as a whole, regardless of their political affiliation.

In a reply to Hyde's speech, Yeats denounced the impracticality of such a proposition, evoking instead the possibility of creating "a national tradition, a national literature, which shall be none the less Irish in spirit from being English in language".[160] For Yeats, Irish hopes of nationhood should not be based upon costly and radical measures; remarking that recasting the national imagination in English would preserve a sense of continuity between past and present, he felt it preferable to utilise translations into English as a source of literary inspiration, rather than dealing solely with the "perishing" Gaelic tongue.[161] He commented, however, upon the necessity of maintaining the "indefinable Irish quality of rythm [sic] and style, all that is best of the ancient literature" in the English texts.[162] To achieve this effect, writers should graft such an "Irish quality" onto their adaptations, rather than simply transposing Irish material into English. His idea of translation as creative adaptation corresponded to complex stylistic mechanisms far removed from the radical cultural subtraction advocated by Hyde.

Putting these ideas into practice proved difficult; Yeats's project to adapt the legend of Diarmuid and Grania for the stage, for instance, displayed scant awareness of the practicalities of translation. The writing process began as a collaborative venture; initially, Yeats proposed to have George Moore write the play in French; this would have been followed by a translation into English, by Lady Gregory, then another, into Irish, by Taidgh O'Donoghue, and yet another, back into English, by Lady Gregory – "and Yeats was to put style upon [it]", Moore concluded.[163] Successive translations would thus enable the exploration of a zone of language far removed from naturalistic conventions of representation, and yet marked by a quintessentially Irish quality due to the Irishness and literary ambitions of its authors. However, had it been implemented, this initial project would have been self-defeating in practice: if specific cultural allusions had been used in any of the translations, they would have disappeared one after another, since it would have been necessary to transpose them with each language change. Cultural specificity would have been gradually erased with each new translation; a form of linguistic neutrality, rather than specificity, would have developed as this form of progressive erasure was put into effect.

Nevertheless, Moore initially took Yeats's project seriously and went to France to draft *Diarmuid and Grania*. For Moore, writing in French was "a way of escape from the English language which [he] had come to hate for political reasons, and from the English country and the English people".[164] This first draft, which corresponds to the first scene of the second act of the play, is reproduced in *Hail and Farewell*, an autobiographical novel much admired by Beckett;[165] Moore justified its inclusion in the published text by claiming that the French fragment broke the harmony of the English narrative.[166] The importance of the draft, however, resides in its heavy reliance upon the strategies of translation adopted by Hyde, although Moore did not speak Irish and considered Hyde's verse and prose translations to be "untidily written".[167] The strong Irish flavour of Moore's French is apparent in the systematic deployment of emphatic structures involving the use of *et* at the beginning of a clause, of *donc* and *si* before adjectives, of *comme* before an exclamation, of *c'est...que* (it is...that). This added emphasis leads to tautological statements in French, as when the two lovers express their yearning for "des landes plus désertes, plus inconnues" (literally, moors more deserted and more unknown).[168] Moore's choice to use the word *landes* instead of the standard, less specific *terres* (lands) hints at an attempt to recreate a stylised Irish landscape. Other phrasings confirm Moore's desire to model syntax on the peasant speech created by Hyde; inversions (for instance, "le pommier des admirables vertus") are used to produce poetic effect.[169] However, such inversions are accompanied by various grammatical oddities and a rather fanciful use of articles and tenses, which undermine the desired effect.[170] The characters' declarations are heavily inflected by English turns of phrase and, often, grammatically incorrect, with Moore using auxiliary verbs based on English rather than French syntax, for instance: "Nous avons passé par toutes les épreuves de la prouesse que l'on nous a demandée".[171] Such lack of fluency has an impact on both the form and the content of the play but enables Moore to achieve an exaggerative effect, namely to heighten the characters' simplicity of thought and manner, and to accentuate their distance from a world left behind. Unsurprisingly, the draft was abandoned and the play was completed solely in English.[172] Upon production in October 1901, it was denounced by Irish nationalists as the ransacking of an Irish theme and as an inconsistent adaptation.[173]

Idiosyncrasies aside, the joint approach to translation of Moore and Yeats provides a precedent for reading the reversals taking place not only in Beckett's trilogy, but also in his later fiction. Indeed, Beckett remained interested in the effect produced by successive translations, and used a similar strategy to elaborate a neutral language in *Company/Compagnie* and *Bing/Ping*. The first version of *Company* was written in English and translated into French; the English text was subsequently revised in the light of the French translation.[174] Likewise, *Bing/Ping* was composed 'backwards': Brian Fitch explains that the published English text corresponds to a stage in the drafting of its French counterpart that precedes the version that had served as the source of the earlier English version.[175] However, the similarities between Beckett's use of translation and Yeats's original project for *Diarmuid and Grania* should not be over-emphasised: the effect of linguistic impoverishment produced by Beckett's successive translations is far removed from that for which Yeats was searching.

Beckett is, perhaps, closer to Flann O'Brien in his uses of translation. O'Brien's novel *The Poor Mouth*, in particular, anticipates Beckett's own use of stylistic features related to translation. Throughout the 1940s, O'Brien explored the ways in which a certain methodology of translation could be used for parodic purposes;[176] this was achieved with particular success in *An Béal Bocht*, which relies upon translation as a method of composition. According to Anne Clissmann, O'Brien initially took an original Irish text, parodied its translation into English and wrote a literal translation into Irish of the parodied translation, which provided a basis for *An Béal Bocht*.[177] He did not wish the novel to be transposed into English; Patrick C. Power's translation appeared only in 1973, long after O'Brien's death.[178] The English translation does not replicate the musical peasant speech favoured by Hyde and Synge; on the contrary, it mocks the pretensions of Hyde's Gaelic League and explores forms of material, cultural and linguistic impoverishment in equal measure. O'Brien's animosity towards the use of stylised speech in order to represent the Gaelic-speaking culture was made clear in his *Irish Times* column, which described Synge's characters as clowns talking a language only intelligible to themselves.[179] He strongly resented Synge's position of superiority towards the native culture, calling him "a moneyed dilettante coming straight from Paris to study the peasants of Aran not knowing a syllable of their language; then coming back to pour forth a deluge of home-made jargon all over the stage of the Abbey".[180]

In *The Poor Mouth*, one is faced with dwindling semantic fields. The gradual disappearance of language affects both form and content; the narrative revolves around a limited number of words, principally potato, pig, rain, misery, hunger and ill-luck, and Gaelic itself becomes meaningless: nothing can be articulated apart from "the question of the Gaelic Revival and the question of Gaelicism". During a feis in the village of Corkadoragha, the president of the feis (known as the Gaelic Daisy) declares:

> I myself have spoken not a word except Gaelic since the day I was born – just like you – and every sentence I've ever uttered has been on the subject of Gaelic. If we're truly Gaelic, we must constantly discuss the question of the Gaelic revival and the question of Gaelicism. There is no use in having Gaelic, if we converse in it on non-Gaelic topics. [...] There is nothing in this life so nice and so Gaelic as truly true Gaelic Gaels, who can speak in true Gaelic Gaelic about the truly Gaelic language.[181]

The use of phrases such as "The Gaelicism of the Gaelic race" illustrates that, from O'Brien's perspective, Revivalist attempts to revive the Irish language were fundamentally sterile, in Irish and in English translation – a failure announced in Hyde's own use of tautological expressions, such as "the Gaeldom of Erin" (*Ghaodhaltacht na h-Eireann*), to celebrate the spiritual purity of ancient Gaelic society.[182] O'Brien's characters remain unaffected by the political changes taking place in Ireland; they live suspended in the past, "in the old Gaelic manner – wet and hungry by day and by night and unhealthy, having nothing in the future but rain, famine and ill-luck".[183] The novel clearly draws upon the introduction to *Love Songs of Connacht*, in which Hyde describes the dire living conditions of the Irish-speaking peasantry in the nineteenth century:

> The life of the Gaels is so pitiable, so dark and sad and sorrowful, and they are so broken, bruised, and beaten down in their own land and country that their talents and ingenuity find no place for themselves, and no way to let themselves out but in excessive foolish mirth, or in keening and lamentation.[184]

While Hyde used translation to create a form of cultural authenticity resting on the assumption that the Gaelic-speaking culture was sovereign and immutable, O'Brien questions the very possibility that ancient mores may have retained meaning: the more unintelligible Gaelic is, the better.[185] O'Brien's construction of a narrative mode that thrives upon its own disappearance and relies on the exaggeration of technical features of translation identifies *The Poor Mouth* as providing an adequate framework for considering certain aspects of Beckett's translation practices.

* * *

Beckett, however, remained at a remove from the debates surrounding the revival of the Irish language; as a young man, he was amused by the frantic Gaelicisation of names in the Irish Free State, and, in a letter of 1933 to Thomas MacGreevy, he joked about the climate of hypocrisy and intellectual snobbery that surrounded the revival of Gaelic, mocking the "newly acquired prudery" of the Irish government and remarking that certain Gaelic names could not be translated literally into English and had to be toned down, due to lewd connotations.[186] Beckett's aloofness from the linguistic debate in post-independence Ireland can be explained by his education; the literary establishment of Trinity College Dublin was initially hostile to the language movement and Revivalist literature at large, leading Lady Gregory to take a swipe at "the Chinese Wall that separates Trinity College from Ireland".[187] In the 1890s, Edward Dowden, Professor of English at Trinity, criticised the sentimentality of Revival literature and argued that the use of Irish themes was often a means to conceal bad writing.[188] Interestingly, Beckett's stance in "Recent Irish Poetry" is not far removed from that of Dowden; he mocks the "antiquarians, delivering with the altitudinous complacency of the Victorian Gael the Ossianic goods" and denounces the parochialism of James Stephen, Austin Clarke, F.R. Higgins and Monk Gibbon, arguing that the use of "accredited themes" merely accentuates the stylistic failures in the poetry of these writers.[189] His notebooks suggest a superficial knowledge of the Revival's literary forefathers: notes from Emile Legouis and Louis Cazamian's *History of English Literature*, for instance, include entries on the Young Ireland movement, Carleton, Mangan, Allingham and Thompson, which are little more than perfunctory lists and suggest little knowledge of the period. The description of Mangan, for example, suggests that Beckett was more interested in his tragic end than in his poetry.[190] Nevertheless, the conclusion of

"Recent Irish Poetry", which refers to Standish O'Grady and Samuel Ferguson, suggests that, for Beckett, the legacy of nineteenth-century writers was problematic; it led to the deployment of Irish folklore as a form of stylistic regulation over the chaos of human experience, itself the adequate subject matter of the modern artist, for Beckett.

In French, Beckett could engage with stylistic devices that were perceived in the context of the Revival period as a potential source of cultural revitalisation, while detaching himself from their cultural and historical weight. French was a language deprived of a core, in which it was easier to "write without style", as he stated in *Dream of Fair to Middling Women*.[191] Something at the heart of English proved an ill fit for his artistic vision, in contrast with French, which he described as a means to "boost the possibility of stylelessness" and to reach "pure communication".[192] Considered in relation to the debates surrounding style during the Revival period, Beckett's statements call into question Yeats's view of an Irish literary idiom: for Yeats, style could be gained and refined precisely through the use of Irish themes and motifs,[193] and he liked to refer, when asserting the importance and originality of the national literature, to Sainte Beuve's idea of nothing in literature being immortal, except style.[194] In practice, however, Beckett's consideration of the necessity of stylelessness collapses entirely; his French remains heavily inflected with constructions that are inspired by English and that may not have occurred to a native French speaker. This feature of his early writings is particularly salient in early drafts of *Molloy*.

* * *

The novel was written relatively quickly, but certain aspects of its genesis were uneasy; it was partially reshaped following the advice of Mania Péron, who disapproved of Beckett's explicit attacks upon Irish political conservatism. An early draft forcefully expresses Beckett's estrangement from the Catholic ideology of the Irish Free State, carrying references to the Huguenots and a history of religious persecution. Molloy's village, Bally, is depicted as a fanciful caricature of a small Irish town; its inhabitants forge a living from the sale of amulets, religious knick-knacks and their own excrement. The 'backwardness' of Bally is measured in relation to the French administrative system, depicted as a model of enlightenment in comparison:

> Ce bourg, ou ce village, comme on veut, s'appelait, disons-le tout de suite, Bally, et X représentait, comme les terres en dépendant, une

superficie de 5 ou 6 milles carrés tout au plus. C'était ça qu'on appelle en F X ce que les Français appellent une commune, on appelle ça une comm En France on appelle ça une commune, je crois, mais chez nous il n'existe pas de terme [?] et générique pour ces [autodivisions?] du territoire, et pour les exprimer avec le maximum de célérité nous avons un autre [?], d'une beauté et d'une simplicité remarquables, et qui consiste à dire Bally (puisqu'il s'agit de Bally) lorsqu'on veut dire Bally et Ballyba lorsqu'on veut dire Bally plus les terres en dépendant et Ballybaba lorsqu'on veut dire les terres de Bally exclusives de Bally lui-même. Ce fut X un prêtre qui inventa X cette X nomenclature, au 16ème siècle, en pleine persécution huguenote, et elle fut reprise, au siècle suivante abandonnée, reprise et abandonnée, [?] des idéologies en présence, jusqu'au triomphe définitif de la vraie croyance.[195]

When Péron annotated Beckett's typescript, she suppressed the passage on religious persecution and justified this elision with one word: "calviniste".[196] She crossed out "en France" and replaced it by "dans les pays évolués", in order to compensate for excising Beckett's hostility.[197] Her suggestions had a strong influence on Beckett's satire of post-independence Ireland:

D'où Ballyba tirait-il donc sa richesse [Péron replaced this by "son opulence"]? Je vais vous le dire [in her hand: "non, je ne dirai rien"]. Des selles de ses habitants. Et cela depuis les [des] temps immémoriaux. Quelques mots à ce sujet. C'est sans doute la dernière fois que j'aurai l'occasion de m'abandonner à ma passion pour la chose régionale, pour cette unique mixture qui donne à chaque terroir son bouquet, pour ce que j'appelle le folklore du sous-sol.[198]

Péron may have thought it necessary to suppress Beckett's aggressive tone due to the likely bewilderment that such directionless hostility might have caused a French audience. In the published text, Beckett followed most of her instructions regarding this particular section: no mention is made of the priest who invented the classification that established Bally, Ballyba and Ballybaba as different locations, and the allusion to the persecution of Huguenots in sixteenth-century France is omitted, as is Beckett's sardonic comment on the true religion, "la vraie croyance". Beckett subsequently suppressed most of the scatological passages, simply stating in the final English text: "What then was the source of Ballyba's prosperity? I'll tell you. No, I'll tell you nothing. Nothing".[199]

Among the significant features of Péron's corrections is their attempt to preserve the sense of the exotic manifested by the use of an Irish locale: she did not change Beckett's phrase "milles carrés" (a straight translation of "square miles") into *kilomètres carrés*, for instance. However, she thought it preferable to suppress Beckett's references to Irish history and politics. Instead, she recommended the use of cliché, adding in the adjective "druidique": "Car à peine un labour prenait-il de l'ampleur, ou un pré, qu'il se cassait le nez sur un bocage [druidique] ou sur une bande de marais".[200] Beckett followed her suggestions; in the published text, evocations of Irish Ireland retain an enigmatic quality, a movement evident in a coded allusion to the "genuine Irish" movement; the handle of the vegetable knife that Lousse's servant gives to Molloy is made of "so-called genuine Irish horn".[201] The knife is, however, of poor quality; in the French version, its exotic "manche en vraie corne d'Irlande, soi-disant" is the sole indicator of its monetary value.[202]

* * *

Mania Péron's comments and corrections indicate that, from an early stage, Beckett found himself under pressure not to hibernicise his French texts. Later, he was also urged to refrain from writing in Irish English; his adaptation of Robert Pinget's *La Manivelle*, for instance, was received unfavourably by Alan Simpson, director of Dublin's Pike Theatre, who found it too close to the kind of Irish English used by Brendan Behan. Simpson pointed out that the Irish actors and actresses who had found success on the London stages were too few to sustain such ventures and argued that, if Beckett continued with this trend, the production of his work in England would become problematic. Irish dialect, he pointed out, was a "handicap" likely to alienate British audiences, given the peculiar nature of British–Irish relations.[203] For Simpson, Donald McWhinnie's dismissal of Dublin English in his television adaptation of *Waiting for Godot* was representative of the immense problems generated by the use of Irish English outside Ireland. Such choices, Simpson pointed out, originated in the likelihood that Beckett's British public might be "confused or prejudiced by the dialect".[204]

Beckett's adaptation of *La Manivelle* is generally regarded as a peripheral venture;[205] it does, however, represent the culmination of a process of stylisation that had preoccupied him since the abandoned adaptation of Samuel Johnson's life into Hiberno-English. The desire to explore the dramatic potential of a stylised form of Hiberno-English was eventually realised with the transposition of Pinget's radio play, which was first broadcast on the BBC in August 1960. *La Manivelle* is a play for voices which revolves around two old men, Toupin and Pommard (Gorman and Cream in Beckett's adaptation, *The Old Tune*), who are sitting by a roadside, evoking common memories. Beckett's transposition of their discussion into Hiberno-English gives more prominence to religion than is granted by the French original: "Pâques" (Easter) becomes the "Holy Week", for instance;[206] certain additions, such as "yes by God", are used as rhythmic markers, reinforcing the musicality of speech.[207] The Irish characters display greater tact than their French counterparts when talking about the dead; elliptical questions such as "Mais dites-moi votre pauvre morte" become "But tell me then the poor soul she was taken then was she".[208] Some passages are toned down; "Madame Pommard est morte il y a vingt ans, Monsieur Toupin" is less blunt in English: "Mrs Cream is in her coffin these twenty years Mr Gorman".[209] In Beckett's adaptation, both characters are associated with certain idiosyncrasies of speech, which makes them easier to distinguish than Pinget allows in the French text; Cream appears to be more disposed to mild eccentricities of speech than Gorman, for instance. Both characters display a greater propensity for swearing in Beckett's adaptation: "de quoi je me mêle" becomes "mind her own damn business".[210] The influence of O'Casey is apparent in Beckett's rendering of "Un bien joli nom" as "Darling name", evoking Joxer Daly in *Juno and the Paycock*.[211] However, Beckett generally avoids the conventions of misspelling adopted by O'Casey, save for a few marginal instances.[212]

Beckett's adaptation may be read as illustrating a uniquely Irish predicament, as the text becomes a reflection upon exile and linguistic displacement in the transfer from French to Hiberno-English. Although the place names used by Pinget are sometimes real, sometimes imaginary, Beckett's use of English equivalents suggests that the characters are exiled Irishmen, a notion reinforced by the sense of nostalgia and relish attached to Hiberno-English expressions. That the adaptation carries more historical weight than the original is apparent in the characters' evocations of their experiences in the army. In Pinget's play, they allude only to military service, whereas in Beckett's adaptation, the allusion suggests Irish involvement in the British army: Gorman joined the army at Chatham – "The Foot, in 1906".[213] Subtle shifts of this nature are not marginal occurrences in Beckett's work; similarly, in the French *Molloy*, Lousse evokes "la pension de guerre de [son] cher défunt, mort pour une patrie qui se disait la sienne et dont de son vivant il ne retira jamais le moindre avantage, mais seulement des affronts et des bâtons dans les roues".[214] In English, this becomes an allusion to Irish involvement in the Great War under the British flag, Lousse remarking upon "the pension of [her] dear old departed, fallen in defence of a country that called itself his and from which in his lifetime he never derived the smallest benefit, but only insults and vexations".[215]

Beckett's decision to adapt Pinget's play into Hiberno-English may be read as an attempt to carve out a territory in which he could freely explore the expressive powers of Irish English without being subject to justification. Indeed, it was with alarming regularity that he was called upon to clarify the meaning of Irish allusions to translators and directors abroad. Alan Schneider, for instance, was puzzled by the word "Avoca", a village in County Wicklow mentioned in *Eh Joe*; Beckett sent him a note indicating the correct pronunciation of the word:

AVOCA (accent on O): stress on *o* long as in po
A as in ma.[216]

In another letter to Schneider, Beckett explained the meaning of his use of "bumper" in *Happy Days*: "'Bumper': brimming glass. Drink a bumper, toss off a brimming glass. It's the 'happy days' toast".[217] In another instance, Ruby Cohn requested a clarification of the origin of his reference to blueband in *Embers*; Beckett explained that it was the name of a brand of margarine.[218] Alterations were thus often required when the work was exported to countries in which such specific allusion may have gone unnoticed, unrecognised or misunderstood. For instance, the reference to the brand of dog biscuit Spratt's Medium in *Endgame* raised problems in American productions; Alan Schneider asked Beckett to change it.[219] Beckett suggested "classic biscuit" (a literal translation from the French text), "standard biscuit" or "hard tack".[220] In another instance, when consulted about a production of *Krapp's Last Tape*, he agreed to relinquish signifiers of cultural specificity and authorised Schneider to replace "reel" with "spool", "weir" with "sluice" or "lock", and "dingle" with "dell", for the sake of clarity.[221]

Beckett's painstaking attention to detail was not limited to the French and English versions of his texts. Elmar Tophoven (who translated Beckett's work into German) claimed that Beckett would reflect carefully upon minute linguistic and phonetic variations,[222] and Beckett's correspondence with Jacoba van Velde (who translated his work into Dutch) reveals a provision of guidance even when the translation involved a language unmastered by Beckett. Intractable problems arose when choosing between transposition and literal translation, and

Beckett negotiated these problems case by case. In some instances, he authorised van Velde to use Dutch equivalents: when clarifying aspects of *Waiting for Godot*, for instance, he explained that La Roquette was "une maison de correction pour jeunes délinquants à Paris", the equivalent of borstal in England; he advised van Velde to replace it by the Dutch equivalent.[223] Regarding the translation of *Krapp's Last Tape*, he recommended adapting Krapp's reference to the Protestant psalm "Now the Day Is Over" to the context of reception:

> J'ai remplacé en français par un cantique protestant français. Ce n'est sûrement pas ça qui manque dans votre chère patrie.
>
> [I replaced it in the French text with a French Protestant psalm. You're certainly not short of them in your beloved homeland.][224]

He also indicated that the jokes and puns in *Happy Days* should be transposed into their Dutch equivalents, if possible:

> Shower (schauen) ou cooker (kuchen) représente le spectateur. Tophoven a donc simplement germanisé les racines anglaises peer and stare. Tu pourrais les hollandiser.
>
> [Shower (schauen) or cooker (kuchen) represents the spectator. Tophoven simply germanised the English roots peer and stare. You could give them a Dutch tint.][225]

Regarding place names, systematic transposition was not advisable, and he suggested using analogies:

> Burrough Green etc: B.G. est un village dans le Surrey. Tu peux le remplacer par un endroit en Angleterre familier aux Hollandais (Dover, par exemple, ou Hawich). Pas une grande ville. Il faut garder le climat anglais – ou bien <u>tout</u> transposer, ce qui n'est pas à conseiller. [...] Bumper: un verre débordant. [...] "Reynolds' News": l'infâme torchon populaire. Pas à remplacer avec l'équivalent hollandais à moins de tout transposer partout. [...] Je te propose "gutter press" ou "courrier du cœur" oder so was.
>
> [Burrough Green etc: B.G. is a village in Surrey. You can replace it by a place in England that rings familiar to Dutch people (Dover, for example, or Hawich). Not a big city. The English climate needs to be preserved – or else *everything* has to be transposed, which is not advisable. [...] Bumper: a glass full to the brim. [...] "Reynolds' News": the

awful popular newspaper. Avoid replacing it by the Dutch equivalent unless you transpose everything everywhere. I suggest "gutter press" or " 'dear John' letters" or something of the sort.][226]

The margin left for manœuvre was, however, reduced, as Beckett signalled to van Velde when discussing *En attendant Godot*:

I am willing to consider whatever modifications you deem absolutely unavoidable for performance or publication in Holland. But some things simply can't be changed. And I prefer no publication and no performance to those of a text that no longer makes sense.[227]

Beckett's manuscripts indicate that his translation methods were extremely strict: almost without exception, they are without trace of linguistic interference between French and English. In general, the first drafts are extremely close to the final versions and contain very few amendments and annotations in the margins. It is, however, difficult to qualify Beckett's approach to translation and writing in general, since fleeting allusions in his correspondence suggest that he underwent periods during which he constantly redrafted his texts and discarded many intermediary versions. In 1958, he wrote to Jacoba van Velde: "J'ai écrit encore un peu en français, encore pour rien. A la corbeille. Il y a deux moments qui valent la peine, dans le travail, celui de la mise en route et celui de la mise en corbeille" [I have been writing a little in French again, to no avail. In the bin. There are two moments that are worthwhile in this job, when it all begins and when it all goes in the bin].[228] His correspondence reveals a writer increasingly weary of the difficulties of interpretation raised by the translation of some of his works. He considered, for a time, leaving *Fin de partie* in French, writing to Susan Manning in 1956: "I am so tired of translations and bad productions abroad and misunderstandings all round that my feeling at the moment is to leave the new play in French for some time at least. [...] It is a difficult unpleasant work and I cannot see it in English".[229] To Alan Schneider, he wrote that *Endgame* would "inevitably be a poor substitute for the original (the loss will be greater from the French to the English *Godot*)".[230]

The realisation that French and English might afford different stylistic effects had haunted him since his days as a lecturer at Trinity College Dublin: during a lecture, he is reported to have claimed that the "English sentence can justify itself by looking well, the French can't. [...] The French, cerebral transmission, statement rare, the English climactory".[231] What he disliked in English was "a lack of brakes";[232] indeed, he stated that he was looking for self-control in writing *En attendant Godot* and that French provided him with a form of authorial detachment: "English was too easy. I wanted the discipline".[233] In 1958, before beginning work on *Comment c'est*, after a long spell of writing in English, he reiterated this thought to Alan Schneider: "I must confess I feel the old tug to write in French again, where control is easier for me, and probably excessive".[234] Beckett's association of French with control and impoverishment is somewhat paradoxical; indeed, French is commonly understood to be a more analytical language than English, while English is considered to be more synthetic than French.[235] His conception of French and English in binary opposition may have been influenced by the outlook of the Revivalists on translation, in particular by Yeats's and Hyde's descriptions of English as a language without vitality, stifled by materialism: ironically prefiguring Beckett's stance, Yeats associated literature in French with authorial control, claiming in 1901 that the National Dramatic Movement should reject the "worn-out conventions of English poetic drama" and "Shakespeare's luxuriance" and embrace the severe discipline of French and Scandinavian dramatic traditions.[236] Beckett's decision to write in both French and English certainly enabled him to reject a Yeatsian attitude to style and subject matter; at the same time, his approach to translation as a method of composition articulated itself in extremely specific ways. His embrace of modernist aesthetics and principles, in French and English, maintains a tenuous link to Revivalist debates around translation and style – debates which entertained an ambiguous relationship with European modernism due to their political tenor and interest in the local. However, the ways in which a range of writers from the Revival and post-Revival periods such as Douglas Hyde, W.B. Yeats, George Moore, Lady Gregory and Flann O'Brien anticipated certain aspects of Beckett's approach to translation suggest that, in moving from one language to another, Beckett was able to signal his simultaneous attachment to and detachment from the contexts formative of his development as a writer, harnessing this tension in order to propel himself forward.

3
Representing Scarcity

Beckett's association with French existentialism has had far-reaching implications for the manner in which his work has been received. The qualities associated with the idea of the 'Beckettian', for instance, derive largely from existentialist approaches to the absurd. Although the adjective does not have the recognised status of 'Pinteresque', 'Beckettian' is widely used to signify a movement towards nothingness and a leaning towards obscure meanings; it also evokes a world of scarcity, on the brink of extinction. These associations result in part from the success of Beckett's early drama; the desolate landscapes of *Waiting for Godot* and *Endgame*, in particular, were received as existentialist documents of the human condition after the Second World War. The idea of lack is visually established as the norm through the use of a minimum of focal points onstage: in *Waiting for Godot*, a tree constitutes the only landmark in a depleted universe where survival depends upon a few carrots, turnips and leftover chicken bones; in *Endgame*, one is presented with a bare stage upon which an elderly couple are spending their final moments in rubbish bins, subsisting on pieces of dog biscuit. Whether *Waiting for Godot* and *Endgame* portray a return to an archaic state of civilisation or the consequences of a brutal historical collapse remains uncertain: linear chronology has disappeared along with all material comforts. Something is certainly "taking its course", as Clov emphasises, although history can no longer be disguised as a teleological movement and can be represented only as *waiting*.[1]

This semblance of regression is central to the power that these plays retain over the Western imagination and to their impact upon twentieth-century philosophy.[2] Indeed, Beckett's presentation of material scarcity as a mode of being had a significant influence on philosophical responses throughout the 1950s and 1960s. During these decades, his work occupied the margins of a series of debates between Bertolt Brecht, Georg Lukács and Theodor Adorno concerning the nature of the avant-garde and the articulation of a form of historical consciousness in literature. Disagreements arose concerning Beckett's relationship to history and the idea of the modern. Lukács made particularly ferocious accusations in *The Meaning of Contemporary Realism* (originally published in German in 1958), criticising Beckett's perversity in his idealisation of "primitive" conditions of existence.[3] In this instance, Beckett's primitive leanings were a sign of his belonging to a modernist avant-garde that Lukács viewed with extreme suspicion: Beckett, along with Joyce and Faulkner, represented a literary current that Lukács identified with depravity and irrationality. The "utmost human degradation" depicted in *Molloy*, in particular, crystallised everything that Lukács resented about modernism: for Lukács, Beckett's novel was a crude manifestation of modernist decadence and an apology for late bourgeois capitalism. Lukács's depiction of Beckett's work as representing a form of regression was not without effect upon philosophical debates regarding modernism: in response to Lukács, Adorno identified the primitive element in Beckett's work as the expression of a "terrestrial catastrophe", arguing: "his primitive men are the last men".[4] In this instance, Adorno's use of the term "primitive" relates to entirely different concerns from those of Lukács: for Adorno, Beckett's portrayals of regression illustrated the avant-garde's estranged relationship to European societies after the Second World War. In his appreciation of Beckett's work, Adorno also registered Beckett's awareness of the concentration camps; the combination of forced labour and starvation evoked in *Waiting for Godot* and *Endgame* led him to describe them as post-Auschwitz plays and to celebrate their significance as historical documents.[5] It is worth noting that, while these plays evidently express states of spiritual disarray and relate to a post-war crisis in moral and social values, for Beckett their symbolic ambiguity was central. The absent Godot, in particular, invited symbolic interpretations of a religious nature, yet Beckett rejected speculation about the meaning of the play, pointing out, in one instance, that the audience would not find in the play a loftier meaning to take home after the performance.[6] He became famous for his ferocious opposition to directorial attempts to diminish the ambiguity of the text and to give realistic motives to the characters.[7] The history of *Endgame* is also marked by disagreements over adaptations and productions that imposed a transparency of meaning upon the text.[8]

Lukács and Adorno both recognised as the most distinctive feature of Beckett's work its problematic relationship with the notion of historical process as a prospective unfolding. Both philosophers also presented Beckett's apparent drive towards ahistoricity as a modernist response to specific historical developments and thus deemed Beckett's primitive leanings to be profoundly historical; interestingly, this aspect of his early drama finds concrete illustration in the production history of *Waiting for Godot*. As David Bradby has pointed out, the play has followed a complex trajectory across the world and has been adapted into various contexts of ethnic, religious, cultural and linguistic conflict. Emphasising the ability of the play to transfer from one politically sensitive situation to another, Bradby discusses productions that took place in South Africa at the height of Apartheid, in Palestine under Israeli occupation, in the context of the cultural debate in Quebec and in a Sarajevo under siege by Serbian forces.[9] It is evident, from Bradby's accounts, that the directors and actors involved in these productions discerned details or references that were germane to their own cultural or linguistic predicament; at the same time, all productions converged at a common point, namely the degree to which states of scarcity remain historically and politically weighted. These productions brought to light a questioning of the relationship between language, culture and history through a portrayal of deprivation, showing that Beckett's casting of a situation of historical stasis channels a form of protest countering, to an extent, the deterritorialised readings that have traditionally been attached to his work. In *Waiting for Godot*, Beckett blatantly refuses to romanticise poverty, exploring a situation of scarcity in which language is as important as food as an instrument of domination (this is equally evident in *Endgame*). This facet of his work was clearly of interest to the practitioners involved in these adaptations: they found their own preoccupations echoed in Beckett's portrayals of impoverishment.

The appeal of these works in such varied situations also suggests that a degree of historical specificity is maintained in Beckett's portrayal of situations of extreme material scarcity, and that his aspirations towards a primitive art form were fashioned by circumstances more specific than those informing the development of modernist movements such as Cubism and early Expressionism (which nevertheless influenced Beckett's artistic awakening). The allusions to Irish culture and history and the shreds of Hiberno-English that recur in Beckett's portrayals of impoverishment are signifiers of this tension between the specificity of the work and its ability to expand beyond the conditions that generated this specificity. The Irish undertones of Vladimir and Estragon's discussions during their wait for "your man" Godot, for instance, are particularly marked, yet these phrases do not serve a narrative purpose and are not aligned with a meditation on Irish history.[10] Their importance lies precisely in their non-consequentiality, as suggested by Beckett's declarations: for a time, he even considered strengthening the Irish flavour of the English text and, when he was told that a Cork production had replaced "to your man" by "to himself" in the late 1980s, he was amused and confided to Gerry Dukes that he had considered changing the line into "to his nibs" in the 1965 revised Faber edition.[11] Nevertheless, echoes of a landlord–peasant template of class conflict bring to mind a specifically Irish predicament; Vivian Mercier, for instance, describes Pozzo as an adaptation of the "wicked" landlord of Victorian melodrama and Lucky as a combination of the French *laquais* and the Irish peasant caricatured in *Punch* cartoons. As he points out, "Pozzo's insistence on the goodness of his own heart and the dog-like devotion to him of Lucky are as familiar in the mythology of the Irish landlord class as they were in that of the plantation owner in the old South".[12] A similar argument can be made in relation to *Endgame*; in fact, Declan Kiberd compares Hamm to the absentee landlords of nineteenth-century Ireland.[13] While the omnipresence of starvation evokes the Great Famine, both plays present a situation which exists largely outside the possibility of history itself and from which no coherent form of historical consciousness can emerge. For Adorno, the historical catastrophe portrayed by Beckett is of such magnitude that it can only remain at the boundaries of verbal articulation: "The name of disaster can only be spoken silently".[14] Scarcity acquires a protean function, simultaneously a mode of existence and a mode of historical representation.

* * *

This aspect of Beckett's work will be contextualised in greater detail below, in relation to Jean-Paul Sartre's exploration of transitional states between regression and suspension. For now, it will suffice to identify the ways in which Beckett's residual primitive dimension relates to his ambivalent response to the Revival. Indeed, even though Beckett's early drama marks a radical departure from the "peasant quality" promoted in Revivalist drama, its representations of historical stasis remain inflected with a specificity that is indebted to Revivalist primitivism. Primitivism is here understood as "the idealization of the primitive", following Sinéad Garrigan Mattar's definition in *Primitivism, Science, and the Irish Revival*, a study of the Revival that establishes the centrality of primitive motifs to the construction of an Irish national literature.[15] To a large extent, *Waiting for Godot* and *Endgame* slough off romanticised undertones of Revivalist portrayals of the primitive and reverse their value as signifiers. Poverty is no longer a guarantee of spiritual integrity; it is imaginatively and metaphysically crippling. Despite their destitution, the characters' love of conversation remains unscathed, and it is precisely in Beckett's juxtaposition of scarcity of food and abundance of words that the influence of certain theatrical practices enshrined at the Abbey Theatre manifests itself.

In her study of the role played by Revivalist representations of the primitive in the political life of the nation, Garrigan Mattar shows how the primitive was cast as sinister or endearing, or else associated with a form of nostalgia, depending on the nature of Irish–English relations. Her analysis highlights the Famine as a catalyst for depictions of the Irish as simian savages, such representations of barbarity and laziness lending credibility to the idea that the Irish were unworthy of exceptional aid and unable to organise themselves politically. The complexity of these representations was heightened in the literature of the Revival, where primitivism became a mode of representation of nation and race in which antagonisms of class and religion could be evaded; the heritage of the past was a "neutral territory" where representatives of the Anglo-Irish gentry, predominantly Unionist, could unite with their Catholic compatriots.[16] Their reasons for associating themselves with the native Gaelic culture, for Garrigan Mattar, were primarily political; an interest in folklore became the means through which they could "give the lie to the idea that their interest in culture was politically neutral".[17]

In early Abbey plays, the use of folk myths and legends operated as a platform for powerful idealisations of social workings. The use of simple decors may have resulted from meagre budgets and concrete limitations in terms of props and machinery, yet this leaning towards what Lady Gregory called the 'picturesque' had greater ambitions in its association of ancient Gaelic Ireland with a sense of cultural regeneration.[18] Rural life acquired an iconic status in representations of the nation and became indicative of a virgin state of civilisation in which the richness and musicality of language countered the effects of material hardship.[19] An immediate example is Yeats's first play, *The Countess Cathleen* (first performed at the Abbey in 1899), in which hunger induces a spiritual expansion of the soul.[20] Set in a famine-stricken Ireland, the play tells of the sacrifice of the Countess Cathleen, who sells her soul to demons in exchange for food for her starving people and is granted divine pardon through her sacrifice, eventually saving her people from death. Simplicity of living was also described as the guarantee of a form of cultural integrity and spirituality in Synge's drama; in *Riders to the Sea*, for instance, Synge drew on the life of the Gaelic-speaking population living on the Aran Islands, with which he was familiar, to portray an isolated fishing community in which material hardship merely heightened endurance and nobility of sentiment. This feature of Synge's drama led Daniel Corkery, the foremost cultural ideologue of the Irish Free State in the 1930s, to praise Synge's portrayal of the native Catholic culture and his intimate connection with the immemorial and the untouched.[21] However, the primitive leanings of Abbey peasant plays were not simply an attempt to imagine a society in which relationships were unoppressive; they reflected a desire to articulate a form of historical consciousness that was distinctively Irish by means of an emphasis on anti-materialism and moral superiority – this association remaining a staple of political discourse from Thomas Davis to de Valera, as Roy Foster notes.[22] Such associations shaped Yeats's definition of an Irish literary canon in the early years of the Revival period in significant ways; in an 1895 review of Standish O'Grady's *The Coming of Cuculain*, for instance, Yeats opposed the "wild Celtic idealism" to the "careful, practical ways of the Saxon".[23] Ironically, when praising the writer he considered the forefather of the Revival, Yeats rehearsed Victorian stereotypes of Irishness, replicating Matthew Arnold's distinction between the Celt's sentimental and impulsive temperament and the Saxon's discipline.[24]

Initially, audiences failed to warm to the stylised speech used by the Revivalists in their adaptations of ancient Celtic myths. In 1901, a critic of the first production of W.B. Yeats and George Moore's *Diarmuid and Grania* objected to its tone: the eloquence of the protagonists did not seem fitting, given their situation of deprivation. For the reviewer, the characters' stylised speech signalled gentility fallen into disgrace: "The stage version lands one in a world of metaphysical meanderings, whose Grania argues as if she took out her M.A. degree in Boston, and then Diarmuid replies with rocks of thought as if he were a deep student of Herbert Spencer".[25] This criticism anticipates arguments deployed against Beckett decades later. To Vivian Mercier, who remarked that the tramps in *Waiting for Godot* spoke as if they had doctorates, Beckett answered: "How do you know they hadn't?"[26]

In the years preceding independence, manifestations of social and political atomisation around the evocation of the primitive became apparent; for James Connolly, for instance, the Revival was primarily a political rather than a cultural movement, and he resented its romanticism, elitism and parochialism.[27] His writings are torn between Marxist and nationalist objectives: his appeals for an anti-colonial struggle sometimes address the entire Irish population and are sometimes confined to the working class alone, in which case national emancipation means breaking the yoke of capitalism.[28] Connolly eventually resolved the tensions among his Marxist, Catholic and nationalist sympathies by advocating a return to the "Gaelic principle of common ownership by a people of their sources of food and maintenance".[29]

Much later, this idea was ridiculed in Flann O'Brien's *The Poor Mouth*, which portrays poverty as a specifically Gaelic virtue. The characters are placed at the limit of a state of regression through a lifestyle lived "in the old Gaelic manner".[30] They dwell on the brink of starvation, but they cannot resolve to eat their pigs and they continue to feed them vast quantities of potatoes; eventually, the overfed pigs take over the family home, one of them even dying of indigestion under the eyes of its hungry owners. Beyond its satire of Revivalist idealisations of Gaelic-speaking Ireland, O'Brien's novel is interesting for its vitriolic attacks upon the idea of 'picturesque' Irishness. Its portrayal of a tramp called Sitric O'Sanassa, who has the misfortune of living in a region densely populated with "Gaeligores" (overly enthusiastic members of the Gaelic League), reads as a jibe against Revivalist attempts to collect folk myths and legends, following the initiative of Lady Gregory and Douglas Hyde to revitalise the oral traditions of the native culture:

> The gentlemen from Dublin who came in motors to inspect the paupers praised him for his Gaelic poverty and stated that they never saw anyone who appeared so truly Gaelic. One of the gentlemen broke a little bottle of water Sitric had, because, said he, it spoiled the effect.[31]

In the novel, accuracy in Gaelic and purity of spirit grow "in proportion to one's lack of worldly goods".[32] Levels of poverty and Gaelic authenticity are also interrelated, both being measured in terms of dress and appearance. Yet the features contributing to distinctiveness of character originate not in a common language, but in dire economic circumstances. At all times, O'Brien's portrayal of an existence ruled by scarcity articulates itself as a response to the debates surrounding Revivalist representations of an Irish national identity; on this point, his position differs fundamentally from Beckett's. Indeed, while both writers construct their work in relation to that which they resist, O'Brien's perspective remains circumscribed by the debates surrounding essentialised representations of Irishness, whereas Beckett's work expands beyond the conditions that created its specificity in the first place – a movement reflected, for instance, in the complex production history of *Waiting for Godot*.

* * *

Beckett's correspondence with MacGreevy during the 1930s reveals that the naturalistic modes of representation central to early Revival drama did not appeal to him, due to their heavy allegorical component. In "Recent Irish Poetry", his attacks are even more ferocious, questioning a self-congratulatory nationalism in which the idea of hardship is romanticised and established as specifically Irish. Here, the canon of writing under attack is essentially Yeatsian, relating to the guidelines issued by Yeats in the early years of the Revival movement. In 1895, in disputes with Edward Dowden, Professor at Trinity College Dublin, Yeats argued that the Irish writer should write about Irish subjects for an Irish public and rejected the idea that the works of Bishop Ussher, Bishop Berkeley, Jonathan Swift and Laurence Sterne were part of Irish literature.[33] Years later, he would amend his views, making Berkeley and Swift part of his own intellectual ancestry in "Blood and the Moon" and "Swift's Epitaph" in *The Winding Stair and Other Poems*. This feature of the volume might have been what spurred Beckett to take an uncompromising stance in "Recent Irish Poetry"; he condemns Yeats's attempt to define a national literary canon and describes Yeats's emphasis on "'the sense of hardship borne and chosen out of pride' as the ultimate theme of the Irish writer" as a manifestation of self-indulgence.[34] This is in fact a misappropriation of Yeats's preface to Gogarty's *Wild Apples*; indeed, Yeats did not make this statement in relation to Irish subject matter but in relation to T.E. Lawrence's leaning towards ethnographic writing, which he read as an inheritance from the Romantics.[35] This suggests either that Beckett misread the preface or, in all likelihood, that he saw this statement as the perfect illustration of everything he resented about Yeats's nationalist persona.

If Beckett rejected the naïve idealism of the early Revival period, he remained attached to its manner of encoding complex political issues within minimalist settings. *Waiting for Godot* and *Endgame* may, in fact, find antecedents in plays firmly grounded in the Revival period; in particular, Lady Gregory's short comedy *The Workhouse Ward*, first produced at the Abbey in 1908, anticipates certain aspects of Beckett's early drama in striking ways. Whether Beckett saw the play during the 1930s remains uncertain; nevertheless, a letter to MacGreevy suggests that he missed the revival produced at the Abbey in January 1931: "I suppose the Workhouse Ward is off?"[36] Although Beckett showed scant regard for Lady Gregory's theatrical techniques in his correspondence,[37] *The Workhouse Ward*, which features two old men trapped in their beds on a bare stage, recalls the forms of historical stasis portrayed in *Waiting for Godot* and *Endgame*, although Gregory's play remains firmly moored in a post-Famine context, as Anthony Roche has illustrated.[38] *The Workhouse Ward* presents a rural community beset by poverty, hunger, illness and a chronic shortage of both workforce and land. Food itself becomes synonymous with starvation: periwinkles are described as a "hungry sort of food".[39] Words are the sole currency of exchange. "All that I am craving is the talk", Michael Miskell exclaims, lamenting: "To be lying here and no conversible person in it would be the abomination of misery!"[40] The coupling of belligerent old men was originally conceived as an allegory for the religious divide in Ireland; Lady Gregory described them as "two young whelps that go on fighting till they are two old dogs".[41] Their light-hearted dialogue contrasts vividly with their situation of deprivation; this particular aspect of *The Workhouse Ward* suggests that the play may be taken as a forerunner of Beckett's treatment of scarcity in *Waiting for Godot* and *Endgame*.

Yeats's late drama provides further comparative material; more precisely, the visual proximity of *Waiting for Godot* to Yeats's play *Purgatory* (1939) suggests points of convergence between the respective searches for economy in Beckett and Yeats.[42] Yeats's play features a tree and the remnants of a "ruined house", figured by a stone; this simple setting is the meeting place of two outcasts, an old man and his son (designated Old Man and Boy).[43] *Waiting for Godot*'s tree and country road recall the bare setting of *Purgatory*, a resemblance cemented by Beckett's addition of a stone to the set in the 1975 production at Berlin's Schiller-Theater Werkstatt.[44] He explained to assistant director Walter Asmus that the play was not visualised to his satisfaction during its conception due to his lack of experience as a playwright.[45] In Yeats's play, this desolate setting is used to dramatise complex social and political changes following the demise of the Anglo-Irish ascendancy in Ireland. The Old Man has no defined place in society, being the son of a stable groom and an Anglo-Irish lady. He is determined to exterminate his bloodline, and the house in ruins becomes the location of a series of murders, the place where the Old Man kills first his father, then his son, in a desperate attempt to free himself from the shackles of history. The cyclical nature of history takes precedence over the particularity of events, as the historical causes of the family's demise are pushed towards the periphery. In a previous version, however, Yeats specified that the marriage between the lady and the groom had taken place in a Catholic Church, suggesting the conversion of the lady to Catholicism as the source of her downfall. The Protestant/Catholic antagonism was portrayed as tribal and not racial, an aspect of the text particularly delicate due to its fascistic undertones, as W.J. McCormack notes.[46] Without doubt, *Waiting for Godot* and *Endgame* are far removed from the problematic undertones of Yeats's play. However, the recurrent appearance of a young boy in *Waiting for Godot* as signal that a new cycle is threatening to begin suggests that Beckett may have had *Purgatory* in mind when conceiving a world characterised by material scarcity. In *Endgame*, Clov also catches a glimpse of a boy, a "potential procreator", when looking outside; however, the threat of a new beginning is no sooner evoked than dissolved into insignificance, any form of life being doomed to disappear.[47]

While certain aspects of Beckett's early plays echo dramatic representations of poverty in Irish literature, his emphasis on the physical consequences of deprivation limits such parallels. His work contrasts sharply with the idealism inherent in the Abbey's representations of social workings; indeed, there is a fine line between generalised scarcity of goods and starvation in *Waiting for Godot* and *Endgame*. In *Waiting for Godot*, the difference between a carrot and a turnip is paramount because there is nothing else; even chicken bones become a matter for debate. For Nell in *Endgame*, the difference between life and death depends upon even less: a few mouthfuls of a dog biscuit. What is important, as Adorno points out, is the maintenance of a transitional state of existence, in which the addition of sand or sawdust to the protagonists' dustbins is of central importance.[48] Bodies bleed, swell, smell and ache; all biological functions are deregulated as an effect of continuing starvation. In *Endgame*, Clov can barely walk, Nagg and Nell are losing their sight and Hamm is incontinent. In *Waiting for Godot*, Vladimir takes garlic in an attempt to support his deficient kidneys – alas to no avail: he has to run offstage to urinate. The emphasis on bodily functions and dysfunctions lends a primal quality to the characters' behaviour which is antithetical to the unspoken etiquette that regulates their exchanges. Indeed, good manners still prevail, even when enquiring after leftover chicken bones, as evidenced in Estragon's request to Lucky: "Excuse me, Mister, the bones, you won't be wanting the bones?"[49] The incongruous juxtaposition of a strict social protocol and generalised material deprivation is dramatically very efficient: it allows for a form of dramatic development that is based not on narration, but on the fluctuating position of the characters towards the social consensus that regulates, or fails to regulate, their behaviour and the world that they inhabit. It remains uncertain whether we are faced with the return to an archaic historical moment, in which men have to fight for the fundamentals to ensure survival, or with the leftovers of a modern civilisation kept in a state of apparent regression. Estragon's choice to introduce himself as "Adam" to Pozzo confirms this ambiguity.[50]

The effects of hunger are merely alluded to in *Endgame*, as this topic is not germane to polite conversation. "Have you had your visions?" Hamm asks Clov. "Less", he answers.[51] Here, the sense that deprivation may lead to spiritual empowerment is deflated, together with the idea that it may follow any discernible logic. For Beckett, Clov's visions indicated the breakdown of his "escape mechanism", and he suggested that this element allowed his perceptions of life (as represented by the rat found in his kitchen and the boy that he sees outside) "to be construed as hallucinations".[52] Beckett's resistance to certain naïve aspects of Revivalist primitivism, in particular its idealisation of the pastoral, is also evident in *Endgame*, in which the very existence of the colour green has become little more than a vague memory. Hamm wonders: "But beyond the hills? Eh? Perhaps it's still green. Eh? [*Pause*.] Flora! Pomona! [*Ecstatically*.] Ceres! [*Pause*.] Perhaps you won't need to go very far".[53] The fauna has been reduced to a lone flea and a solitary rat, the flora to seeds that obstinately refuse to sprout. The weight of material scarcity is so overwhelming that it pushes the characters into a state of civilisation in which historical workings are dissociated from the possibility of progression. Contributing to the paralysis, an implicit process of cataloguing constantly takes place, since evaluating what has disappeared and what remains is a last resort to stave off boredom. All symbols of material comfort, from coffins to bicycle wheels and painkillers, have disappeared; the omnipresence of lack conditions all events taking place and becomes a source of jocularity. Hamm asks: "No phone calls? [*Pause*.] Don't we laugh?"[54] The detritus that remains, including insecticide, a step ladder and a toy dog, exudes something of the lavish. Such lavishness was visually associated with a negativity in early productions of the play, in which the room's sole ornament, a picture, was turned against the wall, reasserting the play's rejection of the conventions of realistic drama.[55] In *Waiting for Godot*, the utter disparity of objects is also striking. Pozzo's possessions include a bag and a picnic basket (both full), a folding stool, a greatcoat, glasses, a pipe, a whip and a slave in Act One. In Act Two, he is entirely dispossessed: the bag carried by Lucky contains only sand.

For Adorno, we are facing a "permanent catastrophe", while, for Beckett, the very notion of catastrophe cannot be articulated.[56] He explained to Alan Schneider that *Endgame* represented "the impossibility of catastrophe. Ended at its inception, and at every subsequent instant, it continues, ergo can never end".[57] Beckett's conflicted relationship with the idea of history as progress was disclosed in a 1955 conversation with Patrick Bowles; he lamented: "What counts is the *spirit* [...]. I cannot see it historically. [...] Ninety-nine per cent of people are out of touch with their spirit [...]. History, for me, it's a black-out. [...] All the rest is frills".[58] This evocation of a dissolving historical spirit can be understood as a coded reference to the gloomy political atmosphere in France at the beginning of the Algerian War of Independence; such an identification of history as a "black-out" also echoes Adorno's assertion that poetry died in Auschwitz.[59] In *Waiting for Godot* and *Endgame*, history is represented as a process constantly weighing itself down and endowed with a capacity to deprive and negate. The correlation between states of scarcity and particular historical processes remains diffuse, yet the historical grounding of both plays was far more salient in early drafts in French: Estragon was called Lévy in the first draft of *En attendant Godot*, for instance,[60] and *Fin de partie* was originally located in Picardy, in a zone where a catastrophe had taken place between 1914 and 1918, drastically affecting transportation and living conditions.[61] The characters lived somewhere by the Manche, or the English Channel, on a rugged coastline that looked onto the "falaises d'Albion", possibly the white cliffs of Dover.[62]

Beckett's practice of representing history through negation is significant in considering his position within avant-garde movements. It is a practice which distances him from Brecht's theatrical strategies: while Brecht treats history as a teleological process, in Beckett's work scarcity is in such excess that the notion of historical process is conceivable only as an alternation between stasis and regression. Early in his reflection on *Verfremdungseffekt*, Brecht pleaded for a historicised theatre in which the use of alienation effects might "underline the historical aspect of a specific social condition".[63] His theory of *Verfremdungseffekt* married Marxist principles with theatrical techniques derived from Eastern drama; as such, it necessitated a careful balance between the familiar and the foreign, as Brecht suggested in the widely read essay "A Short Organum for the Theatre".[64] The self-reflexivity of *Waiting for Godot* and *Endgame* certainly shares a great deal with Brecht's *Verfremdungseffekt*, but produces different results, generating a salutary sense of relief from the characters' plight. The audience is periodically reminded that what is taking place is pure artifice, as when Vladimir laments: "I've been better entertained".[65] His complaint is echoed by Hamm in *Endgame*: "This is not much fun".[66]

It is made evident that the few objects remaining on the stage are theatrical props; for example, Clov replies to Hamm, who fears that his toy dog might have disappeared: "He's not a real dog, he can't go".[67] Objects are exploited to the limit of their capacities: dustbins, a ladder, a hat become sources of entertainment. If certain objects are missing, the corresponding tasks cannot be accomplished: Lucky cannot "think" without a hat on, and the tramps cannot put an end to their plight because they have no rope to hang themselves with.[68] In *Endgame*, material scarcity also affects movement, following an absurd logic indexed to the function of particular objects and their absence. If Clov cannot sit, it is in part because there is nothing for him to sit on. Thus, the function performed by scarcity in these plays indicates Beckett's distance from Brecht; Beckett's concern for the paralysis brought about by the scarcity of objects ultimately marks his divergence from Brecht's theatre of action. These differing approaches to the notion of deprivation also reveal divergent attitudes towards the idea of artistic commitment (in Sartre's sense), recalling Adorno's rejection of Sartrean commitment: for Adorno, Brecht's committed theatre was politically naïve, in contrast to Beckett's drama, whose residual historicity could be read as a critique of the conceptual dimension of existentialism.

Beckett stated that he found Brecht's plays overwrought,[69] a dismissal that contrasts sharply with his admiration for Yeats, whose late drama anticipates Brecht's own pursuit of alienation effects in its reliance upon narrative layers, song, dance and direct audience address. Despite Beckett's distance from Brecht's exuberant drama, the trinkets featured in *Waiting for Godot* and *Endgame* certainly recall the struggle for survival depicted by Brecht in *Mother Courage and Her Children* and *The Caucasian Chalk Circle*. Yet, in Brecht's portrayal of deprivation, we sense history in movement; in Beckett's its stillness – in *Waiting for Godot* and *Endgame*, the emphasis is not upon action but, rather, upon the manner in which scarcity of goods regulates action. Even the presence of objects is a reminder of their scarcity: only decayed remnants are left.

In this respect, Beckett's handling of objects both invites and rejects a Marxian perspective on commodity fetishism, if one adheres to Marx's definition in the first volume of *Capital*, in which the fetishism of commodities is established as originating in the "peculiar social character" of the labour that produces them.[70] However, in the liminal economic zone where *Waiting for Godot* and *Endgame* are located, the overwhelming presence of scarcity creates irreconcilable disjunctions between the use of objects and their value, extending the situation portrayed by Beckett beyond capitalist modes of production. Marxist readings of his early drama have proven problematic: Sean Golden, for instance, reads *Endgame* as a political allegory, with Hamm representing the capitalist bourgeoisie and Clov the proletariat. He points out that some of Beckett's annotations to the play were indicative of an undercurrent of class conflict; in 1967, for instance, Beckett facilitated rehearsals at the Schiller-Theater Werkstatt by cutting the play into two parts, one dealing with Clov's rebellion and the other with Clov's emancipation.[71] Clearly, the manner in which scarcity partially cancels any form of social hierarchy is problematic in Golden's reading; that there is nothing left to exploit, only the traces of previous processes of exploitation, is deemed profoundly shocking.

* * *

The manner in which the residual historicity of Beckett's plays articulates itself, however, is far from straightforward, since these texts are not single but double; their existence as bilingual entities complicates the historical and cultural weight that they bear. The indeterminate location of Vladimir and Estragon's wait for Godot is one such example. It is, at one point, implied that their meeting place with Godot is surrounded by a bog; Vladimir laments: "All the same...that tree...[*Turning towards the auditorium*]...that bog".[72] The mention of a bog has facilitated adaptations of the play into a nineteenth-century context of land dispossession, with Alan Simpson presenting Pozzo as an Anglo-Irish squire and Lucky as an Irish slave in the 1955 Pike Theatre production.[73] Simpson's reconfiguration of the play has influenced subsequent Irish productions, becoming a feature of the most recent 'definitive' Gate Theatre production, for instance, in which Pozzo speaks with an English accent, in contrast to the Dublin accents used by the rest of the cast.[74] If such productions are questionable due to their attempt to diminish the play's non-naturalistic leanings, it is worth noting that Simpson's initial decision to give an Irish flavour to the play was prompted by wider considerations and functioned as a response to the problem of marketing an avant-garde work to a mainstream theatre audience.[75]

Simpson's adaptation also brought to light a dimension of the play that was previously unacknowledged, namely a caricature of Daniel Corkery's Irish Ireland. Bogs, hills and mountains were identified by Corkery in *The Hidden Ireland* (1924) as places in which the native Irish traditionally "lurked" in eighteenth-century representations of Gaelic Ireland.[76] These representations of 'authentic' Ireland also intervene in Beckett's fiction; they are recast as a form of non-representation in *Texts for Nothing*, for instance:

> I'll describe the place, that's unimportant. The top, very flat, of a mountain, no, a hill, but so wild, so wild, enough. Quag, heath up to the knees, faint sheeptracks, troughs scooped deep by the rains. It was far down in one of these I was lying, out of the wind. Glorious prospect, but for the mist that blotted out everything, valleys, loughs, plain and sea.[77]

Similarly, in *Waiting for Godot*, an over-determined signifier such as the bog is turned into a non-space, subverting a pastoral iconography associated with representations of Ireland. The clichéd quality of this representation finds itself annihilated by the dual existence of the text. Indeed, in *En attendant Godot*, the characters are not surrounded by a bog but by a *peat* bog or "tourbière", a term that has more specificity than the English word "bog" and does not carry the same cultural and historical weight.[78] In French, *tourbière* is not a location but reads as a pejorative reference to the audience, accused of insalubrity.

The association between Irishness and non-representation proves tenacious when comparing the French and English texts and informs Beckett's playful approach to meaning. If, in *Waiting for Godot*, Vladimir and Estragon speak Irish English, their nationality remains undisclosed in *En attendant Godot*, in which it remains apparent, however, that they are *not French*. Estragon occasionally speaks in pidgin French:

> Estragon: Est-ce qu'il veut le remplacer?
> Vladimir: Comment?
> Estragon: Je n'ai pas compris s'il veut le remplacer ou s'il n'en veut plus après lui.
> Vladimir: Je ne crois pas.
> Estragon: Comment?
> Vladimir: Je ne sais pas.[79]

Here, Estragon's confused syntax replicates speech patterns commonplace in Irish English: his use of *après lui* reads as a displacement of a construction which signifies immediacy of intention, 'after' followed by the gerund (a recurrent construction in the stylised dramatic language of early Revival plays). Elsewhere in the French text, the characters' familiarity with the English language is made explicit; the stage directions specify that Estragon should use an *English* accent when praising Pozzo's performance as "très bon, très très bon".[80] Ironically, this is reversed in *Waiting for Godot*. Estragon shows off his knowledge of French and exclaims, this time with a *French* accent, "Oh tray bong, tray tray tray bong".[81] This line is one of the few instances in which Beckett adopts conventions of misspelling and may be perceived as a reference to O'Casey's own representation of Dublin speech in *Juno and the Paycock*, in which Joxer Daly is particularly fond of saying "aw rewaeawr".[82] Beckett's characters, however, prefer to use *adieu* when taking leave.[83]

Like Estragon, Vladimir finds French to be an elusive medium of expression. He occasionally struggles to find the right phrase, especially when expressing his dismay at Pozzo's treatment of Lucky: "Après en avoir sucé la substance vous le jetez comme un…(*il cherche*)…comme une peau de banane. Avouez que…".[84] In English, he is less accusative and does not wonder about usage: "And now you turn him away? Such an old and faithful servant".[85] In their French incarnations, the tramps periodically lose fluency and have difficulties in finding the correct word:

> Vladimir: Tu me manquais – et en même temps j'étais content. N'est-ce pas curieux?
> Estragon (*outré*): Content?
> Vladimir (*ayant réfléchi*): Ce n'est peut-être pas le mot.[86]

The tramps' failure to find the right word in French acquires a vastly different meaning in English, as "curieux" becomes "queer" and foreignness is translated into Irishness:

> Vladimir: I missed you…and at the same time I was happy. Isn't that a queer thing?
> Estragon [*Shocked.*]: Happy?
> Vladimir: Perhaps it's not the right word.[87]

Passages suggesting the tramps' estrangement from the French language thus disappear in the English text, the passage from French to English being synonymous with an alteration of the characters' perspective on language. Transposed into English, standard French phrases acquire strong Irish inflections; for instance, "Lève-toi que je t'embrasse" becomes "Get up till I embrace you"; "Assez. Aide-moi à enlever cette saloperie" becomes "Ah stop blathering and help me off with this bloody thing"; "Quel âge avez-vous, sans indiscrétion?" becomes "What age are you, if it's not a rude question."; "J'aimerais bien l'entendre penser" becomes "I'd like well to hear him think"; "Il veut m'avoir, mais il ne m'aura pas" becomes "He wants to cod me, but he won't"; "Alors nous serions baisés" becomes "Then we'd be ballocksed".[88] Estragon's requests to Pozzo for a "louis" and "cent sous" in *En attendant Godot* are modernised in the English version;[89] in English, this reference to antiquated currency becomes: "Even ten francs would be welcome. [...] Even five".[90]

Jokes regarding the English reinforce this complex process of cultural doubling. In *Waiting for Godot*, Estragon briefly adopts an English accent, thus signalling his own distance from standard English and his adherence to another phonetic system: "Calm... Calm... The English say cawm. [*Pause.*] You know the story of the Englishman in the brothel?"[91] In French, this passage has different undertones, confirming Estragon's non-Englishness and indicating his formal education – an indication which is immediately offset by his attempt to tell a bawdy joke: "Calme... Calme... (*Rêveusement*). Les Anglais disent câââm. Ce sont des gens câââms. (*Un temps.*) Tu connais l'histoire de l'Anglais au bordel?"[92] John Fletcher remarks upon the vulgarity of the joke (which remains incomplete, since an irritated Vladimir exits before Estragon reaches the punch line) and reads it as a French joke about the "alleged preference of the English male for sodomy (known in France as *le vice anglais*)".[93] The suggestion of anglophobia is accentuated in the English translation, since the distasteful character of the joke becomes somewhat arbitrary when transposed into English. Another story, albeit less offensive, appears in *Fin de partie* and *Endgame*, this time about an Englishman and a tailor who fails to deliver an order on time (a well-known Jewish joke, as Adorno notes).[94] The joke and its translation differ in purpose, operating as a strong signal of Nagg's non-Englishness in the English text. In addition, the actor playing Nagg is required to respect different instructions in each case. In *Fin de partie*, Nagg takes on a "visage d'Anglais" (an English face) when enacting the part of the English customer, whom the tailor addresses as "Milord", the French title traditionally given to English lords and, by extension, to wealthy and powerful Englishmen.[95] His account of the tailor's reaction becomes all the more affected: "Mais Milord! Mais Milord! Regardez – (*geste méprisant, avec dégoût*) – le monde... (*un temps*)... et regardez – (*geste amoureux, avec orgueil*) – mon PANTALON!"[96] In *Endgame*, the instructions are less precise, yet Nagg's performance remains exaggerated: "God damn you to hell, Sir!"[97] His speech occasionally features fragments of Irish English;

when telling the joke, he emphasises that the tailor "ballockses the buttonholes" and, in another instance, asks for "me pap", a supplication that has been read as threefold in meaning, indicating fatherly authority, Irishness and childishness.[98] In the French play, his request is merely an indication of a regression towards an infantile mode of existence: "Ma bouillie!"[99]

* * *

Complex choices are made in relation to the transposition of specific allusions; these are illustrated in Pozzo's request for his pipe, which is called an "Abdullah" in *En attendant Godot*, linking Pozzo's position of authority and French colonial rule in North Africa.[100] In *Waiting for Godot*, his mislaid *bouffarde* becomes a *dudeen*, more precisely a "Kapp and Peterson".[101] These choices of translation indicate the extent to which Beckett's concern with an Irish historical predicament informed the minutiae of his writing. Indeed, *dudeen* is derived from the Irish and designates a short-stemmed clay pipe, often smoked by women, which goes some way towards explaining Estragon's mirth when Pozzo complains of the loss of his briar;[102] Kapp and Peterson's of Grafton Street and O'Connell Street ranked among Dublin's finest tobacconists, at a time when it was seen as important to 'buy Irish' and shop signs appeared in Gaelic.[103] These respected tobacco manufacturers advertised their products in the programmes of the Abbey theatre throughout the 1930s, and their advertisements usually appeared in the same spot on the front page of the programme: Beckett could not have failed to notice them when he attended Abbey productions during this period.[104]

References to food in *Endgame* also bear the mark of an unstable relationship with issues of colonialism. In the English text, Turkish Delight (which no longer exists, as Nagg notes with nostalgia) and Spratt's Medium, a staple of the characters' diet, provide reference to Irish economic dependency upon English imports, something questioned by Beckett in his attacks upon the censorious Free State.[105] In *Fin de partie*, however, Nagg and Nell eat a nondescript biscuit, a *biscuit classique*, and Nagg evokes his fondness for *rahat loukoum*, rather than Turkish Delight.[106] Nagg's assertion that *rahat loukoum* is his favoured treat introduced provocative undertones in the context of the Algerian War of Independence, as did Clov's habit of wearing *babouches*, embroidered Arabic slippers made of leather.[107] In the French text, Nagg's fondness for *rahat loukoum* and Clov's fondness for *babouches* inflect the relationships of interdependence and oppression developing between Clov, Hamm and his father with a political content, and yet deflect the possibility of articulating a political message: all forms of social order have collapsed under the weight of scarcity.

This tension between Beckett's engagement with and disengagement from Irish culture and history is exposed in his reduction of episodes in Irish colonial history to shadows, as illustrated in the minute facets of *Fin de partie* and *Endgame*. The Great Famine continues to bear upon Hamm's "chronicle", as he tells the story of a starving child he was asked to take care of,[108] and upon the location of the play itself, an outpost looking over the sea. The residual specificity of the setting is illuminated further in Hamm's reference to a place called Kov, situated "beyond the gulf".[109] As Nels Pearson notes, Cobh in County Cork (Cov in English) is a former British military post, where Irish political prisoners were detained before being sent to Botany Bay, a penal colony in Australia; he argues that the reference to Cobh forces one to acknowledge that the hazy past evoked in *Endgame* is, in fact, an illustration of the play's relationship to British colonial domination of Ireland.[110] Cobh was also the port of the Famine ships, a place familiar to Beckett from his travels to Germany.[111] In the French text, Hamm dwells upon the situation beyond the *straits*, bringing to mind the straits between Cork City, Cobh and Cork Harbour: "Je m'enquis de la situation à Kov, de l'autre côté du détroit. Plus un chat. Bon bon" [I asked about the situation in Kov, on the other side of the straits. Not a soul. Well well].[112] This minor difference between the two versions of the play illustrates Beckett's encoding of an Irish dimension within the French text through the use of precise geographical characteristics, which are nonetheless non-specific in French. In this instance, as in the case of certain passages in the trilogy, a return to the French text illuminates the Irish dimension of the English version.

For Pearson, the characters are in alignment with the colonial antagonisms suggested in Hamm's reference to Kov. He notes passages in the play suggesting that Hamm is English and Clov Irish, taking as example Hamm's comment to Clov "You're a bit of all right, aren't you?", which he identifies as British English, and Clov's decidedly Irish response, "A smithereen".[113] Pearson also acknowledges that the exchanges between Hamm and Clov contain vague suggestions that, at one point in their common history, Hamm has taught Clov his language and deprived him of his own. The dialogues reveal semantic shortcomings on Clov's part; to Hamm's great irritation, he renders "laying doggo" as "lying doggo" and asks, bewildered: "Ah? One says lying? One doesn't say laying?"[114] Later, exasperated by Hamm's continuous questions, he remarks: "I use the words you taught me. If they don't mean anything any more, teach me others. Or let me be silent".[115] However, a reading of the play based on an antagonism between coloniser and colonised collapses when one acknowledges the characters' differing attitudes towards the contours of standard English. Nagg's fondness for phrasings such as "ballocks" and "me pap" contrasts with his son's grammatical rigour, as well as that of his wife, who chides him for calling sand sawdust. This divergence in attitudes towards language calls into question, to some extent, linear readings of Hamm and Clov in a Famine context. Indeed, such subtle linguistic variation illustrates the continual re-drawing of the boundary between native and settler, thus eradicating the possibility of realistic motives emerging from Hamm and Clov's master–slave relationship. *Endgame* functions within the structures of coloniser and colonised, master and slave, precisely as it negates them; this, as Michael McAteer points out, is a feature of the play's modernist strategies: "Irishness becomes the vehicle for revealing the dialectic of authority and servility through which the play is structured: a dialectic constitutive of its modernist aesthetic".[116] The scarcity of references to Irish history is thus more significant than their inclusion, since their paucity enables the emergence of an aesthetic of partial erasure. What is called into question, implicitly, is not Ireland as point of origin, but Ireland as the central site of meaning for a situation of historical stasis.

The play's tendency towards accretive meaning, in its bilinguality, prevents the emergence of a stable context of interpretation and distances the historical collapse that it describes from a colonial past. If "Kov" can be read as a coded reference to the Famine, it also operates as an index of measurement, specifying not only the possible Irish origins of the characters, but also the distance they have drifted from these roots; it is also fruitful to acknowledge possible Russian undertones to "Kov", as an allusion to the Gulag, which was at the centre of heated controversies among intellectuals of the French Left in the 1950s. The alteration that Beckett made to the spelling of the word enables him to suggest a combination of forced labour and starvation in both French and English, allowing for an expansion beyond the immediate context of the Famine. Furthermore, the reference to "Kov" figures among nonchalant evocations of major historical bloodsheds: Nell and Nagg evoke the tandem crash during which they both lost their legs, "in the Ardennes", "on the road to Sedan", alluding to sites of major French defeats during the First World War and the war against Prussia under Napoleon II.[117] Here, the double meaning of tandem is played upon – as plane, part of a twentieth-century iconography of warfare, and as bicycle, very popular in France after the introduction of paid holidays in the 1930s.

The multiple meanings encompassed in Beckett's allusion to Kov illustrate the complex processes at work within his portrayals of states of scarcity. History is kept at the stage of suggestion, remaining under the weight of linguistic and cultural interactions. If there are Irish inflections to *Waiting for Godot* and *Endgame*, they are never free-standing, but always re-thought and activated in relation to another context, that of France, and another language, French. Ireland's colonial history thus becomes the springboard enabling Beckett's reflection to reach a form of contextual neutrality, while remaining engaged with a type of power relationship that is held in the shadow of colonialism. If some historical echoes remain in *Waiting for Godot* and *Endgame*, these are never sufficient to indicate the bearing of specific, concrete factors upon the situation of generalised scarcity portrayed. Instead, both plays emphasise the opacity of social workings under the regime of scarcity, portraying not the causes of poverty but the conditions that allow its perpetuation.

* * *

If Beckett's emphasis upon scarcity as a state of being can be read historically, as signifying his distance from the primitivism of the Revival, how can it be read theoretically? Here, the notions best suited to an elucidation of this issue are drawn from Sartre's *Critique of Dialectical Reason*: there is an intimate complicity between Beckett's and Sartre's explorations of situations from which no form of historical consciousness and no stable historical truth can emerge. For the latter, the threat of scarcity is the source of all human violence in history and that which motivates the establishment of social and economic structures. Man is constantly threatened by the prospect of deprivation since, as Sartre emphasises: *"There is not enough for everybody"*.[118] Saluting Marxism as "the untranscendable philosophy of our time", he deploys the concept of scarcity in order to perform a historical reading of existentialism and integrate the human and economic problems arising from colonialism into a philosophical system.[119] His argument is explicitly tailored to address a particular situation, the Algerian struggle for independence; such a discussion of scarcity thus operates on two levels, relating to a philosophical theory of history and to the workings of colonialism in a French political context. However, more relevant to Beckett's early drama than Sartre's approach to colonialism or his perspective on "the hell of daily life" is the protean nature of his concept of scarcity as a conceptual bridge between existentialist and Marxist perspectives on history.[120]

Indeed, Sartre's definition of scarcity as both a mode of existence and a form of historical logic provides a philosophical perspective for examining Beckett's attempt to address a system of power relations related, but not limited, to a particular situation. The Algerian War of Independence plays a double role in the *Critique of Dialectical Reason*: although primarily used as illustration, it ultimately influences the direction of Sartre's argument once the fundamentals of his philosophical model have been established. Yet the political undertones of Sartre's elaboration upon the theme of scarcity are not central to his argument; rather, they emerge from an exploration of society as an ensemble of antagonisms. The study explores the relationship between the individual and the "collective", a term which designates the common existence of men living side by side and deprived of a feeling of community. Utilising the example of people waiting for the bus, Sartre shows that the laws of the collective are conditioned by the experience of scarcity, turning social groups into a "plurality of isolations" through their daily activities.[121] For Sartre, human existence becomes nothing but the manifestation of an ongoing tactical struggle through which man asserts and maintains his dominant position. This principle of human existence originates in the discrepancy between the multiplicity of men and the conditions of their coexistence: as scarcity becomes the basic structure defining human relations within the community, each individual sees the other as a potential competitor.

The *Critique of Dialectical Reason* illustrates Sartre's increasing politicisation as a philosopher; his analysis of the concept of scarcity reads as the transposition into a human and historical system of the concept of nothingness developed in *Being and Nothingness*, in which negation is presented as one of the founding principles of the examination of human existence, one without which no question, including that of existence, can be formulated. In the *Critique of Dialectical Reason*, the concept of scarcity also provides a basis for reconsidering a Marxian definition of alienation.[122] According to Sartre, it is man's inherent violence, and not modes of production, as Marx suggested, that turn human interactions throughout history into a Manichean struggle.[123] Transposed onto a colonial context, the concept of scarcity enables a close association between colonialism and violence; violence is defined as the foundation of the relationship between France and its colonies, characterised by plunder and extermination of the native populations.[124] In this instance, pauperisation and under-nourishment are the results not solely of colonialism, but of a system of "super-exploitation", which Sartre also denounces in his prefaces to Albert Memmi's *The Colonizer and the Colonized* and to Frantz Fanon's *The Wretched of the Earth*.[125]

Sartre was one of the few intellectuals of his generation to actively promote the Négritude movement and to support the Algerian Front de Libération Nationale, and the link forged between scarcity in its existentialist and dialectical materialist senses had important repercussions, especially for African decolonisation movements and for postcolonial theorists.[126] His attacks upon the French government were scathing; in his preface to *The Wretched of the Earth*, for instance, he describes the attitude of the French intelligentsia towards the colonies in vitriolic terms: "We might add, quite between ourselves, as men of the world: 'After all, let them bawl their head off, it relieves their feelings; dogs that bark don't bite'".[127] Upon its publication, French critics greeted the *Critique of Dialectical Reason* with mixed feelings: some thought that the book did not meet the objectives it set out to accomplish,[128] while others admired the visionary potential of Sartre's argument and his capacity to discuss the immediate context of his writing. Raymond Aron, for instance, argued that the critical questions addressed by Sartre stretched beyond a Marxist framework, even though Sartre formulated them in Marxist terms. Nevertheless, Aron expressed strong reservations regarding Sartre's call for violence and accused him of political opportunism.[129]

Yet Sartre's presentation of violence as the only means of overthrowing a colonial system was more abstract than Aron might have assumed. For Sartre, colonialism was a system and not a situation,[130] and, in the *Critique of Dialectical Reason*, he is explicit in claiming his lack of interest in the historical, concrete dialectic of scarcity, leaving this matter to the historian: his own purpose is not to account for cultural and historical particulars but to establish a *formal* dialectic.[131] Nevertheless, he remained conscious of the complex historical tensions shaping the development of scarcity as a system, and his discussion of the relationship between scarcity and the primitive remains inconclusive, shifting between historical and ahistorical perspectives. If scarcity determines the possibility of History, this does not affect all types of human organisation, but excludes societies essentially defined by an agrarian economy "more prone than others to famine or to seasonal depressions of food resources".[132] These primitive societies, which are based on repetition, exist outside History, since Sartre defines scarcity as the basis of the possibility of history.[133] Their temporality remains uncertain, the constancy of material scarcity having absorbed any forward impulse and having induced a process of regression. Pointing out that these societies vary in their ahistoricity, Sartre distinguishes between societies deprived of a history, self-sustained and living in autarchy, and societies "in which historical development [has] slowed itself down and stopped, by turning its power against itself".[134] A footnote reveals that Sartre sought to elucidate the link between the primitive as a concept and colonialism as a system, but the note remains inconclusive; he remarks that primitive societies "have begun to interiorise *our* History, because they have been subjected to colonialism as a historical event. What historialises them, however, is not a reaction to their *own* scarcity".[135]

* * *

Beckett's emphasis upon the importance of a biscuit or the difference between a carrot and a turnip resonates strongly with certain aspects of Sartre's model. In *Waiting for Godot* and *Endgame*, the world of objects is also the world of scarcity. However, while Sartre uses the concept of scarcity to formulate a theory of historical consciousness, in *Waiting for Godot* and *Endgame*, the expression of a state of scarcity is indexed to the reduction of a historical process to a mere trace. Both plays initially appear to portray a universal form of deprivation, but their portrayal of a regression towards a primitive state of existence is linked to a specific literary and historical legacy.

Sartre thought very highly of *Waiting for Godot* and praised it as "the best play since 1945" (a temporal landmark coinciding with Adorno's reading of *Endgame*), but he also suggested that its mixture of expressionism and pessimism made its content, at bottom, "pleasing to the bourgeois".[136] Later, he would clarify his position, pointing out that, while its "alien" quality prevented *Waiting for Godot* from being read as a conservative play, it manifested "a sort of universal pessimism that appeals to right-wing people".[137] This was equally true of *Endgame*, which Sartre considered to be less satisfactory, "far too inflated" and "far too naked" in its symbolism.[138]

Even Sartre's most laudatory comments suggest that he disapproved of Beckett's use of a non-realistic mode of representation to portray deprivation; later, he denounced Beckett's work as an expression of flabby pessimism, suggesting a major incompatibility between Beckett's vision, which did not seek improvement to the condition it portrayed, and his own.[139] Indeed, the form of scarcity depicted by Beckett in *Waiting for*

Godot and *Endgame* is not a regulatory system, capable of mutation and circulation (as Sartre depicts it), but an unavoidable fact that triggers off a gradual regression. In criticising Beckett's depiction of a humanity chained to undefined historical processes, Sartre was not alone; Georg Lukács also showed disapproval of the apocalyptic quality of Beckett's work, arguing in *The Meaning of Contemporary Realism* that it stood for an anomalous, distorted form of historical consciousness. Interestingly, Lukács's opinion of Beckett later evolved from this position of complete rejection, and, in 1967, he discerned elements in Beckett's work that denoted a resistance to capitalism.[140] Yet he still accused Beckett of moral inertia and argued that his decision to portray the meaninglessness of human life as a fatal condition was responsible for generating his success.

It can be argued that Beckett's emphasis on the impenetrability of the factors contributing to human alienation was precisely what Lukács resented, possibly because it was in conflict with his theory of reification. This notion, which Lukács developed in *History and Class Consciousness* (1923), associates human alienation with capitalist modes of production.[141] Lukács takes the internal organisation of the factory as a concentrated representation of the global workings of capitalism; through commodity exchange (the founding value of capitalism, according to Lukács), modes of production split the nature of the object between exchange-value and use-value. This split is communicated to man, who becomes a "a mechanical part incorporated into a mechanical system", separated from other individuals.[142] Due to the impenetrability of the factors causing impoverishment, Beckett's early drama does not easily accommodate Lukács's understanding of alienation: in general, the material needs of Beckett's characters are extremely modest and the zone that they inhabit is far removed from capitalist modes of exchange. Requests for a painkiller, a sugar-plum, a carrot or a radish do not participate in a survival economy but signify a social and historical collapse of immeasurable scope.

Lukács's attacks upon Beckett in *The Meaning of Contemporary Realism* also relate to other concerns, namely his wish to establish a classification of literary modes based upon their representation of history. Taking *Molloy* as an example of depraved primitivism, Lukács chastises Beckett for displaying a lack of concern for the repercussions of history for man. The aspects of modernism to be found in Beckett and challenged by Lukács are its vision of man as an alienated, ahistorical being and its sense of meaninglessness – a "glorification of the abnormal" and an "undisguised anti-humanism".[143] Literature should, Lukács claims, illustrate a process, instead of presenting us with the *disintegration* of a process. As a remedy for the irrationality of modernism, he defines a series of general criteria for appreciation, essentially modelled on the exigencies of classical realism, and proposes to favour the methods of Balzac, Tolstoy and Thomas Mann.

Beckett, it is important to note, did not think highly of the Balzacian realism praised by Lukács, denouncing it as grossly fabricated in a review of 1934, and mocking "the stock-in-trade exactly of the naturalism that Proust abominated", its "uniformity, homogeneity, cohesion, selection scavenging for verisimilitude".[144] His correspondence illustrates an ongoing concern with flaws discerned in nineteenth-century realism; in 1935, he wrote to Thomas MacGreevy:

> Am reading the Cousine Bette. The bathos of style & thought is so enormous that I wonder is he writing seriously or in parody. And yet I go on reading it. I have finished with Adler. Another one-track mind. Only the dogmatist seems able to put it across.[145]

These preoccupations were not confined to his early career: later, he would advise the playwright Robert Pinget to "watch out" for realism, when the latter was writing *L'Inquisitoire*, explaining that writing should simply "take off".[146]

Lukács's long-standing animosity towards Beckett had a strong impact upon debates surrounding the role of the avant-garde in post-war Europe. In particular, his accusations of decadence and anti-humanism operate as a backdrop to Adorno's "Trying to Understand *Endgame*" (1961), an essay dedicated to Beckett.[147] If the title suggests a strong measure of bewilderment in its phrasing, the feeling seems to have been mutual – Beckett complained about the obscurity of Adorno's writing on several occasions and wrote to Ruby Cohn in 1965: "Adorno's philosophy is too difficult for me".[148] In this important essay, Adorno emphasises the ability of modernism to expose modern social traumas in a manner that remains beyond the grasp of committed art, by means of a search for forms that expose the regression of a post-Auschwitz world. Locating *Endgame* within a series of symptomatic responses to the war, he criticises the simplistic character of Lukács's understanding of Beckett. For Adorno, the kind of realism praised by Lukács demands a reality able to sustain stable forms and categories – something no longer existent after the Holocaust.[149] To a large extent, Adorno's analysis of *Endgame* is a defence of the critical insight of modernism into post-war society. He envisages the kind of void exploited by Beckett as symptomatic of a historical catastrophe and of the conditions that allowed it to take place. This catastrophe is doomed to remain nameless, since the consequences of the tragedy are so devastating that the very possibility of its expression is precluded. The work, therefore, challenges the boundaries of existentialist philosophy through its historicity, as the formation of consciousness finds itself confined to stillness and silence:

> [...] Beckett proves to be a pupil of Proust and a friend of Joyce, in that he gives back to the concept of "situation" what it actually says and what philosophy made vanish by exploiting it: dissociation of the unity of consciousness into disparate elements – non-identity. As soon as the subject is no longer doubtlessly self-identical, no longer a closed structure of meaning, the line of demarcation with the exterior becomes blurred, and the situations of inwardness become at the same time physical ones. The tribunal over individuality – conserved by existentialism at its idealist core – condemns idealism. Non-identity is both: the historical disintegration of the subject's unity and the emergence of what is not itself subject.[150]

Adorno did not consider the ways in which Beckett's work might relate to an Irish historical predicament, yet his analysis of *Endgame* does not rule out such readings in its illumination of a specific historical underpinning to the play. This is the point at which Adorno's understanding of Beckett's modernism diverges from Lukács's, as the latter showed little concern for the consequences of colonialism:[151] in essays on Wilde and Shaw, he failed to engage with their Irish background, even when discussing *John Bull's Other Island*, the extended preface of which leaves little doubt as to Shaw's political intentions.[152] Elsewhere, Lukács described Joyce's use of Dublin in *Ulysses* as "little more than a backcloth",[153] leading Adorno to denounce his lack of awareness of Joyce's cultural and historical specificity.[154]

Although Lukács's interests were entirely dissociated from the debates during the Revival period concerning the necessity of articulating a distinctively Irish form of historical consciousness, his long-standing animosity towards Beckett offers an interesting basis for examining the latter's estrangement from the literary canon established in the literature of the Revival. The creation of a norm within Irish literature was one of Thomas MacDonagh's main concerns, for instance: MacDonagh wanted to "clear away certain misconceptions, to fix certain standards, to define certain terms" in relation to the Irish quality of different types of writing.[155] In essays defining the nature, scope and aims of the national literature, Yeats also made clear that he did not want to include all writers who were born in Ireland in his selection, only "those who have written under Irish influence and of Irish subjects".[156] Later, in the 1930s, the criteria for admission into his Academy of Letters depended on the writer's handling of Irish topics.[157] These few examples suggest the existence of *degrees* of Irishness, a function of how closely writers conformed to the demands of traditional poetic, dramatic and narrative forms. Beckett remained exterior to these classifications due to his embrace of non-naturalistic art forms; in fact, when J.C.C. Mays denounced the Irish indifference to Beckett in an article of 1969, he seemed to suggest that the reception of Joyce, Yeats and Beckett in Ireland indicated a form of hierarchy that followed criteria of appreciation based on their realistic use of Irish subject matter. Joyce was regarded with a peculiar form of pride, which Mays identified as familial in nature, Yeats was seen as part of a tradition, and Beckett met with impersonal appraisal.[158]

Finally, Lukács's reading of Beckett provides important illumination of Brecht's response to Beckett's early drama, Lukács's attack upon modernist aesthetics in *The Meaning of Contemporary Realism* being influenced by an ongoing debate with Brecht regarding the purpose of the avant-garde. Their reflections were primarily centred on issues of historical understanding and individual responsibility, but also addressed the relationship between realism and history.[159] In 1938 and 1939, in particular, Brecht wrote several essays criticising Lukács's attitude to realism for being too theoretical and reductive. These essays were not published until 1966, possibly due to Brecht's desire to maintain a united front against fascism: in the late 1930s, both Lukács and Brecht were living in exile, showing unconditional opposition to fascism and support to Communism.[160] In these essays, Brecht argued that Lukács's commitment to realism was conservative and reactionary, his definition of realism too constrained as a literary category. He criticised Lukács's proposals for their remoteness from reality and impracticality, and denounced his neglect of lyric poetry and drama.[161] To Lukács's admonition that the writer should portray history as a driving force, Brecht replied that neither literature nor life is given to command. He emphasised that, as reality changes and new problems appear, the writer must look for the new modes of representation that these changes demand.[162] Deriving a practical definition of realism and guidelines from literary works alone was, for Brecht, unworkable and somewhat ludicrous, since realism was not solely a literary issue but raised major political, philosophical and practical problems; as such, it should be approached as a matter of general human concern.[163]

These attacks upon Lukács's understanding of literature, in turn, informed Brecht's project of adapting *Waiting for Godot*. In 1956, as he was lying in a hospital bed, he began making notes towards what he called a *Gegenentwurf* (a counter-play), but he had to abandon the project due to his illness.[164] Beckett's play was, in this instance, merely an instrument in Brecht and Lukács's debates about expressionism: Brecht believed that expressionism constituted an important vehicle for articulating political protest, while Lukács dismissed expressionism as a pointless formal exercise deprived of a historical underpinning, which had unwittingly contributed to the spread of irrationalism upon which Nazism had thrived.[165] Lukács's uncompromising stance may have influenced Brecht's decision to adapt *Waiting for Godot*, in which, contrary to expressionist drama, the causes of suffering remain unstated.[166]

Brecht transposed the play into a recognisably 'modern' situation, the debilitating effects of scarcity upon man reduced. Clearly, he disapproved of the apparent passivity of the characters and of the absence of a well-defined causal relation governing the action.[167] His annotations have been well documented and show that, in general, he excised what he saw as unnecessary verbal flourishes. He reworked the first half of Act One into a Marxist parable, associating each character with recognisable social origins. Estragon became a "proletarian", Vladimir an "intellectual", Lucky "an ass or a policeman" and Pozzo (whom Brecht renamed "von Pozzo") "one of the landed gentry".[168] The modifications also targeted style. Dialogues were reworked to suppress the sense of meaninglessness; Estragon's cues were rewritten to make him sound vulgar; some of Vladimir's lines were given to Estragon and vice versa. Consequently, as Ulrich Schoenleber points out, the intellectual Vladimir becomes responsible for the pointless waiting.[169] For this adaptation, Brecht used the German translation of the play, which was based on the French text and did not feature the Irish phrases that colour the English version.[170] However, a peculiar irony is at play in this adaptation: if Brecht strove to universalise Beckett's portrayal of alienation, his *Gegenentwurf* illuminates the landlord–tenant relationship central to Irish readings of the play in a nineteenth-century context of land-related conflicts and widespread poverty.

Brecht's modifications suggest that he was attracted to the play's focus on material scarcity, but disapproved of its primitive leanings. In granting deprivation a cause and a possible resolution, he also made the situation of stasis portrayed by Beckett provisional. Clearly, he saw a revolutionary potential in *Waiting for Godot*, but in order to realise this potential, it was necessary to mute the play's primitive tendencies, which, for him, were antithetical to its historical dimension. This is confirmed in his consideration of another counter-play, more politicised and theatrical than its predecessor in its establishment of a direct correlation between deprivation and capitalism, which involved cutting *Waiting for Godot* into several scenes and projecting a film about communist revolution in the background.[171] This idea for a reworking captures a Brecht aware of the visual impact of Beckett's representation of deprivation and wanting to maximise it by utilising a modern medium, cinema. The juxtaposition of film and waiting would, Brecht hoped, induce distantiation as desired and bring universal human concerns to the fore.[172] His intention to use cinema as a medium to historicise the play suggests that he considered something more radical than simple textual reworking necessary in order to rescue the play's historical dimension, and that he objected to Beckett's portrayal of an era whose stance in relation to capitalism remained undefined.

Brecht's concerns were evidently not in keeping with Beckett's intentions. It is commonly recognised that Beckett remained ferociously opposed to interpretations of the play that did not maintain allegorical ambiguity. His repeated refusals to clarify the meaning of the play suggest that he wished to represent a form of human alienation that emerged from an indeterminate position within history, rather than explicit social or political occurrences. Yet Beckett does not seem to have thought Brecht's counter-play worthy of attention, although he was aware of Brecht's revisions and the trying circumstances under which Brecht had decided to rewrite his play. His comments were few; a decade later, he wrote to Ruby Cohn: "I did hear Brecht was rewriting the play or writing an anti-Godot when smoking the final cigars".[173] He also mentioned the matter to Adorno, who was appalled by the idea.[174]

Instead, Beckett preferred to define his search for a minimalist art form as a striving towards "thinglessness". After the success of *En attendant Godot*, he explained in a February 1952 letter to Aidan Higgins that his concern for the idea of nothingness was ruled by motives deeper than even he had previously recognised: "I used to think all this work was an effort, necessarily feeble, to express the nothing. It seems rather to have been a journey, irreversible, in gathering thinglessness, towards it".[175] The phrase "gathering thinglessness" expresses a gradual erasure and negation that recalls Beckett's use of modes of representation central to Revivalist literature. In his early drama, Beckett's emphasis on scarcity enables him to relate to an Irish tradition of representation of nation and race, without explicitly revealing a link to it. Exterior to an

Irish context, his residual attachment to the primitivism of the Revival is also problematic; the overwhelming presence of scarcity becomes, for theorists such as Brecht and Lukács, the manifestation of a failure to provide a historical underpinning to human alienation precisely *because* of the primitive leanings of the work. Viewed in relation to the context provided by the Irish Revival for Beckett's development, the attitudes of Brecht and Lukács towards Beckett provide the possibility for a new framework in which to consider Beckett's so-called ahistoricity. Indeed, their responses highlight the repercussions of Beckett's ambivalent response to the Revival regarding his positioning within European modernism. They also reveal the manner in which Beckett's enduring, if precarious, attachment to certain aspects of a Revivalist legacy influenced his position within the European avant-garde.

4
Writing Disappearance

Throughout his writing career, Beckett remained engaged in active reflection upon the nature of representation. This, in turn, significantly influenced his dramatic practice. His concern for the conceptual intricacies of modern art found articulation in a series of critical articles written about twentieth-century painters for French and English publications between the late 1930s and the early 1960s.[1] These articles reveal a keen interest in the possibilities and limitations of non-representational art. They nuance Beckett's position within the European avant-garde substantially, distinguishing him from playwrights commonly associated with absurdist literature, such as Eugène Ionesco, Alfred Jarry and Arthur Adamov, whose respective divergences from the conventions of realistic drama remained largely subsumed under the representational precepts from which they sought to escape. In contrast, Beckett's movement away from realism was theoretically and conceptually informed: from the 1960s onwards, he perfected dramatic forms bearing scant relation to representationalism, focusing instead upon sensorial and spatial interactions between voices which are either disembodied or on the verge of disembodiment.

This progression was indebted to Beckett's short-lived career as an art critic, during which he paid particular attention to the possibilities engendered by abstraction. His preoccupation with the philosophical and structural problems posed by ideas of abstraction appears in its most concise form in "Three Dialogues with Georges Duthuit", in which he famously argues that the modern painter (and, by extension, the modern artist) should turn away from expressivity and choose instead "[t]he expression that there is nothing to express, nothing with which to express, nothing from which to express, no power to express, no desire to express, together with the obligation to express".[2] Beckett's view of the purpose of representation was informed by conceptual breakthroughs within twentieth-century art; his argument recalls Kandinsky's *On the Spiritual in Art*, published in 1912 as *Über das Geistige in der Kunst*, in which Kandinsky argues that the artist must surrender to the ineluctable impossibility of mastering form: "The artist must have something to say, for his task is not the mastery of form, but the suitability of that form to its content".[3] This parallelism of views suggests a close proximity between Beckett's attitude towards the writing process and modernist theories of composition; Beckett himself referred to explorations of the concept of abstraction in Kandinsky and Schoenberg when suggesting, in a 1969 interview with John Gruen, that he had moved beyond certain concepts of form.[4] In this interview, an intimate complicity between the use of negativity as creative subject matter and the liberation from the duty of figuration and verisimilitude is evoked:

> If my work has any meaning at all, it is due more to ignorance, inability, and an intuitive despair than to any individual strength. I think that I have perhaps freed myself from certain formal concepts. Perhaps, like the composer Schönberg or the painter Kandinsky, I have turned toward an abstract language. Unlike them, however, I have tried not to concretise the abstraction – not to give it yet another formal context.[5]

The complexities of Beckett's statement will be unpacked as the argument progresses; for now, it is important to discuss the motivations underlying his desire to be compared with two artists whose explorations of abstraction determined the direction of twentieth-century painting and music.[6] Beckett had followed their progression with much anticipation; his positive response to Schoenberg's twelve-tone compositional technique, for instance, was immediate: having witnessed a 1949 performance of the *Wind Quintet* in Paris with his future wife Suzanne, he suggested to MacGreevy a preference for Schoenberg's serialist, rather than expressionist, compositions: "Suzanne loathed it, I was very interested, having only read Pierrot Lunaire I think once, without pleasure, and now want to hear some Berg and Webern and more Schoenberg, never or hardly ever played in Paris".[7]

The conceptual rigidity of Schoenberg's twelve-tone system may have influenced Beckett's approach to writing drama; there are similarities between Schoenberg's compositional methods and Beckett's search for new means of conferring expressive force on dramatic forms. Erik Tonning, for instance, evokes Schoenberg's compositional systems when discussing Beckett's use of repetition and its effect in performance.[8] The conceptual similarities between Beckett's drama and Schoenberg's aesthetic project are also evoked in Adorno's essay on *Endgame*. Adorno comments upon the proximity of Schoenberg's twelve-tone system to the philosophical problems posed by Beckett's residual historicity in his approach to form, observing that Beckett's portrayal of historical catastrophe borrows structural elements from atonal music: "In the act of omission, that which is omitted survives through its exclusion, as consonance survives in atonal harmony".[9] For Adorno, the importance of the twelve-tone system originates in its fundamentally levelling effect upon compositional materials. Remarking that the technique resists a conventional interpretation of musical dynamics, Adorno suggests in *Philosophy of Modern Music* that this ultimately prevents the emergence of any form of thematic and motivic development, since "each form of the [tone] row is 'the' row with the same validity as the previous row; no row is more and no row is less".[10] He discerns in *Endgame* a similar absence of teleology operating as a principle of dramatic construction and regulating the individual interventions of Beckett's characters.[11] In this instance, Adorno's comments are part of a wider reflection upon the avant-garde's rejection of expressivity and the primitive dimension of modernism: *Aesthetic Theory*, for instance, discusses the connection between the suppression of hierarchical relationships and the avant-garde's tendency towards forms of apparent regression. Adorno's analysis of modern art's divergence from representationalism stresses the estranged relationship of the avant-garde to society: he establishes the "preartistic" level of art as "the memento of its anticultural character, its suspicion of its antithesis to the empirical world that leaves this world untouched".[12]

While Beckett's awareness of Schoenberg's compositional theory remained largely intuitive, he was certainly more familiar with Kandinsky's theories of abstraction. He became interested in Kandinsky's paintings during a trip around Germany in 1936 and 1937, and was aware of the critical reception of Kandinsky's theories. In 1939, he encountered the art historian Will Grohmann, a specialist in Kandinsky's work, and finally met the painter himself in 1939, describing him as "a sympathetic old Siberian".[13] Beckett's art criticism suggests that he did not view Kandinsky's fascination with Theosophy favourably; in "Three Dialogues", for instance, he dismissed Kandinsky's "every man his own wife experiments".[14] Nevertheless, it is certain that, for the young Beckett, Kandinsky's perspective presented a particular appeal, providing an escape from the pressures of nationalist orthodoxy and the outdated views of Irish art critics. When drafting his review of MacGreevy's monograph on Jack Yeats, for instance, Beckett contrasted MacGreevy's idea of a purely Irish art form with Kandinsky's *Über das Geistige in der Kunst*, concluding: "Since all is mind, inextricably, the eye, the hand, the brush, the site, the earth, the sky, and the po [sic] on the dresser, let it be mind".[15] Here, Beckett's reference to *On the Spiritual in Art* also acts as something of a celebration of Kandinsky's conceptual breakthrough. Indeed, the value of Kandinsky's essay resides in its unconditional rejection of representational painting: for Kandinsky, the connection between different elements in a painting is purely internal, originating entirely from the gaze of the artist and from the free exploration of associations between colours, forms and movements.[16] Kandinsky refined his theory of abstract composition further in *Point and Line to Plane* (1926), in which he evoked the possibility of adopting a new, mathematical vocabulary in order to evaluate the shifts of perception involved in abstract composition.[17] This is echoed in Beckett's "Les Deux Besoins", an unpublished essay of 1938, which utilises a mathematical diagram to represent the tension between the chaos of experience and perception, and the artist's creative energy.[18]

A letter to MacGreevy, dated October 1932, underlines the significant influence of Kandinsky's theories upon Beckett's development. Beckett states that literature should not serve representation, but, rather, a principle of necessity internal to itself. Drawing upon the best of his own poems, Beckett argues that they represent a "necessity" and are distinguished from their less successful counterparts by "something arborescent or of the sky, not Wagner, not clouds on wheels, written above an abscess and not out of a cavity, a statement and not a description of heat in the spirit to compensate for pus in the spirit".[19] Here, Beckett's definition of his poetry in relation to Surrealism and the Wagnerian notion of *Gesamtkunstwerk* appears to be an attempt to evaluate his own artistic enterprise in terms other than the literary. More precisely, the correspondence drawn between artistic necessity and synaesthesia echoes Kandinsky's description of the principle of "internal necessity" in *On the Spiritual in Art* as a basic tenet of modern art: to the idea of art for art's sake, Kandinsky opposes the notion of a spiritual art, rooted in "its own spiritual period" and endowed with "an awakening prophetic power, which can have a widespread and profound effect".[20] Beckett's own interest in synaesthesia, however, remained largely fuelled by a rejection of the hegemony of classical realism.[21] As a budding critic, he perceived the search for synaesthetic effects as an expression of radical dissent from traditional literary forms, arguing, for instance, that

Joyce's *Work in Progress* was not to be read, but to be *looked at* and *listened to*, since "[w]hen the sense is sleep, the words go to sleep. [...] When the sense is dancing, the words dance".[22] Here, Beckett's emphasis upon Joyce's interest in synaesthesia serves a specific purpose: for Beckett, Joyce's integration of a Dublin landscape into a synaesthetic art form is precisely what enables him to resist the nationalist legacy of the Revival.

In drawing a comparison between himself, Kandinsky and Schoenberg, Beckett presented, as a frame of reference, methods of composition which, while exploring the possibility of synaesthesia, sought to eradicate any structural centres of gravity relating to mimesis and tonal music. Indeed, Schoenberg proclaimed the necessity of a "unity of musical space" and an understanding of all musical configurations as "a mutual relation of sounds, of oscillatory vibrations, appearing at different places and times";[23] his concern for the natural tendency of art to gravitate towards the rules that determine its composition manifests itself clearly in his theory of harmony, which emphasises centrifugal and centripetal movements in basic musical constructions.[24] A suppression of the hierarchical relations between various components of the work of art also remained central to Kandinsky's theory of abstraction and, indeed, its application to the theatre. *Point and Line to Plane*, for instance, describes painting as an ensemble of tensions between the colours of the spectrum, the point and the line, defining the existence of the work of art in human consciousness. As in previous essays, Kandinsky postulates an aesthetic understanding that does not take place on a rational plane, but develops from art's emotional and spiritual impact; the correlation between sound and colour is presented as central to the artistic search for new expressive energy, regardless of the medium. The application of these principles to stage composition was explored in a series of theoretical papers and in his own "colour-tone" drama *Yellow Sound*, which developed these elemental laws of composition and connected musical sound, spatial movement and colour.[25]

Kandinsky's emphasis on the necessity of emancipating pure form from representational constraints influenced the ways in which Bauhaus artists such as Oskar Schlemmer and Lázló Moholy-Nagy approached the possibilities of the dramatic medium in their stage workshops during the 1920s. In particular, Moholy-Nagy, praised by Beckett as an "extracteur de quintessence" alongside other proponents of a minimalist aesthetic such as Piet Mondrian and El Lissitzky,[26] reflected upon a "total theatre", the artistic value of which resided in the tension between its logical structure and its "(nonanalyzable) intangible elements, conceivable only by the intuition of its creator".[27] In 1925, he explained that a new approach to technology and the dynamics of space could expose "diverse areas of relationships of light, space, plane, movement, sound, and human being, and with all the possibilities of variation and combination of these elements". New dramatic forms would emerge from the use of the materiality of the stage itself and the presentation of the actor's body as a component of the stage design; synaesthetic drama, hence, would result from the use of intuitive methods of composition in accordance with the rules of abstraction. Moholy-Nagy's idea of a non-logical and non-intellectual drama was concretised in adaptations of Hindemith and Offenbach in which he created complex imaginary spaces relying on optical and kinetic means of expression, and involving projected shadows, folding screens and mechanical props.[28] His call for a dramatic form liberated from the duty of figurative representation anticipated many later developments in twentieth-century drama; Beckett's own experiments may, indeed, be read as echoes of Moholy-Nagy's propositions on the production of a new theatrical space, themselves influenced by Kandinsky's exploration of an abstract synthesis.

In his declaration of kinship with Kandinsky and Schoenberg, Beckett asserted that, while he sought to break from representational constraints, his work was not subsumed in a conceptual reflection, but remained, instead, the organic result of intuitive methods of composition: he took great care to point out that his own formal experiments were deprived of conceptual reins and differed considerably from the "concretized abstractions" of these artists. Yet his motives for placing himself alongside Kandinsky and Schoenberg may have had as much to do with formal concerns as with a desire to neutralise constraints of place and nationality. Indeed, in evoking Kandinsky's and Schoenberg's respective searches for abstract means of expression, Beckett was also comparing his work to art forms that sought to dismantle social and national barriers and erase the boundaries between artistic mediums. This objective is manifest in Kandinsky's rejection of the idea of form as nationally and geographically specific when conceiving the 1912 *Blaue Reiter Almanac*; for Kandinsky, form reflects the *individual* spirit of the artist and bears a stamp of personality beyond nationality.[29] However, Kandinsky's strong aversion to the idea of a national canon did not preclude the use of culturally specific elements; the symbol which he designed for the *Blaue Reiter* group, for instance, clearly draws upon his family's Mongolian roots.[30] His origins influenced his transition from figuration to abstraction in a variety of ways, as illustrated in the painting

"Cossacks" (1910–11), in which Russian cavalrymen feature alongside non-representational elements. Beckett's own comments reveal that he was sensitive to the residual ethnic grounding of Kandinsky's painting, of which he had become aware through Grohmann's work, and he saw its use of Mongolian designs as central.[31]

* * *

For Beckett, the importance of non-representational painting resided in its paradoxical capacity to reflect the concrete through the abstract; in a preliminary draft of his review of MacGreevy's book on Yeats, for instance, he argued that, in overcoming the duty of mimesis, modern art comes closer to the concrete than ever before:

> Kingdom of Nothing has happily more mansions than one, and withdrawal from the official senses, when it becomes wearisome, is not so far an asphyxiating misdemeanour. It is in this sense that painting and sculpture so-called abstract represent perhaps the most passionate effort towards the concrete that the history of art has to its credit.[32]

Beckett's statement echoes Moholy-Nagy's defence of abstract art and his claim that, while it was difficult to see through the 'isms' associated with abstraction, the lowest common denominator of new schools of painting was "the supremacy of colour over 'story'; the directness of perceptional, sensorial values against the illusionistic rendering of nature; the emphasis on visual fundamentals to express a particular concept".[33] The aim of the abstract painter, he suggested, was to find ways of disengaging such visual fundamentals from "the welter of traditional symbolism and inherited illusionistic expectations".

Beckett's own interest in the possibility of non-representation was, nevertheless, nuanced by his awareness of the limitations ruling the conditions of its concrete and conceptual emergence. His concerns find form in two essays on Bram and Geer van Velde; in "Peintres de l'empêchement", for instance, he voices doubts concerning the possibility of objectless painting. For Beckett, speaking of a painting freed from the object, in Kandinsky's fashion, is absurd; he argues that, instead, painting merely freed itself from the illusion that there is more than one object of representation, perhaps even from the illusion that this unique object lets itself be represented.[34] Suggesting that artistic representation is necessarily mediated by an acknowledgement of the ineluctable elusiveness of the visible, Beckett presents the works of the van Velde brothers as illustrations of this phenomenon. Both painters portray a state of deprivation inherent in visual perception, corresponding, for Beckett, to an *empêchement*, or resistance. He distinguishes between two types of resistance, that emanating from the object and that from the artist, and defines two types of artistic approach, one concerned with pure perception and the other with being.

In addressing the conceptual foundations of non-representational painting, Beckett merely shares in Kandinsky's own preoccupations concerning the possibility of abstraction. Indeed, Kandinsky was originally doubtful that the artist could express himself only through colours and forms, and, in 1913, he communicated his fear that the abstract might degenerate into formlessness, wondering: "What is to replace the missing object? The danger of ornament revealed itself clearly to me, the dead semblance of stylized forms I found merely repugnant".[35] Schoenberg also expressed doubts concerning the possibility of non-expressive art forms: "how do you make sure that your music does not express something – or more: that it does not express something provoked by the text?"[36]

Beckett's essays on the van Velde brothers also display the strong philosophical grounding of his questioning of abstraction; a reference to Karl Ballmer's reading of Heidegger in "La Peinture des van Velde ou le monde et le pantalon", for instance, indicates Beckett's sensitivity to the philosophical implications of avant-garde painting.[37] Elsewhere, Heidegger's concept of *choséité* (evoked as *choseté* by Beckett) is integrated into a reflection upon the material equality of all objects within the work of art.[38] The work of Bram van Velde is considered worthy of particular attention; for Beckett, its value resides in the ability to represent the *pure* object, which is necessarily isolated and deprived of life by the artist's need to *see*.[39] Bram van Velde's painting, thus, inaugurates the death of the object, since the represented object dissolves entirely into the process of representation. Beckett's stance recalls Paul Klee's theory that the object itself does not matter, only the artist's perception of its essence; for Klee, the object is "surely dead" and what is of primary import is the "*sensation* of the object".[40] Klee also anticipated Beckett's emphasis upon the act of representation as an attempt to negotiate a form of resistance originating in visual perception itself. For Klee, the function of art is not to reproduce the visible, but to *make* visible: artists should reject their historical forebears when relinquishing the duty of mimesis, in order to create art forms independent of past traditions.[41]

Beckett's concern about the problems posed by abstraction left traces upon both the form and the content of his work. Adorno remarked upon this in *Aesthetic Theory*, tracing in Beckett's plays a residual attachment to realism and comparing it to the ability of abstract painting to retain vestiges of the representationality that it claims to abolish.[42] However, Beckett's interests in abstraction and the conditions of its possibility are, in certain instances, vested with more specificity than is granted by Adorno, the playful evocation of Kandinsky's theories of composition in *Watt* being a pertinent example. After careful observation of an abstract painting composed of a circle and a dot, Watt wonders whether its elements are the results of "some force of merely mechanical mutual attraction, or the playthings of chance".[43] His comments upon visual harmony, colours and effects of perspective read as a satire on Kandinsky's *Point and Line to Plane*. Watt is caught between fascination and bewilderment, and his ambivalence reflects the manner in which the Dublin public received abstract art in the 1920s. The paintings of Mainie Jellett, for instance, sparked a major controversy among the Dublin intelligentsia when they were first exhibited in 1923, as did the New Irish Salon exhibition of March 1924, which was dedicated in part to non-representational painting.[44] Critics wondered whether these paintings had anything to say; George Russell was particularly ferocious towards Jellett's work, describing abstraction as "aesthetic bacteria" and dismissing it as inexpressive.[45] Some of Beckett's acquaintances were affected by these public displays of hostility towards modern art; the painter Cecil Salkeld, whose work was exhibited alongside Jellett's and whom Beckett met on a number of occasions, was also criticised.[46] MacGreevy was heavily involved in these debates, and defended Jellett against Russell's attacks in an article of October 1923, long before he and Beckett first met.[47] When one considers Beckett's vitriolic criticism of Russell in "Recent Irish Poetry", it requires no great leap of the imagination to assume that Beckett would have sympathised with MacGreevy in his defence of Jellett. As he celebrates the modernist acknowledgement of a dislocation between the writer and the world of objects, he laments the paucity of Irish artists willing to address their own estrangement from the visible in their work.

* * *

The formal experiments taking place in twentieth-century literature and painting not only influenced Beckett's artistic development conceptually, but also enabled him to systematise his distrust of the idea of a national art that placed the expression of a sense of community and kinship before that of individual experience. His enduring cynicism towards "the national accident, or the national substance", had a significant impact upon the writing process and his search for non-realistic forms on the stage.[48] His own approach to artistic creation remained inflected with a distaste for such historically and culturally weighted modes of representation long after the publication of "Recent Irish Poetry". The manuscripts of *Eh Joe*, *Not I*, *That Time* and *Footfalls* provide concrete illustration of this, revealing Beckett's efforts to obscure and eliminate any traces of Irishness.[49] These documents reveal a Dublin landscape operating as an obligatory transitional passage and being gradually eroded to produce an apparently indeterminate setting. The form of non-representation that develops from the disappearance of the landscape relies upon a form of dramatic intensity driven not by narrative, but, rather, by the sequential repetition and permutation of elements of sound, light, gesture and speech, in which the occasional appearances of Irish place names and coded cultural references create disruption; a tension between Beckett's desire to embrace fully a non-representational mode and a tendency to retain an Irish imagery for expressive purposes becomes palpable.

Thus, the manuscripts of Beckett's later drama in English suggest that, while a degree of adherence to an Irish setting remained essential in the early stages of composition, such grounding was not entirely appropriate to the experimental mode chosen by Beckett.[50] Irish cultural and historical landscapes are reduced to mere traces over the course of the various drafts and yet remain preserved in the published texts in residual form, maintaining a tension between the figurative and the abstract; this aesthetic of the trace produces the necessary narrative thrust for the plays to function dramatically. The gradual erasure of Irish traits and allusions in successive drafts is thus more important than their initial inclusion: what carries meaning is not their simple presence, but, rather, the specific function that they assumed in the plays' movements away from a logic of composition based upon narrativity. As the initial 'realistic' setting of the works is reduced to a trace, its remnants indicate how far into abstraction the piece has receded. Such a pattern of composition, characteristic of the genesis of Beckett's drama of the 1960s and later, is born out of a lengthy reflection upon the nature of abstraction manifest in his art criticism.

Examining the appearance and disappearance of Irish minutiae reveals a Beckett concerned with the effect produced by eradicating points of narrative gravitation and exposing the result of their erasure;

the manuscript changes made during the respective geneses of *Eh Joe*, *Not I*, *That Time* and *Footfalls* suggest that he may have feared that the use of cultural and geographical features specific to Ireland would divert the attention of the spectator from the pictorial quality of the plays and hinder their synaesthetic aspirations. His instructions to actors during rehearsals confirm that he sought to suppress any elements suggestive of realism; instead, he suggested that the performance of *Footfalls*, for instance, should be understood as an *improvisation* and not as the telling of a story.[51]

This was also a period during which Beckett became more and more involved with rehearsals and, gradually, with directing his own work, beginning with the 1965 production of *He, Joe* for Süddeutscher Rundfunk. He harboured mixed feelings about this development and later feared that directing would prevent him from writing.[52] Nevertheless, his intense engagement with performance had a strong influence on his approach to form and he became more technically adventurous, exploring sensory effects through the use of recorded voices and representations of disembodiment. Paradoxically, such heavy involvement with the theatre led Beckett to write pieces whose status as stage plays can be called into question; upon witnessing the difficulties encountered by Alan Schneider for the New York premiere of *Not I*, Beckett himself wondered whether his play ought to be considered theatre.[53]

The technical and conceptual difficulties encountered when writing *Eh Joe*, *Not I*, *That Time* and *Footfalls* are reflected in the manuscripts, which are heavily annotated and underwent radical modification in the early stages of writing. All four plays are based upon the interaction between a listener and a voice that appeals fleetingly to scenes and memories from the past; emphasis is placed upon the mobility of the voice, rather than the body, and lighting plays a crucial role in reinforcing the expressive impact of the voice and the synaesthetic aspiration of the whole. When drafting the texts, Beckett remained primarily concerned with duration; *Not I*, for instance, should last twenty minutes and *Footfalls* fifteen minutes. Given such lengths, minute adjustments and variations of light, tone and sound were crucial, and the strict choreographies outlined in the texts were later refined in rehearsal. Among the actors involved, Billie Whitelaw was particularly sensitive to the musicality of the texts, describing rehearsals as a succession of shifts between different tempos and commenting that Beckett often "conducted" her performance, "something like a metronome".[54] The pace of speech was also central to *Not I*, as Whitelaw pointed out: "No one can possibly follow the text at that speed but Beckett insists that I speak it precisely.

It's like music, a piece of Schoenberg in his head".[55] There are certainly resonances between *Not I* and Schoenberg's expressionist compositions: in *Pierrot lunaire*, Schoenberg offered a musical representation of a skull being drilled into and stuffed with tobacco, an image that may have infiltrated Beckett's evocations in *Not I* of a buzzing, a "dull roar in the skull...".[56]

As he continued to expand the boundaries of what could be achieved on the stage with the use of light and sound technology, Beckett perfected a form of drama in which understanding was taking place in an emotional and sensory, rather than rational, domain. This departure from an ideal of expressivity based on rationality is illustrated in the instructions provided for those involved with his work. For instance, when the director Hume Cronyn complained that the text of *Not I* would be unintelligible if Jessica Tandy (who was playing Mouth) recited it as requested, Beckett replied: "I am not unduly concerned with intelligibility. I hope the piece would work on the necessary emotions of the audience rather than appealing to their intellect".[57]

The numerous additions and emendations that feature in the manuscripts of *Eh Joe*, *Not I*, *That Time* and *Footfalls* illustrate geneses fraught with uncertainties relating to Beckett's attempts to maximise the correspondence between ear and eye, speech and image. Despite essential differences in form, the compositions of these plays followed similar trends, initially featuring specific allusions to Ireland and, often, Dublin. This Irish landscape acted as a catalyst in the early stages of composition and was gradually dissolved; over the course of the various drafts, the texts move closer to a non-representational mode, and this evolution favours a movement of withdrawal towards states of consciousness which render particulars of time and place non-essential. Due to their residual historicity and attachment to place, references to an Irish setting give a new dimension to Beckett's exploration of the effect of ritual and repetition upon thought processes. These modifications, although preserving some of the specific allusions featured in early drafts, seek to diminish their prominence. Their presence raised problems of balance not only within the text itself, but also in the relationship between text and stage image, a relationship based not on the conventions of classical realism, but on the interaction between sound and image. The careful selection and removal of Irish place names and cultural references eventually produces a movement away from an identifiable setting to a situation of speaking and/or listening that seems to be suspended, divorced from geographical and cultural specificity.

This particular feature of Beckett's writing has been understood as a resistance to autobiography; in particular, S.E. Gontarski emphasises the manner in which Beckett prioritised form over content and wrote himself out of his work, presenting Beckett's movement away from realism as a general characteristic of his approach to writing.[58] However, the resilience of Irish trivia in the manuscripts of the late plays suggests that Beckett's mode of writing is not entirely concerned with self-expression and its curtailment, as Gontarski suggests. It has multiple roots, some in theories of abstract and atonal composition, others in the specific conditions shaping Beckett's development as a writer. Joyce's persistent use of Dublin locations certainly bears upon the work; by using images extracted from the everyday in Dublin, Beckett followed in the footsteps of Joyce, for whom Dublin was a springboard to the universal.[59] However, in an interview with James Knowlson, Beckett famously described his divergence from Joyce as an almost perpendicular movement, arguing that, contrary to the constant expansion of Joyce's language, his own method of composition was "in impoverishment, in lack of knowledge and in taking away, in subtracting rather than adding".[60]

* * *

Beckett's definition of a subtractive aesthetic is especially relevant to the manuscript drafts of *Eh Joe*, *Not I*, *That Time* and *Footfalls*, in which the tendency to erase follows a precise protocol, determined by the gradual erosion of Irish place names and Irish speech patterns. The strategy operates by opposition, rather than inclusion: a Dublin landscape is evoked, only to be gradually eliminated. The radical changes of content brought about by this subtraction have no equivalent in terms of formal modification: Beckett had a clear sense of the visual appearance of these plays from an early stage in their development, and major conceptual emendations to the stage image were rare. However, the historical and cultural weight conferred upon the plays alters radically as they evolve towards their final form. The evocation of a shadowy Ireland becomes associated with the boundaries of articulation and with the uncharted territories of the imagination.

Eh Joe, written for television in 1965, marked Beckett's second attempt at using film as a compositional medium, following *Film*, a silent film in black and white written two years previously. Black-and-white film also proved fitting for Beckett's purposes in *Eh Joe*: in a letter to Alan Schneider, he stressed the importance of using shades of black and grey, a choice which reinforces the dramatic power of Joe's silence and enables fluctuations in the division of space.[61] The emphasis on the importance of using a black background conjures up images of Kandinsky, who stressed the powerful effect of black when discussing the respective functions of different types of colours, lines, movements and sounds. Black is characterised as a "silent" colour in *Point and Line to Plane* and as an "externally toneless" colour in *On the Spiritual in Art* – the only colour against which all others, "even the weakest, sound stronger and more precise".[62]

In *Eh Joe*, a principle of tonelessness applies to movement and speech in equal measure. All physical movements serve the same purpose, conveying Joe's psychological entrapment. At the beginning of the play, Joe walks around a sparsely furnished bedroom – to the window, the door, the cupboard and the bed – searching for the manifestation of a presence, before finally sitting on the bed and remaining still for the duration of the piece; as a ghostly female voice addresses him, the camera edges closer and closer. This gradual movement towards Joe's face corresponds with an increasing aggressiveness on the part of the female voice (simply denoted "Woman's Voice"). Beckett gave strict instructions to Alan Schneider for the 1966 New York production, stating that Joe should not look at the camera and should remain unaware of it: "The eyes are turned inward, a listening look. It is however effective dramatically if at the very end, with the smile, he looks full at the objective for the first time".[63] There is no variation in the tone of the female voice: Beckett specified that it should remain "very low throughout", with "plenty of venom".[64] Joe's facial expression should remain "impassive", yet reflect "mounting tension of *listening*".[65] The resulting tension is coupled with "brief zones of relaxation between paragraphs when perhaps voice has relented for the evening and intentness may relax variously till restored by voice resuming".[66] However, the scene remains dominated by understatement, as Beckett suggested: "Voice should be whispered. A dead voice in his head. Minimum of colour. Attacking. Each sentence a knife going in, pause for withdrawal, then in again".[67]

The play was written for Jack McGowran, a dedication manifest in Beckett's initial choice to call the main character Jack.[68] Writing for the Irish actor influenced early drafts; in the second draft, Beckett gave the Voice an affected and slightly antiquated tone, and an unmistakeably Irish inflection:

> Like that evening in the Green.
> Early on [in our idyll]
> When I ~~told~~ besought you not to rush me

~~Beautiful diction you said I had~~ My elocution enchanted you
[Voice like [Waterford cut glass] to borrow your expression].[69]

In the following draft, Beckett replaced "told" by "besought" in a line later omitted; Waterford cut glass became "flint glass".[70] The inclusion and subsequent elision of "Waterford cut glass" suggests a Beckett reticent about situating the text in an explicitly Irish context. The use of such phrases may have identified him as an Irish playwright for English and American audiences: a fate undesired, as evidenced in his correspondence.[71] Finally, Beckett was aware of the potential problems that Joe's compliment might raise in translation. "Flint glass" retains the merit of direct equivalents; it is translated into "cristal de roche" in the published French text; the German version is equally indeterminate.[72] In English, the phrase also raised delicate issues regarding tone and consistency; it diminished the evocative power of the voice, by bestowing upon it a materiality that did not sit comfortably with its spectral quality.

The play is not explicitly set in Dublin, but allusions to the city nonetheless occupy an important role; from Beckett's first draft of the play, St Stephen's Green is abridged as "the Green", for instance.[73] This abbreviation has the advantage of providing superficial neutrality while maintaining a degree of geographical specificity for a knowledgeable audience. The allusion would not go unrecognised by the Dubliner, but a non-Irish audience might not appreciate the capitalisation of the phrase; those who witnessed the 1966 BBC broadcast, for instance, might not necessarily have recognised the reference to Dublin. Beckett's insider knowledge of Dublin remains evident to a degree in the French translation, which reads: "Comme ces soirs d'été sous les ormes…".[74] In translation, the passage appears to elude cultural specificity, yet a closer examination suggests reference to the elms of St Stephen's Green.

Also of note is Beckett's hesitation when referring to newspaper titles, such as the *Independent* and the *Herald*. These titles, commonplace in the English-speaking world, are also Dublin abbreviations of the *Irish Independent* and the *Evening Herald*. In the first and second drafts, the obituary of an unnamed "green girl", whom Joe drove to suicide, appears in the *Independent*.[75] This later becomes the *Herald*,[76] and Beckett returns to the *Independent* for the final draft.[77] His decision to opt for the *Independent* over the *Herald* has added significance in the identification of both Joe and his female lovers. These newspapers address different sections of the population, the *Irish Independent* being aimed at a conservative, middle-class and Catholic audience, the *Evening Herald* at a popular readership.[78] Other elements confirm Joe and his former lovers (the Voice included) as likely readers of the *Irish Independent*: Joe's middle-class aspirations are apparent in his recommendation to his innocent lover that she should use Gillette razors, for instance.[79] For a time, Beckett toyed with the idea of referring to the British competing brand, Valet Autostrop, but returned to the widely known American company, possibly because the mention of Valet Autostrop would have suggested a preference for specifically British goods on Joe's part – and, in all likelihood, raised complex issues of translation.[80]

A note in the margin of the first draft of *Eh Joe* reveals the Dublin coast to be central to the development of the suicide scene. Beckett originally considered turning the passage describing the suicide attempt of the "green girl" into a drowning scene, which involved a boat leaving from Bullock Harbour in Sandycove and crashing into the Kish lightship:

> What happened to the green one
> 1. [Tried] it lying down on strand with face in it warm night failure
> 2. Boat out from Bullock cap sur Kish sitting in boat facing lights of [land] murmuring Oh Jo Oh Jo…there's love for you etc till end whisper.[81]

This lightship, moored two miles east of Dun Laoghaire, near Bullock Harbour in Dalkey, warned of the dangerous obstacle formed by the Kish Bank at the southern entrance of Dublin Bay. Commissioned in 1811, it was de-commissioned in November 1965 and replaced by a lighthouse shortly after Beckett wrote *Eh Joe*.[82] Beckett's decision to relinquish this geographically specific narrative structure may have originated in an awareness that associating a view of the Kish lightship with a moment of psychological and physical disorientation carried a strong Joycean sentiment. In the "Proteus" episode of *Ulysses*, the sight of the Kish lightship marks the end of Stephen's musings on Sandymount Strand; realising that he has walked too far, he stops on the beach, wondering, before walking back: "Here, I am not walking out to the Kish lightship, am I?"[83]

In subsequent drafts of *Eh Joe*, as in the published text, the itinerary of the "green girl" is much less specific. She attempts suicide along Whiterock Cove in Killiney, referred to in the text as "the Rock".[84] This part of the Dublin coast, known for its distinctive geological features, had remained a landmark for Beckett since his youth. He may have been attracted to the non-specific character of the term, which, in English, mirrors the blank features of the "green girl" herself. In the translation into French, the locational specificity of "the Rock" is partially restored; Beckett uses a synecdoche similar to the translation of "the Green" into "les ormes": "the Rock" is transposed into "vers les grottes".[85] Here, Beckett's initial visualisation of the south Dublin coast has a determining impact on his choice of phrasing: the allusion evokes the two shallow caves between Whiterock Cove and the Vico Road, accessible by foot only at low tide. However, in French, the particularity of the location is replaced by an indeterminacy; the allusion to the caves introduces an enigmatic quality into the Voice's account of the suicide of the "green girl". Concurrently, a generic anglophone setting is preserved in the French text: the name "Joe" remains and the Voice refers to Joe's "thugs", a word that remains untranslated: "Du fil à retordre pour tes thugs…".[86]

The decision to translate "the Rock" into "vers les grottes" and "the Green" into "les ormes" suggests that Beckett intended to preserve the characteristics of certain Dublin locations within the French text, their specificity providing him with an otherness suitable for the exploration of the boundaries of language and representation. His indications to Jacoba van Velde concerning the Dutch translation of *Krapp's Last Tape* confirm that he wanted to preserve a visualised Dublin in some of his works; nevertheless, whether cultural specificity should be maintained in the translation, as in the French and English texts, was not a pressing concern. For instance, when van Velde asked him to clarify his use of the word "weir", he indicated that "weir" did not refer to a "barrage" but to an "écluse", because the canal evoked in the play (which clearly recalls Dublin's Grand Canal)[87] was, in fact, rather small: "Weir = barrage: dont la fonction est de régulariser le débit des voies d'eau. Mais il s'agit d'un petit canal et <u>barrage</u> fait un peu grand. Je propose donc 'écluse', bassin où les péniches changent de niveau" [Weir, whose function is to regulate the water flow. But it is a small canal and weir might seem too big. I therefore suggest "lock", pool where barges change level].[88]

Thus, the Irish setting sketched out in the initial stages of writing is reduced to mere remnants through references to Dublin English and Dublin life: writing becomes a process of erasure. The published version of *Eh Joe* bears few traces of the play's original setting, but features phrases such as "the likes of us" and "His Nibs", and refers to the green girl's "Avoca sack" and its horn buttons.[89] Avoca, a village in County Wicklow, was the location of the well-respected Irish company of the same name, which produced woven fabrics; in the 1930s, the company gained international renown when its tweed designs were used in Schiaparelli collections.[90] The image of the green girl clutching her Avoca sack in the English text is, thus, loaded; it strengthens the Voice's portrayal of her as the easily influenceable, naïve victim of Joe's whims.

The play's residual grounding in an Irish setting also reinforces its very ambiguity: while these references might evoke daily life to a Dublin public, an audience unacquainted with Ireland might remain insensitive to such specificity. Yet the choices made in relation to newspaper names and locations such as "the Green" and "the Rock" reflect a process of displacement and miniaturisation at work within Dublin itself and the language associated with Dublin. If these snippets of information are no longer distinctive when considered independently of Dublin usage and translated into other languages, they are an integral part of daily life in Dublin.

* * *

The text of *Not I* also underwent considerable changes; in fact, the process of erasing its Irish content was central to its genesis. The idea of staging a solitary mouth had preoccupied Beckett for some time: even before the first performance of *Waiting for Godot*, he stated that all he wanted on the stage was "a pair of blubbering lips".[91] Finding a concrete expression for this vision was, however, a long process, which began with an abandoned play of August 1963 entitled "Kilcool", featuring a severed head.[92] Like *Play*, this image provides a direct visual echo of Yeats's *The King of the Great Clock Tower*, which Beckett saw at the Abbey Theatre during the 1930s. Beckett's attempt to write for a severed head may also have been influenced by Buñuel and Dalí's film of 1928, *Un chien andalou*, the filmscript having appeared in a magazine alongside some of Beckett's own translations.[93] He became interested in avant-garde cinema while teaching at the Ecole Normale Supérieure and the film's ending, which features a couple partially buried to their shoulders in sand, appears to have been a powerful source of inspiration.[94]

As Beckett's correspondence illustrates, the composition of "Kilcool", which he referred to as his "face play", raised many problems, principally due to its divergence from classical realism, and he complained that he had never undertaken anything as time-consuming, tenuous and complex.[95] The abandoned fragment proved to be an inconclusive experiment; it featured detailed, realistic evocations of the coast south of Dublin, which were explicitly set in tension with the non-naturalistic stage image. The text, a monologue, described a train journey on the Dublin and Southeastern Railway line, from Dublin's Harcourt Street

Station to "Kilcool".[96] Beckett was familiar with this train line, which was known locally as "the Slow and Easy" and was often diverted near Bray Head due to flooding and coastal erosion – a fact recorded in Beckett's draft, which evokes this section of coastline. The train journey described in the monologue is, in fact, a journey through an Ireland on the brink of disappearance: the Harcourt Street line ceased operation in 1959, shortly before Beckett wrote this monologue,[97] while Kilcoole station, the destination of the journey, was closed in 1964 and subsequently demolished.[98] Despite the play's reliance upon Dublin minutiae, the spelling of the fragment's title suggests a geographical confusion: Kilcoole is situated near Greystones in County Wicklow, while Kilcool is in County Limerick.

The formal tension between the wealth of locational specificity upon which the monologue relied and the non-naturalistic aspirations of the piece as a whole proved difficult to reconcile. For Gontarski, Beckett gave up on this play "apparently because neither a satisfactory shape nor an acceptable artistic distance could be achieved for these images and memories of Ireland".[99] He argues that, when Beckett returned to similar material nine years later with *Not I*, he had no conscious recollection of the discarded fragment. If this is indeed the case, then the revisions and adaptations that marked the genesis of *Not I* in 1972 take on a new significance, and suggest that "Kilcool" may be perceived as a first attempt to explore those formal domains requiring an important degree of technical and visual sophistication.

With *Not I*, Beckett reached a point of equilibrium between the figurative and the abstract, a process enabled by the erasure of all elements suggestive of linear narrative development. The final, published text is a representation of disembodiment; it features a mouth suspended in the air against a black backdrop, "faintly lit from close-up and below", with the rest of the face "in shadow", recounting episodes from a solitary and silent life. Alongside the mouth is a "fully faintly lit" figure, its back to the audience.[100] The mouth is designated "Mouth", and the silent listener the "Auditor". Mouth cannot relinquish the third person when speaking, and the Auditor witnesses the failure to say "I" with "helpless compassion".[101] The play, however, pivots not upon their interaction, but upon a tension between disembodiment and the impossibility of silence, as the mouth speaks itself into non-existence. Of central import is the *pace* of speech and the levelling effect produced by the vision of a mouth speaking without interruption.

Beckett harboured misgivings, for technical and formal reasons, regarding the Auditor character, since the figure proved difficult to position adequately on a theatre stage; the silhouette was discarded from the BBC film version for which production began in 1975 and was also omitted from the 1978 Paris production of *Pas moi*, directed by Beckett.[102] Suppressing the Auditor meant discarding some of the clues that might have enabled Mouth's evocations of sin and punishment to take precedence over other narrative and visual elements. This reinforced the questioning of the possibility of teleological development: in suppressing the Auditor, Beckett ensured that the audience would not be able to interpret Mouth's inability to say "I" as a just retribution for a sin committed and that nothing would divert attention from the speaking mouth onstage.

Maintaining the text at the limit of intelligibility and finding the right cadence proved long and arduous tasks, as reflected in the physical shaping of the text: entire sections were cut from the first two manuscript drafts, yet, in all likelihood, these drafts were written swiftly, and Beckett's hand does not seem to have marked any pauses. The speed of delivery desired by Beckett posed significant problems for his actors and directors, and the process of textual revision actually continued during rehearsals, Beckett being heavily involved in the rehearsals for the 1973 London premiere.[103] The setting was a blackened stage, the words were toneless, and Beckett insisted, in rehearsal with Billie Whitelaw, that there should be "no colour".[104] The toning down of colour was necessitated by the provocative nature of the stage image, suggestive of a vagina. Maintaining this suggestiveness at the edge of the implicit was crucial to the successful dramatic functioning of the play. However, the parallel was unambiguous in the 1977 version of *Not I* for BBC TV, in which a fixed close-up on Whitelaw's mouth was maintained; such unambiguity was probably the reason for Martin Esslin reportedly calling it an "obscenity".[105]

Whitelaw understood Beckett's emphasis upon fastidious details relating to the musicality of speech; she reports that when Beckett worked with her on *Play*, he would also differentiate between pauses, marking half pauses and quarter pauses, and changing some of the three-dot interruptions into two-dot interruptions.[106] A similar process takes place in the successive manuscripts of *Not I*; the length and the location of pauses within the text are carefully identified and occasionally altered.[107] Innocuous though they may seem, these minute emendations are essential to the musicality of the play; the duration and position of these brief silences are as important as the words themselves. A text on the verge of intelligibility prevents the audience from searching for narrative clues and allows greater attention to be paid to the tension between the play's verbal and visual dimensions.

Despite the play's powerful resistance to narrative interpretation, Deirdre Bair suggests that *Not I* developed from Beckett's memories of Ireland and quotes him:

> I knew that woman in Ireland. I knew who she was – not "she" specifically, one single woman, but there were so many of those old crones, stumbling down the lanes, in the ditches, beside the hedgerows. Ireland is full of them. And I heard "her" saying what I wrote in *Not I*. I actually heard it.[108]

In the published text, form, as well as content, is shaped by unusual speech patterns. Mouth repeatedly discerns "peculiar vowel sounds" and recognises that this voice is necessarily that of "she". However, remarking upon such unfamiliarity also forces an acknowledgement of disembodiment, as the mouth acknowledges the disjunction between its existence and what it senses. It is clear that, for Beckett, the peculiarity of Mouth's speech patterns was essential to the play. As early as the initial draft, he began to toy with the idea of adding a note about the pronunciation of vowel sounds, sometimes choosing to include the note as an aside, sometimes deleting it.[109] The comment " 'any': pronounce 'anny' " features in several successive drafts.[110] Another note indicates that "vowel" should be pronounced as "vow-ell", "baby" as "babby", "any" as "anny" and "either" as "eether".[111] In later drafts, this note was retained but systematically crossed out.[112] It nevertheless reappears in a late rehearsal script and in the corrected 1972 Faber proof, for which, after reflection, Beckett also cut the note.[113]

These emendations convey Beckett's uncertainty concerning the manner in which the text might be construed as indicating Irishness; this was something he wanted to avoid, as his recommendations to Alan Schneider indicate. When working on the 1972 New York production of the play, Schneider wrote to Beckett that his note on "anny" had steered Jessica Tandy into adopting an Irish accent; he seemed to think that this could provide for successful interpretation.[114] Beckett turned down the suggestion with elegance: "*Anny*. Simply an example of the 'certain vowel sounds'. No Irishness intended".[115] Indeed, an over-emphasis upon these peculiarities of pronunciation might have created a gravitational centre within Mouth's narrative, emerging not from the permutations of a series of motifs related to issues of perception, but from its perceived Irish inflections. On the contrary,

Beckett's aim was to produce a form of "verbalised image",[116] to borrow Billie Whitelaw's phrase, and the pictorial quality of the stage image had a determining influence on the text's movement towards non-representation.

The subtle corrections which characterise the genesis of *Not I* centre on achieving a balance between a non-figurative mode of representation and a narrative residually based on realistic elements. The finished play bears few references to an Irish setting, apart from the repeated mention of "Croker's Acres": this paucity of geographical references results from a careful process of excision and elision. Indeed, the published text differs sharply from the first draft, dated 20 March 1972, which was firmly anchored in the landscape of the Wicklow Mountains. In this first draft, the narrative relies upon the use of the first person and recounts a birth which might have taken place in the Glen of the Downs in County Wicklow, which is designated "the downs":

> …birth…into this world…this world…of a tiny little thing… 5 pounds…in a godfor…what?…girl?…tiny little girl…into this… in a godforsaken hole…in the bog…named…what?…[the downs…? no] no!…the bog!…in the [godforsaken] bog…named…named… forgotten…to parents unknown…[117]

The reference to "the downs" was added in the margin, and the last paragraph of the manuscript, entitled "analysis", confirms that the idea of referring to a Wicklow setting came to Beckett after he wrote the initial draft. This concluding analysis permits narrativity without referring to particulars: "<u>Birth</u>…hole in bog – name forgotten – parents unknown – premature – no love – waifs' home".[118] The description of the birth as taking place in a "hole" in "the bog" suggests that Beckett initially thought it necessary to create a connection between the stage image and the narrative related by the mouth.[119] However, the potential vulgarity invoked by such a phrase posed serious problems: it required further emphasising of the mouth–vagina parallel and altered the balance between text and image by overloading them with significance.

The inclusion of the allusion to "the downs" within the text required a reworking of the rhythm of the text to accommodate this alteration, as is evidenced in the second draft:

> in the bog…named-…what?…the downs?…godforsaken hole in the downs?…no…no!…the bog…godforsaken hole in the bog… named…named…forgotten…to parents unknown…[120]

Beckett seemed uncertain about the necessity of providing a localised grounding for the dramatisation of a state of consciousness, nevertheless, and he soon suppressed all realistic details. "Five pounds" and "the downs?...godforsaken hole in the downs?..." are subsequently excised from the text; in the third manuscript draft, Beckett also suppresses the "I" used in previous versions and, subsequently, the narrative is told in the third person.[121] Concurrent with the suppression of the "I" is the addition of the figure of the standing Auditor to the script. The coincidence between the textual suppression of "I" and this major formal change suggests that, if Beckett's reflection upon the representation of disembodiment had taken a new turn, he still felt some sense of obligation to retain vestiges of realism.

In the following drafts, the narrative grounding of the play undergoes major alteration. In particular, Beckett replaces "bog" with "godforsaken hole..no matter..."[122] and introduces a reference to "Croker's Acres",[123] the racecourse at which Dubliner Richard Webster Croker trained horses at the turn of the twentieth century.[124] The grounds were within walking distance of Foxrock, and Beckett went there often; the location recurs in many of his writings, from *More Pricks Than Kicks* to *Company*. However, Beckett was plagued by indecision about the addition of a specific place name to *Not I* and he hesitated repeatedly regarding the use of "Croker's acres" or "Croker's meadows".[125] Once the structure of the play was clearer in his mind, however, Croker's Acres became a central location, as shown in a synopsis of the play written later by Beckett.[126] Yet the problems posed by the specificity of the reference emerged once again when Beckett drafted the French translation. "Croker's Acres" went through various changes, with Beckett pondering the necessity of finding a direct French equivalent. For a period, he considered leaving it intact, but the allusion was subsequently crossed out and replaced by a French phrase, "la vaine pâture", which has a specific legal meaning, designating all private land that is not enclosed and upon which grazing rights can be exercised after harvest.[127] In Ireland, grazing rights include only communal land; thus, in this instance, a solution to the problem of translation is found by replacing the geographically specific with the culturally specific.

The stage image of *Not I* draws on multiple pictorial references, including Caravaggio's *Decollation of St John the Baptist*, a painting to which Beckett was exposed in Malta in 1971 and which he described as "a voice crying in the wilderness".[128] When responding to enquiries regarding the origins of *Not I*, he presented Caravaggio as a primary source of inspiration, possibly because Caravaggio's representation of the beheading of St John provided him with a formal precedent for his own distribution of zones of light and darkness on the stage. The bipartite structure of the stage image is also strikingly similar to Man Ray's *A l'heure de l'observatoire, les amoureux* (1932–34), which is divided into two distinctive parts, featuring a suspended mouth floating above a landscape and a recumbent figure, seen from behind, silently observing the floating mouth above.[129] The use of a marker of femininity severed from the female body also recalls Marcel Duchamp's *Prière de toucher* (*Please Touch*), a collage in mixed media of a single female breast made of foam rubber. Duchamp and Enrico Donati made nineteen hundred and ninety-nine of these hand-coloured rubber breasts for the cover of the catalogue *Le Surréalisme en 1947*.[130] It is possible that Beckett came into contact with this image: having established a friendship with Duchamp in the pre-war years, he remained fond of his work.[131]

Other images fed the composition of *Not I*. In a 1972 interview with Deirdre Bair, Beckett reportedly described an everyday scene that he witnessed in Morocco:

> An Arab woman shrouded in a jellaba was hunkered down on the edge of the sidewalk – in Beckett's words, "crouched in an attitude of intense waiting". Every so often, she would straighten and peer intently into the distance. Then she would flap her arms aimlessly against her sides and hunker down once again.[132]

The sources of inspiration evoked by Beckett – Caravaggio's painting, his memories of the incoherent speech of an old Irish woman and a life scene in North Africa – are strikingly discontinuous, and their conceptual combination was a long and arduous process. The final stage image, which reveals Beckett's attraction to abstract art forms, enabled all these source materials to bear upon the creative process equally and allowed an avoidance of the problems posed by direct presentation; the drawing of a parallel between locations in Ireland and North Africa, for example, would have inflected the play with provocative undertones in 1970s France, where mention of the crimes committed by the French army against the civilian population of Algeria remained taboo.

* * *

While integrating Irish subject matter into a non-realistic form in *That Time*, Beckett struggled with similar conceptual tensions. This second "face play", written between June 1974 and August 1975, features an old man listening silently to memories of childhood and adulthood. His only distinctive features are his white skin and "long flaring white hair", which should look "as if seen from above outspread" (his stylised appearance, as James Knowlson points out, recalls Man Ray's *Femme aux longs cheveux*, a photograph of 1929).[133] As in *Not I*, the stage image relies upon the juxtaposition of zones of light and darkness, and the text upon snapshots of a lonely life of observation. The play's thematic and visual resemblance to *Not I* led Beckett to describe *That Time* as a play of the "*Not I* family" and "a brother to *Not I*".[134] Both *That Time* and *Not I* explore the potentialities of the voice as a sustained flow; while the residual Irish inflections of *Not I* are at the limit of intelligibility, in *That Time* Dublin locations and inflections are maintained as a point of departure for a reflection upon memory. Here, Beckett's exploration of the mechanisms of remembrance corresponds to careful geographical and spatial mapping; he wrote the play for the "cracked voice" of the Northern Irish actor Patrick Magee (who also acted as the inspiration for *Krapp's Last Tape*), and, as with *Eh Joe*, writing for an Irish actor influenced the genesis of the work.[135]

The play relies on three spoken parts, A, B and C, which are recited by the same voice and are spatially differentiated, emerging from either side and above the stage. The pace of speech should, Beckett pointed out during rehearsals for the 1976 Schiller-Theater production, be fast.[136] The published text indicates that A, B and C should "relay one another without solution of continuity – apart from the two 10-second breaks. Yet the switch from one to another must be clearly faintly perceptible. If threefold source and context prove insufficient to produce this effect it should be assisted mechanically (e.g. threefold pitch)".[137] The three spoken parts were initially written separately, before being cut into segments and pasted together to form the published text. For Beckett, it was essential to give mobility to the spoken parts via spatial dislocation as well as reference to dissimilar contexts; his wish to establish a contextual differentiation between the spoken parts shaped the initial stages of writing. The main difficulty, nonetheless, remained to "make clear the modulation from one [part] to another, as between attendant keys, without breaking the flow continuous except where silences indicated".[138]

The spatial dislocation that accompanies textual distribution suggests a ceaseless transition between aspects of the psyche associated with memory. Temporal frames also undergo constant shifts between the snapshots of childhood evoked in part B and memories of adulthood recounted in parts A and C. Prior to writing the text, Beckett classified A, B and C according to groupings of characteristics:

A: factual, names, dates, places, confusion
B: mental, conversion of thought
C: affective, conversion of emotion.[139]

Part A enumerates a series of locations with which Beckett was familiar in his youth,[140] telling of a journey from the ferryboat to the train station on Dublin's Harcourt Street via the stop of the Number 11 bus line. The building, which is tenderly described as the "Doric Terminus of the Great Southern and Eastern",[141] ceased operation when the Dublin and Southeastern Railway line closed at the end of the 1950s.[142] The part describes the protagonist's return to the places of his childhood, such as Foley's Folly, which, as Eoin O'Brien points out, recalls Barrington's Tower, situated near the Dublin Mountains.[143] Part B focuses on memories from childhood, anecdotes about love and longing, while part C evokes the protagonist's search for shelter in a museum, a post office and a public library, markers of a city that remains undefined. Although the play is described by a movement towards a non-place and addresses states of consciousness which cannot be subsumed into the geographical particulars that they relate, it is not unreasonable to assume that all sections of the text refer to a Dublin setting; precise Dublin locations are mentioned in part A, and Beckett's description of the textual sections as "attendant keys" suggests that the play was conceived with a certain geographical continuity in mind.[144]

Beckett retained definite ideas about the role of the voice prior to the completion of the text; in preliminary notes, he described the voice as "low, flowing. Unemotional. So low in places as to be unintelligible. Fading effect".[145] He searched for ways of maintaining a consistent tempo throughout, marking pauses and initially toying with the idea of utilising a clock, whose faint tick tock would be "only just audible in silence"; he also considered suggesting the protagonist's eyes be open during moments of silence.[146] His correspondence reveals that he reflected carefully upon the combination of a static stage image with a mobile voice. He retained misgivings about what he called a "disproportion" between the listening face and the text and tried to devise ways of amplifying image over voice. He was, however, forced to abandon such ideas and accept their dissociation as a fundamental component of the play, possibly because any modification raised technical and conceptual problems that could not necessarily be dealt with on a theatre stage. He eventually accepted that the remoteness and stillness of the listening face were unavoidable, pointing out to Alan Schneider, nevertheless, that eye movement, barely audible breath and the final smile were essential and of dramatic value.[147]

The textual tension between Irish and non-specific elements operates as a counterpart to the visual tension between mobile voice and static body. The first draft was marked by a strong Irish flavour, featuring colloquial expressions such as "kip" and "falling to bits", which are commonplace in Irish English but not specific to it,[148] and constructions characteristic of Hiberno-English, such as indirect questions and elision of the word 'if'. The use of these grammatical constructions influenced the cadence of the text, and the repetition of certain groups of words, alliterations and assonances conferred a measure of softness on the protagonist's account of a journey marked by loss and nostalgia:

> [...] what year was that, ~~was your~~ mother still –, ah for God's sake not at all, all gone long ago, where did you stay then, that time you went back to see was the old ruin still there, someone's folly they said it was, ~~Barrington's~~ [Maguire's] was it, ~~Barrington's~~, every bit of the tower still standing, all the rest rubble & nettles, where was it you stayed then, all the trams gone, was it that kip on the front where you went to –, no, that was another time, Dolly was with you then, X ~~or was it Molly~~ no matter [...] terminus of the Southern & Eastern all closed down & falling to bits, gave it up then, and sat down on the steps in the morning [sun].[149]

This passage illustrates the confinement of alliteration to particular sounds, such as wh-, th- or -t word endings. Under the influence of a Dublin accent, these rhythmic patterns become evident, as words such as "night" or "straight" gain prominence.

This feature of the play is consistent with previous works, such as *Not I* and *Eh Joe*, which were also written with Irish accents in mind, as evidenced in their successive drafts. In performance, the faint Irish inflections of these texts encouraged actors and actresses to modify their own speech patterns, and it is certainly no coincidence that the Welsh actress Siân Phillips, cast as the Voice in the 1966 BBC production of *Eh Joe*, found herself unconsciously adopting Beckett's own intonations and soft South Dublin accent (because of this, several sessions and additional takes were needed).[150] Similarly, Peggy Ashcroft chose to adopt an Irish accent similar to Beckett's when playing Winnie in *Happy Days*. She explained that she wished to sound like Beckett because, in order to perform the part, she had to "find a 'voice'" for the role and "heard this one quite distinctly".[151] Beckett, however, refused to sanction this interpretation and, upon hearing of Ashcroft's idea, was not at all pleased – a forced Irish accent precluded the possibility of a toneless, colourless performance.[152]

As *That Time* approached its final form, it adopted a neutrality, in terms of both vocabulary and phonetics. In the first typescript following from handwritten drafts, the text was tightened considerably and lost some of its idiosyncrasies. "What year", for instance, became "when", and "grip" became "bag"; however, "kip" and "falling to bits" were retained. As he rewrote the text, Beckett also altered its tempo, creating the sense of a constant beat, uniting the three voices. Having seemingly given up on an initial intention to utilise a clock as a metronome, he chose to impose rhythm from *within* the text instead of giving it concrete representation outside the text. This was achieved via repetition and effects of acceleration or deceleration:

> till in the end you began finding it hard to believe hard~~er and harder~~
> to believe
> hard to believe
> harder and harder to believe you ever told anyone you loved them or anyone told you ~~so that~~ till it grew to be one of those things you used to tell yourself as you went along.[153]

In this draft typescript, a change of poetic register also takes place. Beckett substitutes "saying" for "vowing", "every now and then" for "every now and again", "sky" for "azure", "sandhills" for "dunes".[154] The expression "not a whit the worse" is replaced by "little or none the worse". The voice describes a visit to the public library in greater detail and recalls "sitting at the big round table with a bevy of old ones poring on their books and not a sound to be heard only the old breath and the leaves turning".[155] The Joycean echoes of "old breath" identify this passage as a parody of Stephen Dedalus's own reflection upon the limited potential of the Irish artist for radical innovation. Stephen remarks upon the "dead breaths I living breathe" when walking along Sandymount Strand;[156] later, he describes the National Library of Ireland as a sanctuary for these dead breaths, reflecting upon the mummified literary heritage of colonial Ireland: "Coffined thoughts around me, in mummycases, embalmed in spice of words".[157]

The second draft typescript of *That Time* sees a radical formal modification; the distribution of the three spoken parts is clearly established and the text shortened. Alongside these structural changes, a number of emendations are made. For instance, "the ruin still there" becomes "still standing"; "all gone long ago" becomes "all gone ages ago"; "Maguire's Folly" (formerly "Barrington's Folly") becomes "Foley's Folly" and, further on, "Madden's Folly"; "stay the night" becomes "sleep".[158] The remaining allusions to a "grip" are replaced by "bag" and "night bag". These transformations are extended in the following typescript, which bears close resemblance to the published text. Several groups of words are elided, suggesting an attempt to further reduce the duration of the play. Some isolated words are underlined, with alternatives suggested above. For instance:

"to the terminus [end of the line]"
"only the old lines [rails]"
"wharf [pier]"
"was that twice or three times [common occurrence (as dirt)] a week"
"boat [ferry]"
"flat stone in the middle of [among] the nettles".[159]

"Sand" becomes "dunes" and "falling to bits" becomes "crumbling away"; importantly, such modifications limit the occurrences of idiosyncratic phrases. As the play approaches a neutral form of English, the function performed by Dublin place names also changes. Initially, evocations of Dublin formed part of an internal textual logic: their erosion banishes memories of Dublin into the furthest recesses of the speaker's mind, and, in the final draft, this Dublin setting is reduced to insignificance, Irish inflections to faint echoes.

* * *

The Irish content of *Footfalls* underwent a similar process of textual erosion, although its extreme paucity of allusions to Ireland and Irish English suggests that, at the time, Beckett may have been weary of the conceptual difficulties arising from the use of explicit geographical and cultural grounding as a point of departure. Work on *Footfalls* commenced in March 1975 and was completed by November of the same year. The play presents a dialogue between a dying, or possibly deceased, mother, whose presence is reduced to a voice alone, and her ageless, ghostly daughter May, who paces outside her bedroom. There is no firm differentiation between spatial and temporal frames or, indeed, between the two voices. Both characters are equally absent and there can be no certainty as to who is narrating whom into existence; what is emphasised is May's seclusion.

The play's divergence from realism is central to both form and subject matter: in rehearsals with Hildegarde Schmahl for the 1976 production of *Tritte* at the Schiller-Theater Werkstatt, Beckett demanded that the actress cease to look for ways of conferring realistic motivations upon May's tone and posture, and that her voice be monotone, colourless and distant.[160] His intentions were undoubtedly understood by Billie Whitelaw, whose appearance in the 1976 production at London's Royal Court Theatre was a perfect realisation of the tension between anguish and tonelessness desired by Beckett. The dressing gown designed for the production reinforced the ethereal quality of her performance: made of several layers of net curtain over a taffeta base, then bleached and dyed, the costume made Whitelaw feel as if she had turned into a stone sculpture.[161] Sensitive to the expressionist quality of the play, Whitelaw later declared that she felt "like a walking talking Edvard Munch painting".[162]

The play required the negotiation of difficulties of a conceptual nature, originating in Beckett's attempt to find a mode of representation suitable for a disembodied voice and a ghostly body. Initially, the main character, May, was called Mary, while her anagrammatic double in the text, Amy, was called Emily. In early drafts, Mary's statuesque appearance provided a central narrative fixture: the mother's voice commented upon her fair complexion, poise and grace.[163] The stage image, as James Knowlson points out, may have been inspired by Antonello da Messina's *The Virgin of the Annunciation*, which Beckett had viewed at the Alte Pinakothek in Munich in 1937: he claimed to have been struck by its "aghast look" and posture.[164] The position of May's hands is also strikingly reminiscent of a famous seventeenth-century statue of Mary Magdalene, *Magdalena Penitente* by Pedro de Mena.[165] The hands of the statue are in a position of imploration, strikingly anticipating May's posture in *Footfalls*. Maintaining such a posture presented serious challenges for performers, some of whom recalled with precision the tension experienced in every muscle.[166]

The first manuscript of *Footfalls* mixed religious references and popular superstition, as Beckett attempted to provide a clear symbolic framework for Mary's movements, utilising words such as "deasil" and "withershins". The voice, counting Mary's steps from one to seven, commented upon the grace of her movement: "See with what grace she wheels, now deasil, now withershins, and, when she halts, how always facing [the wall], to gaze before her with unseeing eyes".[167] Beckett, however, disposed of this idea and struck out the entire section with a thick felt pen. Many years later, he clarified the meaning of "deasil" and "withershins" for Kay Boyle (her enquiry, in all likelihood, was related to *Company*): "Deasil = right-handwise-sunwise clockwise as opposed to widdershins = counter-clockwise".[168] "Deshil" derives from the Irish *deasil* (or *deisiol*), meaning turning to the right, clockwise, sunwise. For the northern Celts, this was a ritual gesture aimed at attracting good fortune, and an act of consecration when repeated three times;[169] Joyce uses this ritual in the opening of "Oxen of the Sun" in *Ulysses*: "Deshil Holles Eamus. Deshil Holles Eamus. Deshil Holles Eamus".[170] Beckett's choice to omit these words from the first draft of *Footfalls* suggests that he did not want to impose a clear symbolic framework upon the play, nor did he want to diminish the expressive tension of May's posture. However, although he removed "deasil" and "withershins" from the first draft, he eventually chose to lengthen May's steps from seven to nine, replicating in diffuse manner the ritual gesture designated by "deasil".[171] This modification certainly emerged from his awareness of the significance of rhythmic patterns, in relation to which, in his view, all else remained secondary.[172] In June 1978, he described the play as being *about* rhythmic sound: "It is about the pacing: nine steps one way, nine steps the other. The fall of feet. The sound of feet. Walking on the ground, as on a tomb. The words are less important, but they are essential".[173]

Preliminary drafts were rich in concrete detail, describing the solitary youth of the main character, known initially as Mary, then as, alternately, Mary and Emily, evoking her "swain" and her refusal to mingle with girls of her own age in their games of hockey and lacrosse details presumably indicative of an upper-middle-class background and education.[174] It is only at a relatively late stage, in the third typescript draft, that Mary becomes May and Emily becomes Amy, as in the final text.[175] At this point, the text is edited down, and details concerning her youth are elided, such as the references to hockey and lacrosse and to the long deceased family physician Haddon.[176] The additional erasure of small sections and phrases bestows an enigmatic quality upon the spoken text: "Dreadfully unhappy" becomes "Dreadfully un~~happy~~...", for example.[177]

Arguably, Beckett's initial decision to erase "deasil" and "withershins" marked a pivotal moment in the genesis of the play, leading him to evoke memories of a childhood that could have equally taken place in Ireland or in England. In rejecting the narrative possibilities that Irish inflections would have enabled within the text, he also refused to provide a stable context of interpretation for the character's religious activity, creating instead a universe in which religious differences between mother and daughter remain as ghostly as the characters themselves. At a relatively late stage of writing, he hinted at a conversion to Catholicism as the main source of disagreement between mother and daughter. Initially, Emily's visits to the local church took place during Evensong;[178] in contrast, in later drafts, it is suggested that Amy no longer shares her family's Protestant faith. Evensong becomes Vespers,[179] the text thus moving from an evocation of Anglican to Roman Catholic prayer: Amy visits the local church alone during Vespers and attends Evensong with her mother. Her claim – that she wasn't "there" during the service – thus becomes laden with new undertones, suggesting a rebellion against familial belief.

This faint undercurrent of religious divide is, however, relegated to the boundaries of articulation, and it is more rewarding to see this aspect of the play as an example of the ways in which Beckett's construction of another "verbalised image" develops from the erasure of a 'realistic' grounding for the relationship between two voices. Nevertheless, this minor change brought in its wake other minute emendations worthy of note; for instance, Beckett was unsure regarding a choice of phrasing from the Book of Common Prayer and, consequently, the end of the play underwent several changes. The phrase "Be with us all, evermore. – Amen",[180] which featured in the 1976 Faber edition, is transformed into: "The love of God, and the fellowship of the Holy Ghost, be with us all, [now, and for] evermore, Amen. (Pause.)"[181]

* * *

If the diversity of subject matter in Beckett's dramatic texts of the 1960s and beyond makes a systematic analysis of their relationship to an Irish context problematic, it is nevertheless extremely fruitful to examine the ways in which the abstract dimension of the voice pieces develops following a preliminary reflection upon the concrete: the gradual subtraction of place names and cultural allusions from the texts expresses both Beckett's attraction towards a specific form of non-representation and his refusal to fully yield to it. In this aspect of his later drama, one may discern a concern with the factors fashioning cultural specificity in artistic production. In correspondence and critical writings, Beckett repeatedly suggested that he did not believe in the existence of a specifically Irish art form; his statements on the painting of Jack Yeats are a case in point.[182] In his review of MacGreevy's monograph, for instance, Beckett questions the idea that Jack Yeats might be seen as the epitome of the Irish artist, comparing his late paintings to those of "the great of our time, Kandinsky and Klee, Ballmer and Bram van Velde, Rouault and Braque" instead.[183] He argues that Yeats's greatness is drawn precisely from an aspiration towards the non-figurative, which transpires in his residual use of figurative elements – the combination of both traits resulting in a striking illumination of the visible. This idea is clearly derived from Kandinsky, whose own discussion of the meaning of art in *On the Spiritual in Art* develops from Schumann's view that "to shine light into the depths of the human heart is the profession of the artist".[184] In relation to Yeats, the reference to avant-garde European painting enables Beckett to question MacGreevy's nationalist leanings and to emphasise the painter's kinship with avant-garde currents in continental Europe.

In according international import to Irish art, Beckett may also have been trying to promote a certain artistic profile for himself; yet, ironically, the criteria of appreciation that he defined for painting are not far removed from W.B. Yeats's aims for the Irish Dramatic Movement: in his annual essays chronicling the development of a new tradition of Irish drama, Yeats emphasised repeatedly that Irish drama should aspire to international standards, comparing the Irish Dramatic Movement to the theatres of Germany, France and Scandinavia. However, in its historical context, Beckett's list reads as pure provocation: Ballmer was unknown, but a friend, while Kandinsky, Klee and Braque were seen as radical artists in 1940s Ireland, and Rouault's work was even more controversial.[185]

These questions are peripheral to Beckett's argument; for Beckett, what remains important and valuable about Jack Yeats's late work is the manner in which its use of colour and repetitive patterns enables a form of dematerialisation. Somewhere becomes nowhere, as all elements, relating to subject or background, are granted similar importance, since the equal treatment of all figurative aspects precludes the possibility of a sequential or narrative development. This leads to a subtraction of meaning: for Beckett, Jack Yeats's artistic vision is one "where Tir-na-nOgue makes no more sense than Bachelor's Walk, nor Helen than the apple-woman, nor asses than men, nor Abel's blood than Useful's, nor morning than night, nor inward than the outward search".[186] In this instance, Beckett distorts the concrete aspects of Yeats's painting, only to express his own concerns regarding questions of form and artistic purpose – concerns manifest as early as the publication of "Recent Irish Poetry" in the early 1930s. His evocation of a conceptual body of non-representational painting in opposition to MacGreevy's nationalist analysis of Jack Yeats illustrates his belief in the irreconcilability of these understandings of art's relationship to society and his comprehension of them in terms of their reciprocal tension. It is precisely in relation to this tension between representational and non-representational forms that the Irish dimension of his own writings articulates itself, as part of a wide-scale experiment with forms of distortion, fragmentation and erosion. If Beckett's use of Irish material remains central to his reflection upon the nature of representation, it is precisely through this reflection that Ireland becomes peripheral, and yet relentlessly present in his bilingual *oeuvre*.

Conclusion

Literary criticism has created many Becketts, from absurdist to poststructuralist, enabling the incessant generation of new meanings and interpretations around the work. The idea of an Irish Beckett has, however, remained encumbered by a degree of reluctance in critical discourses, the notion often being perceived as overly limiting in terms of Beckett's creative endeavours and artistic contexts. This assumption – that the work is culturally non-specific – has fashioned the direction and evolution of scholarship in the field, resulting in largely anecdotal and impressionistic approaches to the specific historical weight carried by Beckett's writing. What remains certain is that whether Beckett should be considered Irish, French or European is of little significance; what deserves to be questioned, however, is the lack of interest in the cultural and historical specificity of modernism revealed in this established critical paradigm. While labels such as Irish, French and European are largely born out of attempts to domesticate a work that escapes generic identification, they also offer points of friction that are germane to critical enquiry, revealing a Beckett unapproachable without the political and cultural frames of reference against which his bilingual *oeuvre* appears to react.

A contextualisation of Beckett's artistic development in relation to the Irish Literary Revival demands that the features that make him so distinctive as a writer take on new currency: considered in relation to primitivist practices within Revivalist literature and Revivalist outlooks on translation, his apparent autonomy from place and nationality, his turn to self-translation and his search for minimalist forms are granted a historical and cultural specificity that is rarely acknowledged, giving credit to the sense of Beckett as an avant-garde artist by means of the manner in which he engages with an Irish context in the very process of *deflecting* it. It is in the tension shaping Beckett's anti-essentialist practices that the fundamental problems raised by the residual presence of an Irish cultural and historical landscape in his work can be located.

The difficulties that arise when one attempts to read Beckett in a post-Revival literary tradition provide, in turn, the seeds of a new critical paradigm which grows in the interstices between differing understandings of artistic commitment and the role of the avant-garde. Indeed, Beckett's attack upon essentialist understandings of Irishness raises fundamental questions relating to representations of historical consciousness in post-war Europe. Debates within Marxism and existentialism provide further illumination of these questions, proving particularly pertinent in examining the fraught question of political engagement in relation to modernism. The diverging views of Lukács, Brecht and Adorno on the historical purpose of the avant-garde, Sartre's attempt to bridge existentialism and dialectical materialism through the concept of scarcity, and Adorno's understanding of modern art as both autonomous and bound to society provide a framework for addressing the politics of the absurd and primitive leanings within European modernism.

It may be objected that contextualising Beckett's relationship with Ireland in relation to post-war reconsiderations of the legacy of Hegelian idealism obfuscates certain aspects of the postcolonial environment formative of the writer.[1] However, the idea of an Irish Beckett is a configuration that is, in equal measures, theoretical and historical, and Beckett's multivalence as a figure of innovation and obscurity should be understood in precisely the same way. When we look at Beckett's work in an Irish literary tradition, dissociating theory from history leads to insurmountable difficulties in contextualisation: indeed, the manner in which Beckett constructs minimalist forms by drawing on an Irish literary legacy also reveals the locus at which much of modern critical theory collapses. Such a breakdown necessitates adequate historicisation in conjunction with the assumptions that surround it. What remains at stake is an assumed alignment between language, culture and writing, an affiliation which continues to dominate much theoretical thinking about twentieth-century literature. This alignment dissolves entirely in relation to Beckett: traditional postcolonial frameworks begin to display signs of fatigue when one acknowledges Beckett's European contexts and avant-garde leanings, due in no small degree to the absence of a theoretical discourse able to accommodate the bilingual form of his work, as well as its simultaneous engagement with French and Irish counter-colonial cultures.

If such theoretical discourse is not yet in existence, the thought of Adorno certainly provides a platform for beginning to imagine how such an understanding might emerge. Indeed, Adorno's perspective on Beckett's historicity illuminates the questions of artistic autonomy and artistic responsibility crystallised around Beckett's relationship to Irishness. For Adorno, Beckett's work remains dependent upon a meaning which it has itself obscured, a phenomenon which results from the way in which his writing both relates to and resists the historical moment that governs its very generation.[2] Such philosophical interpretation is germane to the manner in which Beckett negotiates and dispenses with questions of artistic responsibility central to Revival and post-Revival literature, precisely as a consequence of his refusal to adhere to established aesthetic practices in representing Irish history and culture. Beckett's stance results in the emergence of a peculiar conundrum: the more he attempted to distance himself from an art reflective of social changes in the tradition of Revivalist literature, the more he found himself adopting modes of representation that rely precisely on the articulation of this distance. The Irish trivia scattered throughout his texts are signifiers of this conundrum, their specificity proving insufficient to signify anything other than Beckett's simultaneous engagement with and disengagement from the historical and cultural contexts that fashioned his development as a writer. Such minute linguistic, cultural and historical particulars find multiple and varied lives during the genesis of the texts themselves and, as such, constitute the moment from which Beckett's writing draws its energy.

Abbreviations and Notations

Print Sources

AT: Theodor Adorno, *Aesthetic Theory*, ed. Gretel Adorno and Rolf Tiedemann, trans., ed., and introd. Robert Hullot-Kentor (Minneapolis: U of Minnesota P, 1997).

CDR: Jean-Paul Sartre, *Critique of Dialectical Reason*, Vol. 1: *Theory of Practical Ensembles*, trans. Alan Sheridan-Smith, ed. Jonathan Rée (London: Humanities, 1976).

CDW: Samuel Beckett, *Complete Dramatic Works* (London: Faber, 1990).

DF: James Knowlson, *Damned to Fame: The Life of Samuel Beckett* (London: Bloomsbury, 1996).

Disjecta: Samuel Beckett, *Disjecta: Miscellaneous Writings and a Dramatic Fragment*, ed. Ruby Cohn (London: John Calder, 2001).

EMolloy: Samuel Beckett, *Molloy*, in *Molloy, Malone Dies, The Unnamable* (London: John Calder, 1994).

FMolloy: Samuel Beckett, *Molloy* (Paris: Editions de Minuit, 1951).

Murphy: Samuel Beckett, *Murphy* (London: John Calder, 1993).

NABS: Samuel Beckett and Alan Schneider, *No Author Better Served: The Correspondence of Samuel Beckett and Alan Schneider*, ed. Maurice Harmon (Cambridge, MA: Harvard UP, 1998).

SBC: John Pilling, *A Samuel Beckett Chronology* (Basingstoke, Eng.: Palgrave Macmillan, 2006).

TUE: Theodor W. Adorno, "Trying to Understand *Endgame*", trans. Michael J. Jones, *The Adorno Reader*, ed. Brian O'Connor (Oxford: Blackwell, 2000) 319–52.

Archival Collections

BNF: Bibliothèque Nationale de Paris.

CLC HRHRC: Carlton Lake Collection of Samuel Beckett, Harry Ransom Humanities Research Center, University of Texas at Austin.

HRHRC: Harry Ransom Humanities Research Center, University of Texas at Austin.

RUL: Reading University Library.

SBC HRHRC: Samuel Beckett Collection, Harry Ransom Humanities Research Center, University of Texas at Austin.

TCD: Trinity College Dublin.

Translations and Excerpts from Samuel Beckett's Letters, Notebooks and Manuscripts

All translations between square brackets are my own, unless otherwise indicated. Excerpts from Beckett's manuscripts are noted as follows: additions and emendations to the bulk of the text (which, in the manuscripts, generally feature above the revised line or on the side of the page closer to the altered passage) are signalled by square brackets and inserted within the text. An insertion within an insertion is also noted by square brackets. Passages which were deleted by Beckett and are not fully legible under the pen or pencil marks are marked 'X'. Deleted passages which have remained legible are crossed by a line. The words that I was unable to identify with certainty are noted by a question mark.

Notes

Introduction

1. "Fitzgerald Addresses Assembly of Aosdána", *Irish Times* 15 April 1983: 7; "Beckett Greets Aosdana Honour 'with a Shy Nod'", *Irish Times* 14 April 1986: 9.
2. The aim of the collection is to stress that Beckett's imagination worked within precise historical structures; see Seán Kennedy, "Introduction to *Historicising Beckett*", *Samuel Beckett Today* 15 (2005): 21–27.
3. "Irish Literary Revival", the term used in this book to refer to what is otherwise known as the Irish Renaissance or the Gaelic Revival, is related to a wide array of social, political and cultural factors influencing Beckett's formative years as a writer. My understanding of the period is indebted to recent critical analyses by Sinéad Garrigan Mattar, Michael McAteer, Anthony Roche and Gregory Castle, who contextualise its literature in ways that are fitting to this study.
4. This issue is central to the debates surrounding the development of modernism; for instance, Peter Lasko's *The Expressionist Roots of Modernism* argues that modern art developed through the agencies of German and Eastern European artists.
5. *CDW* 175.
6. *CDW* 173.
7. See Peter Bürger's *Theory of the Avant-Garde*. The aesthetic of the trace discussed in the present study may bring to mind Derridean models of dissemination and erasure; however, such models, being gendered in their original French, prove unsuitable here, given the historical and political tenor of Beckett's work: applied to an Irish context, this gendering of theoretical terms is problematic, due to its disjunction with modes of representation of nation and race which are *historically* gendered in specific ways.
8. Deirdre Bair, *Samuel Beckett: A Biography* (London: Jonathan Cape, 1978) 594. Magee was born in Armagh, Northern Ireland, and found great success in British theatre and film.
9. Samuel Beckett to Bertie Ahern, 22 February 1987, RUL MS 4937.
10. Gerry Dukes, "Beckett's Synge-Song: The Revised *Godot* Revisited", *Journal of Beckett Studies* 4.2 (1995): 103–4. Dukes also addresses this issue in his biography of Beckett.
11. For further comments, see Peter Boxall, "Samuel Beckett: Towards a Political Reading", *Irish Studies Review* 10.2 (2002): 161; Ronan MacDonald, *Tragedy and Irish Literature* (Basingstoke, Eng.: Palgrave, 2002) 141; Richard Kearney, "Beckett: The End of the Story?", *Transitions*, ed. Richard Kearney (Manchester: Manchester UP, 1988) 58.
12. Boxall 161.
13. Mary Junker's *Beckett: The Irish Dimension* discusses Beckett's use of Irish English but fails to register the critical or conceptual difficulties inherent

in historicised readings of Beckett and, indeed, Beckett's peculiar position within the Irish canon.
14. John Harrington, *The Irish Beckett* (New York: Syracuse UP, 1991) 108.
15. Vivian Mercier, *The Irish Comic Tradition* (Oxford: Oxford UP, 1962) 75–76.
16. Vivian Mercier, "Ireland/The World: Beckett's Irishness", *Yeats, Joyce, and Beckett*, ed. Kathleen McGrory and John Unterecker (Lewisburg: Bucknell UP, 1976) 147.
17. Richard Ellmann, "Samuel Beckett: Nayman of Noland", *Four Dubliners* (London: Hamilton, 1987) 79–104; Patrick Murray, *The Tragic Comedian* (Cork: Mercier, 1970) 17.
18. James Mays, "Beckett and the Irish", *Hibernia* 33.21 (1969): 14.
19. James Knowlson, *Samuel Beckett: An Exhibition* (London: Turret, 1971) 20.
20. Critics have commented upon Beckett's ambivalent position in postcolonial readings of Irish literature; see, for instance, Anna McMullan, "Irish/Postcolonial Beckett", *Palgrave Advances in Samuel Beckett Studies*, ed. Lois Oppenheim (Basingstoke, Eng.: Palgrave Macmillan, 2004) 89–109.
21. Clare Carroll and Patricia King's *Ireland and Postcolonial Theory*, for instance, includes a concise analysis of the postcolonial-revisionist debate. It is worth noting that the critical propensity to consider postcolonial theory the only suitable framework for the study of Irishness has been subject to criticism; see Stephen Howe, *Ireland and Empire: Colonial Legacies in Irish History and Culture* (Oxford: Oxford UP, 2000); Colin Graham, "Post-Colonial Theory and Kiberd's 'Ireland'", *Irish Review* 19 (1996): 62–7.
22. Seamus Deane, *Celtic Revivals* (London: Faber, 1985) 131.
23. Deane 130.
24. Declan Kiberd's emphasis on writing as an act of resistance derives from Frantz Fanon's *Black Skin, White Masks*, which presents language as the main site of interaction between coloniser and colonised and, hence, as a site of oppression. For Fanon, any attempt to dissect the mechanisms of language turns language against itself and enables political resistance.
25. Declan Kiberd, *Irish Classics* (London: Granta, 2000) 590–91.
26. David Lloyd, *Anomalous States* (Dublin: Lilliput, 1993) 56.
27. Leslie Hill has pointed out that critical approaches to the idea of Beckett and the political have remained subsumed in post-war debates about commitment, between Adorno and Lukács in particular. Here, certain strands within those debates are used to historicise the tensions surrounding Beckett's anti-essentialist stance and his response to understandings of Irishness emerging from the Revival period.
28. *AT* 24.
29. Anthony Cronin, *Samuel Beckett: The Last Modernist* (London: Flamingo, 1997) 187–88.
30. John Pilling, *Samuel Beckett* (London: Routledge and Kegan Paul, 1976) 1.
31. Beckett's relationship with Joyce has been well documented; see, for instance, Richard Ellmann, *James Joyce*, 2nd edn. (New York: Oxford UP, 1982); Phyllis Carey and Ed Jewinski, eds, *Re: Joyce'n Beckett* (New York: Fordham UP, 1992); Barbara Reich Gluck, *Beckett and Joyce: Friendship and Fiction* (Lewisburg: Bucknell UP, 1979); Kevin Dettmar, "The Joyce That Beckett Built", *Beckett and Beyond*, ed. Bruce Stewart (Gerrards Cross, Eng.: Colin Smythe, 1999) 78–92.

32. *DF* 126.
33. This was a rumour that Beckett heard through Percy (Arland) Ussher and reported to MacGreevy. Beckett to MacGreevy, Saturday [August 1932], letter 31, TCD MS 10402. All excerpts from this correspondence correspond to this manuscript number and are hereafter identified by date and letter number.
34. Beckett to MacGreevy, 11 March 1931, letter 18.
35. Beckett to MacGreevy, 18 August 1934, letter 61.
36. "German Letter of 1937", *Disjecta* 51. This abbreviation recurs in notebooks and letters of the same period.
37. Beckett to MacGreevy, 14 [? July 1932], letter 27. James Mays has pointed out that Eamon de Valera's nationalist project is crucial for understanding Beckett's revulsion towards Ireland; see Mays, "Young Beckett's Irish Roots", *Irish University Review* 14.1 (Spring 1984): 32.
38. Beckett to MacGreevy, 7 September 1933, letter 54.
39. Israel Shenker, "An Interview with Beckett", *Samuel Beckett: The Critical Heritage*, ed. Laurence Graver and Raymond Federman (New York: Routledge, 1979) 147. Critics have expressed doubts concerning the reliability of Shenker's interview; see S.E. Gontarski, *The Intent of Undoing in Samuel Beckett's Dramatic Texts* (Bloomington: Indiana UP, 1985) 6; Ed Jewinski, "James Joyce and Samuel Beckett: From Epiphany to Anti-Epiphany", *Re: Joyce'n Beckett*, ed. Phyllis Carey and Ed Jewinski (New York: Fordham UP, 1992) 164.
40. The complex dynamics of their correspondence have been discussed; see, for instance, Seán Kennedy, "Beckett Reviewing MacGreevy: A Reconsideration", *Irish University Review* 35.2 (2005): 273–87; Susan Schreibman, "'between us the big words were never necessary': Samuel Beckett and Thomas MacGreevy: A Life in Letters", *Samuel Beckett: A Passion for Paintings*, ed. Fionnuala Croke (Dublin: National Gallery of Ireland, 2006) 34–43.
41. Beckett to MacGreevy, 10 November 1951, letter 180.
42. Eamon de Valera, "The Ireland We Dreamed Of", 17 March 1943, *Speeches and Statements by Eamon de Valera, 1917–73*, ed. Maurice Moynihan (Dublin: Gill & Macmillan, 1980) 466.
43. Flann O'Brien, *The Best of Myles: A Selection from 'Cruiskeen Lawn'*, ed. Kevin O'Nolan (London: MacGibbon and Kee, 1968) 382.
44. O'Brien's column appeared wholly in Irish at first and was then published in English on alternate days. The collection *The Best of Myles* covers the first five years of the column and corresponds roughly to the Second World War; however, no dates are given. The reasons underlying this editorial choice are clarified in the introduction.
45. Beckett greatly appreciated O'Brien's humour, as he suggested to Maeve Binchy; see Binchy, "Beckett Finally Gets Down to Work – As the Actors Take a Break", *Irish Times* 14 May 1980: 7. Binchy's article was not authorised and infuriated Beckett; see *DF* 668.
46. Samuel Beckett, *Texts for Nothing* (London: John Calder, 1999) 19.
47. See Beckett's letter to Anne Clissmann, 27 December 1967, quoted in Clissmann, *Flann O'Brien: A Critical Introduction to His Writings* (Dublin: Gill & Macmillan, 1975) 310. It is likely that the meeting took place in 1935 or 1936; Clissmann indicates only that it took place at Niall Montgomery's house in Dublin.

48. See James Knowlson, *Beckett Remembering/Remembering Beckett: A Centenary Celebration*, ed. James and Elizabeth Knowlson (New York: Arcade, 2006) 30; *SBC* 227.
49. Sean O'Casey, *Inishfallen, Fare Thee Well, Autobiographies II* (London: Macmillan, 1963) 86, 114.
50. See O'Casey letters to Anthony Perry of 21 December 1951 and to Margaret Buller of 14 April 1958, *The Letters of Sean O'Casey*, Vol. 3, ed. David Krause (Washington, DC: Catholic U of America P, 1989) 230, 592.
51. The two writers never met, but a meeting was planned in 1958; see O'Casey's letter to Robert Hogan, 12 July 1958, *The Letters of Sean O'Casey*, Vol. 3 614.
52. Nancy Cunard, *Authors Take Sides on the Spanish War* (London: Left Review, 1937) n. pag.
53. John Cooney, *John Charles McQuaid, Ruler of Catholic Ireland* (Dublin: O'Brien, 1999) 329.
54. See O'Casey's letter to the *Irish Times*, 17 February 1958, *The Letters of Sean O'Casey*, Vol. 3 540. O'Casey's response to McQuaid is documented in Christopher Murray, "O'Casey's *The Drums of Father Ned* in Context", *A Century of Irish Drama: Widening the Stage*, ed. Stephen Watt, Eileen Morgan and Shakir Mustafa (Bloomington: Indiana UP, 2000) 117–29.
55. Beckett to Carol Simpson, 27 February 1958, letter 63, TCD MS 10731.
56. Beckett to Alan Simpson, 19 July 1956, letter 36, TCD MS 10731.
57. The circumstances leading to the lifting of Beckett's Irish ban were slightly haphazard; see *DF* 465–66.
58. Beckett to Jack McGowran, 12 September 1965, SBC HRHRC MS 9.3.
59. See Ulick O'Connor, *Oliver St John Gogarty: A Poet and His Times* (Dublin: O'Brien, 1999) 276–81.
60. See Beckett's reply to Ruby Cohn's questionnaire in her letter of 4 August 1975, letter 116, RUL MS 5100.
61. Beckett to Jacoba van Velde, 30 January 1960, letter 63, BNF MS 19794.
62. Beckett quoted in Colin Duckworth, *Angels of Darkness* (London: Allen and Unwin, 1972) 18.
63. See W.J. McCormack, *From Burke to Beckett*, 2nd ed. (Cork: Cork UP, 1994) 386–91.
64. *Disjecta* 19; Beckett to MacGreevy, Monday [? 1929–30], letter 2; *DF* 133.
65. The complex relationship that Beckett's writing maintains to the idea of the political necessitates adequate contextualisation, as Leslie Hill and, more recently, Peter Boxall have pointed out.
66. See, for instance, Beckett to Schneider, 6 March 1968, *NABS* 215; Charles Juliet, *Conversations with Samuel Beckett and Bram van Velde*, trans. Janey Tucker (Leiden: Academic P Leiden, 1995) 159.
67. *DF* 492–95.
68. See Madeleine Chapsal's interview with Sartre, "The Purposes of Writing", *Between Existentialism and Marxism*, by Jean-Paul Sartre, trans. John Matthews (London: NLB, 1974) 15.
69. Fredric Jameson, "Reflections in Conclusion", *Aesthetics and Politics*, by Theodor W. Adorno, Ernst Bloch, Walter Benjamin, Bertolt Brecht and Georg Lukács, ed. Ronald Taylor (London: NLB, 1977) 197.
70. Theodor Adorno, "Commitment", trans. Francis McDonagh, *Aesthetics and Politics*, ed. Ronald Taylor (London: NLB, 1977) 183.

170 Notes

71. Adorno, "Commitment" 180–81.
72. Adorno, "Commitment" 191.
73. Adorno, "Commitment" 194.
74. *AT* 319.
75. *AT* 121.
76. *AT* 154.
77. *AT* 242, 256, 347.
78. *AT* 153.

1 Beckett and the Irish Literary Revival

1. Geoffrey Perrin interviewed by James Knowlson, *Beckett Remembering* 30.
2. Beckett's admiration for *At the Hawk's Well*, which develops from the conventions of Japanese Noh drama, is evident in *Happy Days*, where Winnie refers to the first line of Yeats's play. Scholars have commented upon Beckett's keen interest in Yeats's work: see Ellmann, "Nayman of Noland" 100; Katharine Worth, *Samuel Beckett's Theatre: Life Journeys* (Oxford: Clarendon, 1999) 133; *SBC* 153. *Oedipus the King* was first produced at the Abbey in December 1926, *Oedipus at Colonus* in September 1927 and *The Words upon the Windowpane* in November 1930, when Beckett was teaching at Trinity; see Lennox Robinson, *Ireland's Abbey Theatre: A History, 1899–1951* (Port Washington, NY: Kennikat, 1968) 156.
3. *DF* 56–57, 716 n55.
4. Beckett interviewed by Knowlson, *Beckett Remembering* 30, 268. However, Knowlson did not include this part of the interview in his biography and it remained unpublished until 2006.
5. For a list of the plays that premiered at the Abbey during these years, see Robinson 208–11; Hugh Hunt, *The Abbey: Ireland's National Theatre, 1904–1978* (Dublin: Gill & Macmillan, 1979) 254–59.
6. Beckett to MacGreevy, 11 November 1932, letter 37.
7. Bair 47–48; *DF* 57.
8. Bair 250.
9. Bair 236.
10. *DF* 123–25; Bair 235.
11. Yeats, Synge and the Abbey ranked among Beckett's favourite topics of conversation at the end of his life. See Anne Atik, *How It Was* (London: Faber, 2001) 119.
12. Beckett, letter to George Reavey, 5 August 1938, George Reavey Papers, HRHRC [unnumbered]. I thank Michael McAteer for passing on this reference to me.
13. John Montague, *Company: A Life* (London: Duckworth, 2001) 145.
14. Beckett to Arland Ussher, 17 February 1947, SBC HRHRC MS 9.5.
15. Beckett to Mary Manning Howe, 14 July 1955, SBC HRHRC MS 8.10. *In Sand* premiered at the Abbey in April 1949; see Robinson 212–13.
16. *CDW* 140; Jack B. Yeats, *In Sand*, *The Collected Plays of Jack B. Yeats*, ed. Robin Skelton (London: Secker and Warburg, 1971) 334.
17. Knowlson, *Samuel Beckett: An Exhibition* 14.
18. Garry O'Connor, *Sean O'Casey: A Life* (London: Paladin, 1989) 366.

19. The plot of Balderston and Squire's *Berkeley Square* was inspired by Henry James's posthumously published novel. Beckett to MacGreevy, 29 January 1936, letter 87.
20. Beckett to MacGreevy, 15 May 1935, letter 76.
21. Beckett interviewed by Knowlson, *Beckett Remembering* 30.
22. Knowlson, *Beckett Remembering* 30.
23. Micheál Ó hAodha, *Theatre in Ireland* (Oxford: Blackwell, 1974) 127.
24. Beckett to MacGreevy, 18 October 1932, letter 34.
25. Beckett to MacGreevy, 21 November 1932, letter 38.
26. Beckett to MacGreevy, 11 November 1932, letter 37. Beckett's friend A.J. (Con) Leventhal was part of the cast of *The Wild Duck*; see the cast list in Robinson 210.
27. Beckett to MacGreevy, 5 October 1930, letter 11.
28. See Joyce's "The Day of the Rabblement" (1901) and his review of Lady Gregory's *Poets and Dreamers* (1903). Joyce's response to the Revival has been thoroughly researched; here, my intention is merely to stress that Beckett's stance recalls Joyce's.
29. Beckett to MacGreevy, 5 October 1930, letter 11.
30. See the cast list in W.B. Yeats, *The Collected Works of W.B. Yeats*, Vol. 2: *The Plays*, ed. David R. Clark and Rosalind E. Clark (Basingstoke, Eng.: Palgrave, 2001) 906.
31. Beckett to MacGreevy, 8 August 1934, letter 60. The legibility of the word "thermolater" posed problems and I thank Mark Nixon for his help.
32. Jorge Luis Borges in an interview with Richard Kearney, *Transitions* 52; Vivian Mercier, *Beckett/Beckett* (New York: Oxford UP, 1977) xii.
33. For a discussion of these influences, see Katharine Worth, *The Irish Drama of Europe from Yeats to Beckett* (London: Athlone, 1978).
34. For a detailed overview of the cultural and historical contexts of the avant-garde, see Jean Weisgerber et al., *Les Avant-gardes littéraires au XXème siècle*, Vol. 1: *Histoire* (Budapest: Akadémiai Kiadó, 1984) 22–24, 78–83.
35. In articles such as "Plans and Methods" and "The Irish Literary Theatre" (1899), Yeats argued for the use of "Irish subjects", by which he meant, essentially, Irish folklore and legends.
36. See, for instance, the debates between John Eglinton, W.B. Yeats, AE and William Larminie in *Literary Ideals in Ireland* (1899).
37. If the experimental character of some of the literature produced between 1880 and 1930 was formerly seen as secondary, recent critical studies stress the uneasy circumstances under which this national literature emerged and the prevalence of innovative art forms; see Ben Levitas, *The Theatre of Nation: Irish Drama and Cultural Nationalism 1890–1916* (Oxford: Oxford UP, 2002); Michael McAteer, *Standish O'Grady, AE and Yeats: History, Politics, Culture* (Dublin: Irish Academic P, 2002); Sinéad Garrigan Mattar, *Primitivism, Science, and the Irish Revival* (Oxford: Oxford UP, 2004).
38. Terry Eagleton, "The Archaic Avant-Garde", *Heathcliff and the Great Hunger: Studies in Irish Culture* (London: Verso, 1995) 299, 303, 315.
39. For a review of the genesis of the almanac and the preceding exhibitions, see Wassily Kandinsky, *Complete Writings on Art*, ed. Kenneth C. Lindsay and Peter Vergo (New York: Da Capo, 1994) 109–11, 227–28.
40. Kandinsky, *Complete Writings on Art* 222, 746.

41. Lady Augusta Gregory, *Our Irish Theatre* (Gerrards Cross, Eng.: Colin Smythe, 1972) 20–21.
42. Yeats, *Explorations*, selected by Mrs W.B. Yeats (London: Macmillan, 1962) 182.
43. Ó hAodha 86.
44. Gregory, *Our Irish Theatre* 62.
45. O'Brien requested the suppression of curse words and of the prostitute Rosie Redmond; see his letter to O'Casey, 5 September 1925, *The Letters of Sean O'Casey*, Vol. 1, ed. David Krause (London: Cassell and Macmillan, 1975) 144–45.
46. See Antoinette Quinn, *Patrick Kavanagh* (Dublin: Gill & Macmillan, 2001) 82.
47. Yeats, *Explorations* 254, 257.
48. See Liam Miller, *The Noble Drama of W.B. Yeats* (Dublin: Dolmen, 1977) 231.
49. On Beckett, Yeats and Noh theatre, see, for instance, Keiko Kirishima, "Le Théâtre de Beckett et le théâtre nô", *Critique* 96.519–20 (1990): 691; Christopher Murray and Masaru Sekine, eds, *Yeats and the Noh: A Comparative Study* (Gerrards Cross, Eng.: Colin Smythe, 1990); Yasunari Takahashi, "The Ghost Trio: Beckett, Yeats, and Noh", *Cambridge Review* 107.2295 (1986): 172–76; Minako Okamuro, "Alchemical Dances in Beckett and Yeats", *Samuel Beckett Today/Aujourd'hui* 14 (2004): 87–104.
50. Beckett, "Before *Play*", RUL MS 1227/7/16/6, f. 1.
51. Beckett, "Before *Play*", f. 1; *Play*, RUL MS 1528/3, f. 1; *CDW* 307.
52. *DF* 517.
53. W.B. Yeats, *Collected Plays*, 2nd ed. (New York: Macmillan, 1952) 633.
54. In particular to George Devine, director of the Royal Court Theatre; see *Disjecta* 112.
55. Yeats, *Collected Plays* 703.
56. See Worth, *The Irish Drama of Europe* 99, 110.
57. Yeats, *Explorations* 87.
58. Liam Miller remarks upon this feature of the Noh; see Miller 205.
59. O'Casey, *The Letters of Sean O'Casey*, Vol. 1 xxix.
60. *Disjecta* 82.
61. Sean O'Casey, *Three Dublin Plays* (London: Faber, 1998) 148.
62. *Disjecta* 82.
63. O'Casey, *Three Dublin Plays* 126.
64. *Disjecta* 82.
65. *SBC* 47–48; *DF* 188.
66. According to James Knowlson, by using the name "Belis" Beckett was going back three generations on the side of his mother to his great-grandfather, called Belas (*DF* 3). However, given the immediate context of the article, Andrey Bely is more likely to have been a source of inspiration.
67. See Gleb Struve, "M. Andrey Bely – The Russian Symbolist Movement", *The Times* 26 January 1934, London ed.: D14+.
68. See, for instance, Andrey Bely, "The Emblematics of Meaning", *Selected Essays of Andrey Bely*, ed. and trans. Steven Cassedy (Berkeley: U of California P, 1985) 147–53.
69. See Peter Lasko, *The Expressionist Roots of Modernism* (Manchester: Manchester UP, 2003) 101–3.
70. See the bibliography in J.D. Elsworth, *Andrey Bely: A Critical Study of the Novels* (Cambridge: Cambridge UP, 1983) 246–49.

71. *SBC* 56; Bair 216. Eisenstein never read Beckett's letter; in 1936, he was facing enormous difficulties due to illness and attacks from colleagues. The letter was found much later by his assistant on *Bezhin Meadow* and is held at Reading University Library (RUL MS 5040).
72. See, for instance, George Reavey, "Le Mot et le monde d'André Biely et de James Joyce", *Roman* 2 (1951): 103–11.
73. Beckett's letter is quoted in Reavey's Translator's Note, *The Silver Dove*, by Andrey Biely, trans. George Reavey (New York: Grove, 1974) xi.
74. Trotsky's attacks upon Bely's thought were particularly virulent; see J.D. Elsworth, *Andrey Bely* (Letchworth, Eng.: Bradda, 1972) 107; Elsworth, *Andrey Bely: A Critical Study of the Novels* (Cambridge: Cambridge UP, 1983) 4–5, 220–22.
75. See George Reavey, Introduction, *The Silver Dove* xli–xlii.
76. Beckett to MacGreevy, 8 September 1934, letter 63.
77. Beckett to MacGreevy, 5 June 1936, letter 97.
78. Beckett to MacGreevy, 8 August 1934, letter 60.
79. See Raymond Federman and John Fletcher, *Samuel Beckett – His Works and His Critics: An Essay in Bibliography* (Berkeley: U of California P, 1970) 105.
80. Yeats's definition of Irish literature was, in the 1890s, rather limiting; see "Professor Dowden and Irish Literature – II", *Uncollected Prose by W.B. Yeats*, Vol. I, comp. and ed. John P. Frayne (New York: Columbia UP, 1970) 352.
81. *Disjecta* 70.
82. *Disjecta* 71.
83. James Joyce, *Ulysses*, ed. Hans Walter Gabler, Wolfhard Steppe and Claus Melchior (London: Bodley Head, 1986) 151. This is a reference to Yeats's poem "A Cradle Song"; see Don Gifford, ed., *Ulysses Annotated*, 2nd ed. (London: U of California P, 1988) 194 n9.28.
84. Joyce, *Ulysses* 152.
85. Joyce, *The Critical Writings of James Joyce*, ed. Ellsworth Mason and Richard Ellmann (London: Faber, 1959) 71.
86. Sinéad Mooney, "Kicking against the Thermolaters", *Samuel Beckett Today* 15 (2005): 33–34. Beckett's article has engendered lively critical debate; see, for instance, Terence Brown, "Ireland, Modernism and the 1930s", *Modernism and Ireland*, ed. Patricia Coughlan and Alex Davis (Cork: Cork UP, 1995) 30; Patricia Coughlan, "'The Poetry Is Another Pair of Sleeves': Beckett, Ireland and Modernist Lyric Poetry", *Modernism and Ireland* 173–208; Harrington, *The Irish Beckett* 33.
87. J.C.C. Mays argues that Beckett is correct in identifying MacGreevy as a transitional figure in his essay "How Is MacGreevy a Modernist?", *Modernism and Ireland* 123.
88. *Disjecta* 74.
89. *Disjecta* 75.
90. Beckett to MacGreevy, 1 November 1933, letter 56.
91. Beckett to MacGreevy, 9 January 1936, letter 85.
92. This is a recurrent phenomenon in Beckett's early writings, which John Harrington has carefully documented; Harrington points out that Yeats appears in *More Pricks Than Kicks*, that *Watt* contains a revision of a tale recorded in *Irish Fairy and Folk Tales*, and that *Molloy* is indebted to a story

from *The Celtic Twilight* entitled "The Last Gleeman"; see Harrington, "'That Red Branch Bum Was the Camel's Back': Beckett's Use of Yeats in *Murphy*", *Eire-Ireland* 15.3 (1980): 86.
93. *Disjecta* 70.
94. *Disjecta* 71. The original line read: "We were the last romantics – chose for theme/Traditional sanctity and loveliness"; see W.B. Yeats, *The Poems* (London: Everyman, 1994) 294.
95. Yeats, *The Poems* 302. Here, Beckett replaces Yeats's question mark with an exclamation mark.
96. *Murphy* 52.
97. Beckett reread Yeats's *Collected Poems* often and gave his poetry particular attention during the genesis of *Happy Days*; see Beckett to MacGreevy, 9 January 1961, letter 235. Among Beckett's favourite poems, Anne Atik mentions "Sailing to Byzantium", "Under Ben Bulben", "Girl's Song", "Friends", "A Drinking Song" and "The Old Men Admiring Themselves in the Water"; see Atik 59–62, 68–70. For further comments on Beckett's admiration for Yeats's poetry and plays, see Worth, *Samuel Beckett's Theatre: Life Journeys* 133; *DF* 643; Juliet, *Conversations with Samuel Beckett and Bram van Velde* 137; *SBC* 220.
98. This particular poem was endowed with incredible strength for Beckett; see Atik 68; Gerry Dukes, *Samuel Beckett* (Woodstock, NY: Overlook, 2002) 136; *SBC* 230.
99. *CDW* 422.
100. Yeats, *The Poems* 243.
101. See the drafts of *...but the clouds...* numbered RUL MS 1553/2, f. 10; RUL MS 1553/3, f. 3; RUL MS 1553/4, f. 5.
102. Richard Ellmann dates this meeting to 1932; see "Nayman of Noland" 98. However, John Pilling notes that Beckett dated the meeting to 1934 in conversation with Stravinsky some forty years later; see *SBC* 39, 159.
103. Ellmann, "Nayman of Noland" 98.
104. Beckett to H.O. White, 14 April 1957, letter 15, TCD MS 3777. For a comparative study of Beckett, W.B. Yeats and Jack B. Yeats, see Gordon S. Armstrong, *Samuel Beckett, W.B. Yeats, and Jack Yeats: Images and Words* (Lewisburg: Bucknell UP; London: Associated U Presses, 1990).
105. Beckett's letter to MacGreevy of 5 January 1933 is reproduced in Frederik N. Smith, *Beckett's Eighteenth Century* (Basingstoke, Eng.: Palgrave, 2002) 29. Nevertheless, the story about Stella's tower in "Fingal" is entirely inaccurate, as John Harrington points out; see Harrington, *The Irish Beckett* 61.
106. Beckett, "Alba", *Dublin Magazine* (October–December 1931): 4; W.B. Yeats, "Introduction to *The Words upon the Window-pane*", *Dublin Magazine* October–December 1931: 5–19.
107. This play is the only instance where Yeats adheres closely to a realistic form. The play, however, has distinctly cinematic qualities and was adapted for the screen by Mary McGuckian in 1984.
108. Concerning Swift's influence on Yeats, see Douglas N. Archibald, "*The Words upon the Window-pane* and Yeats's Encounter with Jonathan Swift", *Yeats and the Theatre*, ed. Robert O'Driscoll and Lorna Reynolds (Basingstoke, Eng.: Macmillan, 1975) 176–214.

109. Katharine Worth, "*The Words upon the Window-pane*: A Female Tragedy", *Yeats Annual* 10, ed. Warwick Gould (Basingstoke, Eng.: Macmillan, 1993) 138.
110. Yeats, *Collected Plays* 609.
111. Beckett quoted in Knowlson, *Beckett Remembering* 252. This suggests that the female figure of ...*but the clouds*... may be a generic image for Stella, Maud Gonne and Molly Allgood – to whom Synge used to sign his letters "Your old tramp".
112. Quoted in Anne Saddlemyer, Foreword, *The Playboy of the Western World and Other Plays*, by John Millington Synge (Oxford: Oxford UP, 1995) xvi.
113. J.M. Synge, *The Playboy of the Western World and Other Plays* 61.
114. J.M. Synge, *The Playboy of the Western World and Other Plays* 79.
115. Beckett stated in 1972 that he had seen all the Synge revivals at the Abbey. See *DF* 57; Knowlson, "Beckett and John Millington Synge", *Frescoes of the Skull*, ed. James Knowlson and John Pilling (London: John Calder, 1979) 259. A thorough examination of Synge's drama in the context of the language debates may be found in Declan Kiberd, *Synge and the Irish Language*.
116. *CDW* 194.
117. *CDW* 194.
118. *CDW* 183.
119. *CDW* 176.
120. *CDW* 194.
121. *CDW* 187.
122. *CDW* 183.
123. *CDW* 184.
124. *CDW* 195.
125. *CDW* 172.
126. Dukes, *Samuel Beckett* 47–48; *SBC* 52.
127. Julia Carlson, ed., *Banned in Ireland* (London: Routledge, 1990) 4.
128. Michael Adams, *Censorship* (Dublin: Scepter, 1968) 48, 71; F.S.L. Lyons, *Ireland since the Famine*, 2nd ed. (London: Fontana, 1985) 688.
129. Adams 64, 71.
130. Beckett to MacGreevy, 13 [? September–October 1932], letter 32.
131. See Beckett to MacGreevy, Saturday [August 1932], letter 31; Tuesday [? 1930–31], letter 13; 9 October 1931, letter 20.
132. Adams 247.
133. Montague 123.
134. Beckett to John Calder, 27 July 1960 [24 July 1960], SBC HRHRC MS 8.1.
135. *Disjecta* 87.
136. *Disjecta* 86–87.
137. See Elinor A. Accampo, "The Gendered Nature of Contraception in France: Neo-Malthusianism, 1900–1920", *Journal of Interdisciplinary History* 34.2 (2003): 254.
138. *Disjecta* 87.
139. *Disjecta* 87.
140. *Disjecta* 86.
141. On the cultivation of sugar beet and sugar production in the Free State, see the "Agriculture" section in *The Saorstát Eireann Official Handbook* (Dublin: Talbot, 1932); James Meenan, *The Irish Economy Since 1922*

(Liverpool: Liverpool UP, 1970); Brian Girvin, *Between Two Worlds* (Dublin: Gill & Macmillan, 1989).
142. *Disjecta* 88. It is worth nothing that greedy pigs also feature as symbols of Irish economic and cultural decline in Flann O'Brien's novel *The Poor Mouth*, in which a family home in the Gaeltacht is taken over by a colony of pigs.
143. See Joyce, *Ulysses* 158. Concerning AE's involvement with the cooperative movement, see Robert B. Davis, *George William Russell (AE)* (Boston: Twayne, 1977) 90–104; Darrell Figgis, *AE* (Dublin: Maunsel, 1916) 70; Michael McAteer, *Standish O'Grady, AE and Yeats*, 104–25; Nicholas Allen, *George Russell (AE) and the New Ireland, 1905–30* (Dublin: Four Courts, 2003).
144. James Joyce, *A Portrait of the Artist as a Young Man*, corr. Chester G. Anderson, ed. Richard Ellmann (London: Jonathan Cape, 1968) 208.
145. For a discussion of the problems faced by Joyce, see Richard Ellmann, *James Joyce* (New York: Oxford UP, 1982) 652–53; *DF* 158–59.
146. Beckett to MacGreevy, 8 August 1934, letter 60.
147. Nevertheless, Yeats's article had a direct impact on parliamentary debates: Minister for Justice Fitzgerald-Kenney commented upon Yeats's accusation of "Albigensian heresy" in the *Irish Statesman* during the debate of 18 October 1928; see *Dáil Eireann Parliamentary Debates: Official Report*, Vol. 26 (Dublin: Cahill, 1928) 597.
148. Yeats, *Uncollected Prose by W.B. Yeats*, Vol. II, ed. John P. Frayne and Colton Johnson (New York: Columbia UP, 1975) 479.
149. Yeats, *Uncollected Prose*, Vol. II 480.
150. Terence Brown, *The Life of W.B. Yeats* (Dublin: Gill & Macmillan, 1999) 338.
151. Frank Tuohy, *Yeats* (London: Macmillan, 1976) 198–99.
152. O'Casey, letter to the *Irish Times*, 11 October 1932, *The Letters of Sean O'Casey*, Vol. 1 451.
153. *Disjecta* 71–72.
154. Beckett, *More Pricks Than Kicks* (London: John Calder, 1993) 114.
155. See Lyons 502, 527, 674–76.
156. For instance, Beckett asserted in 1953 that he was not disposed to compromise when Grove Press offered to publish the novel trilogy and *Waiting for Godot* together; see *DF* 391.
157. See Beckett's letter to Schneider, 29 December 1957, *NABS* 24. For an account of the disputes surrounding the premiere of *Endgame* at the Royal Court Theatre, see *DF* 448–51.
158. According to Knowlson, "Censorship in the Saorstat" was written in approximately ten days (*DF* 189). However, it seems that Beckett spent another ten days carrying out background research; references to the article figure in his letters to Thomas MacGreevy of 8, 18 and 28 August 1934.
159. Beckett to MacGreevy, 8 August 1934, letter 60.
160. See Beckett's letters to MacGreevy of 8 August 1934 (letter 60) and of 11 August 1934 (letter 61).
161. "Censorship in the Saorstat" is largely based on the *Dáil Eireann Official Report*, Vol. 28. Beckett's comments develop from Fitzgerald-Kenney's declarations during the debates of 20 and 27 February 1929, during which

Fitzgerald-Kenney attacked *Ulysses* (95, 496). Beckett's references to Alton, Tierney and Byrne are echoes of the debate of 20 February 1929 (109, 104, 105, 240).
162. *Disjecta* 86; see the transcript relating to the debate of 27 February 1929, *Dáil Eireann Parliamentary Debates*, Vol. 28 480.
163. *Saorstát Éireann Official Handbook* 305.
164. *Saorstát Éireann Official Handbook* 18.
165. *Saorstát Éireann Official Handbook* 23.
166. *Disjecta* 87.
167. *Murphy* 47.
168. *Murphy* 69.
169. James Mays, "Mythologized Presences: *Murphy* in Its Time", *Myth and Reality in Irish Literature*, ed. Joseph Ronsley (Waterloo, ON: Wilfrid Laurier UP, 1977) 199.
170. *Murphy* 51.
171. *Murphy* 93.
172. This is reported in a letter from Beckett to Arland Ussher dated 27 March 1938, SBC HRHRC MS 9.5.
173. Review of *Murphy*, *Dublin Magazine* (April–June 1939): 98.
174. *Disjecta* 72–73.
175. *Murphy* 53.
176. Mays, "Mythologized Presences" 199.
177. Beckett to MacGreevy, 5 October 1930, letter 11.
178. Beckett to MacGreevy, 5 June 1936, letter 97.
179. Mays, "Mythologized Presences" 200, 213.
180. *Murphy* 53.
181. Joyce, *Ulysses* 6, 13.
182. *Murphy* 52.
183. Joyce, *A Portrait* 193.
184. *Disjecta* 22.
185. *Murphy* 59. Joyce's own response to the Revival has been thoroughly documented; here, I do not wish to present Stephen as a mouthpiece for Joyce's views, but to emphasise the presence of Joycean echoes in *Murphy*'s parody of the style and nationalist aims of Revivalist literature.
186. Yeats, *The Poems* 64. The poem was included as a song in the 1892 version of Yeats's *The Countess Cathleen*; see *The Variorum Edition of the Plays of W.B. Yeats*, ed. Russell K. Alspach (London: Macmillan, 1966) 65.
187. Joyce, *Ulysses* 8, 41; Gifford 18 n1.239–41; Chris Ackerley, *Demented Particulars: The Annotated* Murphy, 2nd ed. (Tallahassee: Journal of Beckett Studies Books, 2004) 111 n100.2.
188. The letter is reproduced in Sighle Kennedy, *Murphy's Bed* (Lewisburg: Bucknell UP, 1971) 251.
189. Beckett, "Whoroscope" Notebook, RUL 3000, f. 3.
190. At the end of his life, Beckett still remembered the last sentence of *A Portrait of the Artist as a Young Man* by heart; see Atik 106; Knowlson, *Beckett Remembering* 47.
191. Joyce, *A Portrait* 257.
192. *Murphy* 71.
193. *Murphy* 151.

194. Ackerley, *Demented Particulars* 208–9.
195. *Murphy* 154.
196. Kennedy, *Murphy's Bed* 270–71.
197. Ulick O'Connor, *Celtic Dawn* (London: Hamilton, 1984) 266.
198. *Disjecta* 71.
199. *Murphy* 22.
200. See, for instance, Yeats's letter to Dorothy Wellesley of 19 or 20 January 1936, *Letters on Poetry: From W.B. Yeats to Dorothy Wellesley* (London: Oxford UP, 1940) 54. Yeats wrote the introduction to Shri Purohit Swami's 1932 *An Indian Monk: His Life and Adventures* and translated the Upanishads in collaboration with him; see A. Norman Jeffares, *W.B. Yeats: A New Biography* (London: Continuum, 2001) 249; Roy Foster, *W.B. Yeats: A Life*, Vol. 2: *The Arch-Poet* (Oxford: Oxford UP, 2003) 452.
201. *Murphy* 89.
202. Beckett, *Murphy* (Paris: Editions de Minuit, 1965) 114.
203. See Joyce, *Ulysses* 416; Gifford 491 n15.2268.
204. The title of Russell's book is misquoted as *Songs by the Way*; see *Watt* (London: John Calder, 1976) 227.
205. See Beckett to MacGreevy, 1 March 1930, letter 5.
206. Beckett, "Whoroscope" Notebook, RUL 3000, f. 17.
207. *Murphy* 10.
208. Beckett, "Whoroscope" Notebook, RUL 3000, f. 62.
209. Yeats, *Collected Plays* 88. Beckett admired the final lines of the play; see Montague 145.
210. For a concise summary of the political and historical issues fashioning the literature of the period, see Terence Brown, "Cultural Nationalism 1880–1930", *The Field Day Anthology of Irish Writing*, Vol. 2, ed. Seamus Deane (Derry: Field Day, 1991) 519–20.
211. *Murphy* 28.
212. Anthony Roche, *Contemporary Irish Drama: From Beckett to McGuinness* (New York: St Martin's, 1995) 17.
213. John Turpin, "Nationalist and Unionist Ideology in the Sculpture of Oliver Sheppard and John Hughes", *Irish Review* 20 (1997): 73–74.
214. Harrington, "Beckett's Use of Yeats in *Murphy*" 91–92.
215. Yeats, *Poems* 384–85.
216. Beckett was angered by the blurb but failed to get it removed; see Bair 281, 678 n55.
217. Typescript of "MacGreevy on Jack B. Yeats", TCD MS 9072, f. 12.
218. *Disjecta* 177. The translation, in my view, is closer to the intended meaning.
219. Thomas MacGreevy, *Jack B. Yeats* (Dublin: Victor Waddington, 1945) 3.
220. Beckett to Mary Manning Howe, n.d. [December 1937], SBC HRHRC MS 8.10.
221. *Disjecta* 96.
222. *Disjecta* 89.
223. *Disjecta* 97.
224. MacGreevy, *Jack B. Yeats* 5.
225. See Harrington, *The Irish Beckett* 139. Seán Kennedy also reads MacGreevy's argument as the reformulation of Corkery's view of literature as the

repository of national consciousness; see Kennedy, " 'The Artist Who Stakes His Being Is from Nowhere': Beckett and MacGreevy on the Art of Jack B. Yeats", *Samuel Beckett Today* 14 (2004): 62–63.
226. *Disjecta* 89.
227. Eugene Jolas, "Poetry Is Vertical", *transition* 21 (March 1932): 148.
228. Typescript of "MacGreevy on Jack B. Yeats", TCD MS 9072, f. 12.
229. MacGreevy, *Jack B. Yeats* 4.
230. Typescript of "MacGreevy on Jack B. Yeats", TCD MS 9072, f. 13.
231. The square brackets indicate a blank space. Typescript of "MacGreevy on Jack B. Yeats", TCD MS 9072, f. 12.
232. Beckett's account of his experience working for the Irish Red Cross in St-Lô was destined to be recorded, and, according to Dougald McMillan, it was aired on Radio Éireann on 10 June 1946. However, no trace of the recording has been found and the script was "lost" in the archives for several decades. Whether it was censored or simply rejected because of its opacity of style and provocative tone remains uncertain. Beckett did not elucidate the matter when replying to Stan Gontarski's enquiry in 1983. See Dougald McMillan, Introduction, *As the Story Was Told: Uncollected and Late Prose*, by Samuel Beckett (London: John Calder, 1990) 13; Dukes, *Samuel Beckett* 80; Phyllis Gaffney, "Dante, Manzoni, De Valera, Beckett...? Circumlocutions of a Storekeeper: Beckett and Saint-Lô", *Irish University Review* 29.2 (1999): 268; S.E. Gontarski, ed., "Notes on the Texts", *Samuel Beckett: The Complete Short Prose, 1929–1989* (New York: Grove, 1995) 286.
233. Beckett to MacGreevy, 21 December 1945, letter 173.
234. Beckett to MacGreevy, 31 January 1938, letter 155.
235. Beckett to MacGreevy, 31 January 1938, letter 155.
236. O'Casey, *Three Dublin Plays* 85.
237. For a discussion of Fianna Fáil's orientation, see Kieran Allen, *Fianna Fáil and Irish Labour* (London: Pluto, 1997) 44–45.
238. Tim Armstrong, "Muting the Klaxon: Poetry, History and Irish Modernism", *Modernism and Ireland*, ed. Patricia Coughlan and Alex Davis (Cork: Cork UP, 1995) 57.
239. Beckett to MacGreevy, 31 January 1938, letter 155. Although Beckett's letters to MacGreevy often end in this manner, in this case the phrase is clearly used apologetically.
240. Beckett to MacGreevy, Tuesday [? 1930–31], letter 13.
241. Quoted in Peter L. Podol, *Fernando Arrabal* (Boston: Twayne, 1978) 20 [Podol's translation].
242. Beckett, "Lettre pour Arrabal", 20 September 1967, RUL MS 5044.
243. See Eva Kronik, "Interview: Arrabal", *Diacritics* 5.2 (1975): 54–60.

2 Translation as Principle of Composition

1. Beckett to MacGreevy, 18 April 1939, letter 168. Concerning Beckett's turn to French, see, for instance, *DF* 293–94; Ruby Cohn, *Back to Beckett* (Princeton: Princeton UP, 1973) 57–59.
2. Beckett (1968) quoted in Ludovic Janvier, *Samuel Beckett par lui-même* (Paris: Editions du Seuil, 1969) 18.

3. The legible passages suggest an attempt to draft a curriculum vitae or a letter of enquiry. Beckett, MS of *Molloy*, Book 3, MS 4.10, ff. 28–29.
4. Janvier, *Samuel Beckett par lui-même* 46 (Janvier's entries for "bilingue" and "contradiction" coincide); Lois Chamberlain, "'The Same Old Stories': Beckett's Poetics of Translation", *Beckett Translating/Translating Beckett*, ed. Alan Warren Friedman, Charles Rossman and Dina Scherzer (University Park: Pennsylvania State UP, 1987) 17; McCormack 18; Kiberd, *Irish Classics* 590.
5. *AT* 26.
6. Beckett's translations are listed in Federman and Fletcher, *Samuel Beckett – His Works and His Critics* 91–105. However, it remains uncertain whether Beckett translated Kandinsky's essay "Abstract and Concrete Art" into French; see *SBC* 83.
7. See Beckett's letter to John Fletcher of 21 November 1964, Papers of John Fletcher, CLC HRHRC MS 18.8, f. 1.
8. Beckett to Aidan Higgins, 24 March 1959, SBC HRHRC MS 8.9.
9. *DF* 357.
10. Beckett, "German Letter of 1937", *Disjecta* 171–72.
11. Yeats, "Samhain: 1902", *Explorations* 95.
12. Beckett, *Premier amour* (Paris: Editions de Minuit, 1970) 17–18.
13. Beckett, "L'Expulsé", *Fontaine* 10 (December 1946–January 1947): 688.
14. "L'Expulsé" 693.
15. "L'Expulsé" 693, 702.
16. This issue has remained central to debates in Beckett Studies; see, for instance, Harry Cockerham, "Bilingual Playwright", *Beckett the Shape Changer: A Symposium*, ed. Katharine Worth (London: Routledge and Kegan Paul, 1975) 143; John Fletcher, "Samuel Beckett's French", *Samuel Beckett's Art* (London: Chatto and Windus, 1967) 96–105.
17. Her husband died after his liberation from Mathausen.
18. See Knowlson's interview with Nathalie Sarraute in Knowlson, *Beckett Remembering* 84.
19. Beckett to Mania Péron, n.d. (Mardi [1953?]), CLC HRHRC MS 17.19.
20. Beckett to Mania Péron, n.d. (Mardi [1953?]), CLC HRHRC MS 17.19.
21. Beckett, *Malone meurt* (Paris: Editions de Minuit, 1951) 50.
22. Beckett, *Malone Dies*, in *Molloy, Malone Dies, The Unnamable* (London: John Calder, 1994) 202.
23. Marc Fumaroli traces the term "génie de la langue française" back to its context of origin, that of the French Enlightenment. He identifies this purist approach to language as central to French culture; see his chapter "The Genius of the French Language", *Realms of Memory*, Vol. 3, under the direction of Pierre Nora, trans. Arthur Goldhammer, ed. Lawrence D. Kritzman (New York: Columbia UP, 1998) 555–606.
24. For a discussion of the differing syntactical patterns that intervene in narrative descriptions in French and in English, see J. Darbelnet and J.P. Vinay, *Stylistique comparée du français et de l'anglais* (Paris: Didier, 1958) 59–60, 105.
25. *EMolloy* 30; *FMolloy* 43.
26. A detailed analysis of Beckett's translation choices in *Malone Dies* can be found in Linda Collinge, *Beckett traduit Beckett: De* Malone meurt à Malone Dies: *L'imaginaire en traduction* (Geneva: Droz, 2000). Aspects of Beckett's

bilingualism are discussed in Harry Cockerham, "Bilingual Playwright"; Ann Beer, "Beckett's Bilingualism", *The Cambridge Companion to Beckett*, ed. John Pilling (Cambridge: Cambridge UP, 1994) 209–21.
27. See *SBC* 141, 146.
28. *Malone meurt* 126, 179; *FMolloy* 218.
29. *FMolloy* 194.
30. *FMolloy* 218–19.
31. *EMolloy* 7.
32. *Malone Dies* 185.
33. *FMolloy* 189; *EMolloy* 123. As a child, Beckett owned a teddy bear called Baby Jack (*DF* 17).
34. *Disjecta* 73.
35. *EMolloy* 83, 89, 103.
36. *EMolloy* 29.
37. *EMolloy* 159.
38. *FMolloy* 42, 245.
39. "Bally" has also been read as a reference to Ballybrack, a Dublin suburb near Foxrock; see Janvier, *Samuel Beckett par lui-même* 137.
40. *EMolloy* 135. No mention of Blackpool is made in the French text, which remains non-specific.
41. *Malone Dies* 270.
42. Beckett, *L'Innommable* (Paris: Editions de Minuit, 1953) 148, 21.
43. Beckett, *The Unnamable*, in *Molloy, Malone Dies, The Unnamable* (London: John Calder, 1994) 300.
44. *L'Innommable* 80–81.
45. *The Unnamable* 329.
46. *The Unnamable* 408.
47. The earliest extant draft is dated 2 May 1947 and the fourth (and last) notebook 1 November 1947 (Ackerley and Gontarski 377). James Knowlson points out that the first part of the novel may have been written last (*DF* 367).
48. Ackerley and Gontarski 343.
49. Beckett, "Whoroscope" Notebook, RUL MS 3000, f. 82 (no reference is given apart from "Spenser"). The original quotation reads: "[The Irish] have another custom from the Scythians, that is the wearing of mantles and long glibs, which is a thick curled bush of hair hanging down over their eyes, and monstrously disguising them, which are both very bad and hurtful". Edmund Spenser, *A View of the Present State of Ireland*, ed. W.L. Renwick (Oxford: Clarendon, 1970) 50. It remains uncertain when this fragment was jotted down, since Beckett seems to have used the notebook over a long period. On the difficulty of dating the notebook, see John Pilling, "Dates and Difficulties in Beckett's *Whoroscope* Notebook", *Beckett the European*, ed. Dirk Van Hulle (Tallahassee: Journal of Beckett Studies Books, 2005) 39–48.
50. Beckett to MacGreevy, 4 January 1948, letter 175 [Dr. J.: Samuel Johnson].
51. Bair 212.
52. Beckett to MacGreevy, 4 August 1932, letter 28.
53. Beckett, *Murphy* 47.
54. *Malone meurt* 7; *Malone Dies* 179.
55. *L'Innommable* 172; *The Unnamable* 374.

56. *TUE* 330.
57. *Malone meurt* 168.
58. *The Unnamable* 329.
59. Albert Camus, *The Myth of Sisyphus*, trans. Justin O'Brien (London: Penguin, 2000) 13.
60. Jean-Paul Sartre, *Being and Nothingness*, trans. Hazel E. Barnes (London: Methuen, 1957) 628.
61. Sartre, *Being and Nothingness* 629.
62. Martin Esslin, *The Theatre of the Absurd*, 3rd ed. (London: Penguin, 1991) 23.
63. A. Alvarez, *Beckett* (London: Woburn, 1974) 13.
64. *TUE* 348.
65. Beckett to Schneider, 3 March 1959, *NABS* 55; Alan Levy, "The Long Wait for Godot", *Theatre Arts* 40 (1968): 34.
66. *Malone Dies* 275.
67. *Malone meurt* 189.
68. For a discussion of political nationalism in 1920s Ireland, see Richard Kearney, *Postnationalist Ireland* (London: Routledge, 1997) 209–23.
69. Quoted in Kearney, *Postnationalist Ireland* 111.
70. *TUE* 323.
71. *FMolloy* 23.
72. *EMolloy* 17.
73. Juliette Taylor comments on the element of performativity involved in Beckett's use of French in *L'Innommable*, an argument which also applies to *Molloy* and *Malone meurt*; see Taylor, "'Pidgin Bullskrit': The Performance of French in Beckett's Trilogy", *Samuel Beckett Today* 15 (2005): 211–23.
74. *Malone meurt* 19–20.
75. *FMolloy* 37.
76. *EMolloy* 26.
77. *FMolloy* 67.
78. *EMolloy* 45.
79. *FMolloy* 35–36.
80. *EMolloy* 25.
81. *FMolloy* 11.
82. *Malone meurt* 170, 186.
83. For comments upon the analytical nature of the French language, see Darbelnet and Vinay 184–85.
84. *FMolloy* 37; *Malone meurt* 128, 186, 216.
85. Concerning the use of the construction "It is...that..." in Hiberno-English and in the stylised peasant speech of early Abbey plays, see J. Taniguchi, *A Grammatical Analysis of Artistic Representation of Irish English* (Tokyo: Shinozaki Shorin, 1972) 146–81. Critics have remarked upon Beckett's use of this structure in English, which is particularly apparent in *All That Fall*; see T.P. Dolan, "Samuel Beckett's Dramatic Use of Hiberno-English", *Irish University Review* 14.1 (1984): 49.
86. Many passages in the French novels are peppered with sentences in English; for instance, a character called l'Anglais, who speaks English with a strong foreign accent, appears in one of Malone's stories (*Malone meurt* 206, 215). For comments, see Leslie Hill, "'*Up the Republic!*' Beckett, Writing, Politics", *Modern Language Notes* 112.5 (1997): 915.

87. *Malone meurt* 115.
88. *Malone Dies* 236.
89. For comments on the General Election, see Cronin, *Samuel Beckett* 187–88.
90. *EMolloy* 37.
91. Matthew Arnold, *On the Study of Celtic Literature* (London: Smith, Elder, 1867) 100–2, 108.
92. *FMolloy* 54.
93. *DF* 357.
94. *DF* 357.
95. Christopher Ricks, comparing *How It Is* to *Comment c'est*, remarks that the original French version "reads like a highly talented translation of a work of genius, and not as the thing itself"; see Ricks, *Beckett's Dying Words* (Oxford: Clarendon, 1993) 4.
96. For a discussion of the debates concerning the question of translation during the Revival period, see Philip O'Leary, *The Prose Literature of the Gaelic Revival, 1881–1921* (University Park: Pennsylvania State UP, 1994) 355–400.
97. Atik 118.
98. Reported by Robert Pinget in Pinget, "Notre ami", *Revue d'esthétique* (1990): vii.
99. Joyce, *A Portrait* 193.
100. Joyce, *Ulysses* 164.
101. Beckett, *Proust and "Three Dialogues with Georges Duthuit"* (London: John Calder, 1965) 88; *Disjecta* 27.
102. *L'Innommable* 76.
103. *The Unnamable* 327.
104. *The Unnamable* 390.
105. *FMolloy* 44.
106. *EMolloy* 30.
107. Beckett owned a 1919 edition of Synge's *In Wicklow, West Kerry and Connemara*, an edition featuring illustrations by Jack Yeats, which he bought in 1926 (Atik 149).
108. J.M. Synge, *In Wicklow, West Kerry and Connemara*, *Collected Works*, Vol. 3: *Prose*, ed. Alan Price (London: Oxford UP, 1966) 202.
109. *FMolloy* 44.
110. *FMolloy* 151.
111. *EMolloy* 98.
112. *EMolloy* 102.
113. *FMolloy* 158.
114. *FMolloy* 180.
115. Gastronomy is a *lieu de mémoire* central to French culture, as historians have pointed out; see Pascal Ory, "Gastronomy", *Realms of Memory*, Vol. 2, under the direction of Pierre Nora, trans. Arthur Goldhammer, ed. Lawrence D. Kritzman (New York: Columbia UP, 1997) 443–67.
116. *The Unnamable* 355.
117. *L'Innommable* 134.
118. *FMolloy* 8; *EMolloy* 8; *Malone meurt* 95; *Malone Dies* 226.
119. *The Unnamable* 317. *Cul* means "backside" and *jatte* means "bowl", hence Beckett's pun on the literal meaning of the expression.

120. Both Eoin O'Brien and Barry McGovern argue that, upon writing the passage, Beckett had in mind Dublin's Billy. See O'Brien, *The Beckett Country: Samuel Beckett's Ireland* (Monkstown, Ire.: Black Cat and Faber, 1986) 292; Eric Prince, "'Going On': Interview with Barry McGovern", *Journal of Beckett Studies* 2.1 (1992): 110.
121. *L'Innommable* 56.
122. *FMolloy* 27.
123. *FMolloy* 179.
124. *EMolloy* 20.
125. *EMolloy* 116.
126. See Montague 129; Bair 439. However, Bowles's account of his collaboration with Beckett remained neutral; see Ruby Cohn, "Beckett Self-Translator", *PMLA* 126 (1961): 618.
127. *EMolloy* 118.
128. *FMolloy* 181.
129. *FMolloy* 8.
130. *EMolloy* 8.
131. Beckett to Jacoba van Velde, 20 August 1954, letter 29, BNF MS 19794.
132. Ludovic Janvier, for instance, seemed to have mixed feelings; see Janvier, "Au travail avec Beckett", *Samuel Beckett, L'Herne 31*, ed. Tom Bishop and Raymond Federman (Paris: Editions de l'Herne, 1976) 137.
133. See John Fletcher, Notebook 11, Papers of John Fletcher, CLC HRHRC MS 18.1, f. 3.
134. Beckett to Kay Boyle, 17 August 1971, SBC HRHRC MS 8.3. His statements in this respect were often unambiguous; for instance, he stated that the translation of *Comment c'est* was "the most distasteful job [he] ever took on". See his letter to Schneider, 19 January 1962, *NABS* 119.
135. Beckett to MacGreevy on the translation of *Krapp's Last Tape*, 1 October 1958, letter 217.
136. The notebooks are held at Reading University Library (RUL MS 3461/1–3). See *Human Wishes* Notebook 2, RUL MS 3461/2, f. 91.
137. Bair 255.
138. For a discussion of Lady Gregory's reworkings of Molière, see Mary Fitzgerald, "Four French Comedies: Lady Gregory's Translations of Molière", *Lady Gregory: Fifty Years After*, ed. Anne Saddlemyer and Colin Smythe (Gerrards Cross, Eng.: Colin Smythe, 1987) 227–90.
139. Gregory, *Our Irish Theatre* 168.
140. Joseph Holloway, *Joseph Holloway's Abbey Theatre*, ed. Robert Hogan and Michael J. O'Neill (Carbondale: Southern Illinois UP; London: Feffer and Simons, 1967) 123.
141. Synge, *The Collected Letters of John Millington Synge*, Vol. 1, ed. Anne Saddlemyer (Oxford: Clarendon, 1983) 160.
142. Gregory, *Our Irish Theatre* 60.
143. Gregory, *The Kiltartan Molière: The Miser, The Doctor in Spite of Himself, The Rogueries of Scapin* (Dublin: Maunsel, 1910) 230.
144. Yeats, "Irish National Literature, I", *Uncollected Prose*, Vol. I 362.
145. Yeats, "Irish National Literature, I" 361.
146. Yeats, "Irish National Literature, I" 362.
147. Yeats, *Explorations* 95; "The Story of Early Gaelic Literature", *Uncollected Prose*, Vol. I 358.

148. Michael Cronin, *Translating Ireland* (Cork: Cork UP, 1996) 136–37.
149. Yeats, "Samhain: 1902", *Explorations* 92.
150. "Samhain: 1902" 93.
151. George Moore, *Hail and Farewell*, ed. Richard Cave (Gerrards Cross, Eng.: Colin Smythe, 1976) 586–87.
152. Thomas MacDonagh, *Literature in Ireland* (Dublin: Talbot, 1916) 33.
153. MacDonagh 100–1.
154. MacDonagh 103.
155. Douglas Hyde, *Abhráin Grádh Chúige Connacht, or: Love Songs of Connacht*, 4th ed. (Dublin: Gill; London: T. F. Unwin, 1905) v.
156. Declan Kiberd, *Inventing Ireland: The Literature of the Modern Nation* (London: Vintage, 1996) 155.
157. Douglas Hyde, "The Necessity for De-Anglicizing Ireland", *Irish Writing in the Twentieth Century*, ed. David Pierce (Cork: Cork UP, 2000) 3.
158. Hyde, "The Necessity for De-Anglicizing Ireland" 1.
159. Hyde, "The Necessity for De-Anglicizing Ireland" 3.
160. Yeats, "The De-Anglicising of Ireland", *Uncollected Prose*, Vol. I 255.
161. "The De-Anglicising of Ireland" 256.
162. "The De-Anglicising of Ireland" 255.
163. Moore, *Hail and Farewell* 312.
164. Moore, *Hail and Farewell* 249.
165. Beckett read *Hail and Farewell* in 1936, while he was writing *Murphy*; see *SBC* 55. Later, he stated that he enjoyed returning to Moore's *Esther Waters*, *Hail and Farewell* and *Conversations in Ebury Street*; see Melvin J. Friedman, "George Moore and Samuel Beckett: Cross-Currents and Correspondences", *George Moore in Perspective* (Totowa: Barnes and Noble, 1983) 118.
166. Moore, *Hail and Farewell* 254.
167. Moore, *Hail and Farewell* 140.
168. George Moore and W.B. Yeats, *Diarmuid and Grania*, *The Collected Works of W.B. Yeats*, Vol. 2: *The Plays*, ed. David R. Clark and Rosalind E. Clark (Basingstoke, Eng.: Palgrave, 2001) 253.
169. Moore and Yeats, *Diarmuid and Grania* 250.
170. See Moore, *Hail and Farewell* 252–53. For instance, Moore writes: "Les malfaiteurs restent les malfaiteurs. Il retournerait à Finn et il lui dirait que nous sommes ici" (252). Elsewhere, Diarmuid declares: "Dans la bataille je n'ai jamais frappé que mon adversaire et je n'ai jamais frappé que quand il n'était pas sur ses gardes. Et quand il tombait, souvent je lui donnais la main; et j'ai souvent déchiré une écharpe pour étancher le sang de ses blessures" (253).
171. Moore and Yeats, *Diarmuid and Grania* 251.
172. A detailed analysis of the genesis of *Diarmuid and Grania* can be found in J.C.C. Mays, ed., Introduction, *Diarmuid and Grania: Manuscript Materials*, by George Moore and W.B. Yeats (Ithaca: Cornell UP, 2005) xxix–l.
173. M.A.M, "Too Much Grania", *The Irish Literary Theatre 1899–1901*, ed. Robert Hogan and James Kilroy (Dublin: Dolmen, 1975) 105. The article originally appeared in the *Evening Herald* of 22 October 1901.
174. Ackerley and Gontarski 106.
175. Brian Fitch, *Beckett and Babel* (London: U of Toronto P, 1988) 73.
176. Clissmann 234–35.
177. Clissmann 240.

186 Notes

178. On the genesis and contexts of *An Béal Bocht*, see Clissmann, 228–68; Joseph Brooker, *Flann O'Brien* (Tavistock, Eng.: Northcote, 2005) 61–70; Brendan O Conaire, "Flann O'Brien, *An Béal Bocht*, and Other Irish Matters", *Irish University Review* 3.2 (1973): 121–40.
179. O'Brien, *The Best of Myles* 235.
180. Flann O'Brien, *The Hair of the Dogma: A Further Selection from 'Cruiskeen Lawn'*, ed. Kevin O'Nolan (London: Hart Davis; MacGibbon, 1977) 102.
181. Flann O'Brien, *The Poor Mouth: A Bad Story about the Hard Life*, trans. Patrick C. Power (Normal: Dalkey Archive, 1996) 54–55.
182. O'Brien, *The Poor Mouth* 5; Hyde, *Love Songs of Connacht* 2.
183. O'Brien, *The Poor Mouth* 112.
184. O'Brien, *The Poor Mouth* 3.
185. O'Brien, *The Poor Mouth* 44.
186. Beckett to MacGreevy, 7 September 1933, letter 54.
187. Lady Augusta Gregory, Foreword, *Ideals in Ireland*, by AE, D.P. Moran, George Moore, Douglas Hyde, Standish O'Grady and W.B. Yeats (London: Unicorn, 1901) 9.
188. Yeats, *Uncollected Prose*, Vol. I 346–9.
189. *Disjecta* 71.
190. See Beckett, "Notes on English Literature", TCD MS 10970/3, f. 58.
191. Beckett, *Dream of Fair to Middling Women*, ed. Eoin O'Brien and Edith Fournier (Dublin: Black Cat, 1992) 48.
192. *DF* 257.
193. Yeats, "Irish National Literature III", *Uncollected Prose*, Vol. I 382.
194. Yeats, *Explorations* 107.
195. Beckett, *Molloy*, Holograph Notebook 3, SBC HRHRC MS 4.7, pp. 126–28. This passage appears in a different form in the published text.
196. Beckett, typescript of *Molloy* (incomplete typescript, carbon copy with handwritten revisions, some in the hand of Mania Péron), CLC HRHRC MS 17.6, 212/f. 2.
197. Beckett, typescript of *Molloy*, CLC HRHRC MS 17.6 212/f. 2.
198. Beckett, typescript of *Molloy*, CLC HRHRC MS 17.6 214/f. 3.
199. *EMolloy* 135.
200. Beckett, typescript of *Molloy*, CLC HRHRC MS 17.6 213/f. 3.
201. *EMolloy* 45.
202. *FMolloy* 67.
203. Alan Simpson, *Beckett and Behan, and a Theatre in Dublin* (London: Routledge and Kegan Paul, 1962) 176–78.
204. Simpson, *Beckett and Behan* 177.
205. Ackerley and Gontarski 420.
206. Beckett, *The Old Tune*, adaptation of *La Manivelle, pièce radiophonique*, by Robert Pinget (Paris: Editions de Minuit, 1960) 55–56. These differences are all the more obvious in the Minuit edition, in which the two versions face each other.
207. *The Old Tune* 17.
208. *The Old Tune* 11–13.
209. *The Old Tune* 38–39.
210. *The Old Tune* 24–25.
211. *The Old Tune* 12–13.

212. For further comments, see T.P. Dolan, "Samuel Beckett's Dramatic Use of Hiberno-English", *Irish University Review* 14.1 (1984): 55.
213. *The Old Tune* 27.
214. *FMolloy* 48.
215. *EMolloy* 33.
216. Beckett to Schneider, 8 April 1966, *NABS* 203.
217. Beckett to Schneider, 17 August 1961, *NABS* 96.
218. See Beckett's reply to Ruby Cohn's letter of 10 April 1964, letter 15, RUL MS 5100.
219. Alan Schneider to Beckett, 8 November 1957, *NABS* 19, 21.
220. Beckett to Schneider, 21 November 1957, *NABS* 22.
221. Beckett to Schneider, 4 January 1960, *NABS* 59.
222. For instance between "jetzt" and "nun", "Schritte" and "Tritte" in *Footfalls*; see Elmar Tophoven, "Translating Beckett", *Beckett in the Theatre: The Author as Practical Playwright and Director*, Vol. 1: *From* Waiting for Godot *to* Krapp's Last Tape, by Dougald McMillan and Martha Fehsenfeld (London: John Calder, 1988) 318, 321.
223. Beckett to Jacoba van Velde, 24 June 1953, letter 22, BNF MS 19794.
224. Beckett to Jacoba van Velde, 2 March 1960, letter 66, BNF MS 19794.
225. Beckett to Jacoba van Velde, 28 February 1962, letter 85, BNF MS 19794.
226. Beckett to Jacoba van Velde, 9 March 1962, letter 86, BNF MS 19794.
227. Beckett to Jacoba van Velde, 13 September 1953, letter 23, BNF MS 19794.
228. Beckett to Jacoba van Velde, 12 April 1958, letter 53, BNF MS 19794.
229. Beckett to Susan Manning, 2 July 1956, SBC HRHRC MS 9.4.
230. Beckett to Schneider, 30 April 1957, *NABS* 14.
231. S.E. Gontarski, Martha Fehsenfeld and Dougald McMillan, "Interview with Rachel Burrows, Dublin, Bloomsday, 1982", *Journal of Beckett Studies* 11–12 (1989): 10.
232. Beckett (1957) quoted in Clas Zilliacus, *Beckett and Broadcasting* (Åbo, Finland: Åbo Akademi, 1976) 149.
233. Beckett in conversation with Mel Gussow, 24 June 1978, quoted in Gussow, *Conversations with (and about) Beckett* (London: Nick Hern, 1996) 32.
234. Beckett to Schneider, 6 February 1958, *NABS* 37.
235. For a discussion of the analytical properties of French and the synthetic properties of English, see Darbelnet and Vinay 184–85.
236. Yeats, "Samhain: 1901", *Explorations* 80.

3 Representing Scarcity

1. *CDW* 98.
2. An immediate example of this is the title of John Peter's 1987 monograph, *Vladimir's Carrot: Modern Drama and the Modern Imagination*.
3. Georg Lukács, *The Meaning of Contemporary Realism*, trans. John and Necke Maunder (London: Merlin, 1963) 32. Lukács's views were very influential, providing an underpinning for official Soviet cultural policy.
4. Theodor Adorno, "Reconciliation under Duress", trans. Rodney Livingstone, *Aesthetics and Politics*, ed. Ronald Taylor (London: NLB, 1977) 161.
5. Adorno, "Commitment" 190–91; *AT* 153–54.

6. See, in particular, Beckett's letter to Michel Polac of 1952, which has been reproduced in "Who Is Godot?", trans. Edith Fournier, *New Yorker* 24 June and 1 July 1996: 136.
7. Bair 632–33; *DF* 691–96.
8. *DF* 479, 691–92.
9. Daniel Howarth's production in Cape Town was staged in 1980, Ilan Ronen's production in Haifa in 1984, André Brassard's production in Québec in 1992 and Susan Sontag's production in Sarajevo in 1993. For analyses of individual performances, see David Bradby, *Beckett: Waiting for Godot* (Cambridge: Cambridge UP, 2001).
10. Quotations from *Waiting for Godot* feature in Dolan, *Dictionary of Hiberno-English* 3, 24, 58. For further comments on Beckett's use of Dublin English, see Mary Junker, *Beckett: The Irish Dimension* (Dublin: Wolfhound, 1995) 58; John Fletcher, *A Faber Critical Guide: Samuel Beckett* (London: Faber, 2000) 63, 88; Gerry Dukes, "Englishing *Godot*", *Samuel Beckett Today/Aujourd'hui* 14 (2004): 527–29.
11. Dukes, "Englishing *Godot*" 528.
12. Mercier, *Beckett/Beckett* 53.
13. Kiberd, *Inventing Ireland* 377.
14. *TUE* 327.
15. Garrigan Mattar, *Primitivism, Science, and the Irish Revival* 3. The vast question of the primitive in literature is particularly fraught when considered against Ireland's colonial history, and global models such as those developed in James Clifford's *The Predicament of Culture* and Marianna Torgovnick's *Gone Primitive*, which are based on confrontations between Eastern and Western societies, are not adequate when it comes to analysing the complex power relationships that shaped Beckett's primitive leanings. In contrast, Garrigan Mattar portrays the primitivism of Revivalist literature as enabling fluctuating metaphors for English–Irish relations, an understanding of the period that is germane to my discussion of the postcolonial environment formative of Beckett as a writer.
16. Garrigan Mattar, *Primitivism, Science, and the Irish Revival* 14.
17. Garrigan Mattar, *Primitivism, Science, and the Irish Revival* 14. Garrigan Mattar's analysis of the political undertones of Revivalist literature contrasts sharply with Kevin Whelan's view of the Revival movement as a delayed effect, inspired by people born during the Famine. Indeed, Whelan argues that the post-Famine generation sought to reshape Ireland in fundamental ways, generating in the literature of the Revival a melancholy, apolitical view of history; see Whelan, "The Memories of 'The Dead'", *Yale Journal of Criticism* 15.1 (2002): 59–97.
18. On Lady Gregory and the "picturesque", see Sinéad Garrigan Mattar, "Wage for Each People Her Hand Has Destroyed: Lady Gregory's Colonial Nationalism", *Irish University Review* 34.1 (2004): 56–57; Garrigan Mattar, *Primitivism, Science, and the Irish Revival* 186–87.
19. For a discussion of Yeats's representations of the figure of the peasant, see Jacqueline Genet, "Yeats and the Myth of Rural Ireland", *Rural Ireland, Real Ireland?*, ed. Jacqueline Genet (Gerrards Cross, Eng.: Colin Smythe, 1996) 139–57.
20. Beckett greatly admired the play and knew passages by heart; *SBC* 153; Montague 145.

21. Daniel Corkery, *Synge and Anglo-Irish Literature* (Cork: Mercier, 1966) 109.
22. Roy Foster, *Paddy and Mr Punch* (London: Penguin, 1993) 29. This dichotomy between materialism and idealism was also prominent in the discourses of the Catholic Church; see Michel Peillon, "The Structure of Irish Ideology Revisited", *Culture and Ideology in Ireland*, ed. Chris Curtin, Mary Kelly and Liam O'Dowd (Galway: Galway UP, 1984) 51–52.
23. Yeats, "Battles Long Ago", *Uncollected Prose*, Vol. I 350.
24. See Matthew Arnold, *On the Study of Celtic Literature* (London: Smith, Elder, 1867) 97, 124–25.
25. M.A.M. 2.
26. Beckett quoted in Vivian Mercier, "Beckett's Anglo-Irish Stage Dialects", *James Joyce Quarterly* 8.4 (1971): 312.
27. See Kieran Allen, *The Politics of James Connolly* (London: Pluto, 1990) 22–23.
28. James Connolly, "Let Us Free Ireland!", *Collected Works*, Vol. 2 (Dublin: New Books, 1987) 211–12.
29. James Connolly, Foreword, *Collected Works*, Vol. 1 (Dublin: New Books, 1987) 22.
30. *The Poor Mouth* 112.
31. *The Poor Mouth* 88.
32. *The Poor Mouth* 49.
33. See W.B. Yeats, "Professor Dowden and Irish Literature II", *Uncollected Prose*, Vol. I 352.
34. *Disjecta* 72.
35. W.B. Yeats, Preface, *Wild Apples*, by Oliver St John Gogarty (Shannon: Irish UP, 1971) n. pag.
36. See Beckett to MacGreevy, 25 January 1931, letter 15. I thank Mark Nixon for confirming the accuracy of my transcription.
37. Beckett to MacGreevy, 5 October 1930, letter 11.
38. Anthony Roche compares *Waiting for Godot* to *The Workhouse Ward* in "Re-working *The Workhouse Ward*: McDonagh, Beckett, and Gregory", *Irish University Review* 34.1 (2004): 176–79. His analysis focuses on the problem of interdependence, which he describes as, to a degree, voluntary and psychological in both plays. Here, I adopt the opposite view and argue that, since resources have been almost entirely depleted, scarcity is what *creates* interdependence.
39. Lady Augusta Gregory, *The Comedies of Lady Gregory*, ed. Anne Saddlemyer (Gerrards Cross, Eng.: Colin Smythe, 1970) 104.
40. Gregory, *Comedies* 102.
41. Gregory, *Our Irish Theatre* 56.
42. For discussions of the links between *Waiting for Godot* and *Purgatory*, see Roche, *Contemporary Irish Drama* 22; Ellmann, "Nayman of Noland" 100.
43. Yeats, *Collected Plays* 681–82.
44. Beckett, *Theatrical Notebooks*, Vol. 1 9. Echoes of *Purgatory* surface in Beckett's radio play *Embers*; the central character, Henry, summons sounds of hooves, echoing the Old Man's plea in *Purgatory*: "Listen to the hoof-beats! Listen, listen!" (*Collected Plays* 685).
45. Bradby 106.
46. McCormack 343; see also Marjorie Howes, *Yeats's Nations: Gender, Class, and Irishness* (Cambridge: Cambridge UP, 1996) 161–85.
47. *CDW* 131.

48. *TUE* 342.
49. *CDW* 28. Here, Estragon's request draws on syntactical features specific to Irish English. In *En attendant Godot*, however, this line is written in standard French.
50. *CDW* 37.
51. *CDW* 112.
52. Beckett to Schneider, 8 November 1957, *NABS* 22.
53. *CDW* 111.
54. *CDW* 97.
55. The picture was kept in the 1967 production of the play at Berlin's Schiller-Theater Werkstatt, but was suppressed in the 1980 production at London's Riverside Theatre. See Beckett, *The Theatrical Notebooks of Samuel Beckett*, Vol. 2: Endgame, ed. S.E. Gontarski (London: Faber, 1992) 43 n4.
56. *TUE* 329.
57. Beckett to Schneider, 8 November 1957, *NABS* 23.
58. Beckett on 10 November 1955, quoted by Patrick Bowles in Knowlson, *Beckett Remembering* 110.
59. See Theodor W. Adorno, "Cultural Criticism and Society", trans. Samuel and Shierry Weber, *The Adorno Reader*, ed. Brian O'Connor (Oxford: Blackwell, 2000) 210.
60. For a discussion of the manuscript of *En attendant Godot*, see Rosette Lamont, "Crossing Political Parables", *Beckett Translating/Translating Beckett*, ed. Alan Warren Friedman, Charles Rossman and Dina Scherzer (University Park: Pennsylvania State UP, 1987) 79.
61. These preliminary drafts are described in detail in S.E. Gontarski, *The Intent of Undoing in Samuel Beckett's Dramatic Texts* (Bloomington: Indiana UP, 1985) 31–34.
62. Beckett, "Avant *Fin de partie*", RUL MS 1227/7/16/7, f. 14.
63. Bertolt Brecht, "Alienation Effects in Chinese Acting", *Brecht on Theatre: The Development of an Aesthetic*, ed. and trans. John Willett, 2nd ed. (London: Eyre Methuen, 1978) 98.
64. Brecht, "A Short Organum for the Theatre", *Brecht on Theatre* 192.
65. *CDW* 38.
66. *CDW* 98.
67. *CDW* 120.
68. *CDW* 41, 87.
69. In 1956 and 1957, productions of Brecht by the Berliner Ensemble and a selection of Noh plays were staged at the same time in Paris. Beckett preferred to attend Brecht's *Life of Galileo*; while he was impressed by Brecht's staging and admired "the scene with the mirror", he "found it all *trop riche*" (Atik 16).
70. Karl Marx, *Capital: A Critique of Political Economy*, Book 1: *The Process of Production of Capital*, trans. Samuel Moore and Edward Aveling, ed. Friedrich Engels (London: Lawrence and Wishart, 1977) 77.
71. Sean Golden, "Familiars in a Ruinstrewn Land: *Endgame* as Political Allegory", *Contemporary Literature* 22 (1981): 444.
72. *CDW* 16.
73. On Simpson's production, see Bradby 85; Gerry Dukes, "The Pike Theatre Typescript of *Waiting for Godot*: Part I", *Journal of Beckett Studies* 4.2 (1995): 77–91.

74. This includes the 2008 Gate production of *Waiting for Godot*, the first all-Ireland touring production of the play (directed by Walter Asmus).
75. See Christopher Morash's account of the production in his book *A History of Irish Theatre, 1601–2000* (Cambridge: Cambridge UP, 2002) 200.
76. Daniel Corkery, *The Hidden Ireland* (Dublin: Gill, 1967) 19–20.
77. Beckett, *Texts for Nothing* 7.
78. Beckett, *En attendant Godot* 18.
79. Beckett, *En attendant Godot* 47.
80. Beckett, *En attendant Godot* 53.
81. *CDW* 38.
82. O'Casey, *Three Dublin Plays* 96.
83. *CDW* 45.
84. *En attendant Godot* 46.
85. *CDW* 33.
86. *En attendant Godot* 82.
87. *CDW* 55.
88. *CDW* 11, 12, 28, 31, 39, 73; Beckett, *En attendant Godot* 10, 37, 42, 55, 111.
89. Beckett, *En attendant Godot* 54.
90. *CDW* 38. The first Faber text, however, mentioned at first "shilling", then "sixpence"; see *The Theatrical Notebooks of Samuel Beckett*, Vol. 1: Waiting for Godot, ed. Dougald McMillan (London: Faber, 1993) 128 n1040.
91. *CDW* 17.
92. Beckett, *En attendant Godot* 20.
93. Fletcher, *Samuel Beckett* 66.
94. *TUE* 334. The title of Beckett's essay "La Peinture des van Velde ou le monde et le pantalon" is another reference to this joke.
95. Beckett, *Fin de partie* (Paris: Editions de Minuit, 1957) 36.
96. Beckett, *Fin de partie* 37–38.
97. *CDW* 102. John Fletcher points out that the line should be uttered in a "posh" accent by the actor playing Nagg; see Fletcher, *Samuel Beckett* 120.
98. *CDW* 102; Michael McAteer, "Yeats's *Endgame*: Postcolonialism and Modernism", *Critical Ireland*, ed. Alan Gillis and Aaron Kelly (Dublin: Four Courts, 2001) 161.
99. Beckett, *Fin de partie* 23.
100. Beckett, *En attendant Godot* 48. Among the passages referenced here, this is the only one which differs from the first edition of the play, hence my choice to refer to the edition currently in print.
101. *CDW* 35.
102. See Dolan, *A Dictionary of Hiberno-English* 81–82.
103. For a discussion of the state of the economy during this period, see Diarmaid Ferriter, *The Transformation of Ireland 1900–2000* (London: Profile, 2004) 327. Eoin O'Brien comments on Beckett's reference to Kapp and Peterson's; see *The Beckett Country* 253.
104. The design of the advertisement is reminiscent of Magritte's famous painting *Ceci n'est pas une pipe, la trahison des images (The Treachery of Images)* (1928–29). A series of Abbey Theatre programmes from the early 1930s is available for consultation at the National Library of Ireland under the reference number IR 3919 A1.
105. *CDW* 97, 119.

106. Beckett, *Fin de partie* 76.
107. Beckett, *Fin de partie* 79.
108. *CDW* 117.
109. *CDW* 117.
110. Nels C. Pearson, "Outside of Here It's Death: Co-Dependency and the Ghosts of Decolonization in Beckett's *Endgame*", *ELH* 68.1 (2001): 222.
111. Concerning Beckett's journey from Cobh, see *DF* 230.
112. *Fin de partie* 72.
113. Pearson 217, 223. On the origin of "smithereens", see Dolan, *A Dictionary of Hiberno-English* 218. These comments found concrete illustration in a 2004 production of *Endgame* at Belfast's Fisherwick Church (directed by Anna Blagona-Mill for Cello Productions). The play was treated as a meditation upon Northern Ireland's political situation; the actor playing Clov had a marked North Belfast accent, and the actor playing Hamm an English accent.
114. *CDW* 108.
115. *CDW* 113.
116. McAteer, "Yeats's *Endgame*" 161.
117. *CDW* 100.
118. *CDR* 128.
119. *CDR* 822.
120. "The Practico-Inert; or, the Hell of Daily Life" is the title of a chapter by Raymond Aron in his *History and the Dialectic of Violence: An Analysis of Sartre's* Critique de la raison dialectique, trans. Barry Cooper (Oxford: Blackwell, 1975).
121. *CDR* 256–62.
122. *CDR* 66. In the *Economic and Philosophic Manuscripts of 1844*, Karl Marx defined the class system and labour as the seeds of alienation and linked alienation to capitalist modes of production, see Marx, *Economic and Philosophic Manuscripts of 1844*, ed. and introd. Dirk J. Struik, trans. Martin Milligan (London: Lawrence and Wishart, 1973) 106–27.
123. *CDR* 133.
124. *CDR* 723, 123, 150, 717–19.
125. *CDR* 722, 714.
126. Some postcolonial critics, Edward Said for instance, have praised Sartre's integrity, while others have denounced his disregard of African cultural diversity, drawing attention to his over-simplification of the concept of culture in his introduction to Senghor's *Anthologie de la nouvelle poésie nègre et malgache*. See Edward Said, *Culture and Imperialism* (London: Vintage, 1994) 398, 401; Bennetta Jules-Rosette, "Conjugating Cultural Realities: Présence africaine", *The Surreptitious Speech: 'Présence africaine' and the Politics of Otherness*, ed. V.Y. Mudimbe (Chicago: U of Chicago P, 1992) 32; Marie-Paule Ha, "The Narrative of Return in 'Orphée Noir'", *Situating Sartre in Twentieth-Century Thought and Culture*, ed. Jean-François Fourny and Charles D. Minahen (Basingstoke, Eng.: Macmillan, 1997) 100.
127. Jean-Paul Sartre, Preface, *The Wretched of the Earth*, by Frantz Fanon, trans. Constance Farrington (London: MacGibbon and Kee, 1965) 8. Inspired by Sartre's views, Fanon equated colonialism with capitalism, his critique of colonialism thus becoming a plea against capitalism.

128. Edouard Morot-Sir, "Sartre's *Critique of Dialectical Reason*", *Journal of the History of Ideas* 22.4 (1961): 581.
129. Aron 189–92, 195.
130. See Sartre, Preface, trans. Lawrence Hoey, *The Colonizer and the Colonized*, by Albert Memmi (London: Souvenir, 1974) xxv; Sartre, "Colonialism Is a System", *Colonialism and Neocolonialism*, trans. Azzedine Haddour, Steve Brewer and Terry McWilliams (London: Routledge, 2001) 30–47.
131. *CDR* 153 n35.
132. *CDR* 125.
133. *CDR* 125–27.
134. *CDR* 126.
135. *CDR* 125 n16.
136. Jean-Paul Sartre, "Beyond Bourgeois Theatre", *Brecht Sourcebook*, ed. Carol Martin and Henry Bial (London: Routledge, 2000) 53.
137. Jean-Paul Sartre, "Interview with Kenneth Tynan (1961)", *Sartre on Theater*, ed. Michel Contat and Michel Rybalka, trans. Frank Jellinek (London: Quartet, 1976) 128.
138. Sartre, "Interview with Kenneth Tynan (1961)" 128.
139. "Jean-Paul Sartre Speaks: An Interview with Jacqueline Piatier", trans. Adrienne Foulke, *Vogue* January 1965: 94.
140. Wolfgang Abendroth, "Elements for a Scientific Politics", *Conversations with Lukács*, by Hans Heinz Holz, Leo Kofler and Wolfgang Abendroth, ed. Theo Pinkus (Cambridge, MA: MIT P, 1975) 88–90.
141. Later, in 1933, Lukács dismissed the first edition of *History and Class Consciousness*, saying that he regarded it as superseded, and for many years he expressed hostility towards it. See Leo Kofler, "Society and the Individual", *Conversations with Lukács* 73; G.H.R. Parkinson, *Georg Lukács* (London: Weidenfeld and Nicholson, 1970) 15.
142. Georg Lukács, *History and Class Consciousness*, trans. Rodney Livingstone (London: Merlin, 1971) 89.
143. Lukács, *The Meaning of Contemporary Realism* 32.
144. *Disjecta* 64.
145. Beckett to MacGreevy, 8 February 1935, letter 70.
146. Quoted by Robert Pinget in "Our Friend Sam", trans. Robin Freeman, *Eonta* 1.1 (1991): 10.
147. For discussions of Adorno's essay, see Tyrus Miller, "Dismantling Authenticity: Beckett, Adorno, and the 'Post-War'", *Textual Practice* 8.1 (1994): 43–57; Matthew Holt, "Catastrophe, Autonomy and the Future of Modernism: Trying to Understand Adorno's Reading of *Endgame*", *Samuel Beckett Today* 14 (2004): 261–75; Chris Conti, "Critique and Form: Adorno on *Godot* and *Endgame*", *Samuel Beckett Today* 14 (2004): 277–92.
148. Beckett to Ruby Cohn, 28 September 1965, letter 16, RUL MS 5100. Beckett thought that Adorno's reading of *Endgame* was erroneous; see *DF* 479.
149. See Adorno, "Reconciliation under Duress" 176.
150. *TUE* 330.
151. Nevertheless, Lukács's concept of reification clearly exerted an important influence on Albert Memmi and Frantz Fanon: in *The Colonizer and the Colonized*, Albert Memmi describes colonial society as a society that is ruled by a form of capitalism in putrefaction and contaminates everything

it touches, while in *Black Skin, White Masks*, Frantz Fanon comes to a similar conclusion, after a reflection on the signifiers attached to coloniser and colonised.
152. See Lukács's "Oscar Wilde", "Aesthetic Culture" and "Bernard Shaw" in *The Lukács Reader*, ed. Arpad Kadarkay (Oxford: Blackwell, 1995) 120–24, 146–59, 125–40.
153. Lukács, *The Meaning of Contemporary Realism* 21.
154. Adorno, "Reconciliation under Duress" 158–59.
155. MacDonagh vii.
156. Yeats, "Irish National Literature, I", *Uncollected Prose*, Vol. I 360.
157. See Frank Tuohy, *Yeats* (London: Macmillan, 1976) 198–99. However, Yeats's later notes to *The Only Jealousy of Emer* suggest that his perspectives upon Eastern theatrical techniques and Irish myths and legends were informed by an understanding of wider issues relating to the differences between modernist and realist modes of representation; see *The Variorum Edition of the Plays of W.B. Yeats*, ed. Russell K. Alspach (London: Macmillan, 1966) 568–69.
158. Mays, "Beckett and the Irish" 14.
159. For summaries of the debates between Brecht and Lukács, see Stuart Sim, *Georg Lukács* (London: Harvester Wheatsheaf, 1994) 99–104; Eugene Lunn, *Marxism and Modernism* (London: U of California P, 1982) 75–90; Perry Anderson, Rodney Livingstone and Francis Mulhern, "Presentation II", *Aesthetics and Politics* 60–67; David Pike, *Lukács and Brecht* (London: U of North Carolina P, 1985).
160. Lunn 76.
161. Bertolt Brecht, "Against Georg Lukács", trans. Stuart Hood, *New Left Review* 84 (1974): 39, 40–41.
162. Brecht, "Against Georg Lukács" 51.
163. Brecht, "Against Georg Lukács" 45.
164. Käthe Rülicke-Weiler, *Die Dramaturgie Brechts* (Berlin: Henschelverlag, 1968) 155; Clas Zilliacus, "Three Times *Godot*: Beckett, Brecht, Bulatovic", *Comparative Drama* 4 (1970): 3.
165. Werner Hecht, *Aufsätze über Brecht* (Berlin: Henschelverlag, 1970) 122–23; Lunn 76–77.
166. Jessica Prinz comments on the influence of German Expressionism upon Beckett; she identifies a central difference between Beckett's late plays and Oskar Kokoschka's drama (and, by extension, German Expressionism), namely that suffering remains unstated. See Prinz, "Resonant Images: Beckett and German Expressionism", *Samuel Beckett and the Arts: Music, Visual Arts, and Non-Print Media*, ed. Lois Oppenheim (London: Garland Publishing, 1999) 153–71. Beckett's refusal to treat human suffering as resulting from realistic causes may have been precisely what spurred Brecht to adapt the play.
167. Brecht's annotations are partially reproduced in Hecht 118–21; Zilliacus, "Three Times *Godot*" 6–7.
168. Estragon was labelled "ein Prolet", Vladimir "ein Intellektueller", Lucky "ein Esel oder Polizist" and Pozzo "ein Gutsbesitzer". For discussions of Brecht's modifications, see Hecht 118–21; Ulrich Schoenleber, "Baal Meets Belacqua: Une rencontre entre Brecht et Beckett", *Samuel Beckett Today* 2 (1993): 106; Zilliacus, "Three Times *Godot*" 5–6.

169. Schoenleber 107.
170. The play was first produced in Berlin in 1953, the year it was translated from French into German, and caused great confusion among its reviewers; see Wilhelm Füger, "The First Berlin *Godot*: Beckett's Debut on the German Stage", *Samuel Beckett Today* 11 (2001): 57–63.
171. Zilliacus, "Three Times *Godot*" 8; Rülicke-Weiler 155.
172. Rülicke-Weiler 156.
173. Beckett to Ruby Cohn, 30 January 1967, letter 26.
174. Theodor W. Adorno [23 September 1967], *Notes sur Beckett*, trans. Christophe David, introd. Rolf Tiedemann (Caen: Nous Editions, 2008) 19.
175. Beckett to Aidan Higgins, 8 February 1952, SBC HRHRC MS 8.9.

4 Writing Disappearance

1. Beckett's interest in modern art has been well documented; see, for instance, Hannah Case Copeland, *Art and the Artist in the Works of Samuel Beckett* (The Hague: Mouton, 1975); Lois Oppenheim, *The Painted Word* (Ann Arbor: U of Michigan P, 2000); Lois Oppenheim, ed., *Samuel Beckett and the Arts: Music, Visual Arts, and Non-Print Media* (London: Garland, 1999).
2. *Disjecta* 139. On Beckett's friendship with Duthuit, see Rémi Labrusse, "Beckett et la peinture", *Critique* 156.519–20 (1990): 670–80; Labrusse, "Samuel Beckett et Georges Duthuit", *Samuel Beckett: A Passion for Paintings* 88–91.
3. Kandinsky, *On the Spiritual in Art, Complete Writings on Art* 213.
4. Kandinsky first used the word "abstraction" in 1910 to describe Manet's painting and developed the concept further in later publications. Although he did not invent the term, it is widely associated with him and his work; see Kenneth C. Lindsay and Peter Vergo, Introduction, *Complete Writings on Art* 20–1. Schoenberg's theories of composition are developed in *Style and Idea, Structural Functions of Harmony* and *Theory of Harmony*; for discussions of Schoenberg's music in its historical context, see, for instance, Bryan R. Simms, *The Atonal Music of Arnold Schoenberg 1908–1923* (Oxford: Oxford UP, 2000); Juliane Brand and Christopher Hailey, eds, *Constructive Dissonance* (Berkeley: U of California P, 1997). The closeness between Kandinsky and Schoenberg is evident in their correspondence; see *Arnold Schoenberg and Wassily Kandinsky: Letters, Pictures and Documents*, ed. Jelena Hahl-Koch, trans. John C. Crawford (London: Faber, 1984).
5. Quoted in John Gruen, "Nobel Prize Winner 1969, Samuel Beckett Talks about Beckett", *Vogue* December 1969: 210.
6. The impact of Kandinsky's theories upon the subsequent development of modernist currents is documented in Peter Lasko's *The Expressionist Roots of Modernism*, which presents Munich, rather than Paris, as the locus from which theories of abstraction and free expression originated.
7. Beckett to MacGreevy, 27 March 1949, letter 178, TCD MS 10402. Erik Tonning identifies the piece as Op. 6, also called *The Wind Quintet*; see Tonning, *Samuel Beckett's Abstract Drama* (Oxford: Peter Lang, 2007) 63. In the late 1950s, Beckett listened to more pieces by Schoenberg, Berg and

Webern with Avigdor Arikha; see *DF* 496. For further discussion of Beckett and serialist music, see Harry White, "'Something Is Taking Its Course': Dramatic Exactitude and the Paradigm of Serialism in Samuel Beckett", *Samuel Beckett and Music*, ed. Mary Bryden (Oxford: Clarendon, 1998) 159–71.
8. Tonning 62–64.
9. *TUE* 327.
10. Theodor Adorno, *Philosophy of Modern Music*, trans. Anne G. Mitchell and Wesley V. Bloomster (London: Sheed and Ward, 1973) 99.
11. *TUE* 338, 344.
12. *AT* 81.
13. Beckett held Grohmann in high esteem; see *DF* 289; see also his letter to Günter Albrecht of 30 March 1937, RUL MS 5037.
14. *Disjecta* 144.
15. Beckett, typescript of "MacGreevy on Jack B. Yeats", TCD MS 9072, f. 13.
16. Kandinsky, *On the Spiritual in Art, Complete Writings on Art* 202.
17. Kandinsky, *Point and Line to Plane, Complete Writings on Art* 544.
18. *Disjecta* 56.
19. Beckett to MacGreevy, 18 October 1932, letter 34.
20. Kandinsky, *On the Spiritual in Art, Complete Writings on Art* 160, 131. On the history of Kandinsky's concept of internal necessity, see Gillian Naylor, *The Bauhaus Reassessed: Sources and Design Theory* (London: Herbert, 1985) 90.
21. If Beckett's interest in the interdependency of the senses was triggered by the influence of Joyce, it also developed through an intensive reading of Rimbaud. Yoshiki Tajiri draws on Gilles Deleuze's terminology to discuss the influence of Rimbaud and Kandinsky on Beckett; see Tajiri, "Beckett and Synaesthesia", *Samuel Beckett Today/Aujourd'hui* 11 (2001): 178–85. Beckett's interest in synaesthesia is central to Deleuze's essay "L'Epuisé", where Deleuze discusses Beckett's adoption of a synaesthetic language and describes Beckett as an artist dedicated to portraying the exhaustion of his medium.
22. Beckett, "Dante...Bruno. Vico..Joyce", *Disjecta* 27.
23. Arnold Schoenberg, *Style and Idea*, ed. Dika Newlin (London: Williams and Norgate, 1951) 113.
24. Arnold Schoenberg, *Structural Functions of Harmony*, ed. Humphrey Searle (London: Williams and Norgate, 1954) 2.
25. Kandinsky's approach to drama developed over the course of several essays; see, for instance, "On Stage Composition" (1912) and "Abstract Synthesis on the Stage" (1923).
26. Beckett, "Peintres de l'empêchement", *Disjecta* 135.
27. Lázló Moholy-Nagy, "The Coming Theatre – The Total Theatre", *The Bauhaus: Weimar, Dessau, Berlin, Chicago*, by Hans Maria Wingler, ed. Joseph Stein, trans. Wolfgang Jabs and Basil Gilbert (Cambridge, MA: MIT P, 1976) 132. On the context of Moholy-Nagy's theories, see Torsten Blume, "The Historic Bauhaus Stage – A Theatre of Space", *Bauhaus. Theatre. Dessau*, ed. Marie Neumuller (Berlin: Jovis, 2007) 47–51.
28. See Hans Curjel, "Moholy-Nagy and the Theater", trans. Sibyl Moholy-Nagy, *Moholy-Nagy*, ed. Richard Kostelanetz (London: Allen Lane, 1974) 94–96. The essay originally appeared in *Du* 24 (1964).
29. Kandinsky, "On the Question of Form", *Complete Writings on Art* 237.

30. Peg Weiss compares Kandinsky's design to motifs from Mongolian folklore; see Weiss, "Evolving Perceptions of Kandinsky and Schoenberg: Towards the Ethnic Roots of the 'Outsider'", *Constructive Dissonance*, ed. Juliane Brand and Christopher Hailey (Berkeley: U of California P, 1997) 35–57.
31. Beckett, "La Peinture des van Velde ou le monde et le pantalon", *Disjecta* 118.
32. Beckett, typescript of "MacGreevy on Jack B. Yeats", TCD MS 9072, f. 10.
33. Lázló Moholy-Nagy, "In Defense of 'Abstract' Art", *Moholy-Nagy* 44. The essay originally appeared in *Journal of Aesthetics and Art Criticism* 4 (1945).
34. *Disjecta* 135–36.
35. Kandinsky, "Reminiscences/Three Pictures", *Complete Writings on Art* 370.
36. Schoenberg, *Style and Idea* 219.
37. *Disjecta* 118.
38. Beckett, "Peintres de l'empêchement", *Disjecta* 136.
39. Beckett, "La Peinture des van Velde ou le monde et le pantalon", *Disjecta* 126.
40. Paul Klee, *The Diaries of Paul Klee*, ed. Felix Klee (Berkeley: U of California P, 1964) 670. For a discussion of Klee's statement, see Naylor 90.
41. Paul Klee, *The Thinking Eye*, ed. Jürg Spiller (New York: Wittenborn; London: Lund Humphries, 1961) 67.
42. *AT* 81–82.
43. Beckett, *Watt* 127.
44. Bruce Arnold, *Mainie Jellett and the Modern Movement in Ireland* (London: Yale UP, 1991) 78–82.
45. Arnold, *Mainie Jellett and the Modern Movement in Ireland* 64, 80.
46. For a discussion of Salkeld's life and work, see S.B. Kennedy, "An Incisive Aesthetic", *Irish Arts* 21.2 (2004): 90–5; Arnold, *Mainie Jellett and the Modern Movement in Ireland* 85–6. Beckett admired Salkeld's poetry and advised him to send it to T.S. Eliot; see his letter to Arland Ussher, 25 March 1936, SBC HRHRC MS 9.5.
47. For a discussion of MacGreevy's defence of modern painting, see Arnold, *Mainie Jellett and the Modern Movement in Ireland* 82.
48. Beckett, typescript of "MacGreevy on Jack B. Yeats", TCD MS 9072, f. 12.
49. The majority of the manuscripts under scrutiny are held at Reading University Library, with an additional number at the Harry Ransom Humanities Research Center, University of Texas at Austin. Detailed descriptions of the manuscripts held at Reading can be found in Mary Bryden, Julian Garforth and Peter Mills, *Beckett at Reading* (Reading: Whiteknights and the Beckett International Foundation, 1998).
50. For further comments on the genesis of *Eh Joe*, *Not I*, *That Time* and *Footfalls*, see Gontarski's *The Intent of Undoing in Samuel Beckett's Dramatic Texts*. Gontarki's analysis deals with anti-autobiographical strains in Beckett's writing and differs sharply from the present study, whose aim is to contextualise minute aspects of these manuscripts. Unless relevant, the emendations documented in the *Theatrical Notebooks of Samuel Beckett* do not feature in this study. My focus remains on an aspect of Beckett's writing that is salient in early manuscript drafts, written prior to rehearsals.
51. Walter D. Asmus, "Practical Aspects of Theater, Radio and Television: Rehearsal Notes", trans. Helen Watanabe, *Journal of Beckett Studies* 2 (1977): 86.

52. Beckett, 22 June 1979, quoted in Gussow 36. The impact of Beckett's involvement with the theatre upon his writing is documented in S.E. Gontarski, "Revising Himself: Performance as Text in Samuel Beckett's Theatre", *Journal of Modern Literature* 22.1 (1998): 131–45.
53. See Gontarski, "Revising Himself: Performance as Text in Samuel Beckett's Theatre" 135.
54. This remark was made in relation to *Happy Days* but also applies to her experience of *Not I*. Whitelaw in interview with Linda Ben-Zvi, December 1987, quoted in Linda Ben-Zvi, ed., *Women in Beckett* (Urbana: U of Illinois P, 1990) 6.
55. *DF* 598. For comparisons between Beckett and Schoenberg, see, for instance, Daniel Albright, *Representation and the Imagination* (Chicago: U of Chicago P, 1981).
56. *CDW* 378.
57. Beckett quoted in Bair 625.
58. Gontarski, *The Intent of Undoing in Samuel Beckett's Dramatic Texts* xiii–xiv.
59. Joyce to Arthur Power, quoted in Ellmann, *James Joyce* 505.
60. Beckett quoted in *DF* 352. This declaration is similar to Beckett's account of Joyce's artistic project in his interview with Israel Shenker; see Shenker 148.
61. Beckett to Schneider, 7 April 1966, *NABS* 202. His instructions were also respected in the 1966 British production of *Eh Joe*, directed by Alan Gibson and starring Jack McGowran and Siân Phillips, in which the use of three grey panelled curtains reinforced the pictorial quality of the setting and the claustrophobic character of the piece, creating the sense of a flat space. In contrast, Alan Gilsenan's 1986 film production, starring Tom Hickey and Siobhan McKenna, was far removed from the sparse interior initially used. The bedroom, largely dominated by shades of red, green and grey, recalled the Georgian houses with high windows commonplace in Dublin; the suggestion of a Dublin location was confirmed by the actors' marked Irish accents.
62. Kandinsky, *Complete Writings on Art* 578, 185.
63. Beckett to Schneider, 8 April 1966, *NABS* 203.
64. Beckett to Schneider, 11 February 1966, *NABS* 198.
65. *CDW* 362.
66. *CDW* 362. Joe's pose, which conveys extreme anguish and fatalism, recalls expressionist techniques, particularly the self-portraits of Egon Schiele; for a general comparison between the play and German expressionist techniques, see Prinz 157–63.
67. Beckett to Schneider, 7 April 1966, *NABS* 201.
68. See *Eh Joe*, RUL MS 1537/1. This was changed to Joe in the following draft (RUL MS 1537/2), but Beckett hesitated over the spelling of the name.
69. *Eh Joe*, RUL MS 1537/2, f. 3.
70. *Eh Joe*, RUL MS 1537/3, f. 2.
71. See, for instance, Beckett's letter to Schneider, 16 October 1972, *NABS* 283.
72. Beckett, *Dis Joe, Comédie et actes divers* (Paris: Editions de Minuit, 1972) 86.
73. *Eh Joe*, RUL MS 1537/1, f. 3.
74. Beckett, *Dis Joe* 86.
75. *Eh Joe*, RUL MS 1537/1, f. 6; RUL MS 1537/2, f. 4, 7.
76. *Eh Joe*, RUL MS 1537/6, f. 4.

77. *Eh Joe*, RUL MS 1537/8, f. 5; *CDW*, 365. In the French text, the newspaper in which the obituary of Joe's lover appears remains undefined.
78. Beckett himself was a loyal reader of the *Irish Times* and, in France, of *Libération*, the newspaper founded by Sartre. See *DF* 701.
79. *CDW* 366.
80. See *Eh Joe*, RUL MS 1537/5, f. 3; RUL MS 1537/6, f. 5.
81. *Eh Joe*, RUL MS 1537/1, f. 7.
82. Details about the history of the Kish lightship may be found in Bill Long, *Bright Light, White Water* (Dundrum: New Island, 1993) 38–46.
83. Joyce, *Ulysses*, 37. For comments on Joyce's reference to the Kish lightship, see Gifford 57 n3.267.
84. O'Brien, *The Beckett Country* 97.
85. Beckett, *Dis Joe* 90.
86. *Dis Joe* 87.
87. Eoin O'Brien comments upon Krapp's reference to the Grand Canal; O'Brien, *The Beckett Country* 197.
88. Beckett to Jacoba van Velde, 2 March 1960, letter 66, BNF MS 19794.
89. *CDW* 363, 365. The French text is less specific in its depiction of the girl's appearance and does not mention her Avoca bag.
90. See the website of the company.
91. Beckett quoted in Bair 622.
92. Gontarski, *The Intent of Undoing in Samuel Beckett's Dramatic Texts* 132–42. The manuscript is held at Trinity College Dublin Library (TCD MS 4664).
93. See Enoch Brater, "Dada, Surrealism, and the Genesis of *Not I*", *Modern Drama* 18 (1975): 53–54; *Why Beckett* (London: Thames and Hudson, 1989) 100.
94. Images from this film bear upon the stage image of *Happy Days* and upon *Murphy*, which evokes the film's opening, during which a wide-open eye is being slit.
95. Beckett to Schneider, 25 August 1963, *NABS* 139–40.
96. See Gontarski, *The Intent of Undoing in Samuel Beckett's Dramatic Texts* 135–36; W. Ernest Shepherd, *The Dublin and Southeastern Railway* (Newton Abbot, Eng.: David & Charles, 1974) 113.
97. The station was closed down in January 1959 (Shepherd 100) and not in 1958, as argued by Ackerley and Gontarski (531).
98. Shepherd 118.
99. Gontarski, *The Intent of Undoing in Samuel Beckett's Dramatic Texts* 133.
100. *CDW* 376.
101. *CDW* 375.
102. See Gontarski, "Revising Himself: Performance as Text in Samuel Beckett's Theatre" 144. The Auditor is also absent from Neil Jordan's 2000 version for the *Beckett on Film* project.
103. See Bair 624–25; *DF* 596–98.
104. Billie Whitelaw to Mel Gussow, 7 February 1984, quoted in Gussow 84.
105. Gussow 84.
106. See Mel Gussow's interview with Billie Whitelaw of 7 February 1984, reproduced in Gussow 90.
107. See, in particular, the notes relating to rehearsals of *Not I*, RUL 1227/7/12/9 and RUL 1227/7/12/11.

108. Beckett quoted in Bair 622.
109. *Not I*, RUL MS 1227/7/12/1, f. 5.
110. *Not I*, RUL MS 1227/7/12/5, f. 5; RUL MS 1227/7/12/6, f. 6.
111. *Not I*, RUL MS 1227/7/12/6, f. 3, 4, 6.
112. *Not I*, RUL MS 1227/7/12/7, f. 6; RUL MS 1227/7/12/8, f. 6.
113. See the uncorrected rehearsal script of *Not I* numbered RUL MS 1227/7/12/9, f. 9; *Not I*, "Corrected copy for Faber December 72", SBC HRHRC MS 5.3, 9.
114. Schneider to Beckett, [?] 3 September 1972, *NABS* 280.
115. Beckett to Schneider, 16 October 1972, *NABS* 283.
116. Billie Whitelaw to Mel Gussow, 7 February 1984, Gussow 89.
117. *Not I*, RUL MS 1227/7/12/1, f. 2.
118. *Not I*, RUL MS 1227/7/12/1, f. 8.
119. *Not I*, RUL MS 1227/7/12/1, f. 6.
120. *Not I*, RUL MS 1227/7/12/2, f. 1.
121. *Not I*, RUL MS 1227/7/12/3, f. 1.
122. *Not I*, RUL MS 1227/7/12/5, f. 1.
123. *Not I*, RUL MS 1227/7/12/5, f. 3, 4.
124. See O'Brien, *The Beckett Country* 45–50.
125. *Not I*, RUL MS 1227/7/12/5, f. 3; RUL MS 1227/7/12/5, f. 4.
126. *Not I*, RUL MS 1227/7/12/10, f. 1.
127. *Pas moi*, RUL MS 1396/4/27, f. 7.
128. Bair 622.
129. Man Ray's *A l'heure de l'observatoire, les amoureux* (oil painting, 1932–34, private collection) is reproduced in Janus, *Man Ray* (Paris: Celiv, 1990) nb. 17, n. pag.
130. A reproduction of the collage and a discussion of its history feature in Anne d'Harnoncourt and Kynaston McShine, eds, *Marcel Duchamp* (New York: Museum of Modern Art, 1973) 306.
131. *DF* 289, 300–2.
132. Bair 622. In a June 1978 interview with Mel Gussow, Beckett's recollection of this experience was different: he mentioned seeing a mother waiting for her child after school and described the play as being based on "[t]he idea of someone watching the watcher". Beckett quoted in Gussow 34. A similar account features in Knowlson's biography; see *DF* 588–89.
133. *CDW* 388; *DF* 601.
134. Beckett quoted in *DF* 600; Beckett quoted in Bair 636.
135. *CDW* 215; Bair 636.
136. Asmus 92.
137. *CDW* 387.
138. Beckett to Schneider, 8 August 1975, *NABS* 328–29.
139. *That Time*, RUL MS 1447/1, f. 1.
140. O'Brien, *The Beckett Country* 37.
141. *CDW* 391.
142. See the relevant entry in Ackerley and Gontarski 531.
143. O'Brien, *The Beckett Country* 27.
144. The locations of the museum, the post office and the public library evoked in part C remain non-specific, and the setting of the play has been open to debate. Both Deirdre Bair and Stan Gontarski argue that the museum

corresponds to the National Portrait Gallery in London. Eoin O'Brien's interpretation is more plausible and does not suggest a conceptual incoherence; he argues that Beckett had in mind Dublin's National Gallery, the Public Library on Pearse Street and the General Post Office on O'Connell Street.
145. *That Time*, RUL MS 1447/1, f. 1.
146. *That Time*, RUL MS 1447/1, ff. 2–3, f. 1.
147. SB to Schneider, 8 August 1975, *NABS* 328.
148. See Dolan, *A Dictionary of Hiberno-English* 132–33.
149. *That Time*, RUL MS 1447/1, f. 4.
150. *DF* 538.
151. Peggy Ashcroft interviewed by Katharine Worth, quoted in Ben-Zvi, ed. *Women in Beckett* 12.
152. *DF* 604.
153. *That Time*, RUL MS 1477/2, f. 3.
154. *That Time*, RUL MS 1477/2, f. 1, 3, 4.
155. *That Time*, RUL MS 1477/2, f. 6.
156. Joyce, *Ulysses* 42.
157. Joyce, *Ulysses* 159.
158. *That Time*, RUL MS 1477/3, f. 1, 2, 5.
159. *That Time*, RUL MS 1447/4, f. 1, 2, 3, 4.
160. Asmus 86. Beckett frequently gave indications of this kind; see, for instance, *DF* 485.
161. Ben-Zvi 48.
162. Billie Whitelaw in an interview with Mel Gussow, 7 February 1984, Gussow 87.
163. *Footfalls*, RUL MS 1552/1, f. 3.
164. *DF* 256, 625.
165. Pedro de Mena, *Magdalena penitente* (polychromatic wood, 1664, Museo Nacional de Escultura, Valladolid), reproduced in Jean Cassou et al., eds, *L'Histoire de l'art*, Vol. 7 (Paris: Grange Batelière, 1975) 73.
166. Irena Jun in an interview with Antoni Libera, Ben-Zvi 48.
167. *Footfalls*, RUL MS 1552/1, f. 2.
168. Beckett, letter to Kay Boyle, 24 May 1986, SBC HRHRC MS 8.6.
169. See Gifford 408 n14.1.
170. Joyce, *Ulysses* 314.
171. *Footfalls*, RUL MS 1552/6, f. 1. This change, however, was made after Faber had published the play; the first edition was based on previous typescripts, before rehearsals began. Ackerley and Gontarski 202; Samuel Beckett, *The Theatrical Notebooks of Samuel Beckett*, Vol. 4: *The Shorter Plays*, ed. S.E. Gontarski (London: Faber, 1999) 275.
172. Asmus 85.
173. Beckett, 24 June 1978, quoted in Gussow 34.
174. *Footfalls*, RUL MS 1552/1, f. 4; RUL MS 1552/2, f. 3, f. 4.
175. *Footfalls*, RUL MS 1552/4, f. 1.
176. *Footfalls*, RUL MS 1552/4, ff. 3–4.
177. *Footfalls*, RUL MS 1552/4, f. 4.
178. *Footfalls*, RUL MS 1552/2, f. 4.
179. *Footfalls*, RUL MS 1552/4, f. 4.

180. *Footfalls*, RUL MS 1552/3, 4, 5.
181. *Footfalls*, RUL MS 2461, p.12/f. 5.
182. Beckett's tendency to make statements about other artists that also apply to himself is mocked in "Three Dialogues", in which D advises B to bear in mind that the subject discussed is not himself (144). The article is loosely based on Beckett's exchanges with Duthuit and was written by Beckett alone; nevertheless, this line remains appropriate in considering Beckett's perspective on the idea of a specifically Irish art form.
183. *Disjecta* 97.
184. Kandinsky, *Complete Writings on Art* 130.
185. In 1942, Rouault's painting "Christ and the Soldier" was bought for the Municipal Gallery of Modern Art, but was rejected by its Art Advisory Committee; see Arnold, *Mainie Jellett and the Modern Movement in Ireland* 187. Flann O'Brien was among the first to launch an attack against Irish parochialism in his *Irish Times* column, pointing out that the duty of the artist was to *make* his own rules; see O'Brien, *The Best of Myles* 236.
186. *Disjecta* 97.

Conclusion

1. The theoretical configuration developed in this book in relation to Beckett and the politics of identity maintains a conceptual proximity to the interrogation of Hegel's dialectics of identity present in Adorno's and Sartre's writings, Adorno's *Negative Dialectics* operating as a critique of Hegelian idealism and Sartre's *Critique of Dialectical Reason* originating in a questioning of the existence and legitimacy of Hegel's dialectic. For clarifications of Sartre's and Adorno's perspectives on Hegel, see *CDR* 22; *AT* 77; Simon Jarvis, *Adorno: A Critical Introduction* (Cambridge: Polity, 1998) 148–74, 170.
2. *TUE* 348.

Bibliography

Unpublished Sources

Bibliothèque Nationale de Paris
Lettres à Jacoba van Velde. MS 19794.

Reading University Library
"Avant *Fin de partie*". MS 1227/7/16/7.
"Before *Play*". MS 1227/7/16/6.
...*but the clouds*.... MS 1553/2-4.
Correspondence with Günter Albrecht. MS 5037.
Correspondence with Ruby Cohn. MS 5100.
Eh Joe. MS 1537/1-3; 5-6; 8.
Footfalls. MS 1552/1-4; 6.
Footfalls. MS 2461.
He, Joe. MS 3626.
Human Wishes Notebooks. MS 3461/1-3.
Letter to Bertie Ahern. 22 February 1987. MS 4937.
Lettre pour Arrabal. 20 September 1967. MS 5044.
Not I. MS 1227/7/12/1-3; 5-10.
Pas moi. MS 1396/4/27.
Play. MS 1528/3.
That Time. MS 1447/1-4.
"Whoroscope" Notebook. MS 3000.

Trinity College Dublin Library
Letters to Alan and Carol Simpson. Pike Theatre Papers. MS 10731/1-86.
Letters to H.O. White. MS 3777/12-25.
Letters to Thomas MacGreevy. MS 10402/1-280.
"Notes on English Literature". MS 10970/3.
Typescript of "MacGreevy on Yeats". MS 9072/10-13.

Harry Ransom Humanities Research Center, University of Texas at Austin
Correspondence with George Reavey. George Reavey Papers. [Unnumbered.]

Samuel Beckett Collection

Correspondence with Aidan Higgins. MS 8.9.
Correspondence with Arland Ussher. MS 9.5.
Correspondence with Jack McGowran. MS 9.3.
Correspondence with John Calder. MS 8.1.
Correspondence with Kay Boyle. MS 8.3-6.
Correspondence with Mary Manning Howe. MS 8.10-11.

Correspondence with Susan Manning. MS 9.4.
Molloy. Notebook 3. MS 4.7.
Not I. MS 5.3.

Carlton Lake Collection of Samuel Beckett
Correspondence with Mania Péron. MS 17.19–20.
Molloy. Incomplete typescript. Annotated by Mania Péron. MS 17.6.
Papers of John Fletcher. Correspondence 1963–1964. MS 18.8.
Papers of John Fletcher. Notebook 11. MS 18.1.

Published Sources

By Samuel Beckett

Beckett, Samuel. "Alba". *Dublin Magazine* Oct.–Dec. 1931: 4.
——. "The Capital of the Ruins". *As the Story Was Told: Uncollected and Late Prose.* London: John Calder, 1990. 17–28.
——. *Comédie et actes divers.* Paris: Editions de Minuit, 1972.
——. *Complete Dramatic Works.* 1986. London: Faber, 1990.
——. *Disjecta: Miscellaneous Writings and a Dramatic Fragment.* Ed. Ruby Cohn. 1983. London: John Calder, 2001.
——. *Dream of Fair to Middling Women.* Ed. Eoin O'Brien and Edith Fournier. Dublin: Black Cat, 1992.
——. *En attendant Godot.* Paris: Editions de Minuit, 1952.
——. "L'Expulsé". *Fontaine* Dec. 1946–Jan. 1947: 685–708.
——. *Fin de partie.* Paris: Editions de Minuit, 1957.
——. *L'Innommable.* Paris: Editions de Minuit, 1953.
——. *Malone meurt.* Paris: Editions de Minuit, 1951.
——. *Molloy.* Paris: Editions de Minuit, 1951.
——. *Molloy, Malone Dies, The Unnamable.* 1956. London: John Calder, 1994.
——. *More Pricks Than Kicks.* 1934. London: John Calder, 1993.
——. *Murphy.* 1938. London: John Calder, 1993.
——. *Murphy.* 1947. Paris: Editions de Minuit, 1965.
——. *The Old Tune.* Adaptation of *La Manivelle, pièce radiophonique.* By Robert Pinget. Paris: Editions de Minuit, 1960.
——. *Premier amour.* Paris: Editions de Minuit, 1970.
——. *Proust.* 1931. *Proust and "Three Dialogues with Georges Duthuit".* London: John Calder, 1965. 9–93.
——. *Texts for Nothing.* 1974. London: John Calder, 1999.
——. *The Theatrical Notebooks of Samuel Beckett.* Vol. 1: Waiting for Godot. Ed. Dougald McMillan. James Knowlson, gen. ed. London: Faber, 1993.
——. *The Theatrical Notebooks of Samuel Beckett.* Vol. 2: Endgame. Ed. S.E. Gontarski. James Knowlson, gen. ed. London: Faber, 1992.
——. *The Theatrical Notebooks of Samuel Beckett.* Vol. 4: *The Shorter Plays; with revised texts for* Footfalls, Come and Go *and* What Where. Ed. S.E. Gontarski. James Knowlson, gen. ed. London: Faber, 1999.
——. *Watt.* 1953. London: John Calder, 1976.
——. *Watt.* 1958. Trans. Ludovic and Agnès Janvier, in collaboration with Samuel Beckett. Paris: Editions de Minuit, 1968.

——. "Who Is Godot?" Trans. Edith Fournier. *New Yorker* 24 June and 1 July 1996: 136.
Beckett, Samuel, and Alan Schneider. *No Author Better Served: The Correspondence of Samuel Beckett and Alan Schneider*. Ed. Maurice Harmon. Cambridge, MA: Harvard UP, 1998.

Critical Sources

Abendroth, Wolfgang. "Elements for a Scientific Politics". *Conversations with Lukács*. By Hans Heinz Holz, Leo Kofler and Wolfgang Abendroth. Ed. Theo Pinkus. Cambridge, MA: MIT P, 1975. 81–118.
Accampo, Elinor A. "The Gendered Nature of Contraception in France: Neo-Malthusianism, 1900–1920". *Journal of Interdisciplinary History* 34.2 (2003): 235–62.
Ackerley, Chris. *Demented Particulars: The Annotated* Murphy. 2nd ed. Tallahassee: Journal of Beckett Studies Books, 2004.
Ackerley, Chris, and S.E. Gontarski. *The Grove Companion to Samuel Beckett: A Reader's Guide to His Works, Life, and Thought*. New York: Grove, 2004.
Adams, Michael. *Censorship: The Irish Experience*. Dublin: Scepter, 1968.
Adorno, Theodor W. *Aesthetic Theory*. Ed. Gretel Adorno and Rolf Tiedemann. Trans., ed., and introd. Robert Hullot-Kentor. Minneapolis: U of Minnesota P, 1997.
——. "Commitment". Trans. Francis McDonagh. *Aesthetics and Politics*. By Theodor W. Adorno, Ernst Bloch, Walter Benjamin, Bertolt Brecht and Georg Lukács. Ed. Ronald Taylor. London: NLB, 1977. 177–95.
——. "Cultural Criticism and Society". Trans. Samuel and Shierry Weber. *The Adorno Reader*. Ed. Brian O'Connor. Oxford: Blackwell, 2000. 195–210.
——. *Notes sur Beckett*. Trans. Christophe David. Introd. Rolf Tiedemann. Caen: Nous Editions, 2008.
——. *Philosophy of Modern Music*. Trans. Anne G. Mitchell and Wesley V. Bloomster. London: Sheed and Ward, 1973.
——. "Reconciliation under Duress". Trans. Rodney Livingstone. *Aesthetics and Politics*. By Theodor W. Adorno, Ernst Bloch, Walter Benjamin, Bertolt Brecht and Georg Lukács. Ed. Ronald Taylor. London: NLB, 1977. 151–76.
——. "Trying to Understand *Endgame*". Trans. Michael J. Jones. *The Adorno Reader*. Ed. Brian O'Connor. Oxford: Blackwell, 2000. 319–52.
AE, John Eglinton, William Larminie and W.B. Yeats. *Literary Ideals in Ireland*. London: T. Fischer Unwin, 1899.
Albright, Daniel. *Representation and the Imagination: Beckett, Kafka, Nabokov, and Schoenberg*. Chicago: University of Chicago Press, 1981.
Allen, Kieran. *Fianna Fáil and Irish Labour: 1926 to the Present*. London: Pluto, 1997.
——. *The Politics of James Connolly*. London: Pluto, 1990.
Allen, Nicholas. *George Russell (AE) and the New Ireland, 1905–30*. Dublin: Four Courts, 2003.
Alvarez, A. *Beckett*. London: Woburn, 1974.
Anderson, Perry, Rodney Livingstone and Francis Mulhern. "Presentation II". *Aesthetics and Politics*. By Theodor W. Adorno, Ernst Bloch, Walter Benjamin, Bertolt Brecht and Georg Lukács. Translation ed. Ronald Taylor. London: NLB, 1977. 60–7.

Anderson, Perry, Rodney Livingstone and Francis Mulhern. "Presentation IV". *Aesthetics and Politics*. By Theodor W. Adorno, Ernst Bloch, Walter Benjamin, Bertolt Brecht and Georg Lukács. Trans. and ed. Ronald Taylor. London: NLB, 1977. 142–50.

Archibald, Douglas N. "*The Words upon the Window-pane* and Yeats's Encounter with Jonathan Swift". *Yeats and the Theatre*. Ed. Robert O'Driscoll and Lorna Reynolds. London: Macmillan, 1975. 176–214.

Armstrong, Gordon S. *Samuel Beckett, W.B. Yeats, and Jack Yeats: Images and Words*. Lewisburg: Bucknell UP; London: Associated U Presses, 1990.

Armstrong, Tim. "Muting the Klaxon: Poetry, History and Irish Modernism". *Modernism and Ireland: The Poetry of the 1930s*. Ed. Patricia Coughlan and Alex Davis. Cork: Cork UP, 1995. 43–74.

Arnold, Bruce. *Mainie Jellett and the Modern Movement in Ireland*. London: Yale UP, 1991.

Arnold, Matthew. *On the Study of Celtic Literature*. London: Smith, Elder, 1867.

Aron, Raymond. *History and the Dialectic of Violence: An Analysis of Sartre's* Critique de la raison dialectique. Trans. Barry Cooper. Oxford: Blackwell, 1975.

Asmus, Walter D. "Practical Aspects of Theater, Radio and Television: Rehearsal Notes". Trans. Helen Watanabe. *Journal of Beckett Studies* 2 (1977): 82–95.

Atik, Anne. *How It Was*. London: Faber, 2001.

Bair, Deirdre. *Samuel Beckett: A Biography*. London: Jonathan Cape, 1978.

"Beckett Greets Aosdana Honour 'with a Shy Nod'". *Irish Times* 14 April 1986: 9.

Beer, Ann. "Beckett's Bilingualism". *The Cambridge Companion to Beckett*. Ed. John Pilling. Cambridge: Cambridge UP, 1994. 209–21.

Bely, Andrey. *Selected Essays of Andrey Bely*. Ed. and trans. Steven Cassedy. Berkeley: U of California P, 1985.

Ben-Zvi, Linda, ed. *Women in Beckett*. Urbana: U of Illinois P, 1990.

Binchy, Maeve. "Beckett Finally Gets Down to Work – As the Actors Take a Break". *Irish Times* 14 May 1980: 7.

Blume, Torsten. "The Historic Bauhaus Stage – A Theatre of Space". *Bauhaus. Theatre. Dessau*. Ed. Marie Neumuller. Berlin: Jovis, 2007. 22–63.

Boxall, Peter. "Samuel Beckett: Towards a Political Reading". *Irish Studies Review* 10.2 (2002): 159–70.

Bradby, David. *Beckett: Waiting for Godot*. Cambridge: Cambridge UP, 2001.

Brand, Juliane, and Christopher Hailey. *Constructive Dissonance: Arnold Schoenberg and the Transformations of Twentieth-Century Culture*. Berkeley: U of California P, 1997.

Brater, Enoch. "Dada, Surrealism, and the Genesis of *Not I*". *Modern Drama* 18 (1975): 49–59.

——. *Why Beckett*. London: Thames and Hudson, 1989.

Brecht, Bertolt. "Against Georg Lukács". Trans. Stuart Hood. *New Left Review* 84 (1974): 39–53.

——. *Brecht on Theatre: The Development of an Aesthetic*. Ed. and trans. John Willett. 2nd ed. London: Eyre Methuen, 1978.

Breton, André. *Manifestes du surréalisme*. Paris: Gallimard, 1985.

Brooker, Joseph. *Flann O'Brien*. Tavistock, Eng.: Northcote, 2005.

Brown, Terence. "Cultural Nationalism 1880–1930". *The Field Day Anthology of Irish Writing*. Vol. 2. Ed. Seamus Deane. 3 vols. Derry: Field Day, 1991. 516–26.

―――. *Ireland: A Social and Cultural History, 1922–1985.* 2nd ed. London: Fontana, 1985.
―――. "Ireland, Modernism and the 1930s". *Modernism and Ireland: The Poetry of the 1930s.* Ed. Patricia Coughlan and Alex Davis. Cork: Cork UP, 1995. 24–42.
―――. *The Life of W.B. Yeats: A Critical Biography.* Dublin: Gill & Macmillan, 1999.
Bryden, Mary, Julian Garforth and Peter Mills. *Beckett at Reading: Catalogue of the Beckett Manuscript Collection at the University of Reading.* Reading, Eng.: Whiteknights P and the Beckett International Foundation, 1998.
Bürger, Peter. *Theory of the Avant-Garde.* Trans. Michael Shaw. Manchester: Manchester UP, 1984.
Camus, Albert. *The Myth of Sisyphus.* Trans. Justin O'Brien. Introd. James Wood. London: Penguin, 2000.
Carey, Phyllis, and Ed Jewinski, eds. *Re: Joyce'n Beckett.* New York: Fordham UP, 1992.
Carlson, Julia, ed. *Banned in Ireland: Censorship and the Irish Writer.* London: Routledge, 1990.
Carroll, Clare, and Patricia King, eds. *Ireland and Postcolonial Theory.* Cork: Cork UP, 2003.
Cassou, Jean et al., eds. *L'Histoire de l'art.* 10 vols. Paris: Grange Batelière, 1975.
Castle, Gregory. *Modernism and the Celtic Revival.* Cambridge: Cambridge UP, 2001.
Chamberlain, Lois. "'The Same Old Stories': Beckett's Poetics of Translation". *Beckett Translating/Translating Beckett.* Ed. Alan Warren Friedman, Charles Rossman and Dina Scherzer. University Park: Pennsylvania State UP, 1987. 17–24.
Clarke, Austin. "Irish Poetry To-Day". *Dublin Magazine* Jan.–Mar. 1935: 26–32.
Clifford, James. *The Predicament of Culture: Twentieth-Century Ethnography, Literature, and Art.* Cambridge, MA: Harvard UP, 1988.
Clissmann, Anne. *Flann O'Brien: A Critical Introduction to His Writings.* Dublin: Gill & Macmillan, 1975.
Cockerham, Harry. "Bilingual Playwright". *Beckett the Shape Changer: A Symposium.* Ed. Katharine Worth. London: Routledge and Kegan Paul, 1975. 139–59.
Cohn, Ruby. *Back to Beckett.* Princeton: Princeton UP, 1973.
Collinge, Linda. *Beckett traduit Beckett: De* Malone meurt *à* Malone Dies: *L'imaginaire en traduction.* Geneva: Droz, 2000.
Connolly, James. Foreword. *Collected Works.* Vol. 1. 2 vols. By Connolly. Introd. Michael O'Riordan. Dublin: New Books, 1987. 17–25.
―――. "Let Us Free Ireland!" *Collected Works.* Vol. 2. 2 vols. Introd. Michael O'Riordan. Dublin: New Books, 1987. 211–12.
Conti, Chris. "Critique and Form: Adorno on *Godot* and *Endgame*". *Samuel Beckett Today/Aujourd'hui* 14 (2004): 277–92.
Cooney, John. *John Charles McQuaid, Ruler of Catholic Ireland.* Dublin: O'Brien, 1999.
Copeland, Hannah Case. *Art and the Artist in the Works of Samuel Beckett.* The Hague: Mouton, 1975.
Corkery, Daniel. *The Hidden Ireland: A Study of Gaelic Munster in the Eighteenth Century.* Dublin: Gill, 1967.

Corkery, Daniel. *Synge and Anglo-Irish Literature*. Cork: Mercier, 1966.
Coughlan, Patricia. "'The Poetry Is Another Pair of Sleeves': Beckett, Ireland and Modernist Lyric Poetry". *Modernism and Ireland: The Poetry of the 1930s*. Ed. Patricia Coughlan and Alex Davis. Cork: Cork UP, 1995. 173–208.
Cronin, Anthony. *Samuel Beckett: The Last Modernist*. London: Flamingo, 1997.
Cronin, Michael. *Translating Ireland: Translation, Languages, Cultures*. Cork: Cork UP, 1996.
Cunard, Nancy. *Authors Take Sides on the Spanish War*. London: Left Review, 1937.
Dáil Eireann Parliamentary Debates: Official Report. Vol. 28. Dublin: Cahill, 1929.
Darbelnet, J., and J.P. Vinay. *Stylistique comparée du français et de l'anglais*. Paris: Didier, 1958.
Davis, Robert B. *George William Russell (AE)*. Boston: Twayne, 1977.
Deane, Seamus. *Celtic Revivals: Essays in Modern Irish Literature, 1880–1980*. London: Faber, 1985.
Deleuze, Gilles. "L'Epuisé". *Quad, Trio du fantôme,…que nuages…, Nacht und Träume*. By Samuel Beckett. Paris: Editions de Minuit, 1992. 55–106.
Dettmar, Kevin. "The Joyce That Beckett Built". *Beckett and Beyond*. Ed. Bruce Stewart. Gerrards Cross, Eng.: Colin Smythe, 1999. 78–92.
de Valera, Eamon. *Speeches and Statements by Eamon de Valera, 1917–73*. Ed. Maurice Moynihan. Dublin: Gill & Macmillan, 1980.
d'Harnoncourt, Anne, and Kynaston McShine, eds. *Marcel Duchamp*. New York: Museum of Modern Art, 1973.
Dolan, Terence Patrick. *A Dictionary of Hiberno-English*. 2nd ed. Dublin: Gill & Macmillan, 2004.
——. "Samuel Beckett's Dramatic Use of Hiberno-English". *Irish University Review* 14.1 (1984): 46–56.
Duckworth, Colin. *Angels of Darkness: Dramatic Effect in Samuel Beckett with Special Reference to Eugene Ionesco*. London: Allen and Unwin, 1972.
Dukes, Gerry. "Beckett's Synge-Song: The Revised *Godot* Revisited". *Journal of Beckett Studies* 4.2 (1995): 103–12.
——. "Englishing *Godot*". *Samuel Beckett Today/Aujourd'hui* 14 (2004): 521–31.
——. "The Pike Theatre Typescript of *Waiting for Godot*: Part I". *Journal of Beckett Studies* 4.2 (1995): 77–91.
——. *Samuel Beckett*. Woodstock, NY: Overlook, 2002.
Dunsby, Jonathan. *Pierrot lunaire*. Cambridge: Cambridge UP, 2002.
Eagleton, Terry. "The Archaic Avant-Garde". *Heathcliff and the Great Hunger: Studies in Irish Culture*. London: Verso, 1995. 273–319.
Ellmann, Richard. *James Joyce*. 2nd ed. New York: Oxford UP, 1982.
——. "Samuel Beckett: Nayman of Noland". *Four Dubliners: Wilde, Yeats, Joyce, and Beckett*. London: Hamilton, 1987. 79–104.
Elsworth, J.D. *Andrey Bely*. Letchworth, Eng.: Bradda, 1972.
——. *Andrey Bely: A Critical Study of the Novels*. Cambridge: Cambridge UP, 1983.
Esslin, Martin. *The Theatre of the Absurd*. 3rd ed. London: Penguin, 1991.
Fanon, Frantz. *Black Skin, White Masks*. Trans. Charles Lam Markmann. London: Pluto, 1986.
——. *The Wretched of the Earth*. Trans. Constance Farrington. London: MacGibbon and Kee, 1965.

Federman, Raymond, and John Fletcher. *Samuel Beckett – His Works and His Critics: An Essay in Bibliography*. Berkeley: U of California P, 1970.

Ferriter, Diarmaid. *The Transformation of Ireland, 1900–2000*. London: Profile, 2004.

Figgis, Darrell. *AE (George W. Russell): A Study of a Man and a Nation*. Dublin: Maunsel, 1916.

Fitch, Brian. *Beckett and Babel: An Investigation into the Status of Bilingual Work*. London: U of Toronto P, 1988.

Fitzgerald, Mary. "Four French Comedies: Lady Gregory's Translations of Molière". *Lady Gregory: Fifty Years After*. Ed. Anne Saddlemyer and Colin Smythe. Gerrards Cross, Eng.: Colin Smythe, 1987. 227–90.

"Fitzgerald Addresses Assembly of Aosdána". *Irish Times* 15 April 1983: 7.

Fletcher, John. *A Faber Critical Guide: Samuel Beckett*. London: Faber, 2000.

——. *Samuel Beckett's Art*. London: Chatto and Windus, 1967.

Foster, Roy. *Paddy and Mr Punch: Connections in Irish and English History*. London: Penguin, 1993.

——. *W.B. Yeats: A Life*, Vol. 2: *The Arch-Poet*. Oxford: Oxford UP, 2003.

Friedman, Melvin J. "George Moore and Samuel Beckett: Cross-Currents and Correspondences". *George Moore in Perspective*. Totowa: Barnes and Noble, 1983. 117–31.

Füger, Wilhelm. "The First Berlin *Godot*: Beckett's Debut on the German Stage". *Samuel Beckett Today/Aujourd'hui* 11 (2001): 57–63.

Fumaroli, Marc. "The Genius of the French Language". *Realms of Memory: Rethinking the French Past*. Vol. 3: *Symbols*. 3 vols. Under the direction of Pierre Nora. Trans. Arthur Goldhammer. Ed. and foreword Lawrence D. Kritzman. New York: Columbia UP, 1998. 555–606.

Gaffney, Phyllis. "Dante, Manzoni, De Valera, Beckett…? Circumlocutions of a Storekeeper: Beckett and Saint-Lô". *Irish University Review* 29.2 (1999): 256–80.

Garrigan Mattar, Sinéad. *Primitivism, Science, and the Irish Revival*. Oxford: Oxford UP, 2004.

——. "Wage for Each People Her Hand Has Destroyed: Lady Gregory's Colonial Nationalism". *Irish University Review* 34.1 (2004): 49–66.

Genet, Jacqueline. "Yeats and the Myth of Rural Ireland". *Rural Ireland, Real Ireland?* Ed. Jacqueline Genet. Gerrards Cross, Eng.: Colin Smythe, 1996. 139–57.

Gifford, Don, ed. *Ulysses Annotated: Notes for James Joyce's Ulysses*. 2nd ed. London: U of California P, 1988.

Girvin, Brian. *Between Two Worlds: Politics and Economy in Independent Ireland*. Dublin: Gill & Macmillan, 1989.

Gluck, Barbara Reich. *Beckett and Joyce: Friendship and Fiction*. Lewisburg: Bucknell UP, 1979.

Golden, Sean. "Familiars in a Ruinstrewn Land: *Endgame* as Political Allegory". *Contemporary Literature* 22 (1981): 425–55.

Gontarski, S.E. *The Intent of Undoing in Samuel Beckett's Dramatic Texts*. Bloomington: Indiana UP, 1985.

——, ed. "Notes on the Texts". *Samuel Beckett: The Complete Short Prose, 1929–1989*. By Samuel Beckett. New York: Grove, 1995. 279–86.

——. "Revising Himself: Performance as Text in Samuel Beckett's Theatre". *Journal of Modern Literature* 22.1 (1998): 131–45.

Gontarski, S.E., Martha Fehsenfeld and Dougald McMillan. "Interview with Rachel Burrows, Dublin, Bloomsday, 1982". *Journal of Beckett Studies* 11–12 (1989): 5–15.
Graham, Colin. "Post-Colonial Theory and Kiberd's 'Ireland'". *Irish Review* 19 (1996): 62–67.
Gregory, Lady Augusta. *The Comedies of Lady Gregory, Being the First Volume of the Collected Plays*. Ed. Anne Saddlemyer. Gerrards Cross, Eng.: Colin Smythe, 1970.
——. *Ideals in Ireland*. By AE, D.P. Moran, George Moore, Douglas Hyde, Standish O'Grady and W.B. Yeats. London: Unicorn, 1901.
——. *Our Irish Theatre: A Chapter of Autobiography*. Foreword Roger McHugh. Gerrards Cross, Eng.: Colin Smythe, 1972.
——. *The Kiltartan Molière: The Miser, The Doctor in Spite of Himself, The Rogueries of Scapin*. Dublin: Maunsel, 1910.
——. *Selected Writings*. Ed. and introd. Lucy McDiarmid and Maureen Waters. London: Penguin, 1995.
Gruen, John. "Nobel Prize Winner 1969, Samuel Beckett Talks about Beckett". [US] *Vogue* Dec. 1969: 210.
Gussow, Mel. *Conversations with (and about) Beckett*. London: Nick Hern, 1996.
Ha, Marie-Paule. "The Narrative of Return in 'Orphée Noir'". *Situating Sartre in Twentieth-Century Thought and Culture*. Ed. Jean-François Fourny and Charles D. Minahen. Basingstoke, Eng.: Macmillan, 1997. 93–109.
Harrington, John. *The Irish Beckett*. New York: Syracuse UP, 1991.
——. "'That Red Branch Bum Was the Camel's Back': Beckett's Use of Yeats in *Murphy*". *Eire-Ireland* 15.3 (1980): 86–96.
Hecht, Werner. *Aufsätze über Brecht*. Berlin: Henschelverlag, 1970.
Heidegger, Martin. "L'Origine de l'oeuvre d'art". *Chemins qui ne mènent vers nulle part*. Trans. Wolfgang Brokmeier. Rev. ed. Paris: Gallimard, 1980.
Hill, Leslie. "'Up the Republic!' Beckett, Writing, Politics". *Modern Language Notes* 112.5 (1997): 909–28.
Hogan, Robert, and James Kilroy, eds. *The Irish Literary Theatre 1899–1901*. Dublin: Dolmen, 1975.
Holloway, Joseph. *Joseph Holloway's Abbey Theatre: A Selection from His Unpublished Journal "Impressions of a Dublin Playgoer"*. Ed. Robert Hogan and Michael J. O'Neill. Carbondale: Southern Illinois UP; London: Feffer and Simons, 1967.
Holt, Matthew. "Catastrophe, Autonomy and the Future of Modernism: Trying to Understand Adorno's Reading of *Endgame*". *Samuel Beckett Today/Aujourd'hui* 14 (2004): 261–75.
Howe, Stephen. *Ireland and Empire: Colonial Legacies in Irish History and Culture*. Oxford: Oxford UP, 2000.
Howes, Marjorie. *Yeats's Nations: Gender, Class, and Irishness*. Cambridge: Cambridge UP, 1996.
Hunt, Hugh. *The Abbey: Ireland's National Theatre, 1904–1978*. Dublin: Gill & Macmillan, 1979.
Hyde, Douglas. *Abhráin Grádh Chúige Connacht, or: Love Songs of Connacht*. 4th ed. Dublin: Gill and Son; London: T. F. Unwin, 1905.
——. "The Necessity for De-Anglicizing Ireland". *Irish Writing in the Twentieth Century: A Reader*. Ed. David Pierce. Cork: Cork UP, 2000. 1–11.
Jameson, Fredric. "Reflections in Conclusion". *Aesthetics and Politics*. By Theodor W. Adorno, Ernst Bloch, Walter Benjamin, Bertolt Brecht and Georg Lukács. Trans. and ed. Ronald Taylor. London: NLB, 1977. 196–213.

Janus. *Man Ray*. Paris: Celiv, 1990.
Janvier, Ludovic. "Au travail avec Beckett". *Samuel Beckett, L'Herne 31*. Ed. Tom Bishop and Raymond Federman. Paris: Editions de l'Herne, 1976. 137–40.
——. *Samuel Beckett par lui-même*. Paris: Editions du Seuil, 1969.
Jarvis, Simon. *Adorno: A Critical Introduction*. Cambridge: Polity, 1998.
Jeffares, A. Norman. *W.B. Yeats: A New Biography*. 2nd ed. London: Continuum, 2001.
Jewinski, Ed. "James Joyce and Samuel Beckett: From Epiphany to Anti-Epiphany". *Re: Joyce'n Beckett*. Ed. Phyllis Carey and Ed Jewinski. New York: Fordham UP, 1992. 160–74.
Jolas, Eugene. "Poetry Is Vertical". *transition* 21 (March 1932): 148–49.
Joyce, James. *The Critical Writings of James Joyce*. Ed. Ellsworth Mason and Richard Ellmann. London: Faber, 1959.
——. *A Portrait of the Artist as a Young Man*. Corr. Chester G. Anderson. Ed. Richard Ellmann. London: Jonathan Cape, 1968.
——. *Ulysses*. The Corrected Text. Ed. Hans Walter Gabler, Wolfhard Steppe and Claus Melchior. London: Bodley Head, 1986.
Jules-Rosette, Bennetta. "Conjugating Cultural Realities: Présence Africaine". *The Surreptitious Speech: 'Présence africaine' and the Politics of Otherness*. Ed. V.Y. Mudimbe. Chicago: U of Chicago P, 1992. 14–44.
Juliet, Charles. *Conversations with Samuel Beckett and Bram van Velde*. Trans. Janey Tucker. Introd. Adriaan van der Weel and Ruud Hisgen. Leiden: Academic P Leiden, 1995.
Junker, Mary. *Beckett: The Irish Dimension*. Dublin: Wolfhound, 1995.
Kandinsky, Wassily. *Complete Writings on Art*. Ed. Kenneth C. Lindsay and Peter Vergo. New York: Da Capo, 1994.
Kandinsky, Wassily, and Arnold Schoenberg. *Arnold Schoenberg and Wassily Kandinsky: Letters, Pictures and Documents*. Ed. Jelena Hahl-Koch. Trans. John C. Crawford. London: Faber, 1984.
Katz, Daniel. "Mirror-Resembling Screens: Yeats, Beckett and …*but the clouds*…". *Samuel Beckett Today/Aujourd'hui* 4 (1995): 83–92.
Kearney, Richard. "Beckett: The End of the Story?" *Transitions: Narratives in Modern Irish Culture*. Ed. Richard Kearney. Manchester: Manchester UP, 1988. 58–82.
——. "Joyce and Borges: Modernism and the Irish Mind – Richard Kearney and Seamus Heaney in Conversation with Jorge Luis Borges". *Transitions: Narratives in Modern Irish Culture*. Ed. Richard Kearney. Manchester: Manchester UP, 1988. 47–57.
——. *Postnationalist Ireland: Politics, Culture, Philosophy*. London: Routledge, 1997.
Kennedy, S.B. "An Incisive Aesthetic". *Irish Arts* 21.2 (2004): 90–95.
Kennedy, Seán. "'The Artist Who Stakes His Being Is from Nowhere': Beckett and MacGreevy on the Art of Jack B. Yeats". *Samuel Beckett Today/Aujourd'hui* 14 (2004): 61–74.
——. "Beckett Reviewing MacGreevy: A Reconsideration". *Irish University Review* 35.2 (2005): 273–87.
——. "Introduction to *Historicising Beckett*". *Samuel Beckett Today/Aujourd'hui* 15 (2005): 21–27.
Kennedy, Sighle. *Murphy's Bed: A Study of Real Sources and Sur-Real Associations in Samuel Beckett's First Novel*. Lewisburg: Bucknell UP, 1971.

Kiberd, Declan. *Inventing Ireland: The Literature of the Modern Nation*. London: Vintage, 1996.
———. *Irish Classics*. London: Granta, 2000.
———. *Synge and the Irish Language*. 2nd ed. London: Macmillan, 1993.
Kirishima, Keiko. " Le Théâtre de Beckett et le théâtre nô". *Critique* 96.519–20 (1990): 691.
Klee, Paul. *The Diaries of Paul Klee*. Ed. Felix Klee. Berkeley: U of California P, 1964.
———. *The Thinking Eye*. Ed. Jürg Spiller. New York: Wittenborn; London: Lund Humphries, 1961.
Knowlson, James. "Beckett and John Millington Synge". *Frescoes of the Skull: The Later Prose and Drama of Samuel Beckett*. By James Knowlson and John Pilling. London: John Calder, 1979. 259–74.
———. *Damned to Fame: The Life of Samuel Beckett*. London: Bloomsbury, 1996.
———. Foreword. *The Beckett Country: Samuel Beckett's Ireland*. By Eoin O'Brien. Monkstown, Ire.: Black Cat and Faber, 1986. viii–xxvi.
———. *Samuel Beckett: An Exhibition*. London: Turret, 1971.
Knowlson, James, and Elizabeth Knowlson, eds. *Beckett Remembering/Remembering Beckett: A Centenary Celebration*. New York: Arcade, 2006.
Kofler, Leo. "Society and the Individual". *Conversations with Lukács*. By Hans Heinz Holz, Leo Kofler and Wolfgang Abendroth. Ed. Theo Pinkus. Cambridge, MA: MIT P, 1975. 41–80.
Kostelanetz, Richard, ed. *Moholy-Nagy*. London: Allen Lane, 1974.
Kronik, Eva. "Interview: Arrabal". *Diacritics* 5.2 (1975): 54–60.
Labrusse, Rémi. "Beckett et la peinture". *Critique* 156.519–20 (1990): 670–80.
———. "Samuel Beckett et Georges Duthuit". *Samuel Beckett: A Passion for Paintings*. Ed. Fionnuala Croke. Dublin: National Gallery of Ireland, 2006. 88–91.
Lamont, Rosette. "Crossing the Iron Curtain: Political Parables". *Beckett Translating/Translating Beckett*. Ed. Alan Warren Friedman, Charles Rossman and Dina Scherzer. University Park: Pennsylvania State UP, 1987. 77–84.
Lasko, Peter. *The Expressionist Roots of Modernism*. Manchester: Manchester UP, 2003.
Lee, Joseph. *Ireland 1912–1985: Politics and Society*. Cambridge: Cambridge UP, 1989.
Levitas, Ben. *The Theatre of Nation: Irish Drama and Cultural Nationalism, 1890–1916*. Oxford: Oxford UP, 2002.
Levy, Alan. "The Long Wait for Godot". *Theatre Arts* 40 (1968): 34.
Lloyd, David. *Anomalous States: Irish Writing and the Postcolonial Moment*. Dublin: Lilliput, 1993. 41–58.
Long, Bill. *Bright Light, White Water: The Story of Irish Lighthouses and Their People*. Dundrum, Ire.: New Island Books, 1993.
Lukács, Georg. *History and Class Consciousness: Studies in Marxist Dialectics*. Trans. Rodney Livingstone. London: Merlin, 1971.
———. *The Meaning of Contemporary Realism*. Trans. John and Necke Maunder. London: Merlin, 1963.
———. "On Bertolt Brecht". Trans. Rodney Livingstone. *New Left Review* 110 (1978): 86–90.
Lunn, Eugene. *Marxism and Modernism: An Historical Study of Lukács, Brecht, Benjamin and Adorno*. London: U of California P, 1984.

Lyons, F.S.L. *Ireland Since the Famine*. 2nd ed. London: Fontana, 1985.
MacDonagh, Thomas. *Literature in Ireland: Studies Irish and Anglo-Irish*. Dublin: Talbot, 1916.
MacGreevy, Thomas. *Jack B. Yeats: An Appreciation and an Interpretation*. Dublin: Victor Waddington, 1945.
Marx, Karl. *Capital: A Critique of Political Economy*. Book 1: *The Process of Production of Capital*. Trans. Samuel Moore and Edward Aveling. Ed. Friedrich Engels. London: Lawrence and Wishart, 1977.
——. *Economic and Philosophic Manuscripts of 1844*. Ed. and introd. Dirk J. Struik. Trans. Martin Milligan. London: Lawrence and Wishart, 1973.
Mays, J.C.C. "Beckett and the Irish". *Hibernia* 33.21 (1969): 14.
——. "How Is MacGreevy a Modernist?" *Modernism and Ireland: The Poetry of the 1930s*. Ed. Patricia Coughlan and Alex Davis. Cork: Cork UP, 1995. 103–28.
——, ed. Introduction. *Diarmuid and Grania: Manuscript Materials*. By W.B. Yeats and George Moore. Ithaca: Cornell UP, 2005. xxix–l.
——. "Mythologized Presences: *Murphy* in Its Time". *Myth and Reality in Irish Literature*. Ed. Joseph Ronsley. Waterloo, ON: Wilfrid Laurier UP, 1977. 197–218.
——. "Young Beckett's Irish Roots". *Irish University Review* 14.1 (1984): 18–33.
McAteer, Michael. *Standish O'Grady, AE and Yeats: History, Politics, Culture*. Dublin: Irish Academic P, 2002.
——. "Yeats's *Endgame*: Postcolonialism and Modernism". *Critical Ireland: New Essays in Literature and Culture*. Ed. Alan Gillis and Aaron Kelly. Dublin: Four Courts, 2001. 160–65.
McCormack, W.J. *From Burke to Beckett: Ascendancy, Tradition, and Betrayal in Literary History*. 2nd ed. Cork: Cork UP, 1994.
McDonald, Ronan. *Tragedy and Irish Literature: Synge, O'Casey, Beckett*. Basingstoke, Eng.: Palgrave, 2002.
McMillan, Dougald. Introduction. *As the Story Was Told: Uncollected and Late Prose*. By Samuel Beckett. London: John Calder, 1990. 13–16.
McMullan, Anna. "Irish/Postcolonial Beckett". *Palgrave Advances in Samuel Beckett Studies*. Ed. Lois Oppenheim. Basingstoke, Eng.: Palgrave Macmillan, 2004. 89–109.
Meenan, James. *The Irish Economy Since 1922*. Liverpool: Liverpool UP, 1970.
Memmi, Albert. *The Colonizer and the Colonized*. Trans. Howard Greenfeld. London: Souvenir, 1974.
Mercier, Vivian. *Beckett/Beckett*. New York: Oxford UP, 1977.
——. "Beckett's Anglo-Irish Stage Dialects". *James Joyce Quarterly* 8.4 (1971): 311–17.
——. "Ireland/The World: Beckett's Irishness". *Yeats, Joyce, and Beckett: New Light on Three Modern Irish Writers*. Ed. Kathleen McGrory and John Unterecker. Lewisburg: Bucknell UP, 1976. 147–52.
——. *The Irish Comic Tradition*. Oxford: Oxford UP, 1962.
Miller, Liam. *The Noble Drama of W.B. Yeats*. Dublin: Dolmen, 1977.
Miller, Tyrus. "Dismantling Authenticity: Beckett, Adorno, and the 'Post-War'". *Textual Practice* 8.1 (1994): 43–57.
Moholy-Nagy, Lázló. "The Coming Theatre – The Total Theatre". *The Bauhaus: Weimar, Dessau, Berlin, Chicago*. By Hans Maria Wingler. Ed. Joseph Stein. Trans. Wolfgang Jabs and Basil Gilbert. Cambridge, MA: MIT P, 1976. 132.

Montague, John. *Company: A Life*. London: Duckworth, 2001.
Mooney, Sinéad. "Kicking against the Thermolaters". *Samuel Beckett Today/Aujourd'hui* 15 (2005): 29–42.
Moore, George. *Hail and Farewell: Ave, Salve, Vale*. Ed. Richard Cave. Gerrards Cross, Eng.: Colin Smythe, 1976.
Morash, Christopher. *A History of Irish Theatre, 1601–2000*. Cambridge: Cambridge UP, 2002.
Morot-Sir, Edouard. "Sartre's *Critique of Dialectical Reason*". *Journal of the History of Ideas* 22.4 (1961): 573–81.
Murray, Christopher. "O'Casey's *The Drums of Father Ned* in Context". *A Century of Irish Drama: Widening the Stage*. Ed. Stephen Watt, Eileen Morgan and Shakir Mustafa. Bloomington: Indiana UP, 2000. 117–29.
Murray, Christopher, and Masaru Sekine, eds. *Yeats and the Noh: A Comparative Study*. Gerrards Cross, Eng.: Colin Smythe, 1990.
Murray, Patrick. *The Tragic Comedian: A Study of Samuel Beckett*. Cork: Mercier, 1970.
Naylor, Gillian. *The Bauhaus Reassessed: Sources and Design Theory*. London: Herbert, 1985.
O'Brien, Eoin. *The Beckett Country: Samuel Beckett's Ireland*. Foreword James Knowlson. Monkstown, Ire.: Black Cat and Faber, 1986.
O'Brien, Flann. *The Best of Myles: A Selection from "Cruiskeen Lawn"*. Ed. Kevin O'Nolan. London: MacGibbon and Kee, 1968.
——. *The Hair of the Dogma: A Further Selection from "Cruiskeen Lawn"*. Ed. Kevin O'Nolan. London: Hart Davis; MacGibbon, 1977.
——. *The Poor Mouth: A Bad Story about the Hard Life*. Trans. Patrick C. Power. Normal: Dalkey Archive, 1996.
O'Casey, Sean. *Inishfallen, Fare Thee Well. Autobiographies II*. 2 vols. London: Macmillan, 1963.
——. *The Letters of Sean O'Casey*. Vol. 1. 3 vols. Ed. David Krause. London: Cassell and Macmillan, 1975.
——. *The Letters of Sean O'Casey*. Vol. 2. 3 vols. Ed. David Krause. New York: Macmillan, 1980.
——. *The Letters of Sean O'Casey*. Vol. 3. 3 vols. Ed. David Krause. Washington, DC: Catholic U of America P, 1989.
——. *Three Dublin Plays:* The Shadow of a Gunman, Juno and the Paycock, The Plough and the Stars. Introd. Christopher Murray. London: Faber, 1998.
O Conaire, Brendan. "Flann O'Brien, *An Béal Bocht*, and Other Irish Matters". *Irish University Review* 3.2 (1973): 121–40.
O'Connor, Garry. *Sean O'Casey: A Life*. London: Paladin, 1989.
O'Connor, Ulick. *Celtic Dawn: A Portrait of the Irish Literary Renaissance*. London: Hamilton, 1984.
——. *Oliver St John Gogarty: A Poet and His Times*. Dublin: O'Brien, 1999.
Ó hAodha, Micheál. *Theatre in Ireland*. Oxford: Blackwell, 1974.
Okamuro, Minako. "Alchemical Dances in Beckett and Yeats". *Samuel Beckett Today/Aujourd'hui* 14 (2004): 87–104.
O'Leary, Philip. *The Prose Literature of the Gaelic Revival, 1881–1921: Ideology and Innovation*. University Park: Pennsylvania State UP, 1994.
Oppenheim, Lois. *The Painted Word: Samuel Beckett's Dialogue with Art*. Ann Arbor: U of Michigan P, 2000.

——, ed. *Samuel Beckett and the Arts: Music, Visual Arts, and Non-Print Media*. London: Garland, 1999.
Ory, Pascal. "Gastronomy". *Realms of Memory: Rethinking the French Past*. Vol. 2: *Traditions*. 3 vols. Under the direction of Pierre Nora. Trans. Arthur Goldhammer. Ed. and foreword Lawrence D. Kritzman. New York: Columbia UP, 1997. 443–67.
Parkinson, G.H.R. *Georg Lukács*. London: Weidenfeld and Nicholson, 1970.
Pearson, Nels C. "Outside of Here It's Death: Co-dependency and the Ghosts of Decolonization in Beckett's *Endgame*". *ELH* 68.1 (2001): 215–39.
Peillon, Michel. "The Structure of Irish Ideology Revisited". *Culture and Ideology in Ireland*. Ed. Chris Curtin, Mary Kelly and Liam O'Dowd. Galway: Galway UP, 1984. 46–58.
Peter, John. *Vladimir's Carrot: Modern Drama and the Modern Imagination*. London: Deutsch, 1987.
Pike, David. *Lukács and Brecht*. London: U of North Carolina P, 1985.
Pilling, John. "Dates and Difficulties in Beckett's *Whoroscope* Notebook". *Beckett the European*. Ed. Dirk Van Hulle. Tallahassee: Journal of Beckett Studies Books, 2005. 39–48.
——. *Samuel Beckett*. London: Routledge and Kegan Paul, 1976.
——. *A Samuel Beckett Chronology*. Basingstoke, Eng.: Palgrave Macmillan, 2006.
Pinget, Robert. *La Manivelle, pièce radiophonique*. English text by Samuel Beckett. Paris: Editions de Minuit, 1960.
——. "Notre Ami". Spec. issue of *Revue d'esthétique* (1990): vii–viii.
——. "Our Friend Sam". Trans. Robin Freeman. *Eonta* 1.1 (1991): 9–10.
Podol, Peter L. *Fernando Arrabal*. Boston: Twayne, 1978.
Prince, Eric. "'Going On': Interview with Barry McGovern". *Journal of Beckett Studies* 2.1 (1992): 99–114.
Prinz, Jessica. "Resonant Images: Beckett and German Expressionism". *Samuel Beckett and the Arts: Music, Visual Arts, and Non-Print Media*. Ed. Lois Oppenheim. London: Garland, 1999. 153–71.
Quinn, Antoinette. *Patrick Kavanagh: A Biography*. Dublin: Gill & Macmillan, 2001.
Reavey, George. Introduction. *The Silver Dove*. By Andrey Biely. Trans. George Reavey. New York: Grove, 1974. xxi–xlii.
——. "Le Mot et le monde d'André Biely et de James Joyce". *Roman* 2 (1951): 103–11.
——. Translator's Note. *The Silver Dove*. By Andrey Biely. Trans. George Reavey. New York: Grove Press, 1974. xi–xxvii.
Rev. of Samuel Beckett's *Murphy*. *Dublin Magazine* April–June 1939: 98.
Ricks, Christopher. *Beckett's Dying Words*. Oxford: Clarendon, 1993.
Robinson, Lennox. *Ireland's Abbey Theatre: A History, 1899–1951*. Port Washington, NY: Kennikat, 1968.
Roche, Anthony. *Contemporary Irish Drama: From Beckett to McGuinness*. New York: St Martin's, 1995.
——. "Re-working *The Workhouse Ward*: McDonagh, Beckett, and Gregory." *Irish University Review* 34.1 (2004): 171–84.
Rülicke-Weiler, Käthe. *Die Dramaturgie Brechts: Theater als Mittel der Veränderung*. Berlin: Henschelverlag, 1968.
Saddlemyer, Anne. Foreword. *The Playboy of the Western World and Other Plays*. By John Millington Synge. Oxford: Oxford UP, 1995. vii–xxi.

Said, Edward. *Culture and Imperialism*. London: Vintage, 1994.
Saorstát Éireann Official Handbook. Dublin: Talbot, 1932.
Sartre, Jean-Paul. *Being and Nothingness: An Essay on Phenomenological Ontology*. Trans. and introd. Hazel E. Barnes. London: Methuen, 1957.
——. "Beyond Bourgeois Theatre". *Brecht Sourcebook*. Ed. Carol Martin and Henry Bial. London: Routledge, 2000. 50–57.
——. "Colonialism Is a System". *Colonialism and Neocolonialism*. Trans. Azzedine Haddour, Steve Brewer and Terry McWilliams. London: Routledge, 2001. 30–47.
——. *Critique of Dialectical Reason*. Vol. 1: *Theory of Practical Ensembles*. Trans. Alan Sheridan-Smith. Ed. Jonathan Rée. London: Humanities, 1976.
——. "Jean-Paul Sartre Speaks: An Interview with Jacqueline Piatier". Trans. Adrienne Foulke. *Vogue* January 1965: 94–5; 159.
——. Preface. Trans. Lawrence Hoey. *The Colonizer and the Colonized*. By Albert Memmi. Trans. Howard Greenfeld. London: Souvenir, Press, 1974. xxi–xxix.
——. Preface. *The Wretched of the Earth*. By Frantz Fanon. Trans. Constance Farrington. London: MacGibbon and Kee, 1965. 7–26.
——. "The Purposes of Writing". *Between Existentialism and Marxism*. Trans. John Matthews. London: NLB, 1974. 8–32.
——. *Qu'est-ce que la littérature?* Paris: Gallimard, 1948.
——. *Sartre on Theater*. Ed. Michel Contat and Michel Rybalka. Trans. Frank Jellinek. London: Quartet, 1976.
Schoenberg, Arnold. *Structural Functions of Harmony*. Ed. Humphrey Searle. London: Williams and Norgate, 1954.
——. *Style and Idea*. Ed. Dika Newlin. London: Williams and Norgate, 1951.
——. *Theory of Harmony*. Trans. Roy E. Carter. London: Faber, 1978.
Schoenleber, Ulrich. "Baal Meets Belacqua: Une Rencontre entre Brecht et Beckett". *Samuel Beckett Today/Aujourd'hui* 2 (1993): 99–110.
Schreibman, Susan. "'between us the big words were never necessary': Samuel Beckett and Thomas MacGreevy: A Life in Letters". *Samuel Beckett: A Passion for Paintings*. Ed. Fionnuala Croke. Dublin: National Gallery of Ireland, 2006. 34–43.
Seanad Éireann Parliamentary Debates: Official Report. Vol. 12. Dublin: Cahill, 1929.
Shaw, George Bernard. "Preface for Politicians". *John Bull's Other Island*. Ed. Dan H. Lawrence. Harmondsworth, Eng.: Penguin, 1984. 7–52.
Shenker, Israel. "An Interview with Beckett". *Samuel Beckett: The Critical Heritage*. Ed. Laurence Graver and Raymond Federman. New York: Routledge, 1979. 146–49.
Shepherd, W. Ernest. *The Dublin and Southeastern Railway*. Newton Abbot, Eng.: David & Charles, 1974.
Sim, Stuart. *Georg Lukács*. London: Harvester Wheatsheaf, 1994.
Simms, Bryan R. *The Atonal Music of Arnold Schoenberg 1908–1923*. Oxford: Oxford UP, 2000.
Simpson, Alan. *Beckett and Behan, and a Theatre in Dublin*. London: Routledge and Kegan Paul, 1962.
Smith, Frederik N. *Beckett's Eighteenth Century*. Basingstoke, Eng.: Palgrave, 2002.
Spenser, Edmund. *A View of the Present State of Ireland*. Ed. W.L. Renwick. Oxford: Clarendon, 1970.
Struve, Gleb. "M. Andrey Bely: The Russian Symbolist Movement". *The Times* 26 January 1934. London ed.: D14+.

Synge, John Millington. *In Wicklow, West Kerry and Connemara. Collected Works.* Vol. 3: *Prose.* Ed. Alan Price. Robin Skelton, gen. ed. London: Oxford UP, 1966. 185–343.
———. *The Well of the Saints. The Playboy of the Western World and Other Plays.* Ed. Anne Saddlemyer. Oxford: Oxford UP, 1995. 51–94.
Tahakashi, Yasunari. "The Ghost Trio: Beckett, Yeats, and Noh". *Cambridge Review* 107.2295 (1986): 172–76.
Tajiri, Yoshiki. "Beckett and Synaesthesia". *Samuel Beckett Today/Aujourd'hui* 11 (2001): 178–85.
Taniguchi, J. *A Grammatical Analysis of Artistic Representation of Irish English.* Tokyo: Shinozaki Shorin, 1972.
Taylor, Juliette. "'Pidgin Bullskrit': The Performance of French in Beckett's Trilogy". *Samuel Beckett Today/Aujourd'hui* 15 (2005): 211–23.
Tonning, Erik. *Samuel Beckett's Abstract Drama: Works for Stage and Screen 1962–1985.* Oxford: Peter Lang, 2007.
Tophoven, Elmar. "Translating Beckett". *Beckett in the Theatre: The Author as Practical Playwright and Director.* Vol. 1: *From* Waiting for Godot *to* Krapp's Last Tape. By Dougald McMillan and Martha Fehsenfeld. London: John Calder, 1988. 317–24.
Torgovnick, Marianna. *Gone Primitive: Savage Intellects, Modern Lives.* London: University of Chicago Press, 1990.
Tuohy, Frank. *Yeats.* London: Macmillan, 1976.
Turpin, John. "Nationalist and Unionist Ideology in the Sculpture of Oliver Sheppard and John Hughes". *Irish Review* 20 (1997): 62–75.
Weisgerber, Jean, et al. *Les Avant-gardes littéraires au XXème siècle.* Published by the Centre d'Étude des Avant-Gardes Littéraires de l'Université de Bruxelles. 2 vols. Budapest: Akadémiai Kiadó, 1984.
Weiss, Peg. "Evolving Perceptions of Kandinsky and Schoenberg: Towards the Ethnic Roots of the 'Outsider'". *Constructive Dissonance: Arnold Schoenberg and the Transformations of Twentieth-Century Culture.* Ed. Juliane Brand and Christopher Hailey. Berkeley: University of California Press, 1997. 35–57.
Whelan, Kevin. "The Memories of 'The Dead'". *Yale Journal of Criticism* 15.1 (2002): 59–97.
White, Harry. "'Something Is Taking Its Course': Dramatic Exactitude and the Paradigm of Serialism in Samuel Beckett". *Samuel Beckett and Music.* Ed. Mary Bryden. Oxford: Clarendon, 1998. 159–71.
Wingler, Hans Maria. *The Bauhaus: Weimar, Dessau, Berlin, Chicago.* Ed. Joseph Stein. Trans. Wolfgang Jabs and Basil Gilbert. Cambridge, MA: MIT P, 1976.
Worth, Katharine. *The Irish Drama of Europe from Yeats to Beckett.* London: Athlone, 1978.
———. *Samuel Beckett's Theatre: Life Journeys.* Oxford: Clarendon, 1999.
———. "*The Words upon the Window-pane*: A Female Tragedy". *Yeats Annual* 10. Ed. Warwick Gould. London: Macmillan, 1993. 135–58.
Yeats, Jack B. *In Sand. The Collected Plays of Jack B. Yeats.* Ed. Robin Skelton. London: Secker and Warburg, 1971. 333–76.
Yeats, William B. *Collected Plays.* 2nd ed. New York: Macmillan, 1952.
———. *Diarmuid and Grania.* Written in collaboration with George Moore. *The Collected Works of W.B. Yeats.* Vol. 2: *The Plays.* Ed. David R. Clark and Rosalind E. Clark. Basingstoke: Palgrave, 2001. 557–607.
———. *Explorations.* Selected by Mrs W.B. Yeats. London: Macmillan, 1962.

Yeats, William B. "Introduction to *The Words upon the Window-pane*". *Dublin Magazine* October–December 1931: 5–19.
———. *Letters on Poetry: From W.B. Yeats to Dorothy Wellesley*. London: Oxford UP, 1940.
———. *The Poems*. London: Everyman, 1994.
———. Preface. *Wild Apples*. By Oliver St John Gogarty. Dublin: Cuala, 1928. Shannon: Irish UP, 1971.
———. *Uncollected Prose by W.B. Yeats*. Vol. 1: *First Reviews and Articles, 1886–1896*. 2 vols. Comp. and ed. John P. Frayne. New York: Columbia UP, 1970.
———. *Uncollected Prose by W.B. Yeats*. Vol. 2: *Reviews, Articles, and Other Miscellaneous Prose, 1897–1939*. 2 vols. Comp. and ed. John P. Frayne and Colton Johnson. New York: Columbia UP, 1975.
———. *The Variorum Edition of the Plays of W.B. Yeats*. Ed. Russell K. Alspach. London: Macmillan, 1966.
Zilliacus, Clas. *Beckett and Broadcasting: A Study of the Works of Samuel Beckett for and in Radio and Television*. Åbo, Finland: Åbo Akademi, 1976.
———. "Three Times *Godot*: Beckett, Brecht, Bulatovic". *Comparative Drama* 4 (1970): 3–17.

Index

Adamov, Arthur, 127
Adorno, Theodor W., 107, 125, 162–3
  Aesthetic Theory, 9, 19–20, 56, 129, 135
  "Commitment", 19, 108
  Philosophy of Modern Music, 129
  perspectives on the avant-garde, 4, 9, 18–20, 56, 97–8, 108
  responses to Lukács, 97–8, 122, 162–3
  responses to Sartre, 19, 108
  "Trying to Understand *Endgame*", 63, 66, 67, 97, 99, 105, 107, 112, 119, 121–2, 129
Ahern, Bertie, and *The Beckett Country*, 4
Apollinaire, Guillaume, 56
Arikha, Avigdor, 196 n7
Arnold, Matthew, 72, 101
Aron, Raymond, 118
Arrabal, Fernando, 16, 53–4
Ashcroft, Peggy, 153–4

Ballmer, Karl, 134, 159
Beckett, May, 12
Beckett, Samuel:
  and the arts in Ireland:
    and the Abbey Theatre, 21–4, 29–30, 47, 100, 104, 113, 144
    dialogue with MacGreevy on Jack Yeats, 12–13, 50–3, 133, 158–60
    and Dublin literary circles, 11–12, 31–5, 40–1, 46
    and the Gate Theatre, 21–2, 23–4, 46, 109
    on the Irish Academy of Letters, 43
    and nineteenth-century Irish writers, 34, 87–8
  biography:
    friendship with MacGreevy, 11–12, 13, 50
    and the Gogarty trial, 16
    interest in Dublin theatres, 21–4
    perception of London, 63
    at Trinity College Dublin, 11, 21, 87, 94
    trip to Nazi Germany, 12, 129
    turn to French, 55–6, 57, 72, 94–5
    upbringing in Foxrock, 10, 12
    work with the Irish Red Cross, 52
    works censored in Ireland, 40, 41
  contextualisation:
    on abstract painting, 127–8, 133–5
    on Theodor Adorno, 121
    on Andrey Bely, 32
    on Bertold Brecht, 108, 125, 190 n69
    on Austin Clarke, 33, 40, 45–6
    and French existentialism, 20, 64–8, 96, 127
    on Lady Gregory, 24, 103–4
    on James Joyce: *A Portrait of the Artist as a Young Man*, 46, 47; *Work in Progress*, 56, 131
    on Wassily Kandinsky, 128, 129, 130, 133
    on Lázló Moholy-Nagy, 131
    on Flann O'Brien, 14
    on Sean O'Casey, 14, 23, 29–31
    on George Russell (AE), 40, 42, 48
    on Arnold Schoenberg, 128
    on J.M. Synge, 22, 23, 37, 38, 72, 75
    on Jack B. Yeats, 36, 50, 51, 53, 158, 159
    on W.B. Yeats, 13, 14, 36, 40, 42, 43, 48, 103; poetry, 35–6, 46, 174 n97; drama, 21, 22, 24
  politics:
    and the Algerian War of Independence, 7, 17–18, 107, 113, 150
    banning of own work in Ireland, 15
    on the Irish Free State economy, 24, 41–2, 113

Beckett, Samuel: – *continued*
   and Irish Free State politics, 5, 8, 10, 11, 12, 40–1, 44–5, 49, 53, 87, 88
   and nationalist understandings of art, 50–2, 135–6
   and the 1929 Censorship Act, 40–4, 45
   and the revival of Irish Gaelic, 38–9, 87
   and the Spanish Civil War, 15
   support to Fernando Arrabal, 54
   reception of:
     and Aosdána, 1
     critical reception in Irish studies, 5–8
     historicisation of, 2, 5–6
     as Irish cultural icon, 1
     postcolonial readings of, 6–8
     problematic classification of, 2–3, 5–8, 123, 161
   writing and translation:
     articles and reviews:
       "The Capital of the Ruins", 52
       "Censorship in the Saorstat", 12, 40–5
       "Dante... Bruno. Vico.. Joyce", 17, 31, 46
       "Les Deux Besoins", 130
       "The Essential and the Incidental", 29–31
       "Homage to Jack B. Yeats", 50
       "MacGreevy on Yeats", 13, 50–1, 52, 158–60; preliminary typescript draft, 51–2, 133
       "Peintres de l'empêchement", 133–4
       "La Peinture des van Velde ou le monde et le pantalon", 134
      Proust, 73
       "Proust in Pieces", 121
       "Recent Irish Poetry", 14, 31, 33–5, 39, 43, 45, 46, 48, 50, 57, 61, 87, 88, 103, 135; genesis of, 33; use of pseudonym, 31, 33
       "Three Dialogues", 7, 127, 129, 202 n182

   drama:
     Act without Words II, 29
     All That Fall, 3–4, 38–9
     ...but the clouds..., 36–7
     Dis Joe, 141, 143, 199 n77
     Eh Joe, 92, 136, 137, 139–44; drafts, 140–4; Irish contexts of, 92, 140–4; performance of, 139–40, 198 n61
     En attendant Godot, 94, 95, 110–12, 113; draft, 107
     Endgame, 9, 63, 66, 92, 94, 96–9, 103–9, 119–20, 129; cultural indeterminacy, 112–13; historical underpinning, 107, 113–16
     Film, 139
     Fin de partie, 94, 107, 112–14; draft, 107
     Footfalls, 136, 137, 138, 139; drafts, 156–8; influences, 156; performance of, 156, 157
     Happy Days, 22, 92, 93, 153
     He, Joe, 137, 141
     Human Wishes, 79, 90–1
     "Kilcool", 144–5
     Krapp's Last Tape, 4, 15, 92, 93, 143, 151
     Not I, 136, 137, 138, 139, 151; contexts of, 144–5, 147, 150; difficulties, 145–6; manuscripts, 144, 147–9; performance of, 137, 146; pictorial influences, 149–50
     The Old Tune, 72, 90–1; *see also* Pinget, Robert
     Pas moi, 149
     Play, 27–9; and W.B. Yeats, 27–9; drafts, 27–9
     That Time, 136, 137, 138, 139; contexts of, 151; difficulties, 151–3; drafts, 152–5; pictorial influences, 151
     Waiting for Godot, 5, 9, 24, 41, 90, 93, 94, 96–9, 101, 105–9, 119–20, 124–5, 144; cultural indeterminacy, 109–12; historical underpinning, 107, 113, 116; production history,

Beckett, Samuel: – *continued*
  98, 109; and *Purgatory*, 104–5;
  and *The Workhouse Ward*,
  103–4
 fiction:
  Bing/Ping, 85
  Compagnie/Company, 85,
   149, 157
  *Dream of Fair to Middling
   Women*, 88
  "L'Expulsé", 57, 58, 78
  First Love, 8, 57
  L'Innommable, 60, 62, 63, 73, 76
  Malone Dies, 9, 41, 61, 62, 63,
   64, 66, 76
  Malone meurt, 9, 13, 59–60, 62,
   63, 64, 67, 69–70, 76, 78
  Molloy (English), 9, 41, 60,
   61–2, 68, 69, 71, 72, 74–6,
   76–8, 97, 120
  Molloy (French), 9, 13, 55, 61–2,
   67, 68, 69, 70, 74–6, 76–8, 91;
   genesis of, 62–3, 88–90
  More Pricks Than Kicks, 11, 16,
   37, 40, 41, 43, 149
  Murphy (English), 9, 35, 45–50,
   63, 78; genesis of, 48–9; and
   *A Portrait of the Artist as a
   Young Man*, 46–7; and Irish
   nationalist iconography,
   49–50; use of caricature,
   45–6, 47–8
  Murphy (French), 48
  Premier amour, 8, 57
  Texts for Nothing, 14, 110
  The Unnamable, 9, 60, 62, 63,
   64, 73–4, 76–7
  Watt, 41, 48, 78, 135
 and hibernicisation, 68, 70, 72–3,
  76–7, 78, 90, 91–2, 99, 110,
  112–13, 153
 and linguistic misuse, 56, 57,
  58–9
 poetry:
  "Alba", 37
  *Echo's Bones and Other
   Precipitates*, 32
  "Whoroscope", 36
 and self-translation, 55–6, 78–9

 and translators, 56, 78, 93–4
 and use of Irish English, 3–4,
  38–9, 70–1, 76–7, 78, 79,
  90–2, 99, 105, 110–13, 114,
  143, 147, 153–4, 156–7
 and use of Irish locations, 3,
  38–9, 49, 53, 61–2, 64, 88–90,
  92, 113, 141, 142, 143, 148,
  149, 152
Beckett, Suzanne, 128
Behan, Brendan, 90
Bely, Andrey, 31–2
Berg, Alban, 128, 195 n7
Bion, Wilfred, 31
Borges, Jorge Luis, 24
Boucicault, Dion, 13
Bowles, Patrick, 78, 107, 184 n126
Boyle, Kay, 78–9, 157
Braque, Georges, 159
Brecht, Bertold, 18, 19, 97, 107–8, 126
 debates with Lukács, 123–4
 rewrites *Waiting for Godot*, 124–5
Breton, André, 56
Buñuel, Luis: *Un chien andalou*, 144
Butor, Michel, 18

Camus, Albert, 65–7, 68
Caravaggio, 149–50
Chekhov, Anton, 21
Clarke, Austin, 11, 33, 40, 46, 47, 87
 The Hunger Demon, 46
 and *Murphy*, 45–6
 Pilgrimage, 46
 and "Recent Irish Poetry", 33
Coffey, Brian, 35
Connolly, James, 101–2
Corkery, Daniel, 51, 101, 109–10
Cosgrave, William Thomas, 12
Craig, Edward Gordon, 27
Cronyn, Hume, 138
Crowder, Henry, 17
Crowe, Eileen, 24
Cunard, Nancy, 15, 17, 56
Cusack, Cyril, 15, 22

da Messina, Antonello, 156
Dalí, Salvador, 144
Davis, Thomas, 101
de Rivarol, Antoine, 59

de Valera, Eamon, 10, 12, 13, 43, 49, 101
Devlin, Denis, 35
di Mena, Pedro, 156
Dowden, Edward, 87, 103
Duchamp, Marcel, 16; *Prière de toucher*, 150
Duthuit, Georges, 7, 56, 202 n182

Edgeworth, Maria, 6
Edwards, Hilton, 23
Eisenstein, Sergei, 32, 173 n71
Eluard, Paul, 56

Fanon, Frantz, 118
Ferguson, Samuel, 34, 88

Giacometti, Alberto, 16
Gibbon, Monk, 40, 87
Gogarty, Oliver St John, 16, 40, 103
Gregory, Lady Augusta, 15, 24, 26, 49, 70, 72, 83, 87, 95, 100, 102
  Dervorgilla, 24
  The Workhouse Ward, 103–4
  translations of Molière, 79–80
Grieg, Edvard, 24
Grohmann, Will, 129, 133

Havel, Václav, 16
Heidegger, Martin, 134
Herder, Johann Gottfried von, 26
Higgins, Aidan, 78, 125
Higgins, F.R., 33, 87
Holloway, Joseph, 80
Hyde, Douglas, 72, 87, 95, 102
  Love Songs of Connacht, 80–2, 86, 87
  "The Necessity for De-Anglicizing Ireland", 82–3
  reception of, 80, 81–2, 83–5

Ibsen, Henrik, 21, 23–4, 25
Ionesco, Eugène, 66, 127

James, Henry: *The Sense of the Past*, 23
Janvier, Ludovic, 78
Jarry, Alfred, 127
Jellett, Mainie, 135
Johnson, Samuel, 63, 79, 90
Jolas, Eugene, 11, 51

Joyce, James, 6, 7, 11, 14, 15, 31, 32, 33, 34, 42, 43, 46, 56, 73, 97, 122, 123, 131, 139
  "The Day of the Rabblement", 34
  A Portrait of the Artist as a Young Man, 42, 46–7, 73
  on the Revival, 24, 34, 73
  Ulysses, 15, 34, 42, 46, 48, 73, 122, 142, 154, 157

Kafka, Franz, 19
Kandinsky, Wassily, 10, 52, 56, 128, 129, 131, 132, 133, 195 n4
  Blaue Reiter Almanac, 26, 132
  interest in folk art, 26, 133
  and internal necessity, 130
  limits of abstraction, 134
  Point and Line to Plane, 131, 135, 140
  On the Spiritual in Art, 128, 130, 140, 159
  Yellow Sound, 131
Kaun, Axel, 56, 57
Klee, Paul, 52, 134, 159
Kleist, Heinrich von, 26

Leventhal, A.J. (Con), 24, 45
Lissitzky, El, 131
Lukács, Georg, 4, 9, 18, 97, 126, 162
  and Bertold Brecht, 123–4, 126
  History and Class Consciousness, 120
  and Irish literature, 122
  The Meaning of Contemporary Realism, 97–8, 120–1, 122

MacDonagh, Thomas, 82, 122
MacGreevy, Thomas, 11, 12–13, 22, 23, 33, 35, 36, 37, 40, 42, 46, 50–3, 63, 78, 79, 87, 103, 121, 128, 130, 133, 135, 159, 160; and *Jack B. Yeats*, 50–1
MacLiammóir, Micheál, 23, 24
Macnamara, Brinsley, 21
MacSwiney, Terence, 66–7
Maeterlinck, Maurice, 25, 28
Magee, Patrick, 4, 151
Magritte, René, 191 n104
Mallarmé, Stéphane, 25
Mangan, James Clarence, 87
Manning (Howe), Mary, 22, 23

Manning, Susan, 94
Marc, Frantz, 26
Marx, Karl, 108, 117
McGowran, Jack, 15, 140
McQuaid, John Charles, 15
McWhinnie, Donald, 90
Memmi, Albert, 118
Moholy-Nagy, Lázló, 131–2, 133
Mondrian, Piet, 131
Montague, John, 41
Moore, George, 47–8, 72, 82, 95, 185 n165; *Diarmuid and Grania* (French draft), 83–5, 185 n170
Murray, T.C., 21

O'Brien, Flann, 13–14, 15, 95
  and *Irish Times* column, 13–14
  The Poor Mouth, 85–7, 102, 202 n185
  on J.M. Synge, 85
O'Brien, George, 27–8
O'Casey, Sean, 13, 14–15, 21, 22, 23, 27, 29–31, 43, 51
  Autobiographies, 14–15
  Juno and the Paycock, 22, 30–1, 53, 91, 111
  The Plough and the Stars, 27, 30
  view of Beckett, 15
O'Flaherty, Liam, 11
O'Grady, Standish (James), 34, 88, 101

Pelorson, Georges, 22
Péron, Alfred, 56, 58
Péron, Mania, 58–9, 88–90
Phillips, Siân, 153
Pinget, Robert, 72, 73, 78, 121; *La Manivelle*, 90–1, 92
Pirandello, Luigi, 21
Pound, Ezra, 27
Proust, Marcel, 47, 73, 121
Pudovkin, Vsevolod, 32
Purohit Swami, Shri, 48

Ray, Man, 150, 151
Reavey, George, 32
Rimbaud, Arthur, 44, 56, 59
Robbe-Grillet, Alain, 18
Robinson, Lennox, 21, 22
Romains, Jules, 21
Rouault, Georges, 159, 202 n185

Russell, George (AE), 34, 40, 42, 48, 49, 135; *The Candle of Vision*, 48

Salkeld, Cecil, 135
Sarraute, Nathalie, 18
Sartre, Jean-Paul, 8, 9, 20, 66, 99, 108, 120, 162
  and Algeria, 116, 118
  on Beckett's early drama, 119
  Being and Nothingness, 65
  and colonialism, 117–18
  Critique of Dialectical Reason, 116–19
  Qu'est-ce que la littérature? (What Is Literature?), 18–19
Schlemmer, Oskar, 131
Schmahl, Hildegard, 156
Schneider, Alan, 17, 79, 92, 94, 95, 107, 137, 139, 140, 147, 153
Schnitzler, Arthur, 21
Schoenberg, Arnold, 10, 128, 129, 131, 132, 134, 138; *Pierrot lunaire*, 128, 138
Schumann, Robert, 159
Schwartz, Jacob, 4
Shaw, George Bernard, 22–3, 40, 122
Sheppard, Oliver, 49
Simpson, Alan, 15
  on Beckett's use of Irish English, 90
  production of *Waiting for Godot*, 109
Sinclair, Henry Morris, 16
Soupault, Philippe, 56
Soutine, Chaim, 52
Spenser, Edmund, 62
Stalin, Joseph, 32, 33
Swift, Jonathan, 6, 36–7, 44, 103
Synge, John Millington, 21, 22, 25, 37–8, 39, 49, 70, 72, 73, 75, 80, 85, 101
  Deirdre of the Sorrows, 23
  The Playboy of the Western World, 22
  Riders to the Sea, 101
  The Well of the Saints, 22, 37–8
  In Wicklow, West Kerry and Connemara, 75

Tandy, Jessica, 138, 147
Tierney, Michael, 44; *Saorstát Éireann Official Handbook*, 44
Tophoven, Elmar, 92, 93

Ussher, Percy (Arland), 11, 22, 40

van Velde, Bram, 133–4, 159
van Velde, Geer, 133–4
van Velde, Jacoba, 16, 79, 92–4, 143

Wagner, Richard, 25, 26, 130
Webern, Anton, 128, 196 n7
White, H.O., 36
Whitelaw, Billie, 137–8, 146, 148, 156
Wilde, Oscar, 28; *Salomé*, 28
Wilson, R.N.D., 40

Yeats, George, 22
Yeats, Jack B., 12–13, 50–3, 158–60; *In Sand*, 22
Yeats, William B., 6, 13, 14, 15, 18, 25, 29, 32, 33, 34, 36, 37, 38, 39, 40, 45, 49, 72, 95, 108, 123, 159
  and the Abbey Theatre, 26–7
  drama:
    Cathleen Ni Houlihan, 49
    The Countess Cathleen, 100
    The Death of Cuchulain, 28
    Diarmuid and Grania, 101
    At the Hawk's Well, 21, 22, 27
    The King of the Great Clock Tower, 24, 28, 36, 144
    Oedipus at Colonus, 21
    Oedipus the King, 21
    Purgatory, 21, 22, 27, 104–5
    The Resurrection, 24, 42
    The Words upon the Window-pane, 21, 37
  and Douglas Hyde, 82, 83
  interest in the esoteric, 48
  and Irish Academy of Letters, 43, 123
  and Irish censorship, 40, 42–3
  and Japanese Noh drama, 27, 28, 29
  and Jonathan Swift, 36–7
  meeting with Beckett, 36
  national literature, 25, 26, 33, 83, 101, 103, 123, 159
  poetry:
    "The Statues", 49–50
    "Three Movements", 35
    "The Tower", 36
    "Vacillation", 35
    "Who Goes with Fergus?", 46
    The Winding Stair and Other Poems, 35, 103
  project for *Diarmuid and Grania*, 83–5
  and translation, 80–1, 82, 83–4
  views on style, 25, 56–7, 83, 88, 95